MW00814256

When the Perfect Comes

The Deverell Series
Book ~1~

Susan Ward

Copyright © 2014 Susan Ward

All rights reserved.

ISBN: 0692305521
ISBN-13: 978-0692305522

DEDICATION

To my bugs and my bug from another mother. There is a piece of each of you contained in this story. Bug number one's infectious laughter and wild spirit. Bug number two's beauty of person and heart. Bug number three's fragility, faith, innocence and hope. Bug from another mother's idealism and politics. And even from me a piece: the simple joy of irritation.

"When the perfect comes, the partial will pass away."
1 Corinthians 13:10

This is a work of fiction. Names, characters, places, and incidents either are the product of the author's imagination or are used fictitiously. Any resemblance to actual persons, living or dead, events, or locales is entirely coincidental.

PROLOGUE

Cornwall, England, September 1813

For twenty-five years, Lucien Merrick, the Duke of Dorset, lived with his family in a simple cottage orné named Bramble Hill. To the west lay Land's End and to the east, the village of Falmouth. A six-day journey by coach, in the North Country, was the ducal estate with its beautifully landscaped parks and gardens. There Lucien had been raised as a boy, and lived until he had married Rhea.

Bramble Hill possessed none of the manicured formality of the ancestral home of the Merricks. The slightly aloof elegance of Grecian summer houses and velvet lawns of sternly perimetered flower beds, edged in topiary, would have been a garish intrusion amid the graceful naturalness of the landscape here.

While the house was large, as befitted a man of such great stature, there was nothing of awe-inspiring grandeur about its simple lines. No emblazonments of rank or wealth, to betray to a casual on-looker that this house belonged to a family as rich in history and importance as the Merricks were.

Yet, the gloriously blooming wild flowers and ancient tress lent an aura of delicate glamour to the humble dwelling built facing the shore. It instantly drew the eyes. Every weather worn, sun-drenched inch screamed out that happiness dwelt here. No

1

other estate was more beloved by the Merrick family.

It was why Rhea insisted upon living here. It was a working farm, one of the loveliest farms on the coast of Cornwall. She had spent the last decade of her life, before marriage to Lucien, on a modest farm in Virginia. Poverty and necessity, forced the unexpected change of circumstance for this woman of impeccable birth and breeding. She was a blend of noble English lady and American spirited girl, somehow making it work.

She was adored by the society she rarely ventured into, her style and social graces admired, her tiny flashes of unconventional whim always forgiven. Even her strange proclivity to raise her children outside the rigid formality of the rank they'd achieved by the simple act of birth, had long ago been forgiven by even the strictest members of the ton.

Criticism of Rhea would achieve nothing, not unless one's intent was to provoke Lucien's fury. Lucien indulged Rhea's every whim. Rhea was happy here. Rhea was Lucien Merrick's happiness.

The London season had ended some months earlier. It surprised Lucien that with each passing year his eagerness to return to Cornwall only increased, when he had once spent all his days in London. England was a country at war. On the continent of Europe, they were submerged in their sixth year of war with France, and across the seas a series of petty squabbles had catapulted them into war with their former rebellious colonies, The United States. They were in their second year of war in America, stalled and no closer to peace than they had been when it started. The negotiations and peace talks between Whitehall and the American delegation were little more than farce. They'd been tedious to endure, since he was not a man who found it easy to tolerate ineffectiveness.

Even in his comfortable mansion in Mayfair, the effect of

war on England had been impossible to miss in London. The streets were lined with posters lampooning Napoleon, President Madison, the regent and much to his displeasure, himself. He had been vocal in his disdain over the conflict with America. Now, the walls of that fashionable city, of the country he'd served in loyal dedication for five decades, boasted pictures of him burned in effigy. Hanging from the American flag, no less.

Twenty thousand people were unemployed in London. The streets were littered with thin, dirty, and shabbily dressed bodies. In row upon row of houses poor families lived in a single room. Less fortunate families were homeless, seeking shelter under bridges, in parks, and the streets of London's dirty slums. The result of an economy hurt by war. His sympathies were with the masses, all his energies devoted to peace, and what it would bring them all, and now they burned him in effigy.

The social season had been a tedious bore of entertainments, long grown stale. Within the fashionable drawing rooms and clubs of London, in their high pillared mansions, the upper ranks of society were untroubled by the suffering around them as they danced and gossiped. Even in the never-ending social whirl, the worries of England's wars had beset Lucien. The prince regent sought his council and never followed it. He'd been vastly relieved to return at the close of the season to his simple dwelling in Cornwall.

Staring out the casement windows, Lucien's eyes swept the rough terrain with its windblown trees and cob walls. He took in the jagged tumble of cleft boulders, the water that surged in relentless tides against the cliffs, and then, the green pasture meadow until spotting a familiar form. He settled his gaze on the tiny figure of his daughter, Merry. The only war in Cornwall to beset Lucien was Merry.

CHAPTER ONE

Lady Meredith Ann Merrick, affectionately known as Merry, glided across the moist, fragrant grass in a graceful flurry, her sapphire blue eyes dancing with poorly concealed amusement as she stared into the nervous gaze of her opponent.

An hour ago, after a stern lecture from her father regarding her poor conduct at last night's country ball, she had come from the house. She was prim and proper, in her lavender silk, her waist length curls piled elegantly atop her head, determined to prove that she could deport herself every bit as ladylike as her cousin, Kate.

Now, her raven tresses dangled loosely about her shoulders, her pearl studded combs and brass hair pins were held in place only by the knots in her curls. Her delicate cheeks were bright with color, and her gown boasted an unsightly grass stain.

She had no idea how charming the effect of her dishevelment was, or that Rensdale, even in his annoyance, thought her uncommonly fetching. Nor would she have cared if the viscount had given voice to the compliment. It was never her intent to charm Rensdale now, or at any time.

Her only intent had been to put Rensdale in his place after he had prowled the grounds with Philip, in search of her as he sought to impress her with his expertise in foils.

"Merry, please. You must stop," Kate begged over the sound of clanking metal, as an angry foil soared dangerously close to her young cousin's cheek. "What if your mother should see? We're still in view of the house."

Kate looked anxiously over her shoulder. The house seemed to smile down at them from the small rise above the pasture, and little deserved Kate Merrick's fretful stare.

Merry laughed when Rensdale nearly stumbled after her cleverly made forward thrust. Kate, however, was not amused, sure that it was only a matter of time before the duke and duchess learned of Merry's latest lapse in propriety.

She knew that a certain measure of their disapproval would fall on her. It was, after all, her duty to help keep Merry in line. *To save Merry from herself,* as Uncle Lucien was want to put it, though, how they expected her to manage such a mammoth task by herself, Kate would never know.

Certainly three grueling seasons in London should have shown that it was an exercise in futility. Any respectable match to be settled on her wild cousin would have to occur with a sleight of hand manipulation of Merry's less attractive qualities, and a healthy share of divine intervention.

If only Merry had a husband to take her in hand. Hence, Rensdale's advent into their close-knit ranks at Bramble Hill.

"Good Heavens, Merry, haven't you taken this far enough?" Kate admonished, her sweet face stern with reproof. "Perhaps you're inclined to spend the afternoon with a stern lecture from your mama, but I assure you I am not. You know very well this escapade will make its way through Bramble Hill before supper. Aunt Rhea is going to be furious."

Seated on a low cobblestone wall, Merry's brother, Philip, was more amused than worried. "Hush up, Kate. She's got him on the run. Don't distract her."

Kate's eyes flashed at her cousin. "You should be ashamed of yourself, Philip Merrick. This is your doing. I will not see you laughing if Merry is hurt."

"It is our viscount there who warrants your concern, Kate."

Gnawing her lower lip, Kate had to admit that it did look as if the Viscount Rensdale were in trouble.

Laughing, Merry made her final lunge, sweeping her foil in a furious, circular motion that unsettled Rensdale's weapon from his hand, and brought the deadly point of her shiny instrument to rest on the material covering his heart. She'd gone so far as to take the guard off the tip.

"Merry!" Kate screamed, "Put that sword down before you hurt someone. What has come over you?"

"I think you owe me an apology, Rensdale," Merry said, easing the point, ever so slightly, forward. The sight of him red faced and winded made her giggle. Lightly tracing the deadly tip across his chest, she added, "Or perhaps your heart would do better."

"Get that blasted thing away from me," Rensdale demanded furiously, nearly stumbling over a bush as he hurriedly backed away from her. "You go too far this time, Merry."

Merry cocked her head, fighting back her laughter.

"A gentleman would not make sport of a lady. You were insulting in your manner when you offered to..." mimicking his voice, "...*Instruct me in the fundamentals of fencing.* Clearly I did not need instruction."

"This is a man's skill to master, not a lady's," Rensdale pointed out pompously, taking another step back. "You would do well to practice the waltz and become my equal on the dance floor. Then, Lady Gillian would not call you the 'charging cassock' and I would not have bruised feet to contend with after every ball."

"If you consider me not up to snuff on the dance floor, I suggest you seek out another girl as your partner."

"As your future husband, it is my obligation to give you counsel. You are grace itself with that foil in hand. If you could only learn to move so surely when we dance."

"In this matter I would say that it is Merry who should give you counsel, my friend," Philip said dryly. "Perhaps you should fence on the dance floor instead of attempting the waltz. I dare say, Lady Gillian wouldn't laugh at our Merry, then. Michael, no good ever comes from criticizing Merry. I have eschewed the practice."

"What say you, Kate?" Merry asked. "Should I run him through? He was cruel to tell me what Lady Gillian said."

"I think last night's ball was punishment enough," Kate answered, her eyes twinkling as she met her cousin's gaze. She battled not to laugh as she recalled the sight of Lord Rensdale hobbling across the lawn, a victim of the waltz via Merry.

"If you apologize I will put down the sword, Milord."

"I am not ready to forgive you, at all. I hate this habit you have of making a spectacle of yourself. You do not behave, at all, in a manner that befits your birth."

"Spectacle. I am not a spectacle. For that I will settle for nothing less than my sword through your wicked heart."

"Don't do that, nestling," Philip advised sagely. "You've managed to scare off all your other suitors. Rensdale deserves mercy for his sheer tenacity and nerves of iron."

"I dropped my pursuit of Merry, long ago," Lord Rensdale said stiffly, cautiously keeping his eye on his raven-haired hellion. "They're wagering at White's, five to one, that the Merrick chit will not marry this season. I have bet a hundred pounds, myself."

"If you are the best England can offer me, I suspect you've won your wager," Merry taunted, never missing a chance to insult His Lordship. "As it is, you stand to collect nothing if I decide my foil would better rest in your chest."

7

Philip sprang smoothly from the wall, shoving the foil away from Michael's chest after his sister made the blade bend slightly from added pressure. "Oh, will you stop it. What will our father say, Merry, if you let the viscount's blood here in our pasture?"

"He'd say 'Drat, our last hope has gotten away. Darn, Rensdale for his untimely death. How shall I ever marry my daughter off at this rate,'" Merry said flippantly.

Philip grimaced. "Idiocy and melodrama. No wonder you're nearly twenty and still unwed. No man wants to take a lunatic as wife."

A giggle escaped Kate, despite her valiant efforts not to laugh.

"Don't encourage her," Philip chided. *"You* are supposed to be a proper influence. Another year and she'll be on the shelf."

"Once Merry becomes my wife, she'll come to tow," said Rensdale firmly. "Your sister just needs to be taken in hand and instructed on the proper mode of behavior."

"She'll more likely bite your hand off," Philip commented wryly.

"Take me in hand? I am a woman, not a horse. Can you credit what you're hearing, Kate? Barbaric."

"All spirited animals are alike. They need be taught who is their master," Rensdale remarked firmly.

"Do you think you are up to the challenge, my lord? You weren't for today's," Merry countered.

"We shall see. Once I have collected my wager. Why lose five hundred pounds if I can have your sister and the purse in the bargain?" Michael quipped, earning an approving slap against his shoulder from Philip.

"Spoken like a man of reason," Philip concurred, amused that, for once, Rensdale wasn't letting himself be dragged

8

around by Merry. "Besides, she is soon to pass a marriageable age. Who will want the chit then? We'll have to content ourselves with a doddering old fool, willing to take her off our hands for her dowry. She'll be yours for the asking, Michael. That is, unless you come to your senses, and ask for our fair Kate."

Kate blushed from chin to hairline. She knew very well that her golden hair and green eyes were no match for Merry's dark beauty. It was no wonder the elegant Rensdale was determined to have Merry, in spite of her cousin's irritating, exasperating treatment of him.

"Of course, Merry shall wed Lord Rensdale," Kate said. "We will never find another who is willing to tolerate her. We all know that the contracts are drawn and only wait for Uncle Lucien's signature."

"And my consent," Merry added pointedly, knowing very well, that the contracts would not be signed by her father unless she agreed to the marriage.

Which she would not. Hadn't she spent the better part of two years trying to get Rensdale to cry off?

Under sooty lashes, Merry examined the Viscount Rensdale. His amber eyes settled on her. She felt her insides itch with irritation.

Even after a fortnight at Bramble Hill, he had not shed his icy London formality. She stared with real loathing at his intricate white cravat and meticulously tailored trousers.

It was not that Rensdale was an unattractive man. At thirty and two, his face was a pleasant blend of strongly carved features and his hair a mass of expertly groomed blond curls. It was just that he was wrapped in so much condescension, as were too many men of their class. Merry could abide arrogance and stuffiness no more than she could abide the hypocrisy of London society. There was a stiff-neck formality in everything the man did, which was hardly appealing to a girl who loved to run in meadows shoeless.

If I ever decide I want a husband, it would certainly not be Rensdale, she thought, glaring at him.

"Marriage is nothing more than the morally sanctioned enslavement of women," Merry said determinedly. "Why would any woman consent to that? I will never marry. It is my choice and I choose not to."

"If you spend the season in London as scandalously as the last, you'll find yourself wed with nary a chance to object," Philip said sagely.

Rensdale's eyes narrowed on her, knowing that by the end of this season the victory would be his. One more season and Merry Merrick, her delightful little body, her fortune, and her lands, would be his. With or without her consent.

"Where is Lord Andrew? I had expected to see him today. Did he not return last night?" Rensdale asked.

"Uncle Andrew returned near midnight," Merry said, "but has not spent a moment with us, since his return. He's locked away in the study with my father. Something very serious is afoot, I think. Do you know what your father is about, Kate?"

Kate shook her head. She knew nothing of what business drew her father away from Bramble Hill so often. Not that she faulted her father for being away so much. He was an important man, and with his wife long dead, had no reason to ground himself in Cornwall.

"It is best not to question my father on his activities," Kate said properly.

"They're putting their heads together trying to find one man, in all England, cork brained enough to wed my sister," Philip put in mockingly. Merry stuck her tongue out at her brother. "Charming."

"Do you think that Captain Morgan is the reason for your

uncle's preoccupation," Rensdale asked, expertly masking his anxiousness to discover if that were the case. "I heard a rumor in Falmouth, yesterday, that the *Corinthian* was in Swansea a fortnight ago. And now, Lord Andrew has returned so suddenly and mysteriously. More than a coincidence I think. Is that the urgent business your uncle has been about?"

"*Corinthian?*" Merry piped up excitedly. "*THE Corinthian?*"

Rensdale was clearly surprised by her interest. "You've heard of Morgan?"

"Of course," Merry countered indignantly, shaking her dark head anxiously. "Just because I am a woman doesn't mean that I know nothing of the world. Who hasn't heard of Morgan? His exploits live in the *Times*. I would rather read about Morgan than our ghastly war with America. One is a fascination. The other intolerable."

Morgan. Merry turned the name over in her brain, feeling a nervous bubble of excitement swell within her. Of course, she had heard of him. What a foolish question. Rensdale was so condescending in his opinion of what should occupy a lady's mind.

Morgan was one of the most vicious pirates who had ever plundered the sea. She had spent years following his exploits in the *Times*, reading every tidbit she could find on him. His mystery and villainy, caused a fascination that bordered on obsession with her. He'd been committing atrocities against Britain for nearly a decade. The man was a legend.

"What did Morgan do in Swansea?" Merry asked eagerly.

"Damn, Michael, you should know better than to bring gossip back for Merry. We don't need to have her pretty head filled with more nonsense. Her politics are scandal enough. I doubt strongly that my father would approve. Uncle Andrew's flying trips have nothing to do with Morgan, or anything else of such serious import. It's the deuced lack of entertainment in

Cornwall that sends Uncle Andrew off, not pirates and their petty intrigues. Let's discuss the matter no further."

"Don't listen to Philip," Merry ordered, her brows lowering in a frown above her blue eyes. "With Uncle Andrew gone for the past two months and now playing least in sight, things have been deadly dull around here. I am so bored... but, Rensdale, you must tell me everything you heard." She planted her elbows into the lush green, setting her chin on her open palms. "I promise to hang on every word," she assured him. Those sparkling blue eyes stared at him. Rensdale felt both anger and desire rocket through him, simultaneously.

Merry was so confident of her power over him. He relished the day he would no longer play the besotted fool, when he would hold the whip. The Merrick haughtiness and pride would not save her once she was his wife.

"There's little to tell," Rensdale began, his interest gone, now that he realized nothing would be learned from bringing this matter before the Merrick younger ranks. "A fortnight ago, Morgan's ship was seen in Swansea. Sailed it right into the harbor as if he belonged. The *Corinthian* was filled from bow to stern with smuggled goods from the colonies. He stayed for three days. Bought off the customs officials, so no one would know he was there until he was gone. Like in Bristol, he just disappeared in the night."

Merry glared. "There's more, isn't there, My Lord. I want to hear everything. Did he ransack the village? Burn the village to ash? Carry off the women? What mischief was he about this time? Don't worry about Kate. She is used to being shocked."

"What nonsense," Philip stated brusquely. "He's a pirate. A criminal. You prattle on about his exploits as if he's one of those heroes in those ridiculous novels you read."

"You have to admire the man for his audacity," Merry said in quick defense. "There's not another pirate who has been more successful against mighty England. I doubt he's the evil villain you purport him to be."

"What an idiotic child you can be," Philip countered grimly. "The man is a pirate. He would as soon murder you as look at you, if it suited his fancy. Don't let yourself be carried away with fanciful notions of romantic heroes, Merry. Morgan is a criminal. It won't be long before he hangs from the gibbet."

"They'll never catch Morgan," Merry rebuked harshly.

"Morgan's villainy, like his fame, is soon to expire," Philip flung with brutal force. "You would do better to occupy your mind with thoughts of a husband, rather than pirates."

Merry stared at him, the picture of wide-eyed sisterly concern as she said, "And you would do better to stay out of the gaming-halls in Falmouth and Molly Saunder's arms. You should go about finding a wife to breed an heir, so they would have less worry about me. Or, was that not your discussion with Papa, last night?"

Philip's entire face reddened. "You go beyond the limit, Merry. To skulk around the house spying is shameful enough, but to make mention of your petty eavesdropping before Michael and Kate is beyond tolerance. I can't imagine why Michael puts up with you. 'Tis no wonder you've become a scandal and you're not married."

"'Tis no wonder you're not," Merry countered sweetly.

"Please, Merry, don't ruin this lovely day with your temper," Kate suggested quietly. "Your brother has every right to be displeased with you."

"You can't mean to take Philip's side."

"I am on the side of these delicious blackberry tarts. I can't enjoy them if you two are scowling at one another."

Philip choked on the laughter he tried to subdue. Kate, as always, was simplicity and sweetness itself. Smiling at his sister he said, "Come on, Pet, smile at me so Kate can enjoy her feast.

It's terrible of us to fight in front of the good viscount. We are giving him a terrible impression of your sweet and docile nature."

"You were hateful and you know it," Merry said peevishly.

"Yes, I was," Philip agreed generously, "but only because I am deuced uncomfortable in this coat. Now smile, Sweeting. I am sorry I lost my temper with you."

Reluctantly, Merry smiled. She could never stay angry at Philip. "Whatever will we do when Rensdale leaves us? We won't have a reason to end our quibbles."

"You should have no worry then, Merry," Lord Rensdale said with steely determination. "I thought you would come to accept that I have no intention of leaving."

Her blue eyes sparkled. "Ah, but of course you are leaving, Rensdale."

The trotting rhythm of hoof beats pushed their discussion from Merry's mind.

Lifting a hand to shade her eyes, she looked toward the narrow gravel drive, to see Lord Warton making his way toward the simple brick cottage.

"It's Warton. How marvelous," she announced unnecessarily, charging unceremoniously through a lilac bush.

She gathered her silk skirt into her hands, mindless that in doing so she revealed her slim ankles and bare feet, and jogged lightly across the green meadow to the road.

"Lord Warton. Hallo. Greetings," she cried excitedly, smiling brightly up at her father's friend. "What brings you here from London?"

Grinning, Warton slipped from the saddle, doffing his hat from his graying tawny mane. "I came to see you, of course. The sight of your pretty face is the only thing in England worth braving the wilds of Cornwall to see."

"If that is true, then why do you not join us more often,"

she accused lightly. "Surely you know that you've been missed."

"Missed? With the elegant Rensdale to keep you occupied?" He smiled down at her, knowing very well how his comment irritated her. "Am I finally to be replaced in your affections by our gallant young viscount?"

Merry fairly bristled at the question. "Rensdale is a conceited oaf. For the life of me I can't understand why my parents would agree to a match with him. Or, why he persists in this courtship." Dismissing Rensdale from her mind, she asked, "Why have you come to Bramble Hill?"

"To see how our poor Rensdale fairs, of course. I can think of no greater amusements than watching you torture him while putting him through the paces."

Only urgent business of the Foreign Office could force the genial Warton from the comforts of London.

Slipping her arm through his, they climbed the stone steps toward the main entrance of the house.

"I wish it were a social call that has brought you to Cornwall. Uncle Andrew only recently returned from his latest mission. I should hate to see him leave again, so soon. If only the Americans and the French would stop making war. Kate sees little enough of her father. Can't Whitehall give him even a moment's peace? Is it serious?"

"Nothing to trouble your mind about, Merry."

Regardless of his denials, Merry wasn't diverted. For Warton to have traveled such a great distance, something important must be happening, maybe peace with America? Had the peace talks finally become un-stalled? The Merricks were unified in their opposition to the war with America. Warton was here for only one reason, to deliver information from the Foreign Office to Uncle Andrew. Andrew was one of Whitehall's best agents.

A thought came to her, out of nowhere, arousing her

curiosity despite its absurdity.

"The *Corinthian*. Is that why you've come? Is Uncle Andrew now trying to root out pirates, instead of spies? We heard that Morgan was in Swansea a fortnight ago."

Warton laughed to hide his shock. "What a fanciful mind you have, Merry. Pirates, indeed. There isn't a pirate within two hundred miles of Falmouth. As for a blackguard like Morgan, he's not Lord Andrew's interest."

"Then whose interest is he? Surely Whitehall has set someone to the task of capturing this man."

"Of course they have. Never doubt it. But it would hardly require one of England's best operatives to capture a common criminal, especially during this time of war. There is nothing for you to be frightened of, Merry."

"Frightened? You should know better than that, Warton. My father believes I haven't an ounce of fear in me, or sense for that matter."

"And have you?" Warton teased affectionately.

"Sense? Don't doubt it. But fear, no I can't say that I do. How could anyone be afraid with such gallant men as you and Uncle Andrew protecting England?"

"Don't work your flirtations on me. I am on to your tricks. I have learned from experience they only mean trouble. What is it you want, Merry?"

"A chance to choose my own fate," Merry admitted softly.

Wharton laughed quietly. "As if anyone could force your hand."

"Can't they?" Merry's wide blue eyes searched Warton's face.

If her father was making plans for her future, Warton would surely know.

"Has my father grown weary of me and decided to settle my future himself? Do you think he intends to marry me to

Rensdale, though I have expressly told him that I don't wish it?"

"Really, Merry, what has your father ever done to make you distrust him?"

"Nothing," she admitted, though she could not shake the feeling that something was about to happen.

"Then, your suspicions do him a disservice. His Grace is one of the finest men I have ever known. Stop your worrying, Kitten. He only wants your happiness, as do we all."

It wasn't until much later that Merry realized that Warton hadn't answered her question, at all. But by then, it was too late. He was locked away in her father's study and the chance to press him for the truth was lost.

~ ~ ~

Rensdale's sharp gaze fixed on the heavy double doors Merry disappeared through. Her cool dismissal of him was intolerable.

"Staring at the door won't make her return," Philip said glibly, pushing away from the wall. "Let's ride to Falmouth. We can share a few glasses of ale and you can tell me your woes." A wicked grin twisted his lips. "Or better still, a bottle or two of *Grave's End's* famous Blue Ruin? That will grant you a moment's peace from your courtship of my exasperating sister. You did wish to go there as I recall. Though what amusements Jack Shelby and his rough lot can afford, is beyond me."

Michael forced his thoughts behind an expression of lovesick woe before turning to face Philip. "I doubt even Jack Shelby's Blue Ruin could push your vexing sister from my mind."

Philip's laughter was low and amused. "We will try, my friend. And if not, I know a place in Falmouth where..." his voice died off as they made their way toward the stables.

Kate stared after them as her cousin and the viscount disappeared across the lawn. What she had seen on Rensdale's

17

face made the pit of her stomach grow cold. For a moment, she had caught sight of something in the viscount's eyes, as he stared after Merry, which she had never seen before. A hint of malevolence mingling with his annoyance. It was not the look of a man hopelessly in love. It was a look that boded ill and suddenly she was very afraid for Merry.

~~~

There was quiet from the study. Merry waited anxiously in the small day room beside her father's study, huddled beside the open window.

"Something has happened, hasn't it, Warton?" Lucien Merrick asked. "Your message stated it was urgent."

"Yes, Your Grace. I would not have come otherwise." The voice belonged to Lord Warton. "I knew this matter was of particular interest to you, Andrew."

There was a rustling of paper, and then her uncle's voice said in a calm tone, "Yes. I have chased after the bastard, the length of the Atlantic many times over. How accurate is this information?"

"From Castlereagh, himself," said Warton.

"Who knows of it?"

"No one," Warton assured Lord Andrew in a determined voice. "We thought it best to keep the information among ourselves. Castlereagh trusts no one. We've not discovered the identity of the spy in the Foreign Office. The information Morgan is receiving comes from very high up. How else would the blackguard know our every move? Sails in and out of British ports as if he belongs. He's giving intelligence fits."

"My Kate could give British intelligence fits," Andrew put in sardonically. "It's been damn poor, lately."

"Morgan's spies have infiltrated at the highest levels," the duke agreed blandly. "It does not take luck when one knows exactly which ports to avoid. Have we made any progress in finding out who our traitor could be?"

"No," Warton informed him unhappily. "That is why I could not trust this information by courier. We thought it best to meet here."

There was a heavy silence. "How will you precede, Andrew?" the duke asked.

"What do you know of Sir Atterby, Lucien?"

"Impoverished. Desperate. The perfect makings for a traitor. I could never understand how anyone on Wilbrook's staff could find use for the wretch."

"Then, you have confidence that this information is accurate?" Lord Andrew asked of his brother. "You think Sir Atterby might well be a spy? That he is selling information to Morgan, and will assist him to land his cargo on his lands tonight?"

Merry's eyes widened in shock. *Morgan!*

"I haven't a problem believing that Atterby is selling information to Morgan," the duke said. "You've only scratched the surface. Atterby has not the position to unearth as much information as Morgan possesses. I should think that much of it is coming from higher up than Atterby. Much higher."

"Atterby is a good start," her Uncle Andrew stated in displeasure.

"Only a start, Andrew," the duke said with quiet certainty. "Morgan. He seems a man of great capabilities. He wouldn't trust a man like Atterby with knowledge of himself."

"Then, I had better make sure that nothing goes awry and we capture Morgan tonight," Andrew stated arrogantly. "No outsiders, Warton. I don't trust anyone these days. Morgan seems to be aware of what my next move will be, even before I have plotted it."

"With your permission, Andrew, I would like to ride with you as well," Warton said.

Lucien Merrick and his brother laughed heartily.

"Like old times, eh, Warton," the duke murmured in amusement. "I wish I could join you both."

"There is much we must accomplish before nightfall," Andrew Merrick announced, rising from his chair. "My men, thankfully, are all in Falmouth awaiting new orders. They should be in fine form for this adventure. They were most frustrated by our last failed attempt to bring Captain Morgan to justice. How we missed him at Swansea..."

His words trailed off with his thoughts. He would never know how Morgan managed that.

"I wish that I could join you both on this rout," the Duke of Dorset said ruefully. "Morgan reminds me much of myself. I can't help but wonder if England would not be better served by turning this man to her side, rather than to settle for his death."

"You sound as if you admire the man," Warton exclaimed incredulously.

"He's been a worthy adversary. How can I not admire a man who has had the three of us running in circles for over a year?"

That comment naturally brought Merry to Warton's mind. Grinning, he exclaimed, "Ah, Your Grace, I almost forgot. In London I acquired a dispatch to be delivered to you."

"Morgan?" Andrew asked, studying his brother.

The Duke of Dorset smiled. "No. Whitehall has their problems and I have mine."

"But yours grows more beautiful each day, Your Grace," Warton said in amusement.

The Duke of Dorset laughed. "Morgan can't compare with the trials to be endured at the hand of a blue eyed filly, with too much spirit, and not enough sense."

"She is, after all, your daughter, Lucien."

"That she is, Andrew, but with enough of Rhea in her to

make up for that."

"I should be off to Falmouth," Lord Warton announced, rising from his chair.

"I shall see you at nightfall, Warton. Perhaps we'll have an end to the deuced annoyance," Andrew Merrick announced, seeing his friend to the study door.

"A bit of good luck, at last, Andrew," the duke murmured.

"We will see how long our luck holds. I have nearly had Morgan three times and he's escaped. He should not have escaped me in Swansea. I still don't know how he managed to know my moves there."

"You will succeed, Andrew. Castlereagh has faith in you, and so do I."

Andrew laughed gruffly. "Castlereagh would rest easier if you were to take this matter in hand, Lucien. I know very well, he thinks me second best."

"I have my own problems, Andrew. Would that I could trade them for yours."

Andrew Merrick smiled with wry understanding. "Merry?"

"What else? Another season. Another scandal. I won't have it. Not again."

The steely determination in her father's voice was impossible to miss. Merry tensed. "What is that you have, Lucien?" Andrew asked.

Lucien Merrick sighed. "Perhaps the solution for my dilemma."

Andrew scanned the papers. "Good God, Lucien, how could you even consider this?"

"She's had her pick among the dandies at court. I won't tolerate Merry's delays any longer. She is left to choosing from these two fates in my hand. It is past time for her to marry, and marry she will. Last season, for all the interest she stirred, not a single offer was forthcoming. If left on her own, it will not be

21

long before not a single respectable family will receive her. Her actions grow more scandalous. I live in dread of her every whim."

"Her escapades, though reckless and foolish, are not so shocking or serious, Lucien. You exaggerate it all out of proportion."

Lucien Merrick smiled grimly. "Do you forget what she did at Carlton House? Would you be so tolerant if it were your Kate?"

"It was youthful foolishness and the regent was not greatly miffed."

"Only because Brummel laughed. It galls me to no end that I owe my daughter's continued good grace in society to that man. She is my daughter and a Merrick. It has come to this. That upstart, that bounder shielding her against her actions, when the name of Merrick can no longer accomplish that feat. You know how I detest Brummell. Now, I am in his debt and the blackguard knows it."

"Dear Lord, Lucien, you make it sound like she engaged in treason."

"People have had their head on Traitor's Gate for less. We are at war with America. If Prinny hadn't settled on tolerance because of Brummel's amusement, there would have been nothing I could have done to protect her. You know that, Andrew."

"She sang 'The Rich Lady Over the Sea'. That's all. Of course, it was not wise to do so with Prinny and half of London in attendance to hear. But, it can hardly come as too great a shock when the street pamphlets bandy about your opposition to the war with America. It is common knowledge how the Merricks feel about this matter, Lucien, and you have hardly been silent. She is nothing, if not loyal to her politics. Both you and I openly oppose England's Orders in Council. She is a

Merrick, after all. What she did, it was not so shocking or a scandal."

"I opposed the Orders in Council. I oppose the blockade of American ports. I don't expound treason in the midst of social gatherings with the regent, no less."

"Neither does Merry."

"Not yet, but I have come to accept that I can put nothing past her."

Merry's cheeks burned. Did her father really think her capable of treason? How could he have misunderstood her so completely?

The lampoons plastered on the streets in London had been horrible, expressing outrage at the Merrick's well-known politics, opposing the war with America. It had seemed a reasonable reply at the time. Rensdale had been so obviously shocked by her brother's suggestion, that the thought of not doing it had never entered her mind. She had wanted only to irritate Rensdale, and to tell London to go to the devil with their opinions of the Merricks. She hadn't thought of the implications of her acts.

How could her father react so strongly when their politics were the same? How could he think her capable of treason?

"I think you make too much of this," Andrew said sagely.

"What about her other follies? Her blatant association with the young radical set in London, spouting their anti-monarchal rhetoric, wanting to bridge the classes and the sexes. She exercises absolutely no caution in voicing her sympathies for the cause of the Americans, and openly expounds the fairness of the destruction of the aristocracy. Her absolute lack of decorum is how she deports herself in all circumstances. At Bramble Hill, her conduct is no better than a common farm lass. Spinning, weaving, plaiting straw, and running bare foot through meadows. All eliminate the possibility of an excellent marriage. She stubbornly refuses to behave in a manner that befits her birth, or by settling herself in marriage. The London scandalmongers make sport of her, Andrew. Am I to wait until no respectable family in England will have her, until she brings about her complete ruin?"

"She is a spirited girl who enjoys living, Lucien. Her position is secure."

"I mean to see it remains that way."

"I can't believe that you will truly do this, Lucien."

There was no softening in the duke's voice. "I have decided upon this course. We all must accept certain standards of conduct for our own wellbeing. Merry seems incline not to. Only this afternoon, she was clashing swords with Rensdale in the front pasture. How much more do you think Rensdale will tolerate from her? Who will I find to replace him, once his interest is pushed to the limit? Rensdale has made his suit. The terms are both generous and fair. She needs a husband and children to settle her down. Rhea and I—" his voice broke with regret, "—we have been too indulgent with her in the past. I can't afford to indulge her whim any longer."

"She loathes Rensdale, Lucien."

"Merry sees Rensdale, not as a man, but a threat to her independence. Once she marries him, she will see her fight will do her no good. And what will indulging Merry bring her? Unhappiness in the end, when she finds herself a social outcast. Without a husband, without her reputation, or a choice. Then, what will her life be? I can't allow that, Andrew. She forces me to leave her to either Rensdale or Windmere. I will sign her into marriage this very week, with one or the other. She will have no choice but to honor my selection and my seal."

"But Windmere, Lucien. How can you even consider giving the care of your daughter to that man?" The intense dismay in her uncle's voice made Merry shiver.

"Rhea has always approved of him, Andrew. Even though the tragedy nearly broke her heart, she would never allow anyone to speak a word against him in her presence. After he was forced to quit England, when the rumors would not wane, she went to Windmere to let him know she had never once thought ill of him. She knew the canaille was unjust in their prosecution of him. Even after ten years, my wife is still his loyal friend and will not tolerate old gossip to add to Windmere's grief."

"That does not change the fact, that it has never been learned, what truly happened. My God, Lucien, how can you so quickly dismiss what he was accused of doing, without proof that this man will not bring harm to Merry? We don't even know where he's been this past decade."

"Do you have so little faith in me, Andrew? If I can't trust Rhea with the welfare of our daughter's future, who should I trust?"

"I can't accept that things are so desperate that you and Rhea would force Merry's hand into marriage, with such a man as Windmere. He is twice Merry's age, old enough to be her father."

"Rhea and I are in agreement on this, Andrew. It is for Merry's sake that we are committed to this course. If Merry proves too contrary to accept a match with Rensdale, I will wed her to Windmere. As much as it pains me, I can't ignore the truth. Merry's conduct has ruined any chance we have of making her a decent match. Rensdale is a fine man. I have no reason to distrust Rhea and believe that Windmere is, as well."

There was a long, tense pause. "I think you will rue this decision, Lucien. Merry is young. She'll be terrified of Windmere, for all her bravado with the dandies. You should not be so quick to act in this matter, Lucien. What harm will time cause any of us?"

"A rather good situation, all things considered. Another year, Andrew, and even Rensdale and Windmere may not want my daughter."

"You might very well push the girl too hard with all this. Have you considered that, Lucien?"

"I will see this matter set before she leaves for London. No more delays. When she goes to London for the season, it will be to prepare for her marriage."

CHAPTER TWO

Merry glided into the west drawing room and immediately went to the windows facing the front drive. Beneath her feet the subtly warped polished surface of the floor held a pleasant coolness, telling her that the fog would roll in thickly this night.

This room held none of the splendor of a ducal estate. The walls were hung in a pretty buff yellow tabby. The furnishings, lavish in purchase, were winsomely comfortable and without even a mild effort at pomp. Every inch was cleverly and informally arranged. The only efforts her mother had made with her style of decor were those to please a family.

Merry sighed, her eyes searching the dramatic view of the coast and water. It was always the Channel that claimed her undivided attention this time of night. The darkness descended across the Heavens and the blue-starred sky was gently obscured by a thin rolling of mist that would suddenly thicken, as though by magic, to block out all view of the world beyond.

But this night Merry found no pleasure in this familiar sight. Searching the rosy sandstone drive, fully obscured by darkness, panic rose in her senses. Her father's words weighed heavily upon her mind.

How could he mean to force her into marriage? He knew how she felt about Rensdale. He had gone so far as to draw up contracts with a man she had never met to force her hand. What was she going to do?

If only Rensdale were here, she could find a way to get rid

of him once and for all. But how? How to stop it? She had done everything she could think of, in the past two years, to get Rensdale to cry off of his offer for her hand. Nothing worked and the thought of marrying him sent a cold chill through her soul.

No, she would not marry Rensdale. And, she would not marry this Windmere person. How could her father have devised such a scheme? Was he so desperate to see a match settled for her that he would actually resort to such under-handed means?

The nervous churning of her stomach intensified as she recalled her uncle's words. Who the devil was Windmere?

Uncle Andrew had said he was a man old enough to be her father. He fled England when she'd still had been a young girl, to avoid a scandal so wicked it was not even known to her.

What could Windmere have done that was so nefarious, that she, who was privy to all the gossip of the ton, had never heard either his name or a whisper of the scandal surrounding him? Did her father mean to use this wicked bounder as a whip over her head, to frighten her into doing his bidding?

It was beyond belief. There was no amount of coercion possible to get her to agree to become Rensdale's wife.

She frantically searched the drive. Where were they? Knowing Philip, they might well be half-way to London by now. She needed Rensdale here, needed to make him withdraw his suit, to stop this terrible event from occurring.

Once the contracts were signed, even Merry would be unable to stop it. She would have to go after Rensdale. There was no other way.

Merry was unaware that her mother had been studying her, for quite some time, from her seat on the settee. Her quill and note cards were forgotten, lying in a disorderly heap on the lap desk as she wondered what thoughts occupied her daughter's mind and made her appear so unhappy.

"Ah, no wonder you can come into a room so quietly. You've forgotten your shoes."

Blushing, Merry looked down at her toes, still speckled with dirt and wisps of grass. She should have washed them.

"How scandalized Rensdale would be by my latest lapse in decorum."

"I, however, am not scandalized, my dear," Rhea said, in sweet loving tones. "I am only concerned. After that cold you suffered last month I prefer you not to run barefoot. You are not fully recovered."

"I prefer the feel of grass on my feet rather than the feel of shoe leather."

Arming her nerves, Merry turned toward her mother. As always, she was struck by the sharp contrast between them. Her mother was a small, elegant vision, stylishly turned out in coral silk, artfully arranged short brown curls, and dancing chocolate brown eyes. Her looks, Merry had inherited from her father while her inner composition was a mystery unresolved.

"Merry? What troubles you, dear?"

"Nothing, Mama," Merry answered abruptly.

"You are very quiet tonight. You've not said two words since supper. Has something happened to distress you?"

She sank into a chair, curling her legs up in front her. "I am not upset, only bored."

Rhea ran her glance over her daughter's inappropriate posture, knowing it was a useless effort to chide her on this. As outrageous as it was, she curled in a chair even at Carlton House with the regent.

It was little wonder that society bent an unkind eye on Merry. But, there was something charming about her graceful naturalness that always kept Rhea from responding severely with her daughter. They had given Merry too much free reign in her upbringing. She had been raised in the country and as a result her daughter possessed a county girl's heart and manner.

Only yesterday, she had spent the afternoon with Jane Coleman, the wife of their under-coachman, making black pudding, no less. She had come home filthy and in disarray at dusk. She had spent only ten minutes on her toilette for the Sanderson's country ball they attended that night.

Bathed, hair still damp and scented of roses, tied in a simple knot on her shoulder, she had pulled on a modest gown of white on white muslin and had climbed into the carriage without her shoes. They'd had to keep the team standing and send Moffat off for them.

Rensdale had been outraged. However, even thusly turned out, Merry's beauty put any other woman to shame. The viscount's outrage hadn't lasted the carriage ride. No displeasure from any of them ever lasted a carriage ride with Merry in amusement. Merry could charm the devil with her laughter.

Elegant, composed, and sophisticated her daughter was not. She was little changed from the girl they had sent to London, three seasons ago, for her coming out into society.

In the secret chambers of Rhea's heart, she was pleased that Merry was as she was, regardless of the difficulties it created for all of them. She was a whirlwind of joyful movement, temper flashes, laughing storms, and a constant source of bliss at Bramble Hill. To Rhea's pride, to her joy, to her exasperation: she was Merry.

The duchess picked up her quill. "Do you look forward to your return to London?"

"No. I find the season a tiresome chore. I much prefer the simple pleasures of our life here, rather than the smothering bustle of London."

"You must attend the season, Merry. There is little hope of you finding a husband here. We are so isolated at Bramble

Hill."

"I do not want a husband," Merry snapped furiously.

"Merry, you are nearly twenty," Rhea said patiently. "It is time for you to marry. To have a home, children of your own, and your own life. Don't you want that, dear?"

"Were you in love with Papa when you married him?"

Rhea laughed softly. "I could not help but love him. Your father is a most persuasive man. I did not start out loving him, but in the end he left me little choice."

"Would you have married him without love?"

Rhea put down her quill. "It was an arranged marriage. I would have honored my father's promise, even if I had not fallen in love with your father. It is my duty as a woman."

Just as I am expected to do, Merry thought derisively. *My duty as a woman. Captivity to a man.*

"Why are you and Papa so determined to see me wed to Lord Rensdale, when you know that I don't love him? Am I asking too much wanting my freedom, rather than settling to marry a man, whom I will never hope to be happy with?"

"Rensdale will make you a fine husband, Merry."

"I did not say that he would not. I said that I do not love him."

"Love comes after marriage for some women," Rhea put in sagely.

"I don't want love or marriage," Merry countered stubbornly, rising from her chair and going to the window. "I have no want of a husband. I have no wish to live my life in servitude to a man, trying to be things that will not make me happy."

Rhea studied her daughter, her heart filled with a mother's worries. Were they doing the right thing? She had agreed with Lucien that the matter of Merry's marriage could not be put off for another season. But was it right to see it settled this way?

It would take a man with a firm hand, a tender heart, and unshakeable self-confidence not to crush Merry's spirit. A man, who could see through her spirited facade, a man who would not be put off by her tempers and her airs or blinded to the gentleness, of the fragile heart buried within. A man just like Lucien, thought the duchess tenderly. Few men had such a blend of strength and tenderness.

Windmere came clearly into Rhea's mind. She wondered if the passage of time had changed him, if he were still so handsome and sure of himself. Had the sorrow and bitterness finally left his heart? Had the pain lessened enough that he would, at last, return to England? Was that why, after ten years, he had come from out of nowhere to make an offer to take Merry to wife? Was he aware of Merry's censure? Did the old suspicions still haunt him? Would he accept their daughter, despite her current lack of favor in society, to gain a wife of good family and birth to start anew?

How any could accuse Windmere of the tragedy was beyond her. She would more trust Windmere than Rensdale, with Merry's heart. She wondered if Rensdale knew of this unexpected offer and what his reaction would be. Rensdale was a pale shadow beside Windmere. It was hard to credit that they were related by blood.

Next to Lucien, Windmere had been the finest man she had ever known. Whereas Rensdale... Rhea frowned. Was it only Rensdale's great difference to Lucien that made her think less of him than Windmere?

"Am I so wrong not to want Rensdale? To want more? To want more than be the wife of a dandified lord in London, who thinks only to be my master? Why can't I have a grand tour of Europe as Philip did? Why can't I journey to America as I long to? Why can't I determine my own fate? Why, as a woman, is my only option marriage? I would rather stay with you here, than to live my life with a man I can't love. Deporting myself as someone I am not, doing things that have no meaning, and being all the things I despise, so I do not offend his or society's eye. Am I wrong to want more?"

Rhea studied her daughter's lovely passionate face, amused by her melodrama and saddened by her innocence.

Such hope belonged to the young, but her daughter could not fight the ways of the world forever. There were no other options, in polite society, for a girl of Merry's birth. All roads eventually would lead to marriage, whether her daughter accepted that or not. Her fate had been set at the moment of her birth with the sex that God had granted her.

"No, Sweetheart, you are not wrong, but perhaps you have set your expectations too high. Marriage is your duty. You refuse to give any man, even a fair chance to see if they may be what it is you desire. You are too impatient. You want conformation, at first glance, that they will be all you wish them to be. Even the finest man is a blend of both good and bad, a man of strengths and weaknesses. None of us are without faults."

"I have Papa to blame for my high expectations. Next to him, I find all men sadly lacking."

Rhea laughed. "I imagine you would."

"Perhaps, if I could find one whom I could develop affection for, who can accept me as I am, then perhaps, I would become his wife. But, Rensdale is not that man, and he never will be."

~~~

Lightening illuminated the blackening skies beyond the tall casement windows. A brilliant flash highlighted the lone figure seated in the center of the rug. The candles had long been doused, the servants sent off for the night, but Rhea Merrick did not abandon her wait in her private salon. Her daughter's words replayed themselves, over and over again, in her head.

"Rhea?"

Startled, Rhea cried out. For a moment, she imagined that the portrait had spoken her name in a husky whisper, instead of the man she had yet to see looming in the doorway.

Rhea stared up into the handsome face of her husband. The years had hardly touched him at all, she thought. She remembered all those years ago, when she had first fallen in love with Lucien Merrick.

He was still tall, still lean, a touch of gray mixing with his jet black waves, and though there were more lines on his face to mark the passing of time, she could image no man affecting her as deeply as Lucien was now, with the barest glimmer of a smile hovering at the corners of the his lips.

It amazed her now that she had once been frightened of his commanding figure. She had completely missed the tell-tell mirth-light in those imposing blue eyes and had not been able to see the soul deep gentleness she had come to know, so well.

"What are you doing here alone in the dark?" Lucien asked, crossing the flowered carpet, sinking down beside his petite wife.

Rhea smiled tenderly. "I was thinking back to the first day you brought me here to Bramble Hill. Of this room, and what happened in it."

Lucien grinned wickedly. "You seduced me, as I recall it."

"You would remember it that way," Rhea laughed, playfully poking her husband in the ribs. "I was not thinking so much about what we did, but how I felt. How much I loved you. We were so happy then, Lucien, in our honey month."

"Were? Are you no longer happy as my wife, Rhea?"

"Foolish man. How can you ask such a thing? I was thinking of Merry. Do you think she'll ever know with Rensdale, even a measure of the happiness we had when we were young?"

Understanding came to Lucien with the ease that came from having loved Rhea for over two decades. "We are still young," he countered in amusement, pulling her tiny form up against him. "There are times I find it hard to believe you old enough to share my bed."

"Rensdale will not make her happy, Lucien."

"You can't know that for certain, Rhea."

"I know." Rhea rested her head against Lucien's shoulder. "If you had not loved me, would you have married Jane as the marriage contract ordered?"

"How could you even ask such a thing, after all this time?" Lucien was clearly shocked by the question. "I loved you from the moment I first set eyes upon you, Rhea. I was determined to have no other. It would not have mattered how many contracts bound me to Jane, I could marry no other."

"Merry is every inch your daughter, Lucien." Rhea pointed out sagely. "She will not bend. She will not marry Rensdale. Your will or not."

Lucien frowned. "You can't compare Merry and Rensdale to us. I loved you, Rhea. There was no doubt of what was in my heart."

"I was twenty when we wed," Rhea reminded her husband calmly, "and until we met, I did not think myself capable of finding love. But, I knew what I wanted. What my heart hungered for." Rhea moved back a little, her huge brown eyes wide and glistening, as she stared up at him. "I wanted you, Lucien. Though I did not know your name, or if you even existed, at all. I wanted you. I would not have settled until I found you. You can be certain of that, my love."

Lucien was quiet. Too quiet, Rhea thought. After a long pause she felt him relax, his long fingers closing over hers, and she smiled to herself.

"Letting Merry have her way will bring no good, Rhea. You know that I am determined to see Merry wed to Rensdale, this year. Yet, you disarm me without my even seeing the danger of your words. You are a devious woman, Rhea Merrick."

Rhea shook her head. "A happy woman and that is what I want for our daughter."

Lucien sighed. "You want me not to settle Merry's future?"

"Give her another year, Lucien. To find what we have found. If we give her time, she will settle on her fate. She can't escape being a woman forever. She will not run from the right man. Even her stubborn heart will find a man she can't dismiss by will, just as my heart could not dismiss you. Let her find what I have found with you."

With a graceful gesture, Lucien lifted his wife upon his lap. Pulling her back against him, his hands slowly parted the bodice of her gown as he breathed in her ear, "Impossible, Rhea. What we have found happens only once in a century."

"I am sure you are right," Rhea whispered, her heart beating wildly. His hands slipped inside to cup her breasts, as his lips pressed fiery kisses along her suddenly bare shoulder. "Lucien," she objected huskily, feeling her husband's rising passion along with the heat spreading through her own limbs. "What if someone should come looking for us?"

He turned her in his arms, silencing her with his lips. "They would not dare," he breathed against her mouth as he gently lowered her to the floor. "As I recall, this is where it happened that first night."

"I love you, Lucien."

"Enough words, Rhea. Show me."

~~~

Merry carefully buttoned the battered white shirt, tucking it into the baggy breeches she had stolen from the servants wash.

The clock on her bedside had just chimed midnight, and she knew it was pointless to wait any longer. Rensdale and Philip were not coming home, and there was no choice but to go after them.

I will never marry Rensdale, Merry vowed to herself, drawing back the curtains. She peered restlessly out into the darkness. If it took all night she would find Rensdale and put a stop to her father's plotting.

Twisting her ebony curls into a knot, she shoved the wooly cap atop her head. She tucked a small pouch of coins into her waistband, before carefully slipping a dagger into her boot.

Merry opened the window and climbed up onto the sill.

"Merry. Where the devil are you going?"

Kate was standing in the doorway.

"I thought you'd gone to bed."

"Oh, Merry, what foolishness are you chasing this time?" Kate closed the door, taking in her cousin and her curious manner of dress.

"Really, Kate. There is no need for your drama. I am going for a ride that is all."

"Melodramatic, am I? I am not the one about to drop two stories. One usually leaves through the door, unless they are up to no good."

Merry shrugged, hoping she looked more composed than she felt. "You know how my father has forbidden me riding at night. He would stop me if he knew."

"The truth, Merry. What in Heaven's name are you up to?" Kate demanded with uncharacteristic sharpness. "I am going to get Uncle Lucien."

"No," Merry cried, springing from the windowsill and going to Kate's side. "Don't. Please, you can't. I beg of you. Tell no one."

"What is happening, Merry? What is wrong?"

"I am going after Rensdale. It is necessary that I speak with him tonight and since he has not returned, I must go after him."

"What could be so urgent that you can't wait until morning...?" Kate lost all color. "The marriage contract has been drawn, hasn't it?"

"Yes, but my father has not signed it. He won't, if I have any say in the matter. That is why I must find Rensdale. To get him to withdraw his offer. I won't marry him, Kate."

"Oh, Merry, I don't think there is anything you can say that will get him to withdraw his offer. He seems a most determined man where you are concerned."

"I must at least try, Kate. My father means to force me into the marriage. You would not believe the plot he has concocted to force me to consent."

"Force you? Merry, surely, you've misunderstood your father. He would not force you wed that horrible man."

Merry was shocked by the venom in her cousin's voice.

"You don't like Rensdale either, do you? Why? I thought it just me."

"He frightens me. The way he looks at you, Merry, when he thinks no one is watching him. I don't understand it. It makes me afraid for you. You can't go after him, Merry. Something terrible will happen if you should find yourself alone with him."

Merry laughed aside her fear. "Do you think I can't handle Rensdale? What harm could he possibly do to me, except bore me to death with that insipid drivel he spouts from morning till night?"

"No. I won't allow you to do this. The thought of you alone with him terrifies me. And if, by chance, you are seen? It would be disastrous for you to be caught meeting with the viscount alone. You would find yourself wed, no matter your objections."

"Be sensible. Philip is with him. What harm could he do me with Philip there?"

"And Philip is known for exercising good judgment? Do you expect me to trust that they are still together, and that Philip will see you safely in this?"

"I will not sit idly by and let my father seal my fate," Merry replied with a toss of her head. "I have little to lose. Unless I find Rensdale, tomorrow I will find myself betrothed to that man."

"I think you are acting rashly, Merry, and no good will come of it. Uncle Lucien would not do what you accuse him of, and Rensdale would like nothing better than a scandal to serve his ends. Can you not see how little sense there is in you going after the viscount?"

"Can you see how little sense there is in doing nothing?" Merry countered firmly, meeting her cousin's worried gaze.

With a ragged sigh, Kate had to admit that Merry was right.

Reluctantly, Kate murmured, "If you are determined to go after Rensdale, then I am going with you, Merry, to see that you come to no harm."

"Kate, you can't come. The only way out of the house is the tree outside my window. You couldn't even manage it when we were children. How do you expect to now? You could never manage it."

Kate lifted her chin stubbornly. "I am going, and there is nothing you can do to stop me. Besides, you will never find Rensdale without my help. I know where they have gone."

"I won't allow you to come."

"You are in no position to allow me anything, Merry," Kate said calmly. "I will not tell you where they have gone,

unless you take me with you. I don't trust Rensdale, and I won't
have you risk meeting him alone."

"Really, Kate. Can't you see how absurd it is for you to
think you can protect me? What do you plan to wear? You can't
ride into Falmouth clad only in your dressing gown."

"I am going with you, Merry, and that is that," Kate said,
going to the closet and pulling out her cousin's blue riding
habit. "If you dare to step a foot from this house without me, I
will go to Uncle Lucien. I promise you, I will tell him the whole
of it."

With a frustrated sigh, Merry sank down on the bed,
waiting for her cousin to change.

"You have a stubborn nature, Kate Merrick," Merry
pointed out unkindly.

"It is the one trait we share," Kate countered, stepping
from the dressing room and hastily finishing the fastenings on
her garments.

Kate followed her young cousin to the window.

"You must not look down," Merry warned. "You will fall
if you look down. Move out onto the sill and grab the branch. It
is not as far as it looks, Kate. Truly."

With the grace of a cat, Merry pushed off, catching the
branch of the large oak beyond. Merry quickly made her
descent, half climbing, half slipping, until she dropped the final
few feet to the ground. Her hands burned from rubbing against
the bark, and she shook them wildly, trying to sooth her
throbbing flesh.

"It's not so difficult."

Kate's arms and legs refused to cooperate as she tried to
push off as her cousin had done. Good Lord, what had she
gotten herself in to?

It was a fool's errand Merry was forcing her to join. Even
if they found Rensdale, no good would come of it. Rensdale

would, most likely, tell Lucien Merrick the entire affair to suit his own ends. There'd be the devil to pay for this night's work if they were caught. Furthermore, what would Uncle Lucien think, if he learned her part in this reckless escapade?

She was supposed to help keep Merry's conduct in line, provide a good example, and try to harness some of that impulsive spirit.

Merry running amuck and me running amuck with her, Kate thought fretfully.

Holding her breath, Kate lunged for the tree.

Merry watched in amusement, as her cousin followed the same path down the tree and could not contain a laugh as Kate plopped to the earth, landing unceremoniously on her backside.

"Are you all right?" Merry asked. "I told you not to look down."

"I could have done very nicely without that last five feet."

"I did not think you would do it, at all."

"I couldn't let you go off alone. That's what you'd have done if I hadn't followed."

"You said you knew where Rensdale and Philip had taken off to," Merry reminded her impatiently.

"Some ridiculous tavern called *Grave's End*," Kate replied absently, rubbing her tender backside.

Merry's eyes rounded. "*Grave's End*. Are you sure, Kate?"

"For some vile concoction called 'Blue Ruin'." Kate nodded, her pale brows puckered on her forehead. "What the devil do you imagine that to be? And, why are you looking at me like that. I am sure they said *Grave's End*." Kate stared hard at Merry, dread filling her stomach. "Have you heard of a tavern called, *Grave's End*?"

"Of course, I have. Merciful Heavens, Kate, how could you have lived your entire life in Cornwall and know nothing of *Grave's End*. It's the devil's lair. A smuggler's den."

"Smugglers and Lord Rensdale to contend with. Wonderful, Cousin. Oh, Merry, what have you gotten us into?" Kate moaned.

~~~

Dark, gray tendrils of fog enveloped the coast, making it impossible to see the edge of the jagged cliff. Merry urged her horse to a faster pace, riding by memory the treacherous path that ran between Bramble Hill and Falmouth.

A glance over her shoulder assured her that Kate was still following behind. For all her cousin's frailty, Merry had to admit that she was an exceptional rider.

It was well into the night before they caught sight of the steeply slanted roof of *Grave's End.*

A hundred years ago the gray stone building, with its small mullioned windows, had been a favorite stop for weary travelers journeying to Land's End. But, years of neglect and the constant assault of the sea air did not lend an impression of welcome.

"*Grave's End?*" Kate murmured fearfully, staring at the square board sign boldly decorated with the scull & crossbones. "Oh, Merry, you will not go into that place."

Merry stared at the structure in dismay. "I must admit I didn't expect it to be so bad. Now do you understand why I didn't want to bring you along?"

"Oh, and it would have been better for me to let you come here alone."

Merry slid from the saddle, carefully tucking her hair up into the smelly wool cap she'd lifted from the stables.

"Merry, no. This will not do. This is even more foolishness than you can manage. We can wait here for Rensdale, if you must. I will not allow you go in after him."

"Not go in? There is no cause to panic, Kate." Merry leaned forward to retrieve the dagger from her boot. "But, I think it best, Kate, that you stay with the horses. No one will know I am a woman dressed this way. But you, Kate? You could not help but to cause trouble inside. If someone so much as takes a step toward you, ride off, Kate. Don't worry about me. Ride to Saint's Cove and I will meet you there."

"Oh, Merry, I don't think this is at all wise," Kate rushed anxiously.

"Don't fret, Kate. Philip is inside. He would never allow harm to come to me."

"Can Philip protect you from smugglers and thieves? Do you have any idea what will happen if they realize that you are a woman?"

Merry didn't even want to consider it, or that Philip would not be inside. The ugly possibility of finding herself alone, in *Grave's End* was too terrible to contemplate.

Hesitantly, Merry approached the weather worn structure. Lightly placing her hands on the scarred door, it pushed forward the tiniest bit. The raucous buzz of conversation and laughter floated out to her.

If I let them see my fear, I won't last a minute, she chided herself, trying to steady her nerves.

Taking in a deep breath, she leaned her weight against the door, almost falling when it instantly gave way. It was designed to swing, and once through, it fell quickly back from her, leaving her trapped on the inside.

Merry eased back against the far wall, trying to blend into the background, as she quickly tried to orient herself to her surroundings.

The scene was not at all what she had been expecting. It was worse. In front of the door, a group of truculent Irish seamen had staked out their territory. Their heavily accented voices made the candle's flame beside her head gut, as they alternately toasted and threatened each other. The only light, in the narrow, high-ceilinged room, came from the smelly tallow candles set in brass sconces widely spaced along the smoke-discolored walls. The only heat against the chill sea air, from a single log burning in the hearth. A sudden pop and crackle of wood made her jump. The shower of sparks sent an uneasy glow over the group of rough-looking men, huddled over tankards of ale at the crude assortment of tables and chairs.

The tavern was much larger than it looked from outside, with the dim light she could see but a few feet. A quick inspection of the tables near her confirmed that Philip and Rensdale were not nearby. She would have to move from the door if she hoped to find them, but the thought of stepping even a foot forward on the gritty, sand-laden floor...

The door was pulled quickly back. She skittered out of the way, to allow a nasty looking brute with a crude heavy face and red rimmed eyes to move past her.

The fresh night air, which had been trapped deeply in her lungs since entering, pushed out of her throat and Merry raised her hand to cover her trembling lips. The room held the stale, sour odor of sweat and unwashed bodies, the pungent aroma of *Grave's End* gin and cheap perfume that nearly suffocated her. A bottle crashed from a nearby table. Merry whirled toward the sound to find the nasty looking newcomer harshly glaring her.

"Get yer arse frem behind me chair, ya young wretch," he growled. "It's bad luck ta stare at a mon's back, less'n you mean ta put a knife in it."

Merry mumbled what she hoped was an appropriate response, and made a hurried flight to the bar. As she settled against the roughly made counter, her shaking hands knocked over a flagon of gin.

Frightened, she pulled a coin from her belt and tossed it carelessly onto the counter. It rolled about and finally made a soft clank that drew the barkeep's attention.

"Little young ta be out on a night like this, eh lad," he said, his deep-set eyes giving her a sharp appraisal beneath thick bushy brows. "Gin or ale?"

"Neither," Merry muttered, keeping her face averted. "I am looking for someone."

The bartender laughed. "Are ye, now? Yer too small a fish ta be thinking about a hop with me ladies, so it's a drink ye'll be getting and nothing else if yer meaning ta stay." The bartender slid a flagon of gin at her. "Blue Ruin. Drink."

Merry flinched from the barked order. "I said..."

"And I said drink, laddie. We don't like troublemakers here."

With a defiant tilt of her chin, Merry raised the glass and took a deep pull on the vile brew. It burned from her throat to her stomach and it took every ounce of self-control not to spit the hideous concoction out

Merciful Heavens, I am going to be sick, she thought with welling panic, trying to hold both her stomach and the hard gaze of the coarse-featured laughing man before her.

"It's a wonder they don't kill you for serving swill like this," Merry muttered under her breath.

One hairy, muscular arm snaked out and pulled Merry up against the counter. "Ye've had yer drink, lad, and I suggest ye leave. Yer not a big enough tub ta stand on yer own bottom with this lot. Someone is gunna want ta have a little fun with ye. They use squirts like ye fer target practice, and that's only if yer lucky enough not ta be used for something else. Be on yer way. A little maggot like ye means only one thing. Trouble. I don't mean to have me establishment ruined over the likes of ye. Damn messy business when they get a mind ta have a little live sport."

The iron fingers tightened fiercely on Merry's arm.

"Let go of me. I am not leaving before I find who I am

looking for," Merry countered firmly.

His yellow eyes rounded with surprise. "Hell's bells, ye ain't no lad. If ye came here fer a job, why didn't ye say so, lass? Ye'll do. We don't get young lassies like yerself here, too often. I bet ye got something sweet and juicy hidden under yer britches."

Understanding came to her in rapid shock waves. Did this horrid man actually think she wished to become a *doxie*? The terror of being found out didn't match the flood tide of fury cursing through her veins.

"Let go of my arm," Merry spoke in a soft, yet commanding voice. Better to die game than cowering. "Or you'll live to regret it."

"Uppity, ain't ye. A little spirit will do ye good, a man likes a few bumps with the ride, but ye best mind yer tongue."

"If I were you, I would listen to what I have to say or rue the day you didn't. You are grievously mistaken if you think I have come here to be in your employ. If you place your hands upon me again, you'll see my dagger in your heart. Understood?"

Swiftly, she pulled the knife from her belt. Light flashed off of the blade that was clutched fiercely in Merry's tiny fingers, but her carefully enunciated words, which told Jack Shelby that she was a lady, were what had just rescued her.

"By God, what kind of craziness is this, m'lady," Jack swore, anxiously looking past the girl to see if any of the men had taken note of the exchange.

A gently bred female, unprotected in this group, was like putting a match to a powder keg. And gently bred she was. A closer look at that delicate face was all Jack needed to know that she was a blue blood. What she was doing here? He couldn't fathom for the life of him, but one thing for sure, he had better get her out before all hell broke loose. If anything should happen, he'd have the authorities swarming over him and a one-way trip to Newgate.

"If they catch wind of this, there won't be nothing left of yer bonnie hide or me tavern when they're through."

"I am looking for a gentleman. My brother. I was to meet him here. He was with another gentleman, but I don't see them. Perhaps you can tell me where they've gone."

The ways of nobility were strange to Jack, but this was the damnedest coil he'd ever stumbled across. A gentleman. He didn't have to search his brain to know whom the lass was talking about. *So the whelp who'd accompanied Rensdale was her brother,* Jack Shelby thought in dismay. *Damn Rensdale fer bringing this trouble ta him. What craziness had possessed them ta have the lass come here?*

"Aye, they were here. Got flush up on me ale and set ta brawling. They could see that they were court'n more trouble than they could handle. They had the good sense ta leave afore nightfall. *Grave's End* is not a safe place for the respectable after dark."

"Do you know where they have gone?"

"I don't ask questions, and they don't be offering answers. Now if ye don't want ta see both of us dead, m'lady, ye'll get yer arse out of here, afore someone takes note of ye."

Gone. *What am I going to do?* Merry wondered desperately. Finding Rensdale had been her only hope. Until this moment, she had not believed that her father would have his way or that she would fail. Now, Rensdale and Philip were off God knows where and she realized that finding them was an impossibility.

A lifetime as Rensdale's wife, it would have been better to be plunged into Hades than to accept that fate, she thought.

"If ye start ta bawl'n, yer done fer," the barkeep said solemnly, seeing the despair on the tiny lass's face. "There's no needing ta be afraid. Ye got yerself in here on yer own and ye can get yerself out, as well. Jack Shelby won't be let'n any harm come ta ye, so long as you high tail it out of me tavern. Just get yerself gone from here quickly."

"Thank you. You've been very kind," she said, tucking the knife back into her belt.

Jack breathed a sigh of relief as the tiny lass turned from the counter. It would be all right. She'd be gone, with none the wiser and, to his surprise, he was grateful that no harm would come to the girl.

The wee lass had such bonnie eyes. The bluest eyes he'd ever seen, and pluck, too. Damn, Rensdale for this. There weren't many women, lady or common strumpet, who'd be brave enough to come into *Grave's End* alone.

Then, the scrapping of chairs and low rumble of voices caused Jack to look up. The blood quickly drained from his face. His front door had been opened without a sound. Inside his establishment stood the most frightening figure ever to set foot on the dry earth.

Jack Shelby recognized him instantly. *Bloody hell*, he thought. The little lass's luck had just run out, and she didn't even know it.

CHAPTER THREE

"If ye have a care ta live, ye'll be silent," Jack warned in a low voice from behind.

"What is wrong?" Merry demanded anxiously.

The only answer she got was a painful squeeze on her shoulder and her body jerked roughly back to the counter.

Then, she saw that the door to *Grave's End* was opened wide, and two men had stepped in with a chill of fresh night air. It was too dark to make out their faces clearly, but it was obvious that the inhabitants of *Grave's End* did not need to. Whoever these men were, they were recognized by all, their effect on the crowd unmistakable.

Merry stood, transfixed, staring at the door. A moment ago the gathering had been laughing, drinking, and brawling. Now, they were frozen. The silence around her was unearthly. These men, who feared nothing, were terrified. But why? What on earth could this lot fear?

The deathly silence did not break until something forced the rough Irishmen by the door to pull apart in a rush. And then through the center cut a boy, his strides brisk and menacing.

Merry could tell that the figure, beneath the poor light of the tallow candles, was not like any boy she'd ever seen. A mass of jet black hair cascaded in loose waves down his back, and his body, clad in faded denims and a battered leather jerkin, was lithe and finely boned. He stood only a handful of inches taller than her, and carried himself with an arrogance that inspired fear despite his size.

He brushed past Merry as if he knew, very well, that no

49

one would block his path. She caught a quick glimpse of his face. It was startlingly young, the features so perfectly formed that the word 'angelic' came to Merry's mind, but he was most decidedly male. She watched in amazement as the brawny, towering men withdrew in a flurry to let him pass.

The boy did not stop until he was at the table nearest the hearth. The men sat huddled over their tankards, not daring to lift their faces.

The boy raised his booted foot, kicking the table over with a sure and graceful blow. The bottles shattered against the grimy floor. With a subtle command, from the boy's scarred hands, the two men who had been seated there jumped from their chairs setting the table aright before hurrying away.

The boy turned back toward the doorway.

Merry estimated him to be about her own age, maybe a year younger. For all his youth, there was nothing that could be considered boyish about his face. His eyes were dark, cold, soulless, and fixed keenly on the room.

Staring at the boy in unwilling fascination, Merry had to fight back a gasp when she noticed that the ugly scars on his hands extended up his arms and across the corded chest. Ridges of healed flesh stood white against that darkly sun-bronzed skin. Even his face had not been spared. Across his cheek, a wide scar etched its way from beneath his left eye to the corner of his mouth, adding a sinister cast to what would have been arresting features.

What manner of man could have done such a thing? Merry wondered, horrified, and then, she knew. When the sound of boots against the sand sprayed floor pulled her attention back to the door.

The man who stood in the darkened doorway stepped in, the dim glow of the candles falling across his face. All at once, Merry could see him clearly. The blood roared in her ears.

Nothing could have prepared her for the magnificence of this man's face.

This man was more than handsome, he was perfect, in a ruthlessly masculine way that was more than a little frightening. His features were intense and strongly chiseled, as though carved in smooth stone. The firm line of his jaw was arrogant, with a hint of superiority and mockery in the sensually twisting lips. His hair was sable, thick across a high, noble forehead and the glowing eyes, above the aristocratic nose, were darker than any she had ever seen. They were black, without a hint of hue to soften them.

His stealthy footsteps were an eerie sound in the otherwise silent room. His eyes surveyed the crowd in a lazy float, his keen gaze missing nothing and settling nowhere. He was moving through the crowd with the ease of supremacy, his powerfully built body relaxed, and latently dangerous at once.

He stood well above the rest of the men, his wide shoulders straining against his black muslin shirt, the firmly sculptured chest covered by a dark mat of curling hair. His muscular torso tapered down to lean hips, snugly encased in black breeches that were tucked into wine colored boots, cut high to the knee. From the top of his head to the tip of his toes, this mountain of a man was dressed in black.

The boy inspired raw terror with his presence, but there were no words to describe this man's effect. His name formed in her mind in fast, furious shock waves. She did not need anyone to tell her that the man, who had just brought *Grave's End* to a terrified halt, was the infamous Captain Morgan. The most vicious pirate ever to plunder the seas. No other man would have dared to make such a brazen entry among this savage order of men.

Any belief that Morgan's reputation was the result of myth or exaggeration died the instant Merry looked at the boy, standing obediently behind his chair.

Her heart hammering in her chest, she made a panicked check of the door.

"Stay still, lass, if ye a care ta live," Jack whispered fiercely. "One step ta the door and those devils of Morgan's will snap yer neck like a twig."

Merry nodded, realizing the futility of trying to make an escape. The men Jack was referring to were almost as tall as Morgan, but twice as wide. Around their thick middles large leather belts rested, boasting a variety of sinister looking weapons.

"No one comes. No one goes. Not while Morgan is here, not ever. Ye've got nothing ta fear unless ye stir Morgan's notice." He shoved a filthy cloth across the counter toward her trembling hands. "Take the rag. Set yerself ta cleaning the bar. Ye don't want ta be caught watch'n them."

Slowly activity resumed around her. Merry carefully slipped around to the back of the bar, feeling foolishly more relieved to have the rickety plank of wood as an added barrier between her and the pirates.

Carefully focusing her attention on the impossible task of cleaning the counter, she was unaware that her movement had caught Morgan's notice, until she looked up to find his black eyes focused on her face. The heat of his stare made her burn, a sensation she found bewildering. She knew that the longer she met the contact, the more the danger, yet she couldn't seem to find the will to lower her gaze. She felt as though she were drowning in those dark depths, like a sailor beguiled by the sea, drawn too far out and left helpless.

Bound by a pounding urge of fascination, Morgan held her gaze as effortlessly as he silenced the crowd. Merry had the sickening feeling that Morgan knew perfectly well she was not a lad. He ran her form once in a thorough, efficient stare. When his sharp appraisal returned to her face, he sent her a grin. To her horror, Merry felt a hot blush rise to her cheeks.

"Fer God sake, lass, don't be let'n that devil get ta close of look. Ye don't wanna know what Morgan does ta his women."

"Please, you must help me. The militia...."

Jack stopped her words cold. "There's no way out, lass. Ye best hope he has other matters ta occupy his mind than what he thinks ye got beneath yer breeches."

Time slowed to a crawl for Merry, though the men of *Grave's End* attempted to carry on in a normal manner, despite Captain Morgan's ominous presence. Jack raced about the bar, refilling tankards with frantic speed, as the noise grew to a deafening pitch. For Merry's part, she did as Jack ordered, cleaning the bar and refilling the heavy tankards.

She prayed that Kate had seen the pirates and ridden hell for leather to Bramble Hill. She tried to divert herself, from her terror bent thoughts by making a list of the mistakes that had brought her to this point, vowing that if she lived never to repeat them again...

The hair on the back of Merry's neck stood up. Silence.

"Oh lass, we've got trouble," Jack muttered fearfully.

"What is it?"

She looked across the room to find Morgan sitting at his table as he had for the past hour. For a man about to cause mayhem, he was amazingly indifferent about the whole thing.

"Not him. HIM." Jack said, inclining his head toward the long-haired boy with the nasty scars. The terrifying boy-pirate had moved from behind his captain's chair to the ugly brute that had barked at her for staring at his back. "The little blackguard, what does Morgan's dirty work, has made his move. It's Blackburn they've come for."

"Come for? You mean kill? Right here. With witnesses?"

"Morgan warns only once. Blackburn should have

listened when he had the chance."

Blackburn rose with deceptive calm from his chair, but from Merry's vantage point she could see his fingers slide to his belt and grab the cold hilt of his knife. Morgan had but three men with him. She tallied at least a dozen on Blackburn's side. Blackburn lunged for blood. Swift as quicksilver, the boy darted out of his way, brandishing the knife with deadly skill, as the room shook with the sound of overturning tables, shattering glass, and hastily drawn steel.

Through the melee Morgan never moved. He sat at his table, staring into his drink, setting it to swirl slowly with the air of man slightly bored.

A bottle whizzed through the air, dangerously close to Merry's head. Thankfully, the riotous commotion of the room swallowed her scream. Jack grabbed her arm, pulling her down behind the bar.

"Beyond that door is a storeroom. If there's a chance of ye getting out of here, it's while no one be watch'n. Ye can go out the window afore Morgan and his men even notice ye gone. Hurry, lass. The last time Morgan and his cutthroats brawled in *Grave's End*, there was little enough left of me tavern and only meself alive ta tell the tale."

Scrambling on her hands and knees, Merry made her way across the wet gritty floor littered with broken glass and battered bodies. She carefully darted beneath the hastily hung cloth that acted as a door for the storeroom, and spotted the window on the far side of the room.

Frantically, she tried to push open the pane. Good Heavens, how many centuries had passed since the window had been open? The jamb was frozen solid and the stuffy room held the dank odor of mold, filth, and air that had not been circulated for a decade.

With all the strength she could muster, she attempted

again to force it open and realized that she was trapped. The tavern was in total bedlam, but did she dare to break the window to get free? Would someone hear the sound and come to investigate? The thought of being trapped in this cramped space with one of Morgan's cutthroats—no, better not think of that.

Her frantic musings came to a screeching halt when she became aware of ruffling, coming from the other side of the curtain. Desperately, she searched for a way out. She was about to pick up a chair and knock out the window when she noticed a large, empty crate only a foot away.

She dashed toward it, and hastily climbed in. There was no room to spare, her arms were pinned at her side, and the interior of the crate was still damp. At least it was a hiding place. If there were an ounce of goodwill in the Heavens left for her, she would gladly stay put, until it was safe to leave the tavern, rather than falling prey to the dangers beyond.

Trembling, she laid her cheek on her knees, determined to wait out the threat. Much to her dismay, she felt tears sting her eyes. She hated to cry. The tears angered her, but she was frightened. What was the point of pretending otherwise? No one was here to see her cry. Just that rat she could hear scuffling across the room.

Scuffling? She lifted her face and peeked through the crack in the crate. Captain Morgan was less than an arm's length from the crate and he wasn't alone.

"What a flair you have for creating diversions, Varian, but was that gruesome little knife fight really necessary?"

Merry tilted her head to get a better look through the crack. Confusion hit her, as she recognized the man with Morgan as the Earl of Camden. What the devil was the foppish Camden, dressed in the garb of a common fisherman, doing here at *Grave's End* with a notorious pirate?

"Blackburn has become a nuisance of late," was Morgan's off hand reply. "He has been poaching along English shores flying my flag. I should be accused of sinking the Fleetwood before long."

Morgan's voice brought her up sharply. Low and sensual, it was the distinct English accent that made her heart turn in surprise: English and decidedly aristocratic. By all accounts, she had assumed him to be an American. At least that was what the *Times* had concluded because of his ruthless penchant for attacking English ships. Never, ever, had she heard a hint of speculation that he was one of their own countrymen.

"And here I thought you staged it all for my benefit," the Earl chided glibly, before settling his bulk down on the crate. "Did you have trouble getting into the cove?"

Morgan's low laughter filled the room. "Not a British patrol in sight."

"Damn tedious bit of work this smuggling. Developed a prodigious thirst from it all. Though, it's too much to hope that Jack Shelby has anything lying about fit for consumption. Really, Varian, why *Grave's End?* Couldn't you have picked a more comfortable locale for this meeting? You have such a grim fancy for drama."

"I have kept your comfort in mind. There are a few amenities I can't do without."

Morgan walked over to a crate and pulled free a bottle, tossing it with amazing accuracy to the earl. Camden raised the bottle to his lips, taking a long pull, before a satisfied smile twisted his thin lips.

"Ah, French cognac." The earl took another noisy swallow. "A fortnight ago, you were in Swansea with a cargo of riches from America. Now this. Smuggling out of France. Your recklessness has me on the verge of apoplexy."

"I would have thought you'd consider smuggling a sign of

my reforming character. In times of war, doesn't it tend to be considered more honorable than piracy?"

"I don't think English law carries a distinction. Two runs in one month. I know waiting bores you, but you must be more careful. You have the devil's own luck, but there is always the chance that your charms might lose out against currency."

"I never depend on luck or charm thanks to you, Brian."

"I am afraid I have precious little information for you. The thugs I hired were successful in their search of your cousin's estate. Unfortunately the documents you hoped to find were not there. They did, however, find these." Balancing the bottle in the crook of his arm, Camden reached inside of his coat pulling out a bundle of age-yellowed papers. "They're not enough to prove your cousin had anything to do with the sinking of the *Carolina*, but interesting none the less."

Morgan scanned the papers the earl had given him. "It seems that our fine lord is planning on another shipment from the Caribbean. Fifty thousand pounds, he has insured this cargo for."

"Quite an accomplishment, considering that his warehouses, as you well know, are empty. He is an expert at insurance fraud. It is still not enough to settle his debts. They are monstrous. Even I was shocked by the extent of them. A small fortune he has made in his last four crimes, but it will take a fortune two times that to see him clear."

"Five ships. I was too late to catch the *Sandow*. A total loss."

"Survivors?"

"Not a one. It is nothing less than a miracle that Indy survived the explosion on the *Carolina*."

"You must not continue to blame yourself, Varian."

"Do you think that I can forget that I was his target?"

"You have done more than anyone could ask of you to set

right that tragedy, Varian. You will bring our scoundrel to justice. He will pay for those deaths. His cargo is set to go on the *Hampstead.*"

"When is it set to sail?"

"That information is proving more difficult to obtain. Whitehall is concerned with the secrecy of such information, considering the heightened fighting on the seas, due to this foolishness with America."

"Have his rooms in London searched. If we can't prove his involvement in the sinking of the *Carolina* then we must content ourselves with foiling his plan for the *Hampstead* and bringing his ruin with that. How long will it take to have his rooms searched?"

"There is no point in that, Varian. It has been many months since our scoundrel has seen London. He is in hot pursuit of another interest these days."

"Indeed," Morgan mused thoughtfully. "I did not think he ever journeyed far from London. My estates lay in ruin from his neglect."

"You can credit his absence to a pretty filly with an enormous dowry."

"Rich, you say?"

"Enormously so, enough to settle the last of his debts. And the girl is beautiful, to boot. The marriage will gain him a powerful alliance. If I were ten years younger, I would make a play for the gel myself, just to annoy our scoundrel. When last I saw him, he was practically drooling in anticipation of getting his hands on the poor pretty child and her fortune."

"And when is the happy nuptial to take place?" Morgan asked scathingly.

Brian chuckled softly. "There seems to be considerable question as to that. The girl has formed quite a dislike of our scoundrel. She's had him on the run, but it seems our poor girl is about to run out of luck. Rumor has it that the engagement will be announced this season."

"Well, I wish our young filly a hearty wind in her sail."

"I have set a curve or two into your cousin's pursuit myself."

Morgan's great dark eyes flickered with amusement. "Really?"

"Yes, indeed," Camden replied, obviously pleased with himself. "It was my hope that another offer would come of its own for the girl's hand, if nothing but to delay his lordship's pursuit. As it seemed she was about to run out of room to escape the altar, well, to put it simply, you've made an offer for the lady's hand. If nothing else it should infuriate our pup to no end when he learns."

Morgan threw back his dark head, the room shaking with his laughter. "How did you manage that, you scoundrel?"

"A word here, a word there. Your seal and a forged signature on a marriage offer. It was simple, I assure you, and it afforded me no small amount of amusement."

"Yes, I can see that it has."

"Have you any doubts? You'd be hardly misused if they accepted your offer. Your cousin would be enraged beyond reason. You'd acquire a proper English bride, with a beautiful face, a fat purse, and a touch of wild spirit to match your own. A rather good stroke of fortune, all things considered."

"What a ridiculous fancy, Brian. The sheer amusement of it all … it is well that I have no want of a wife."

"Not even to foil our scoundrel's careful planning? Think how crushed he'd be, all these years standing behind you in succession, and you getting about the business of breeding an heir. I am disappointed in you, Varian. Think of the poor girl."

"I can better help our filly by seeing my cousin to the gallows." Morgan strode over to the doorway, pulling back the cloth to peer out at the ravaged room. The girl was gone. "Jack Shelby's new helper? What do you know?"

Merry felt her heart plummet to her feet.

"Helper? I wasn't aware he had one. You don't think..."

Morgan's eyes sharpened. "Whitehall?"

"No, I am sure of it. I would know if Andrew Merrick had put his own agent in here. They know nothing of your past visits here. They believe the tales of you coming to Cornwall are little more than fishermen folklore. Your legend is growing like a wild thing among the masses, often with you popping up in three places at once, doing villainy, terror and debauchery. You should really try to temper it down, Varian, for your own wellbeing. This blasted notoriety, you seem so amused on feeding, in the end might work against you, though it does have its benefit at times."

"Then the bar help's connection to Shelby could only mean one thing."

"If you're aware of Shelby's connection to your cousin, why do we meet here? Why haven't you done something about him?"

"Shelby is our only link between the hirelings who burned the *Carolina* and my cousin. I have my own man in *Grave's End*. He lets me know when they meet, and sees to Shelby's continued safety." Morgan's glowing eyes shifted back to the Earl.

"Whitehall owes you a great debt. When the time comes, if only you would permit me to lay this matter before Andrew Merrick...."

"You would sing my praises to Andrew Merrick and see yourself to Traitor's Gate? Brian, when are you going to accept that my destiny is no longer bound to England?"

"If I explain to him the circumstances, you could have England's support in this, as well. Merrick could prove an invaluable ally. He could get you pardon of your crimes."

"Ah, but Andrew Merrick provides one of my greatest amusement. What would I have to concern myself with without Andrew Merrick's artless pursuit of me?"

"Just because you can outmaneuver Andrew Merrick, doesn't mean that he wouldn't prove valuable to your quest. You've always been more clever than most by half."

"I have no wish of England's pardon. My home is my ship. It is the life I have chosen, Brian. You know why. Let it go."

"As you will. You will be contacting me soon?"

"I have business in Galway. Plan to meet me a fortnight from now."

The words roared, again and again in Merry's mind, with the force of an exploding rocket. They would meet in Ireland in a fortnight. The Earl of Camden was Morgan's spy in the Foreign Office. The problem of how she would forward this information to Uncle Andrew, without betraying how she'd come by it, didn't diminish the thrill of such heady power.

"The boy. Jack Shelby's new accomplice. Do you want me to make inquiries?"

Morgan's next words sent her back to earth with bruising speed. "I will set Indy to take care of Shelby's mysterious friend. We can't risk questioning Shelby. If the boy knows anything Indy, will have the truth from him."

In front of Merry's eyes the world froze. She knew very well how Morgan intended to deal with her. A vision of that horrible knife with the jagged edge rose in her mind.

Her body became one quivering mass, and try though she might, she could not still the frightened shaking of her limbs. She heard the crate creak from her quaking.

Hold steady, she chided her trembling form, but her shocked nerves didn't seem intent on obeying the dictates of her mind. The trembling continued as did the subtle creaking of the crate.

"God's speed, Varian, and good hunting."

The men clasped hands and the earl departed through the curtain.

"Blackburn?" Morgan inquired, with the air of a man without a single scar on his conscience. He was peacefully reclined on a crate less than a foot away from her, black eyes glittering, sipping from the half emptied bottle of cognac.

"We won't be troubled by him again," the sinister boy-pirate replied without emotion. "Should I return to ship?"

"No, there is another matter you have yet to deal with."

Indy arched a brow questioningly. Morgan studied the storeroom, then his long strides carried him purposely toward the crate. Every part of Merry went limp. There was no chance even to panic before the lid to the crate was slapped fiercely back in place, trapping her inside.

"Take it to the beach," was Morgan's cryptic order before going calmly from the room.

CHAPTER FOUR

Merry braced herself inside the crate as Morgan's two pirates carried her toward the beach. Reality lay cold and heavy on her terror dulled senses. It was hardly a comfort to admit she had no one to blame but herself for her current predicament.

Her panic-wracked brain conceded that she was about to become the pirate Indy's next victim. There was little she could do to stop them. Not the least of her problems, was the annoying frequency that her handlers dropped her. They dropped her more than once, the force of hitting the ground making her bones crack and ache.

After each fall, she pounded vigorously on the lid, hoping to remind them that a living organism was trapped inside. She'd given up her protest after the fourth unfriendly decent to the dirt.

It was obvious that simple decent care was too much to expect from pirates.

"Damn it, Shay, get a better hold of it. We don't want the lad dead before I can have a chance to question him. Morgan will have our hides if you bungle this one."

"Yer only worried that ye won't have a chance to take the knife to him. Ain't one butchery enough fer you? A damn bloody mess you made of Blackburn."

"Not nearly enough."

"But the lad? What if he ain't got nothing to do with...?"

"He does," Indy cut across harshly. "Why else would

Morgan bother with him? The lad should have thought twice before deciding to cross Morgan."

Distraught, the rest of their conversation was lost to Merry. She had to get out. This was all a horrible mistake. She wasn't in league with Jack Shelby and his nefarious activities.

Pressing her palms against the solid confinement of the crate, her mind frantically searched for a means of escape. There had to be a way. She banged an angry fist against the lid, to her amazement, feeling it yield slightly before being slapped harshly back into place.

She could hear the Channel water crashing against the shore, feel the sense of moving downward, instead of across level earth. They were making the decent from the cliffs to the beach.

She knew the path by memory, the steep slope, the treacherous footing. If there was a chance to get out, it was now, when it would be no easy task to maintain their balance with a struggling cargo. With sudden purpose, she began to crash her body side to side inside of the crate, taking heart that her captors were having no easy time keeping hold of her.

"Hold still, you maggot. Do you want us to drop you over the cliffs?" came the anxious voice of one of the pirates.

Milord, pirates, why do you think I am doing this? Merry thought furiously, deciding her last moments of life wouldn't be better spent inside the crate than on the beach as the boy-pirate's hapless victim.

Redoubling her efforts, she threw her body against the side. The crate jolted. Again. Then, all the sudden she heard cursing from outside the crate. The darkness inside became a dizzying spinning hollow that turned faster and faster with each passing second.

Trying to steady herself inside, she had the horrifying impression of how a fly must feel trapped on a pinwheel in a windstorm. Round and round, until the senses in her body blurred, until all thoughts, all reactions, became lost in the constant whirling.

Thump.

The crate hit hard a rock, bounced, and landed with a heavy drop into the sand.

Stillness.

Merry waited dumbly for the motion to start up again, her vision still spinning relentlessly. The hard drop had knocked the wind from her, but her arms and legs were moving.

She scrambled out. Springing to her feet, she began to run across the beach.

The path was less than ten yards away, and as each step brought her closer, she began to believe more and more in the possibility of escape.

That was easy. Really easy, Then, somewhere in the middle of her self-congratulations, she felt something grab hold of her legs. She was thrown forward into the earth.

As she tried to rise, a booted foot landed painfully atop her buttocks, forcing her back downward into the sand.

"Let me go," Merry screamed, trying to wiggle free beneath the pirate's leg.

"Hold still, you miserable wretch. I ought to feed you to the sharks. You don't want to learn how little patience I have for the likes of you," the boy-pirate warned calmly, moving his boot.

Furious, she scrambled on her belly until she did the only thing that came to her mind. She bit him. Desperately, she clamped her jaws shut around his calf.

The leg moved an angry jerk, dragging her across the sand like a rag doll.

"What the hell do you think that'll accomplish?" he growled. She was unprepared for the painful grasp of his dark fingers that jerked her carelessly to her feet. "We can do this two ways, you little fool," the boy pirate hissed, "quick and with a minimum of pain or..."

"Go to the devil," Merry screamed, kicking him in the shin with all her might. "If you don't let me go this instant I will see you hanging from the gallows by morning."

The pirate ruthlessly clasped both her fists in one hand, jerking her several inches from the earth, and gave her a snapping shake to silence her.

"If you don't stop that racket now, I will break both your arms with a single snap."

To emphasize his words, his fingers tightened like iron bands around her wrists. Merry went limp from the pain.

"You're hurting me," Merry accused heatedly.

"What did you expect? You've been a damned nuisance so far."

How dare he blame her for his brutality?

"I suppose you wouldn't mind being rough handled. Unhand me now, or be prepared to suffer the consequences."

The boy's smirk let her know just how greatly she'd failed in intimidating him, and how foolish she had sounded.

"Let me go," she demanded again, replacing the dramatic, with cold menace. "Or you'll be dead by morning."

The other pirate reached them, huffing and puffing as he leaned forward, hands braced on his knees. His blond head tilted upward, and his large green eyes sparked with mirth. Smile lines fanned his youthful features as a lopsided grin held his lips.

"Quick as a salmon, ain't he?" he laughed, tossing his long gold hair back over his shoulder. "Thought he'd be off to the sea before ye could get to him."

"Do you think I'd let him scamper off to raise the militia?"

Frantic, Merry struggled violently against the iron hold of the pirate, trying to strike his companion with the wild motion of her legs. "I wasn't going after the militia."

"Weren't ye now? Of course ye were, you little maggot. Would have tried it meself if I were in yer shoes. The militia is camped on the other side of Falmouth, in case ye weren't knowing that." The jovial pirate laughed good-naturedly. "So ye see, it's just ye, us and the owls. We just want to be having a talk with ye."

A talk. Did they think her a fool? "This is all a mistake. A terrible mistake."

"Ye shouldn't have spied fer Shelby, unless ye were willing to dance the piper. A man has got to pay fer his friends. He ain't one ye should have bothered with."

"I didn't bother with him. I don't even know the man."

"Ye were willing to spy on Morgan fer a man ye don't know? There's no point in denying it now. Ye were caught red-handed, lad. If ye stop acting like a bloody fool, I promise that Indy will leave nary a scratch on ye. But if ye keep up this madness..."

He let the threat hang in the air. Merry gathered every scrap of the coldness that was flooding the linings of her digestive tract, weaving it into a chilling voice, as she said, "I don't know anything. If you touch one hair on my head my father will kill you."

Indy took a handful of her shirt, shaking her back and forth before his sneering face. "Will he? Is he tucked away in the crate, as well?"

How rude of him to make jest of her. "You're as good as dead if you don't let me go immediately," she snapped.

"Give it up, young'n. Tell Indy what he wants to know. He can be bloody ruthless with that knife, when he's got a mind to be. He'll not be leave'n without answers."

In spite of herself, Merry trembled, allowing images of how Indy had dealt with Blackburn to slip into her mind.

She turned her anxious gaze on the sinister long-haired pirate. He was calmly polishing the ugly blade against his pants.

Frantically, she turned back to his less terrifying companion. "Let me go this instant. This is a mistake. I don't know Jack Shelby. I don't know anything."

"The hell ye don't. I saw it with me eyes, ye working fer Shelby. Could hardly miss it. Damn worse drink pouring I ever saw. Where the hell ye learn to poor drinks, lad? If ye don't know Jack Shelby, what the blazes were ye doing in his tavern and why did he send ye into the storeroom to spy on Morgan?" came the boy's rambling inquiry.

"He didn't send me to spy. He thought I could escape through the storeroom window, only it wouldn't open."

The boy's eyes were cold and disbelieving.

"It's the truth," she insisted fiercely. "I just wanted to get out, but the windowpane was jammed. Then Morgan came in and I hid in the crate. Truly, that's what happened."

One jet brow eased upward on Indy's sinister face. "Off to raise the militia, were you?"

Merry's cheeks flushed with fury. "No. I only wanted to leave. It's the truth."

The pleasant pirate's hands took hold of her arms, jerking her with painful force. "We haven't got time to waste here listening to fairy stories. Ye best start talking, lad, or Indy will see that ye do."

"But, I have already told you everything. Why won't you believe me?" Merry demanded frantically.

Indy's sneering face came within inches of her own. "Because Shelby knows no one is to leave while Morgan is at the tavern. Why would he risk his life to help you?"

"I don't know. He helped me because..." her voice broke off. She'd been about to say because he knew that she was a woman. The boys hadn't figured out she was a girl, yet. What a blunder that would have been. "I don't know."

"You had better start to know and quickly," the boy-pirate advised, pulling his knife from his belt. "Hold him steady, Shay."

Merry's eyes locked on the knife as she began to struggle furiously within the pirates grasp. "No. Please. I have told you the truth."

She didn't see Indy's other hand moving toward her, until it was too late. She was too busy trying to ease back from the knife pressed against her neck. She was unprepared for the blast of chilled night air hitting her warm trembling flesh as the front of her shirt was rented down the middle. Moonlight spilled across her lace bound breasts. She cried out in horror, wanting desperately to cover herself, but Shay would not relax his grip.

"Bloody Hell. This ain't no lad. It's a woman."

Trembling with embarrassment and rage, the last scattered drops of good reason gone, she began to thrash wildly in Shay's hold. Humiliation tore through her middle as she struggled to cover herself with the battered remains of shirt. Both the choking sobs and useless flailing motions of her limbs, strangers to Merry, seemed beyond her control. Head spinning, it felt as if the explosion of fluid would drain every cell in her body.

"Christ," Indy growled. "Cease that racket you fool or I will silence you myself."

"Go ahead," she screamed, making frantic, useless efforts with her hands to pull her tattered shirt in place across her quivering flesh. "I told you I wasn't one of Jack Shelby's accomplices. I have told you the truth. You refused to believe me."

"Well, how were we to know you had tits beneath your shirt instead of..."

Seeing the effect of his words and Shay's pointed stare at

the girls well-endowed front, he cut his sentence abruptly off. Cursing under his breath, he tore off his vest and pulled it in place quickly over her quivering flesh. The last thing he needed this night was a fight with Shay over this miserable girl.

"If you'd stop crying for a minute," Indy hissed, irritated, "perhaps we could figure out what to make of this tangle."

Merry brushed the uncontainable tears of her humiliation from her cheeks, and lifted her chin to stare daggers at Indy. "No tangle. A mistake. Your mistake."

"Bloody hell," Shay exclaimed, noting her face for the first time. "She's little more than a child, a damn pretty little piece at that. Ain't seen nothing this juicy at *Grave's End* before. Is Morgan off his tub? Why would he want us to harm this girl?"

"She unwisely decided to listen in on Morgan's meeting. Remember?"

"Christ, girl, what possessed ye to make an enemy of Morgan?"

Indignant at being continually misjudged, Merry exclaimed fiercely, "I wasn't out to make enemies of Morgan. I was just hiding, that's all. A perfectly logical thing, since you were out committing murder and mayhem."

"Who the hell are you?" Indy asked, staring hard at the delicate face.

Before she could stop herself, Merry bit out, "Who are you? What were you doing with Shelby? Why did you murder Blackburn? How do you like to be questioned? The devil take you, and your questions. I wasn't spying and that is the last time I will tell you that. If you don't release me this instant I will ..."

Over her simmering tirade, Indy barked, "If you don't stop that screeching, I will stop it for you. Keep a lid on it or someone is apt to hear you and come to investigate. Morgan has men all over the coast. So, unless you want to be the sacrificial lamb at a pirate debauchery, shut up. If the crew comes there'll be no question you'll be harmed."

Somehow she managed to recognize the faintest traces of worry on the boy's scarred face, though it was hard because his expression never changed. She sank her teeth into her lower lips, fighting her panic. Whatever else happened, she didn't need more pirates to contend with. The two boys were trouble enough.

"You, of course, would be desolate if that were to happen," she sneered, not able to stop herself.

"You're yipping up the wrong tree, if you have the idea that I care what happens to you," said the boy, smoothly emphatic. "I just don't want to have to kill one of my own to protect your hide until I make reason of this mess, and decide what to do with you."

Behind him she heard the blond pirate say woefully, "Damn Morgan fer dumping this bit of work on me. I don't go fer harming women, Indy and she a bonnie one at that. We should let the lass go before the others see her, lad. She's just a poor scared little thing. Morgan would be the first to have other thoughts than harming her on his mind, if he could see what a fion bit of fluff she is, if ye ask me."

"Well, I didn't ask you, you damn stupid Irishman," the boy said irritably.

"Damn ye fer the cold-blooded maggot ye are. Even ye should be able to recognize a harmless, frightened girl when ye see it."

Shay clamped his beefy hands on Merry's cheeks and spun her around to face the boy with such swiftness that her cap flew off, fully revealing her face for the first time.

"Plague rot it, look at her. Do ye mean to tell me that ye could take your knife to this? What's become of ye, lad? There was a time I thought ye had some human heart in ye."

A minute passed before Indy reluctantly looked at the girl. He made a short inspection of her face and if this little exercise was supposed to have some effect on her fate, clearly it did not. His eyes, narrowed and hard, were quite simply soulless.

The boy's voice was chilling. "What I see is trouble," was all he said, knife in hand. "If you have no stomach for this, I suggest you go to the skiff and wait for me."

"Damn it, lad, let her go." His voice had taken on a wheedling edge, but he surrendered the girl to Indy's hands. It was clear that in a battle between the two boys, the sinister pirate would win without a struggle.

Then, when she was beginning to feel as though all hope was lost, fighting helplessly in the boy's arms, something flickered on his face, quickly, then gone. The knife retreated from her as swiftly as it had closed in. He ruthlessly seized her face in the cup of his hand and pulled her more closely beneath him, his eyes taking on a sudden sharpness.

"Bloody Christ," he cursed. With an irritation and a quickness that caught Merry off guard, his scarf was in her mouth. She was gagged before she could muster a resistance. He was only an inch or so taller than her, his lithe body a collection of gracefully knit muscles, but he was much stronger than Merry had anticipated.

"Hell's teeth, Indy. Do ye mean to torture the lass before ye butcher her?"

"Take a look at her, damn it," Indy barked.

"I told ye she was just a poor, scared girl."

Indy's hard impassive mask flickered briefly with intense annoyance. It defied logic that Shay didn't recognize this pale, aristocratic face, but then Shay was annoyingly idiotic at times. They'd seen the girl, only a bare handful of times, during that long spring month when Morgan had sent them to London, in worthless surveillance of his lordship's activities. Inquiries had provided her name, which had been as much of a shock as was her connection to him, and the villain it had become his mission to destroy.

Staring at the girl, he suffered a brief regret for having been so rough with her. He couldn't begin to reason why she had been at *Grave's End*, dressed like a boy and cavorting with Shelby and pirates. He was sure the answer would be a stupid one. Indy knew this girl, too well.

He had indulged an unfathomable curiosity last spring, by spending as much of his time watching her as he did his target. He had observed her often enough never to expect her to conduct herself in a manner that was anything but idiotic. He knew, whatever the truth, it would be nothing evil and merely absurd.

He was certain of only two things. This girl had nothing to do with Shelby, and no power on earth could force him to harm her.

The strongest impulse inside of him, surprisingly, was to release her now, to lie to Morgan, and let his discovery remain his own. But, the girl had been witness to that farce at *Grave's End* and had seen too much. He knew with her exposure to the upper ranks of British aristocracy, she had certainly recognized the man poorly disguised, as a fisherman, had been the Earl of Camden. There was no telling what dangers could come of that. If he let her go, he would be doing so at the risk of Morgan and the ship. However, killing her was just not an option.

He could give her to Morgan's care, but that meant only one thing: in the least captivity on a pirate ship, most probably Morgan's bed. That option was equally disturbing.

He knew if he dumped the girl and the truth at the captain's feet, he could save her from all of these unpleasant fates. He knew Morgan would neither keep, nor harm her.

SUSAN WARD

She'd be safely home before morning.

But what would save them from the girl?

She'd heard too much. Now in her hands were enough pieces that the truth about the pirate captain could come together. What could save them from her? Only her death, Indy conceded grimly, unless...

He looked at her face with its delicate aristocratic lines, cursed himself a fool, and fought the rapid clicking reasons why he would never have a chance at success in all this. He could never play a game with Morgan that Morgan didn't win. As strange as it all seemed, the more he gave it all thought, the more he wondered if perhaps the gods were smiling on him in this.

What it would require was simple sleight of hand manipulation. Iron determination. Fearless, emotionless battle. One wrong move would sink them all...

"Get the skiff," Indy announced unexpectedly.

"Ye ain't thinking what I think yer thinking. Are ye crazy, lad?"

"Unless you mean for me to kill this girl I suggest you start moving quickly."

"Bloody hell. Morgan will have both our hides' fer this. I wanted ye to let the lass go, not to see us dead. Ye know very well, we can't take her aboard the *Corinthian*. Why there isn't a pirate crew on the seas that'll take a woman on board. It's bad luck, boy."

"Superstitious nonsense. Morgan takes on women all the time."

"Morgan is bloody charmed. He can tempt a little bad luck."

"Get the ropes. If she jumps from the skiff, we'll never find her in this darkness. If she kicks up a scuffle, the crew will be on her before we can get her to Morgan's cabin."

Merry's eyes rounded in horror. Did they mean to take her aboard the *Corinthian*? Frantic, she began to struggle, her arms and legs flailing wildly about, as she tried to kick at her captors and wiggle away from the ropes they held in their hands.

"Feisty bit of fluff, ain't she?" Ian Shay laughed, holding her legs for Indy to bind. "Look at her try to claw ye. Morgan will have his work cut out mounting this one."

She pulled free a leg and kicked the Irishman soundly in the gut. To Merry's dismay, he only laughed.

The pirate Indy was not so amused. In a flashing second the knife was back in hand, that horrible jagged blade before her. He pressed the edge against her throat, the coolness of the metal making her freeze instantly.

His fingers snaked through her hair and jerked her head back cruelly. "For Christ sake, stop being such a bloody nuisance. Do you think fighting will accomplish anything?"

"Listen, Peaches, we just want to tie ye up so ye won't be harming yourself. We can't be fighting with ye, and trying to row back to ship at the same time. We'll all end in the drink, if ye don't behave. The Channel ain't no place to take a dip at night. Let Indy bind yer feet. That's a good girl. I promise I won't let him harm ye."

Not harm her. Did he think her an idiot?

Her thoughts clear in her eyes, the jovial young pirate laughed and tossed Merry roughly over his shoulder. None too gently, he dropped her into the small boat, resting his booted feet on her backside once he took his place for rowing.

"What do ye suppose Morgan will do to her?" Shay asked.

"If we're lucky, he'll bed her. If we're not lucky, we'll find ourselves chained in the brig. We best hope she's a damn good..." he used a crude word that Merry had never heard before "... or we'll be wishing we never laid eyes on Morgan."

Merry's heart skipped several beats and then began to race

again at a frenzied pace.

"Ain't no reason to fret, Peaches," Shay assured Merry. "My money is on ye, if that means anything."

It didn't. Not to Merry.

"Morgan is a hard man, but a fair one. Give him what he wants and ye ain't got nothing to fear."

She could feel the small craft pulling away from the shore, the swells of the waves making them lurch and sway. Sea spray saturated her clothing, making her skin burn. She struggled to hold her chin up, so she wouldn't drown in the pool of water beneath her.

"Do ye think we could take off the gag? The poor little lass is turning blue."

"From the cold." Indy looped his fingers into her hair and jerked her head harshly up until her face was before him. "If you make so much as a peep—I can see you understand." He pulled the gag from her mouth. "One yap and the gag goes back."

Choking back her tears, she knew that each stroke of the oars took her farther from Cornwall, and closer to the *Corinthian*. Merry Merrick, whether she wished it or not, was now on her way to a pirate ship. She had wanted free of Rensdale and it seemed she was about to be granted her wish. Only she had not imagined that the answer to her prayers would come at the scarred hands of a sinister boy pirate and the infamous Captain Morgan.

CHAPTER FIVE

The water slapped against the bow of the small craft as it jolted through the fog. Merry lay trembling in the stern of the boat, her garments soaked with sea spray and her hair snarled in her face.

Frozen and terrified, she felt a wave of pure panic when she spotted the *Corinthian* rearing from the water.

Beneath the towering triple spires of the masts and the Grecian figurehead, the boy angled the bouncing craft against the curved underbelly of the great ship. He let go a piercing whistle into the inky darkness. A rope came spinning down, and with sure hands the boy worked to uncoil the tangled line of what looked to be a ladder.

Merry's sodden garments were no protection against the cold wind that dug like nails into her skin. She felt her nerves begin to give way and fought hard against her escalating panic. She reminded herself as bad as things stood, it could have been worse.

She could have been alone at *Grave's End*. Kate must have seen what had happened. In no time at all, her father would find her. Lucien Merrick was nothing, if not a thorough and capable man. She knew that he would leave no stone unturned until his daughter was returned. She would be rescued. She would not allow herself to believe otherwise. The other possibilities were too horrible to consider.

The young pirate jerked Merry from the skiff's floor and set her with a painful drop over his shoulder. Indifferent to her struggles, he climbed the rope ladder, unaware that his hard bone shoulders jabbed painfully into her stomach as he pulled her weight upward.

The boy sprang down on the deck and released her without ceremony. The moment his rough, scarred hands left her, she fell hard against the damp deck, and then thrashed about its slippery surface like an eel.

"What a nuisance you are."

Merry's fury surged upward in a floodtide of flailing, bound arms and legs struggling his direction.

"I would like to see you keep your balance with your hands and feet tied after being jostled about like a dead Christmas goose," Merry countered indignantly, making a desperate, feeble attempt to rise. "If you don't release me this instant, I will ..."

It was her misfortune to find her knees, for they instantly deserted her. She made another loud thump against the deck.

"Hopeless," Indy mutter the single word, packed with enough contempt that it was by far the cruelest comment anyone had ever directed to her.

No power on earth could have made her accept his outstretched hand. She was nearly to her feet, when the ship suddenly came to a creaking pause, suspended, and then the floor dove suddenly, pulling her down with the force to land hard on her chin and stomach.

"Jesus Christ. Can't you exercise even the slightest common sense?"

This time his arm snaked around her without being offered and jerked her to her feet.

Blue eyes snapping, Merry exclaimed, "Let me go, you barbarian. You'll pay for humiliating me like this. If you don't untie my arms this instant, I will scream."

"That," said closely to her ear, "will only draw sharks. Human sharks. But, it's entirely up to you how you choose to die. Damn. Stop screaming. Be silent, you miserable, bedraggled wretch, unless you want Morgan's crew topside within a thrice.

I am not going to rape you, you stupid girl. Only move you out of sight, before someone else sees you and gets into their mind to—"

He didn't need to finish the thought. It was clear the moment she understood him because the fight went from her body in a single gush.

She might have weighed nothing for how little effort he spent dragging her poorly resisting body from the ships rail. He deposited her into a sitting position on the deck, with a crate supporting her back, obviously trusting her disobliging limbs less than she did.

Curt and dismissing, he commanded, "Stop squirming and be still. Do you want me to spend the rest of the night pulling splinters from your backside?"

"You, of course, would be heartbroken," Merry snapped sarcastically, but her voice didn't rise above a low, fierce hiss. "There is not enough kindness in you to sink a flea."

The boy returned to the rail as a puffing Shay sprang over the side of the ship. Indy's low, harsh curse momentarily drowned out the vibrations of footsteps and voices wafting upward from the men below decks.

"Damn it, Shay, I told you to secure the skiff," Indy growled, watching the craft drift away from the *Corinthian*. "Morgan will have our hides, if you're not able to retrieve it."

"Yer worried about trouble over a skiff with herself sitting there, staring daggers at us? Damn it, mon, with the trouble we're in, there won't be enough left of us fer Morgan to flail over the loss of that bloody skiff."

Indy pulled a stiletto from his belt. Terrified, Merry cried out, trying to scurry away. As Indy grabbed for her hair, Shay put his bulk between them. The knife, just missing his ear, made a ruthless slice through the red bandana tied above his lobe.

"Damn it, lad, be careful with that bloody thing. An inch

higher and it would have been me ear on yer pretty blade. Can't ye see the lass if afraid. It's all right, lass. Calm yerself. Do ye think Indy would have taken ye from the beach if he meant to butcher ye?"

She was still trying to scurry away, even as Indy seized her ankles to cut the ropes on her legs. In a gracefully rapid slash, before her horrified eyes, her bonds were removed.

"Get up," Indy ordered, giving her a hard pull.

Reluctantly, Merry obeyed. He took her bound hands, obviously not trusting her to navigate the ship's darkness on her own and snapped her body forward.

Merry scrambled to keep pace as the pirates moved with practice ease toward the stern of the ship, and down a tiny passage of stairs. A lantern flickered on the far wall, casting a nightmarish glow over the companionway. Thoughts of escape soared in and out of her mind like shooting stars, but she knew better than to attempt one.

Shay followed closely behind her. Even if she managed to escape the boys, the thought of being discovered by the crew of the most villainous pirate ship ever to sail the seas, was intimidating enough to stop her. Caution, a voice she seldom listened to, reminded her that only Indy and Shay were aware of her presence aboard the *Corinthian* and she should take every precaution to see that it remained that way.

They halted before a doorway. Indy briefly release her as he rummaged through a pocket for the key. Pushing the red oak door wide with his foot, he ruthlessly tossed her into the cabin of Captain Morgan.

To Merry's annoyance, she lost her footing, again. This time, her toe catching the edge of Morgan's Persian rug and she fell with a painful thump to the floor.

"Does it flatter your manly ego to toss me about like a sack of meal? If you don't have a care, *you'll* do away with me and deprive Morgan of the pleasure."

He clamped her mouth shut with iron like fingers on her cheeks. "And if you don't learn to lower that bloody screech, I will put the gag back in."

It was Shay who helped her up. "Ye would do better to save ye breath if yer're hoping to find a tender heart in Indy. He likes to stay clear of trouble, that one does, and ye lass, are more trouble than two lifetimes can take. Ye don't know what fear is 'til ye've suffered the razor side of Morgan's temper."

"If you're afraid of trouble, why don't you stop jawing with the girl and make yourself useful, you lazy Irish porker. Get the tub and some water from the wardroom," Indy barked. His clever dark eyes darted to Merry. "Don't even think it," Indy grumbled, aware of the open cabin door, though he hadn't looked. "Do you think you can out run me?"

It was hardly likely. Not with the way her body seemed to have no intention of cooperating and the unsuspected difficulty of maintain her balance on the sharply shifting deck.

Schooling her face into what she prayed were innocent lines, she conceded, reluctantly, that now was not the time to attempt a daring escape. Especially since daring was the last thing she was inclined to feel near Indy. Like a wet sugar cake she felt her body give way as she sank down on the dark, patterned rug, which had conspired against her only a moment ago.

For the first time she turned her full attention to the room. Staring about in wide-eyed surprise, Morgan's private haven was not at all what she expected. She had expected something sinister and wicked. What she found was a room clean as a pin, amazingly luxurious, opulently comfortable, and tastefully decorated from floor to beam.

Soft light shimmered from the clear crystal globes of gimbaled candlesticks and wrought iron sconces, lending a cozy glow to her surprisingly elegant surroundings. The air held the spice of warm wood musk, the faint but pleasantly blending scents of tobacco and.... *wintergreen?* She drew a small measure of comfort from the scent for it was one, ironically, instantly associated with her father.

Her fertile imagination conjured an image of Lucien Merrick storming Morgan's men like a thundercloud, to rescue his rash and reckless daughter. Brutal, morbid reality mocked her that, more likely than not, Morgan would kill him.

She turned her attention back to Morgan's cabin, trying to stem her mounting hysteria. There was a real bed of polished mahogany, spread with a heavy velvet coverlet of a rust hue. Matching brocade pillows lined the gallery's window bench beneath the diamond-shaped glass of the stern windows. On one side of the sturdy, but inviting bed, bookshelves lined the wall. Wing chairs made cozy by lambskin were positioned before the books, and across from the bed was a handsome table and chairs. The expert carving of mahogany wood reminding her of a table in her mother's own private sitting room. Along the walls were certainly a priceless collection of European masterpieces, carefully encased in glass to protect them from the sea mist. Morgan's desk was a well-organized mass of charts and navigational tools. Most of which she could identify from the time she'd sailed—*or rather, stowed away*—at the age of nine on a ship with Uncle Andrew bound for the American capital, no less.

She leaned forward, picking up a divider, lightly tapping the pointed end of the instrument against her fingers. She was fervently inventing ways to use this simple navigational tool as a weapon against her young captor. Meanwhile, Shay returned from the wardroom, dragging an attractive baroque hipbath behind him.

"You had better not have taken so long because you were

regaling the crew of our exploits with the girl," Indy said, tossing the garment he'd removed from a lacquer chest onto the bed.

Shay's pleasant face curled with indignation. "Do ye think I want them—" he jerked his head in the far direction of the ship. "—to know we've got herself sit'n there. Ye may think I am a dumb Irishmen, but credit me wi' some sense. Ye and I, lad, ain't likely to win, not fer all your fancy blade dancing and me being the fion strong lad that I am."

"Don't bother to heat the water. Two buckets should do. There isn't much of her to wash. And be quick about it. It won't be long before Morgan and the others return."

Wash. Merry, who had only been half listening to their exchange, sat up in alarm.

"You're not getting me into that thing," Merry declared, springing away from them.

She held the divider in hand, its shiny point directed at Indy. As far as weapons went, it was damn pitiful. The point couldn't deliver a mortal wound, but it would hurt like the devil, if wisely used. Wouldn't it?

Obviously, Indy didn't think so. Contempt simmered unpleasantly in his black eyes.

"Christ, what do you plan to do with that? Chart my course?" In an instant, she was disarmed. "What an imbecile you are. For God's sake, don't touch anything else. Nothing annoys Morgan more than having his possessions moved."

"I have every right to defend myself," Merry hissed wretchedly

"Don't count on Morgan seeing it that way. Do you think we brought the tub in here to drown you? If you leave the stench of the Channel and splotches of sand in Morgan's sheets, he's likely to give you the backside of his hand. You won't last two minutes with Morgan in the shape you're in. There's no telling what vermin you've got crawling on you after Shelby's."

Merry sputtered with outrage. "Vermin, indeed. There is no need to get insulting. I won't bare the last of my dignity, before you two young villains and lull about in a tub that's seen more men, than a public convenience."

Shay, who had been filling the tub, let out a howl of laughter at that.

"Bare the last of yer dignity? Ye have to admit, Indy, she does talk pretty fer one of Jack Shelby's girls."

"I am not one of Shelby's girls. This is a mistake, I tell you."

"It wouldn't matter if ye were the Queen of England, lass. If Indy's got a mind to put ye into the tub,"—he made a comical diving motion with his hands— "then, in ye go."

Scowling, Indy snapped, "Christ, it's not like you've got anything I haven't seen a thousand times before."

"Well, pardon me for not wanting to be a one thousand and one. I repeat..."

Unceremoniously, he picked her up, ignoring her frantic protests, and dumped her fully clothed into the water. Pulling the knife from his belt, he cut free her wrists.

"Can I trust you to do the rest or are you going to make me strip you?"

Humiliated, Merry stared up at him with eyes bright with fury and tears. Holding her arms wide, she glared at her garments. "I suppose you've a plan on what I am to wear now."

For that complaint, she earned his fingers snaking through her hair and a sharp tug backward of her head.

"Do you want me to finish the job myself?"

She did not doubt for a moment he would. He held up a bar of soap in front of her, which, much to her surprise, smelled of roses.

"Is privacy too much to expect?"

"Christ, what a nuisance you are. Do you think the sight of your rosy ass is going to make me...?" he broke off.

It was useless. His cold eyes watched her face color, from chin to hairline, in every shade from pink to scarlet. He wondered if he'd ever been hampered by such modesty and was heartily pleased he couldn't recall a time.

Cursing under his breath, Indy turned toward the door. "Five minutes. Be done or I will finish you."

Merry sat, shivering in the tub, watching him disappear from the cabin. Anxiously, she shed her clothes vaguely disappointed in herself when her icy fingers closed around her dagger.

Why hadn't she remembered the weapon when it could have done her some good? Tossing her pitiful little blade on Morgan's desk, she grabbed the scented soap and the cloth Indy had left her.

The fresh water was soothing after the harsh saltwater spray. She welcomed the comfort to her flesh. Her skin burned from the frantic motions of her hands, but when she climbed from the tub every inch of her was clean and scrubbed.

She found a linen towel atop of Morgan's trunk and wrapped her shaking body within it, then took the comb he'd left. She was huddled before the stove that Indy had lit before leaving, trying to untangled her locks before the fire, when the boy returned.

"You're making it worse," was all he said when he saw her tangle Morgan's comb in her dark curls. He sank cross-legged behind her, lifting the comb from her hands. He began to work the knots from her hair with careful strokes that would have rivaled even a mother's.

Noticing her shiver, disgusted he said, "You should have grabbed the quilt if you were cold. What a helpless creature you are."

"I am not helpless," Merry protested hotly, trying to keep her teeth from chattering. "This cabin is drafty, the water was cold and you specifically told me not to touch Morgan's possessions. You left me a towel, not a dressing gown. Of course I am cold."

"Well forgive me, did you enjoy the feel of saltwater bleeding into your pores?"

"No."

"Stop complaining. After all your trouble, you're lucky I didn't leave you to suffer."

His scarred hands closed on her again and jerked her to her feet. He silenced her protest with a hard shake. Merry admitted to herself, it was pointless to fight with the boy. She might have been a gnat for all the power she had against him. Her struggles were ridiculously ineffective. In the end, he would do as he pleased.

Trembling and humiliated, she suffered through the indignity of having her body patted dry.

"What a bunch of nonsense over a little flesh."

Tears of humiliation trickled down her pink cheeks. "Perhaps the girls you are acquainted with think nothing of allowing a strange boy to stare at them, but I assure you I am not in the habit of undressing in front of anyone."

He took no affront at her calling him 'strange' and surprised her by saying, "Did I say you were? But all your high minded sentiments won't do you a bit of good here." His low voice was muffled, as a decidedly feminine nightgown was being pulled quickly over her shriveled, pink body. However, he allowed her the towel to remain in place around her until she was covered by the gown. "You had best forget your delicate notions and start figuring out a way to save your hide. They're not going to help you with Morgan."

Her eyes fixed on his face curiously. His tone hadn't been

exactly kind, but neither had it been cruel. She had the strangest feeling that he knew, perfectly well, she wasn't one of Jack Shelby's doxies.

That look in his eyes, before he had pulled back his knife from her face, had been surprise and annoyance. Who was this boy? And what did he know?

His callous fingers fastened the small pearl buttons on her bodice, because her shaking hands couldn't master it. When he finished, he released her without pause. He was really quite a bizarre boy. Her nervous gaze locked on his scarred hands, remembering when he had pulled off his vest on the beach that his back had been such a horrid collection of healed ridges she had felt a lump rise in her throat. She wondered how he had become so disfigured.

Was it this torture that had made him so cold, as if he had no soul left at all?

Merry frowned as her eyes followed a neatly swirling pattern of healed flesh that ran across, what would have been, quite a lovely chest. "How..." she faltered, but only momentarily. "How did all that happen?"

His cold black eyes whipped her delicate face. "Oh, this? I was beaten of course. What the hell do you think happened? People aren't born this way. Beaten and burned."

Merry trembled. They might have well been talking about the weather, for all the feeling in his voice. There was no doubt, in her mind who had beaten him.

"Not very pretty, is it? Doesn't it make your skin crawl to look at them?"

"No, my skin isn't crawling. It's just... they make me sad, that's all."

"You should save your pity for yourself. It's the memory of these scars and how I got them that gave me the will to survive."

Survive what? The beatings? Morgan's undoubtedly cruel treatment?

She scrambled away from him, huddling on the window seat, and watched as he quickly went about tidying the cabin. Anxiously, she tried to arrange the ice blue lace more modestly over her front, but the gown was having none of her prudishness. That it was two sizes too small in the bodice helped, not at all. It was meant to be provocative and highly sophisticated. What was such a garment doing in Morgan's decidedly male domain?

With an anxiety she couldn't hide, she asked, "What will Morgan do with me?"

"It depends on how silver-tongued you are," said the boy as he continued to tidy the cabin. "Morgan can see clear inside a person's skull. If you've got something to hide, you had better pray he doesn't sense it."

"You have to help me. If Morgan finds out who I am, he'll peel me to the bone."

"Then, you best make sure he doesn't," Indy said dispassionately, but his dark eyes were severely warning and shrewd. "As for helping you, pay attention this time. I am the one who brought you here. Remember? I have got trouble enough of my own. Morgan is likely to feed me to the sharks when he finds you here."

She stared at him, her bluebell eyes like buckets, her face pale as parchment.

"Don't look at me like that. What lunacy possessed you to cross paths with Morgan?"

"I didn't cross paths with him on purpose," Merry shouted back. "Do you think I would have gone to *Grave's End*, if I had known Morgan would be there? Do you think I am insane enough to look for that kind of trouble?"

Annoyed, Indy abandoned the effort to keep his tone civil.

"Going into *Grave's End* wasn't a sane thing to do, at all. How am I to know what manner of lunacy you're capable of?"

"Nevertheless... What am I to do now?"

Mildly, he jeered, "Christ, haven't you even a notion of self-preservation?" Meeting her defiant stare, he cursed and added, "Don't expect me to help you with every coil. Don't spit daggers at me, if you don't like what you hear. From where I sit, you've got two choices with Morgan. Tell him nothing and pray he doesn't kill you, or tell him nothing and take him to bed."

He gave this advice so matter-of-factly, that for a moment, Merry wasn't certain she had heard him correctly. She stared down at the gown, realizing that the boy, for whatever reason, had decided the truth was not an option. He had taken providence into his own hands.

"I won't do it." Merry was screaming, without knowing it. "I can't. How could you think for a moment I would ever consider such a ghastly plan?"

"It's your life. You are perfectly capable of doing it," he told her simply.

"Understand this—never. Not even if my life depended on it."

Those may have been brave words, but she couldn't have chosen them less wisely. The grimness of the boy's eyes told her the seriousness of her fate.

"You should be damn glad you have the kind of look that stirs a man's softer side. You can be certain Morgan won't be moved by that sharp tongue of yours."

Never, thought Merry, *never, never, never.*

So much for cool-headed logic. The minute Indy turned his back, she sprang for the open door. She was almost out of the cabin, when the boy caught her. He lifted her effortlessly from the ground, and flung her cruelly down upon Morgan's bed. As she struggled beneath him, he held her in place with his body.

"Let me go," Merry screamed, twisting and clawing at the dark face above her. "Get off of me this instant. I demand that..."

"Damn it, keep your voice down," Indy warned, breathless from the struggle. "They can hear your screams from poop to f'cle. Do you have any idea how many men are on this ship, who would love a chance at your haughty ass?"

"I won't stay here," she cried, trying to kick him. "I want to go home. I won't do what you want me to do. I won't."

"I didn't save your worthless neck... stop that. Do you think it'll do any good to bite me? You stupid girl, there is no way off this ship. And you will do exactly what it takes to save your life. Damn it. Use your head. You're here. Accept it."

"Accept it?" she spat, as he held her squirming body in place. Helpless tears dribbled down her face and weakly she said, "I hate you. Why did you bring me here for this?"

"I thought *you* might prefer to live," Indy countered with brutal coldness and a less than gentle shake. "You got yourself into this complicated mess. What I have done is provide you the chance to get out of it, hopefully living."

"Bloody hell. I heard ye two all the way from the wardroom," Shay warned, puffing from his run back to Morgan's cabin. His eyes rounded when he saw Indy spread eagle atop the girl. "Should I come back?"

"Don't be stupid," Indy said, grabbing her wrists and jerking her to a sitting position. "Start using your head, girl. If you take off, like a hare before hounds, with Morgan, he'll know in an instant you've got something to hide. If you continue to cry, he's apt to shove a sock in your mouth. It's a damn annoying sound. You don't cry at all pretty like most women."

"Hell's teeth, lad, ye don't have to be so hard on the lass. Can't ye see she's frightened? There's no need to be frightened, lass. Do ye think Morgan's some demon, what's going to steal yer soul? I don't know what those shellbacks did to ye at Shelby's, but Morgan's got a rare hand with the lassies. Ain't nothing to be afraid of if ye catch his fancy. Treats them all well. God's teeth, it might be best fer us all."

Swallowing her frustration at being misunderstood, she gave them a hostile stare and snapped, "Understand this. I would rather die than become Morgan's mistress. It disgusts every feeling."

"Then tell him that. We'll make sure your body pieces are buried all in one spot," Indy hurled at her callously. "That is, if Morgan's hasn't heard you already. Christ, why is he always so bloody punctual?"

From far away voices came to her and Merry's fury shifted to terror. Her nerves pricked to Morgan's nearness, even before he entered the cabin.

The door opened and the entire chemistry of the room was that easily altered. With a negligent wave in Indy's direction, Morgan, his mind on business, leaned one hand on his desk, flicked over a page, and entered something in the logbook. His presence filled the cabin with humming energy. She couldn't shake the sensation of being watched by him, even though his eyes never sought her.

Several minutes passed before Morgan unclasped his flowing black cape, tossed it to Indy, and turned to face Merry's trembling form huddled on his bed. Every organ from throat to toes started to scream. He was even more frighteningly large, more disconcertingly handsome, than she remembered.

Shivering beneath his penetrating stare, she wished she could read the thoughts carefully hidden behind those intimidating black eyes. His features revealed nothing, not even surprise at finding her here.

Holding herself still beneath the terror of Morgan's notice, she half expected him to lunge across the cabin, cutlass in hand, either to strip her bare or slit her throat. Morgan did neither. He poured some wine and then settled on the edge of his desk.

Struggling desperately not to fall to pieces, as his eyes slowly roamed her from head to toe, Merry tried to remind herself he was only a man. She dismissed her thoughts for the foolishness they were.

Morgan was no mere mortal. He was the stuff of myths and nightmares. She had a sudden impression of how she must look to him, helpless, frightened, and to her dismay, pathetically awe-struck. As afraid as she was, she could never forget the legend of this man. The uncontainable fascination of seeing, with her own eyes, that he was not some specter of fantasy, but real, and despite every speculation, no one had touched even a faint hint of the reality.

Across the cabin, someone moved. Merry felt a moment of pure relief as Morgan's eyes lifted briefly from her.

"Tom, come. Don't be shy. See what the lads have found for us."

Turning her head, Merry noticed for the first time that Morgan had not entered the cabin alone. The man was as tall as Morgan, but of slighter build and greater age. She would have thought him unremarkable, in all, except for the sharp scar that ran from hairline through pointed brow, which possessed the most curious jig-jag pattern. His lips were narrow and tight, as if he had never known a smile, his eyes strict and without kindness. He did not conceal his thoughts with the same care as Morgan, though she wished he had.

What she found in his expression was clear and oddly insulting. In a single word: *Irritation.*

"What mischief have you lads been up to now? Have you taken to stealing the Falmouth lasses from their beds for sport?" His short laugh had nothing to do with humor, as he arched a brow and turned to his captain. "Or have I forgotten your birthday, Varian?" Pouring himself a glass of wine, he settled in a chair at Morgan's table, his eyes never leaving her. "Well, Varian, this is a night of surprises, is it not? Though I must admit that this one is more pleasant than the last. Such a beauty. Where do you suppose she came from?"

Morgan's long mouth developed a soft Byronic twist. "The short version, if you will. I don't think our frail flower will last through the unabridged tale." With suave mockery, he said to Merry, "I command you to stay alive, Little One. At least until I decide otherwise." Morgan's dark gaze locked on the boy and with a dramatic wave of his hand: "Speak."

'The crate," was all the boy said, in way of explanation.

"Ah." The brief flicker of light died in the captain's eyes. "Indy, why isn't she dead?"

There was a short intense silence that Merry spent shaking like chimes in a windstorm, wondering the same thing. She knew very well what Morgan's orders had been. Nothing could convince her Indy had spared her life for pity's sake alone.

Morgan arched one dark brow severely, and the boy's response came instantly.

"Give me a chance before you blister my hide. Look at her. Isn't she a dead ringer for the wench we hauled off with in Cadiz? And she was with Shelby. I thought..."

"You didn't think," Tom broke in with undisguised annoyance, "or else you'd realize the mess you've left us with. You don't imagine she sprang from a mushroom patch, do you? We don't need anyone connecting her disappearance with our visit to Cornwall. I can't wait to hear how you connect this girl to what happened in Cadiz."

"A spy," Morgan supplied, his deep voice sending shivers down Merry's spine. "You remember the girl from Cadiz, Tom. The one the crew killed, while having a bit of sport, before the lad got a chance to get some answers from her. This one we found tucked away in a crate at *Grave's End.*"

Tom looked at the boy with open disgust. "Of all the muddle-headed notions. What you two morons have here is a child. You do realize that bringing her aboard ship changes nothing? You should have killed her at the beach and been done with it."

"With the patrol hot on our heels to witness the deed," Indy snarled, speaking the lie so convincingly, that it took Merry a moment to register that he was lying and to wonder why.

"Patrol? What nonsense are you trying to pull, young'n? There wasn't any patrol."

Indy met the furious stare without flinching so much as a single hair.

"That chit who slipped through your fingers, rode off hell for leather and must have run to raise the men. If you hadn't been so stupid as to let her get away, none of this would have been necessary."

"I will take no more impudence from you. Keep a civil tongue, lad, or I will cut it out."

Equally menacing, Indy flung back, "I don't take orders from you. We could have been killed because of your damned, bloody incompetence."

"And here I thought the rest of my night would be deadly dull, Tom," Morgan put in lightly. Amid the crackling tension of the room, his gaze shifted from Indy, focusing on Merry, and began to sparkle.

He knows Indy is lying, she thought desperately, terrified of what he would make of that.

"You have had an adventure, haven't you, lad?"

"Bloody Christ. Don't tell me you believe this nonsense, Varian?" said Tom.

"Of course I do," Morgan stated blandly, while pouring

himself more wine. "The lad knows better than to lie to me. Don't you, Indy?"

Indy met Morgan's black stare. Whatever the game between them was well beyond Merry's comprehension.

"You still haven't explained why the girl isn't dead, *now*," Tom demanded and added with sharp sarcasm, "Or is the patrol tucked in the hold?"

Indy pulled the dagger from his belt and tossed it in the center of the table. "You slit her throat, if you have a mind to do it. The girl need be a problem to no one then."

Across the room, Morgan's dark glittering gaze moved swiftly and unnoticed among his companions.

Grinning a little, he collected Tom's cool glance and said, "Can we blame the boy for wanting to delegate this atrocity? I admit, I never suspected she'd be so young and pretty. So, if there is any blame to lay anywhere for her being here now, I suppose it's mine. I would more than gladly discuss the matter with you in private, Tom, if you have a care to." Not waiting for Tom's response, Morgan's dark eyes swiveled to Indy. "And if you desire to see the girl dead, lad, you should have tossed me the knife. Otherwise, your posturing is really quite useless, and overly dramatic. Since it's obvious you wish to see the girl live, pick up that damn dagger before I decide she's more trouble than she's worth."

With comical quickness that would have made Merry smile if her life hadn't been hanging in the balance, Indy retrieved the knife and tucked it into his belt.

Suddenly Morgan's features resolved themselves into a smile. "You needn't worry, Tom. Our pretty hostage need be a bother to no one, but me. And if she becomes a bother, we'll settle it then. She's really quite lovely, as you would see if you gave her a good stare, and stopped your scowling. Obviously, our tender-hearted lad thought to procure me a little sport and kill two birds with one stone. You know how wonderfully economical Indy's thought processes tend to be. And as this discussion is getting us nowhere at all," he said with a dramatically crafted sigh, "the two of you may leave. You, Indy, will stay..." Morgan's dark gaze moved smoothly back to Merry. "...and of course, you, Little One."

Morgan settled back at his table as the others filed from the room. His black eyes settled nowhere, not on Indy hanging up his cloak or Merry quaking on his bed. He slowly swirled the wine in his glass and seemed intent on simply watching it. His voice suddenly broke the silence, completely devoid now of the polite fiction of tolerant amusement he had maintained in front of the others.

"Was I not clear, lad? I wanted the girl dealt with at the beach."

Those cunning eyes watched the boy, who for his part bothered not to respond and continued stone-faced to carefully put Morgan's possession away.

Morgan indulged the silence, studying the boy who betrayed nothing at all. Waiting until the boy was near, he ruthlessly grabbed his chin to jerk his face so that eye contact was impossible to avoid. "Speak."

Indy's gaze met Morgan's squarely. "I won't harm her." That simply, he defied Morgan.

Morgan's gaze began to shimmer. "Oh my, you do dive straight to the heart of things, don't you?"

Irritation whipped the boy's face, as he broke free of Morgan's hands. "What the hell is that supposed to mean?"

"If you wanted the girl for yourself, you need not have put her in my bed first. Your sacrifice and generosity are unnecessary and insulting. Every boy deserves a pet. Did you really fear I wouldn't let you keep her, if you did not let me have her first?"

"I want her, not at all. You better than anyone should know where my tendencies run."

"Your tendencies, as you so quaintly put them, are a matter we should discuss later. I hardly think our Little One is up to the rigors of it. To be honest, tonight, neither am I." Those clever eyes sharpened. "Who is this girl to you?"

"Two tits and a..." he used a vulgar word that Merry had never heard before. Yet, something in the sound and way he said it, made her blush from chin to hairline.

"If that were true, lad, you would have raped her on the beach and slit her throat to ear. You know very well what disobeying my orders means, though it seemed not to have been much of a deterrent in this case. You've gone to considerable trouble to make her sufficiently appealing to me. Which means you want me to bed her, so not you or anyone else, is likely to harm her. However, bedding her, no matter how much confidence you place in what you call my gluttonous tendencies and her visually obvious merits, won't change a thing. I might very well bed her, then give her to Tom's capable hands, just to teach you a grim lesson about the necessity of trusting me with the truth. Something you fail to do with enormous frequency, I little deserve. So when I ask you who this girl is, don't insult me with your silence, when obviously, it would serve you better simply to tell me."

"She's nothing to me. I know her, not at all. I don't consort with genteel young girls."

"You know her not at all, lad, and yet you know her to be genteel," Morgan commented shrewdly. "A considerable leap in logic given where we found her."

"You, more than anyone, should know that environment is not all defining."

Morgan's smile took on an appreciative edge. "Ah...point taken, lad. Whatever you're trying to hide, the truth will come

97

out in time. It always does."

Morgan poured himself another drink and continued to watch the boy sharply. Whatever their relationship was, and Merry wasn't certain that she wanted to know *that* any more than she wanted to know exactly what they meant by *tendencies*. She was sure it was a complicated one she would never make reason of.

The boy was confident enough to dare Morgan's scrutiny and his displeasure without an ounce of fear. He went about his business with the same quiet efficiency he seemed to do all tasks, as though Morgan's burning gaze following him was a matter of no concern.

"You know, of course, that Tom won't stop until she's dead. He's right in this. She's a witness to my meeting with the good earl at *Grave's End*. For that reason alone, she should die. An unpleasant reality, as young and as beautiful as she is."

"Tom may be an excellent quartermaster, but he's a damn extremist. He'd depopulate half the planet, if you'd let him. At any rate, you'll do as you please with the girl, regardless of Tom's panicking or my wishes. They have never seemed to grant a moment's importance to you, for all that you continually hound me that they do."

"You've made your wishes overly complicated, if I am missing them and failing you. You should have released the girl at the beach, if you wanted to spare her. There would have been no time for me to check that you'd handled this matter wisely. Shay, miserable wretch that he is, would have lied to protect your hide, with the sincerity of a defrocked priest trying to steal the collection basket. It was clear you felt you couldn't free the girl. If your secret turns out to be an unpleasant one, there is nothing I can do to help you, lad."

There was a short, unfriendly silence where neither man betrayed any emotion. Every fear revealed itself on Merry's face.

"I am really getting tired of asking you these questions, lad. Who is this girl and why is she here?"

"I thought you had decided that I would be overly complicated in this," the boy sneered. "Wouldn't explaining myself tend to ruin that? If you want to bed her, you'll bed her. If you want to kill her, you'll kill her. Don't pretend with me it could ever be otherwise. I thought we had agreed long ago to abolish that fiction. You'll do what you will, you always do, and explaining myself won't in the end change a thing."

Delicate surprise augmented the sparkle in Morgan's black eyes. There was a short laugh, a lifted eyebrow.

"So now we're really digging deep at the marrow of things, and not bothering to dance around it civilly. What benefit you think either of us will gain from this grim little exercise is beyond fathoming. Your ability at reasoning is somewhat in disarray, if you think turning this girl into one of your obscure adolescent tests will change anything of our relationship. You've still got a lot to learn, not the least of which, the weapons you choose to toss at me. If I decide to dispose of the girl, I will. You've let it be clear, without explanation, it is your wish to spare her. You never seem to grasp, Indy, is that what you constantly set in motion is *failure.*"

Indy leaned over, retrieved Morgan's discarded boots, and returned them to the lacquered chest bolted to the wall.

"My," Morgan said in a civil way. "A symbolic show of obedience and all. You have gotten better at this, haven't you, lad?"

There was a short unfriendly silence in which the boy obviously revealed he wanted the matter to end. Morgan, having decided it best to let things simmer awhile, turned his attention to Merry.

"Come here, girl, and let me get a look at you," Morgan said, into the hysterical buzzing in Merry's head. "Let me see if you're worth all the bother you've caused me this night."

Even if God had ordered her to do so, Merry couldn't have found the will to move from her embarrassingly poor place of safety on Morgan's bed.

The effect of his full attention, paralyzed Merry. His black eyes held neither kindness nor malice. Yet, she could only manage to meet the burning power of his stare for the briefest of moments, before quickly, fearfully dropping her eyes to concentrate on the clasped hands that lay in her lap.

"Put your chin up, girl, and let me have a look at you." When she didn't comply, Morgan said softly, "Oh my, we are going to have to teach you to obey an order, aren't we."

Merry was unprepared for the harsh clutching of hands that jerked her from the bed. Recognizing the scarred fingers on her pale flesh, she exploded into fury, and screamed, "Let me go, you barbarian. You loathsome son of a..."

It was not the first time she had let loose her temper at Indy. His reaction, however, was different. The words clogged in her throat as his scarred hand went mid-air ready to strike her. Closing her eyes and struggling to break free, Morgan's voice was lost to her as was the quiet move of his body.

"Really, Indy, there is no need for that. Let her go."

Caught unaware by the swiftness of her release, Merry could not rally her numb muscles. As her knees buckled beneath her, it was Morgan who caught her up, supporting her as she fell against his towering form. The movement, thankfully, had brought her face and eyes to be hidden against his slowly heaving chest. She longed to pull back, but would have rather died than to look at him.

She felt strong fingers in her hair, tensed because she feared he was about to grab it. Frightfully, she looked to find Morgan delicately taking a handful of her raven tresses and touching them to his lips.

Softly, he said, "Scented of roses. The boy has been busy with you, hasn't he?"

Merry forced herself to look into his eyes then. "Please, don't kill me. Please."

Her plea made Morgan smile. "Is there a reason why I should want to kill you?"

Merry had not intended to speak at all. The words had simply come, from a force of their own. With grim disappointment, Merry wondered why they had to be so nakedly pathetic. She was ashamed of her cowardice, her shivering, and the whimper in her voice. She had never lacked for spirit, but then, she had never met Morgan either.

"There is no need to abandon hope, Little One. I won't harm you. Not unless you give me a reason to. Right now, I will settle on just a good look."

In a clever, effortless movement, Morgan tilted her face, his broad palm at the base of her throat, her hair tangled through his long fingers. He studied her while his other hand lightly explored her body.

The blood began to pound in Merry's throat at his touch, which moved with leisurely, efficient thoroughness. His palm left no spot of her body unexplored, as he traced the contour of her hip, climbing lightly up its slope until his fingers spanned her stomach.

She cried out when his palm slipped to the soft cup of the underside of her breast. It was shocking and embarrassing, that queer response to his finger's work. His eyes opened just a trifle, the slow grin telling her he knew exactly the response of her body to his touch.

"Who would have thought such a beauty lay hidden in a crate at *Grave's End*? I was wrong to underestimate you, lad. As far as efforts go, this ranks among your best."

Merry turned her face away, not wanting him to see as she

bit her lower lip, to try and soothe the unfamiliar sensations caused by his expert touch.

Morgan's soft laughter told her that the effort had been worthless. "Why is there something elusively familiar to all this?"

"The gown," Indy supplied dryly. "Only the girl is new."

"Ah, wrapped and everything. You have made your best effort, haven't you, lad?"

The girl blushed from chin to hairline. Morgan's gaze traveled her features. Her alabaster skin which contrasted so dramatically with the unfashionably long, wild ebony curls; her clear bluebell eyes; the haughty little nose which carried the stamp of good birth; and those soft red lips. Her beauty was undeniable. Her soft, cultured voice one of breeding. Was it possible the girl was as innocent as she looked?

What had she been doing at *Grave's End* with Jack Shelby? What did Indy think to accomplish with him using this mere slip of a girl?

Perhaps it was the wine he'd consumed tonight, but Morgan felt a nagging displeasure from the fear in her eyes. He wondered if this poor frail vassal was truly as frightened as she looked.

Even with the mantel of his reputation many years set, he was unused to women fearing him. Every woman he had ever wanted, had been his for the asking. Yet, Morgan sensed that if he meant to have this girl, at all—which was clearly what Indy intended for reasons obscure—it would be no small effort to get her into his bed willingly. She was afraid of him. That alone made her different from the others.

"Who are you, lass?" he asked softly.

Merry knew she ought to have been anticipating the question and was dismayed with herself for not having thought of a suitable lie beforehand. If it needed one thing only to make her situation worse, it would be for Morgan to learn she was Andrew Merrick's niece. What was she going to say? She had paused too long for him to believe any answer she managed. So, she reasoned her best course would be to keep her mouth tightly shut.

Morgan repeated the question. When she didn't answer, his fingers found her chin, and gave a gentle tug on her lower lip. "Oh my, I would have thought, by now, even you would have realized the necessity of getting away from me, as quickly as possible. Do you think your silence will serve you at all, girl?"

She sank her teeth into her lower lip and jerked her face away.

"We're under full sail, Little One. Though, our route is somewhat circuitous, we a have destination in a fortnight. So, unless it is your wish to sail with me to Ireland, you had better explain yourself quickly. If you drag this out any longer, we'll be too far from Cornwall for me to do anything about returning you home, before they know you're gone."

"Ireland?" The words burst through the burning fibers of Merry's mouth. "No. You can't. You can't take me with you to Ireland. I won't allow it."

"Won't you? If you'd like to go topside and convince Tom— you remember Tom don't you? He's the one who wants me to kill you— regardless, if you think Tom will consent to turning the ship around, be my guest. Though, I doubt he'll be agreeable with a dozen British patrollers roaming the coast."

Staring up into those opaque eyes, she knew it was hardly likely that any aboard ship would cross Morgan to help her. But to sail to Ireland with Morgan and his pirate ship....*No, no, no. She would have to stop him. But how?*

Merry forced herself to look into his eyes. "Please. You must take me back. Please."

"I would be more than happy to see you safely back to

shore, but that depends on how much you're willing to cooperate. We've reached an impasse and I have only asked you your name."

Merry swallowed hard, more frightened of answering his question than defying him. She whispered on a voice, embarrassingly thin, "Is it necessary to have a woman's life history before you rape them?"

His black eyes suddenly brightened. "Not always, Little One, just when I find myself curious. It tends to prove beneficial when one has a whim to have intimate conversation after the raping. Are you ashamed of who you are?"

The girl puffed up like a suddenly inflated balloon, those bluebell eyes flashing daggers at him. It almost worked before she dropped her gaze to focus on her knitted fingers.

"Ah, a mystery. I will learn them all before you leave my ship, count on that, Little One."

Again silence. Something had shown in her eyes that told Morgan the answers he wanted wouldn't come unless he beat the girl. The last thing any man would want to do is beat this girl, beautiful and fragile as she was. She was frightened to death, but not so frightened as to tell him what he wanted to know.

His long, tanned fingers reached to touch the slope of her cheek. "There's no reason for your fear, girl. I only asked to see you home. How am I to know where to take you, if I don't know who your people are?"

If this were an act, it was a damn good one. The man could drip sincerity when he chose to. Merry—weary, frightened, and desperate to return home, before she was in any more trouble than she was sure she was already in—felt a moment of dreadful uncertainty.

When he spoke again his words came to her low and kind. "Whatever you're trying to hide, your silence won't help you. It will only force my hand to keep you. There's no question which one of us will enjoy that situation more. What will your stubbornness gain you, but a fair deal of me, and your continued captivity? I can't release you, until my curiosity is satisfied as to who you are and why you were with Shelby spying on my meeting. If your answers are as innocent as I suspect they are, you have nothing at all to fear. Contrary to the ravings of hysterical fisherman, I don't make a habit of murdering young girls. At least not when I can help it. Why not spare us both quite a bit of bother and cooperate?"

Merry concentrated on showing nothing and his gaze remained steady and probing.

Feeling her tremble, Morgan ran a hand up her arm, noting it was icy, and understood instantly.

"Indy, bring me some wine. While I appreciate the effort, the girl is half frozen. This gown is hardly sufficient rigging for the Channel on a foggy night."

Lifting her chin with long tapered fingers, Morgan put a wineglass to her lips. When she had taken several swallows, he set the glass aside to lightly brush the droplets from her lips.

His fingers lingered on her lower lip as his intense jet gaze studied her again. "Better?"

Several minutes passed before Merry could manage a small nod. The gentleness of his touch made her head spin, the unwilling response of her body was unnerving. The play on her lips was not the kind of gesture she had even remotely conceived of from a man. It was humiliating the way her body responded to this meager contact.

As if he sensed her discomfort, his fingers slowly began to move, once again. Finally, in a weak voice she hardly recognized as her own, Merry whispered, "Please."

His black eyes began to sparkle. "Please what, Little One? I don't think I could deny you anything at the moment. Should we send the boy from the cabin?"

"Please, take your hands from me, sir," she demanded, her voice a blend of poorly concealed embarrassment and absurd politeness, given her circumstance.

Morgan smiled. "Not the answer I had hoped for, Little One. But as you said 'please' and called me 'sir'—" His unfinished thought hung in the tension laden air and then, to her utter amazement, he released her.

She watched nervously as Morgan moved from her to stretch in a chair, crossed his stocking feet at his ankles and reached for the glass of wine he had fed her with. Hot color flooded her cheeks at the memory of his fingers touching her lips. Before she could conceal her thoughts, he put the glass to his lips, in a light erotic contact swallowing the remaining wine in a single savoring effort.

Into her breathless silence of fear and unwilling fascination, she heard him say, "Do you have any idea how you flatter me, Little One? I have never made a lady blush by simply drinking from her wineglass. Whatever do you do when a man kisses you? Do you turn the colors of the rainbow from head to toe?"

Merry's spirit, poor errant thing though it had been since Morgan had entered the cabin, returned to her in a senseless floodtide.

Before she could think better of it, she snapped, "Whatever colors I may turn, you will never see them. If you so much as touch me again, I swear, I will scratch out your eyes."

Her words seem only to please him. "Ah, so there is a touch of spirit beneath that useless show of hand wringing and whimpering. Even better, Little One. I have a feeling I am going to thoroughly enjoy being scratched by you, my dear. Somehow, I don't think it will be my eyes you'll be reaching for."

Easing his elbows onto the arms of his chair, Morgan touched his own lips with the steeple of his fingers.

"If you are agreeable to suggestions, I know exactly where I would like you to begin." Before she could stop herself, Merry's eyes did a frantic flight to the door. "You don't have to run away from me, yet, Little One. For the moment, you're much safer here. Whatever shameful things you're imagining I may want to do to you, I can do only so often. My crew can do it endlessly. Would it help you to relax, if I told you I haven't at all made up my mind yet, what it is I want to do with you?"

Wishing she could match his ease, Merry said, "You could let me go."

"Yes, I could, but that would tend to limit the scope of my options rather early on. I may not have made up my mind, Little One, but I never said I wasn't considering it."

"Whatever you may be considering, sir, I can guarantee it won't happen, not if I have a say in the matter," she hissed with sudden, flashing rage.

"You don't, as a rule, Little One. The hostage's options are rather limited. Would you like me to explain them to you, since you seem so determined to be my hostage?"

"You and your explanations can go to the devil. Let me inform you of another option to consider. I will kill you before I let you kiss me." She had delivered her threat with her best menace and was unprepared for his reaction.

His black gaze ate the details of her angry face, and then, to her bewildered dismay, he began to laugh softly.

"Be fair, Little One, you're the one determined on silence and staying. If it's not your desire for me to consider anything beyond your quick return to Cornwall, it would have served you better to have moved away from the light and to answer my questions promptly. I can see through your sleeping gown, and unless you correct it, I shall have no choice but to believe that situation pleases you and continue our relationship accordingly."

The instant horror on the girl's face was nothing less than comical. Morgan watched as she tried to pull the shockingly thin fabric more protectively around her. She was by far the most absurd creature he had ever run across.

For her part, she did try. But the hurried motions of her hands only succeeded in exposing more of her bosom than the plunging neckline already revealed. Although, the sight of it was pleasing, his humor suddenly diminished as his pity increased for this poor amusing girl. He thought better of letting this continue, at least for the moment.

He smiled, moved from his chair, took something long and white from a drawer, and handed it to Indy. "You had better put her in this, lad. It's clear she doesn't understand, at all, what she is doing. Another moment, and we'll find her nude."

The boy's expression spoke nothing, as he took the shirt and went to her. It was clear she misunderstood his intent, because her hands moved in a defensive swing that only narrowly missed Indy. She was beyond listening when Indy tried to explain. It was Morgan who had to take her in hand, and bring her sudden flash of struggle to a quick halt.

"Silly girl. Stop fighting. I am not proposing he tie you up with it. Though, I can't guarantee we won't have that later. Right now I only want you covered. If I leave you to your own devices, you'll have yourself naked in a trice, poor, miserable things that your hands are. While the thought is appealing, if you want me to be able to consider any other course than putting you in that bed and sending the boy away, you had best start cooperating quickly."

His words made her melt in Indy's arms with frantic quickness. With steady hands the boy pulled the shirt in place, warned her against panic again, and set her in the chair beside the captain.

The gamin face stared at Morgan with wide-eyed anxiety, but her gaze was remarkably direct and clear, as transparent as a child's. For the hundredth time, he wondered if it were possible the girl was as innocent as she seemed and then knew in an instant she was.

Morgan's gaze began to simmer. "I can see now, lad, why you were reluctant to harm her. Though, I am not pleased beyond half that she's here. Can you imagine what her reaction would have been, if she knew that I was considering more than a kiss a moment ago?"

"I suspect it would have burned the topgallant right off the mainmast."

"And, I suspect that you realize by now, if you are reluctant to seeing our topgallants aflame you had better explain who this girl is. I also suspect the truth of who she is, has as much to do with her fear, as why you brought her here. It's pathetically obvious she's no threat to us. Whatever she was doing with Shelby, had nothing to do with us at all. Do you really want to put the girl through all this when the truth might very well stop it? How far are you willing to let this go?"

"What makes you think I can put a stop to it?"

"Which leads me to wonder what such innocence was doing at *Grave's End* and how the devil Shelby got a hold of her? It is also worth noting that while innocence may be refreshing, you wouldn't bother to bring her here because of it. Guilty or innocent, you would have taken care of the girl at the beach. For the simple fact that you are nothing less than thorough in your actions, and she witnessed my meeting with the earl. There is no reasonable motivation, at all, for what you've done, lad, in bringing this girl to me and offering her like a sacrificial lamb on an altar. Unless..." Morgan's thoughts seemed to hang, with a heavy sense of unpleasant speculation that Merry cared for not at all. "Rensdale."

Rensdale? The shock of hearing his name, in this of all surroundings, was like being dropped into a tank of icy water. Before Merry realized that Morgan had said the name in a tone that should have warned danger, her round, disbelieving eyes fixed on the pirate captain.

Noting the error too late, she had only a frantic moment to wonder, *Dear Lord, what does Rensdale have to do with Morgan? And what have I stepped into now?*

Her face was jerked swiftly to meet that burning black stare.

Before Merry could speak, Morgan silenced her. "Oh, no, don't bother to pretend the name means nothing to you, Little One. Your face lit up like a Roman candle at the mention of it. I should have seen Rensdale mixed into all this." Morgan's voice was heavy with sudden weariness and displeasure, as his gaze moved to the boy. "She has his type of look about her. Young, tender fruit. Who is this girl to Rensdale? There's no point in denying the connection, lad, or the sudden clarity of why she is here. Did you really expect me to bed this girl, to allow you some measure of obscure, petty revenge?"

"Why not?" the boy snapped irritably. "It's precious little revenge I have had thanks to you. It's providence she slipped into my hands, at all. Should I deny myself a gift when it's given?"

Morgan leaned back in his chair and studied the boy with the sharpness of a surgeon's scalpel.

"Why involve me in all this? If you wanted revenge, you could have raped the girl on the beach and sent her back to him deflowered. There's more to all this, then you're telling. It's only half about Rensdale, isn't it? You want to strike at me in this, as well. You had better answer me, lad," Morgan demanded in a voice of tightly controlled unpleasantness.

Frightened to a depth she had not thought possible, Merry could only listen in muted terror to their bewildering discourse. She knew whatever would become of her, might very well rest in this complicated struggle between man and boy.

Her anxious eyes turned to the boy. Whatever he saw in her face had the power to turn him away from the captain when Morgan's displeasure didn't.

"Do you truly believe putting this innocent, young girl in my bed, to be ruined, will accomplish what you want in your struggles? Do you think Rensdale would even care if I ruined her? Look at her. All the man wants to do is ruin her himself. Beyond that, I can't see any fascination this girl could have for him, or any man over twenty, for that matter. She's young, she's idiotic, and she's beautiful. There is nothing for a man to want from her, except bedding her. I can't see what effect beyond a passing amusement you think it will have on me, if I should decide to indulge her for my pleasure. Has it ever occurred to you I may not let you use this girl as a weapon of war between you and Rensdale, or a weapon of war between you and me?"

The boy swung around and faced the pirate captain with hard, glowing eyes.

"Has it ever occurred to *you,* that perhaps, that is the point of all this? *Your* unwillingness to use the girl. You are so consumed with your complicated web of moral contradictions that not only is killing the girl not an option, neither is having pleasure from her. Tell me, what part of all this has changed what she is to you, when only a moment ago I could deal with her however I wish? Is it that she is gently born, or that I've made her fate now yours to deal with? You may very well deny the existence of that part of your soul that disdains this grim little conflict, but you can't escape it. The self-discovery of that should be blindingly obvious, even to you. You can't accept the truth of what you are. Or, the truth of what I am. Nor, that you can't change any of it with the power of your will or this insane sense of obligation you feel toward me. It is past time that you free the both of us from this gruesome fiction you've created."

"It's always been more than obligation. It is you who refuse to accept that. Has it ever occurred to you that what I may disdain is you're not so subtle manipulations to force my hand in ways I don't wish to have it forced?"

"Then, give me the girl now and my manipulations will be at an end. You wanted the girl dead before, I will give her to the sea and we can be done with this."

Morgan couldn't give the order to kill the girl, and the boy knew it.

Morgan's eyes narrowed. Oh, but it would be foolishness not to expect there to be more to the trap than this: proving that he couldn't kill the girl. Or, was Indy trying to prove he was capable of killing her, forcing on him all that meant...?

It couldn't be that. Dear God, don't let it be that....

Morgan looked at Indy and felt despair in the center of his soul, a despair he had learned through the years to keep carefully hidden from the boy. Time had not softened the boy. The years had only made him harder. He was no closer to bringing the boy back to what he should be than he had been that first day he found him. Farther, in fact, every day a little farther.

He looked at the girl, young, beautiful, and desirable. What power did the boy imagine this mere slip of girl would have over him, and what the boy termed too often, 'his inability to escape the truth of himself'? An insignificant scrap of flesh with a blurry tie to Rensdale. Very blurry, since clearly the girl was untouched and well born.

What plot was the boy weaving? Indy did not weave weak plots. Clearly the boy was weaving again. There was more,

112

much more.

Morgan's head rested back against the lambskin. His eyes were closed. "Leave the girl and get out."

CHAPTER SIX

Merry Merrick's first night aboard the most infamous ship, ever to sail the seas, passed in the cabin of its legendary captain unmolested, unharmed, and pretty much unnoticed.

Alone with Captain Morgan, the only exchange of words she had with her mysterious captor was an off-hand suggestion she should take a quilt, if her intentions were to sleep on the window bench.

She awoke, her first morning as Morgan's prisoner, warm beneath a heavy quilt, lightly scented of wintergreen, which had somehow come to be tucked high under her rosy cheeks and still with her innocence in hand. She gave credit to the pirate captain for neither of these charitable turns, chastised herself for having fallen asleep, and wondered how she could have let the night pass without even attempting an escape.

Charged with sudden purpose and a hazy plan to escape, she climbed from her comfortable bed of pillows. Cursing the chill in the air, she tried the cabin door.

Of course, it was locked. She wondered why she had ever expected it to be otherwise. *A key. What she needed was a key.*

Dismissing Indy's prior warning about not touching Morgan's possessions, she began her frantic search. One by one she tried each lock, the cabinets, his desk, everything. Only his drawers were unlocked. She was both embarrassed and disappointed to find only his shirts and his unmentionables.

Sinking to her knees, she dropped before his sea chest. She wondered at the usefulness of trying it, because the man had locked up everything else tighter than Grandmamma Merrick's corset. She was unprepared for the slight creak as the heavy lid lifted beneath her prodding fingers.

Afraid to speculate on Morgan's reaction if he should find her, instead she concentrated on the contents. There were papers, books, and a bag of coin. Pulling it out bit by bit, the contents were dumped around her in annoyance.

In spite of how much the chest held, what it didn't hold was a key. After having spent a ridiculous amount of time pulling papers upward, she continued out of frustration more than hope. Her eyes suddenly fixed on a box wrapped in cloth on the bottom.

Common sense told her to leave it alone and to clean her mess up quickly. She had no interest in what was surely little more than stolen plunder, but having come this far...

She lifted the box, set it in front of her, and removed its cover. Any chance she would return it undisturbed died an instant death.

The box was made of fine-grained leather, elaborately tooled, expensive, and inlaid in gold was a large crest Merry did not recognize. It wasn't very deep or large. It was clear whatever was within it mattered enough to Morgan to keep it elegantly safe. The box had a tiny gold lock of its own.

She couldn't help herself. She took the divider from Morgan's desk and pried the lock. She worked carefully, surprised when she actually managed to spring it.

Lacking the repugnance for this invasion of his privacy, she stared at the strange collection in pure fascination. It was an oddly sentimental gathering for a man like Morgan.

There, lying on a bed of red velvet, was a single rose, dried by age and fragile, a man's heavy signet ring, engraved with the same crest as the box, and a small gilt framed miniature of a woman.

It was the picture her gaze fixed on. Picking it up, she stared down with uncontrollable curiosity. It was a pretty face, young and spirited, with lively brown eyes that seemed to carry a hint of a smile. There was something oddly familiar to the face. She studied it. She was sure she had never seen the woman before. But those eyes...

There was something about those eyes that pricked her memory, as if she were being unaccountably slow by not recognizing them.

Who she was? Merry wondered, staring at the face not much older than her own. Her heart knew from some unfathomable sense this girl was dead.

Perhaps it was because of where she had found it, laying neatly beside that faded bud. She was swept with a strange feeling of sadness having this girl in her hands. Surely, it was her own fertile imagination making more of this than she should.

Morgan was a complicated creature. She did not, for one moment, believe him sentimental. *Devils simply had no sentiment.*

Therefore, she was unprepared for the sight of his undisguised fury as he lifted her cruelly from the floor. All prior experience with Morgan had displayed him above such human failings as uncontrolled anger. Clearly, he was not. Obviously, the devil had made his creature, at least in small part, man.

"Damn you. What the hell are you looking for?"

She had never been more frightened in her life. Morgan's fury was a thing beyond imagination. He was clearly enraged and manufacturing none of his suave manipulations to hide it.

"Please," she whispered desperately, fearing he would crush her in his hands.

He shook her hard. "What were you looking for? Tell me, girl, or by God..."

"A key," she exclaimed, too terrified to lie. "Only a key. Did you expect to find me waiting meekly in your cabin to be raped?"

Morgan devoured her face in a single, glittering look. His fingers tightened and she yelped in pain.

All at once, a spasm rocketed down her arms, every muscle one-by-one going limp. The tiny portrait slipped to the floor shattering at their feet.

"It was an accident," she rushed desperately, "I did not mean to drop it. Truly."

Morgan's eyes lowered to the floor. In his fury, he had missed what had claimed the girl's interest. Then he saw the papers, those documents so painstakingly gathered, lying discarded and untouched in a disorderly heap around him. If she had been sent by Rensdale to destroy them, surely they would not be here now.

The papers...he saw the girl, pale and shaking before him, and suddenly let her go.

He watched her sink at his feet to gently lift the gilt frame with trembling hands. "Damn you," he cursed in a voice low.

The girl met his gaze, her eyes fearful under sooty lashes that cast delicate shadows on her pale cheeks. She looked so tiny on the floor, huddled beside his feet, her dark curls a tangle about her shoulders, her youthful face a wash of concern.

"The portrait isn't broken. I have only damaged the glass," she assured anxiously. "I did not mean to break it. Truly. You frightened me or else I would have never dropped it."

"What a vexing child you are," Morgan sighed. "If I had any sense at all, Little One, I would lock you in the brig and leave you to the rats."

"Then, lock me in the brig. I would much prefer the rats to you, sir," Merry snapped.

Morgan might have managed not to smile, if she hadn't been so damn in earnest.

"Would you really prefer a hundred rats in the darkness nipping on your toes, Little One, over one big rat nipping

117

SUSAN WARD

elsewhere?"

It sounded theatrical, even to him. Most probably he would have felt ridiculous saying it, if it didn't suit, *to* perfection, this doe eyed girl. The blush that answered him swept her face, charming as it brightened the color of her eyes.

"I prefer not to be nipped, at all," she announced, haughty and indignant.

Morgan began to laugh softly. He lifted one of her curls and laced his fingers through it.

"Someday, Little One, I suspect you'll find that nipping is not so bad. Haven't you been tempted even once to lay with a man?"

As much as Merry hated his vile question, she couldn't escape the sudden memory of her few failed explorations into passion. She couldn't imagine what it was that made women submit to men. The few kisses she had allowed, stirred nothing more in her than a strange sensation of annoyance.

Being kissed by a man, in her experience, was about as exciting as flattening your lips to a dead fish. Hard mouths and stiff hands, half wanting to excite, half worried to offend. What she had learned about passion only made her more determined to avoid it.

Where was the pleasure in letting a man get heated up, while you went cold, so he could do what he wanted with your body? *Tempted, indeed.* Men, how unfathomable they were to think temptation brought women to them.

"Tempted? You have an overrated opinion of your sex, if you think it's temptation that brings women to your bed, instead of duty, greed, and the forced submission of marriage."

What Morgan forced into submission was his impulse to gently seduce her, now. Those flashing sapphire eyes betrayed that she was absolutely serious.

Instead he found himself cupping her chin as he said,

"Little One, I think I am going to keep you forever, if for no other reason than the men where you're from don't deserve you."

With that, his hands moved to gently lift her from the ground. As he felt her protests, he laughed softly and said, "Stop squirming. No man would force his unwanted attention after such an eloquent speech. You are surrounded by glass in case you hadn't notice."

Morgan set her in the center of his bed. He tried to recall what had brought him to the cabin, in the first place. He went to his drawers, seeing that she had rummaged there as well, and bent her a sternly lifted brow.

Unexplainable to Merry, it had the power to instantly make her lower her eyes in belated shame over snooping.

"We're not going to get along well, at all, if you continue to paw my possessions."

It was a warning, no matter what prosaic gloss he covered it in. Merry lifted her head and looked in the direction of his voice. She was about to bite off a curt rejoinder, when the words suddenly failed to come.

Morgan had moved to the far side of the cabin. He stood draped in a stunning shower of light, pouring through the long lines of squares of glass behind him. What her eyes fixed upon, rendered her speechless.

It was hardly Merry's habit to study the male anatomy, *but oh*, she had never seen a specimen like Morgan. *Somehow*, he had come to be naked from the waist up. She was alarmed to feel the rapidly rising heat of her cheeks.

His chest had a masculine beauty a Michelangelo sculpture would have envied. The firm rise of muscles seemed to have a life of their own. They moved with a grace that even in her limited experience with men she recognized was sensual. The shapely play of line, curve, and muscle caught the eye, no matter how modest his actions were.

Merry was about to thank God he had rather quickly covered himself with a new shirt. The motion of his hands working the buttons had brought to mind the sensation of those same long, tanned fingers touching her.

He was doing nothing at all, truly. She could not imagine why she was suddenly reminded of his touch. Feeling the hot embers of that same confusing blend of wakefulness and excitement, she tried to concentrate on anything. The number of buttons, the length of time between each one, how many were left, anything.

She had been halfway to believing his legend with women had all been myth and exaggeration, but that was before seeing him half exposed, in all his demon splendor. No one needed to tell her the man was magnificent.

Convinced that she desired Morgan, not at all, Merry could not convince herself that Morgan, as a man, was not desirable.

She was gratefully saved from the discomfort of her thoughts when he said, "I feel rather ridiculous always calling you 'Little One'. What do you think of a compromise? There's no harm in giving me your first name, girl, at least so I know what to call you."

"Merry." It took several minutes to realize she had spoken her name, and not merely thought it. She looked up in alarm and wondered if he heard her. By the expression on his face, it was clear he had.

He was finishing his work with the shirt when the key turned in the latch. Indy entered, carrying a breakfast tray. "Merry has an exceedingly curious nature," Morgan said, tossing a grin at her as he moved toward the door. "See that you lock everything."

Indy surveyed the room in a single glance and found the girl huddled in the middle of Morgan's bed. That she was still wearing her nightdress told him everything. As he set the tray on the table, his black eyes took note of the papers strewn across the floor.

"What a circus," the boy grumbled, sinking down to carefully return Morgan's items into his sea chest. "What the devil were you looking for anyway?"

"A key."

"Haven't you the slightest shred of common sense? What good would a key have done you? We've been under full sail all night. Do you imagine you could have swam your way back to Mother England?"

Of course it was absurd. Still: "I have every right to want my freedom."

"Don't count on Morgan seeing it that way. Oh, Christ, what mischief have you gotten into this time?" He snatched the picture from the floor. "Was he very angry?"

The memory of Morgan's face made her shiver. "Very."

He tucked the broken frame back into its velvet box and secured the latch. "You've got a way of seeing and hearing exactly what you shouldn't. You would think, with all the trouble you're in, you would learn to behave yourself."

She ignored his slight, sensed a mystery and asked, "Who is the girl anyway?"

"She was his wife, Merry," Indy said emotionlessly.

"His wife?" Stunned, Merry sat back on her heels and studied the boy alertly. "But, whatever did he do to her? Did she displease him? Did he make her walk the plank?"

"Idiocy," the boy whispered under his breath. "Why do you have to be so childish? I can see it was a mistake to tell you. Morgan didn't do a damn thing to her. She died."

"But, Indy—"

He cut her off. "But nothing, Merry. Enough. I suggest you don't ask him about it because he'll blister my ears for

121

having told you this. Nothing rankles Morgan more than having people groping around in his private affairs. As for you going through his things, you're lucky he didn't beat you."

The anger she had held, tightly in check with Morgan, surged upward now she was alone with the boy.

"Heavens above, we shouldn't offend Morgan's right of privacy, now should we," Merry sputtered furiously. "Little matter that my own rights have been so grievously abused. That even the right to my freedom has been taken from me."

"You're alive."

"In such lovely circumstance. I suppose you want me to thank you."

"Did you hear me asking for thanks? You have no one to blame but yourself for this mess. You have no one, but yourself, to get you out of it."

That he was right did nothing to lessen Merry's indignation.

"So what," Merry asked stiffly, "will Morgan do with me now?"

"It depends on how much trouble you are. If you don't behave, he's apt to toss you overboard for the sharks. And if you really try his patience he might sell you."

Sell? For a moment she wondered if she'd heard him correctly.

"He wouldn't sell me," Merry said, sure the boy was just trying to frighten her. "Why would anyone wish to buy me? I thought I was vexing and a nuisance."

"I can think of at least a dozen reasons. You're temperament isn't one of them."

Surely the boy was jesting, though it was impossible to tell. His face revealed nothing.

"It's obnoxious of you to try to frighten me," Merry exclaimed.

Propping her chin on one of Morgan's brocade pillows, she watched the boy as he moved about the cabin. His long black waves were in a braid today that swished with each step. She stared at him in fascination.

There was something so blatantly different about the boy, a difference that proved compelling and baffling. As amazing as it was, she no longer feared him. She wondered at his strange relationship with the pirate captain.

"Is that how Morgan came to have you? Did he buy you?"

If he was insulted by the questions, it didn't show on his scarred face.

"Oh-ho, you do come up with the damnedest notions. What are you imagining in that foolish, simple mind of yours? Do you think that I am Morgan's fancy boy?" The instant blush betrayed her. "What a child you are. Do you really have so little instinct about men? Morgan may be a man of wide dissipations, but I assure you it does not extend to *that*. Morgan is a skirt man, through and through."

There was nothing about Morgan that wasn't virile, strong, and male. Still, he had not even so much as kissed her.

Surely, a man of such shocking morals would have at least done that, if women were his fancy. Or was it her? Was there something about her that failed to stir his fancy?

Irritated with herself for allowing that last thought, she looked at the boy and asked, "So, how did you come to be with Morgan?"

"Morgan found me chained in the hold of the vilest British warship ever to sail the Atlantic," he said lightly. "Pure filth. I don't know how long I was there. Quite a while, I think." His eyes were savagely cruel as they fixed on her. "Would you like to know what your fine fighting men of Britain do to young boys on their ships?"

Merry shook her head, shuddering. The way he said it, left

little doubt in Merry that she didn't want to know.

"If Morgan hadn't found me when he did, I would be mad by now or dead. As it was, I nearly died the first month aboard this ship. Withdrawal from opium intoxication is a gruesome thing, almost as bad as the slow return to clarity of mind, and the sudden undiluted picture of things that have been done to you. There are times I wonder, if it would not have been more merciful to spare me my rescue and simply shoot me."

Staring at the scarred face, with its soulless plains, Merry was consumed by an awareness of the suffering hidden beneath it. It was little wonder that the boy was so bitter and strange.

"So is that why you are so loyal to him, despite his nefarious self? Because he showed you a simple human kindness, and did not leave you there to rot? You feel you owe Morgan something for saving your life?"

One black brow arched severely. "You have an exasperating mind. Nefarious self? Do you imagine Morgan is the devil? He's a man, Merry. A better man than any I found on that warship. Some good. Some bad. Flesh and blood like everyone else."

Merry lifted her dainty noise an inch. "You will never prove that to me."

"Share his bed, then, Merry. If you can't find proof there, that he is a flesh and blood man, far be it from me to try to convince you with mere words."

He was going toward the door, key in hand. "Please," Merry cried, springing to her feet. "You can't keep me locked in here alone, forever."

"If you weren't such a bloody nuisance—" Seeing her face fall, Indy swore under his breath and added, "I will work on Morgan for you. But for the love of God, Merry, try to exercise some common sense."

~~~

Day one passed in an endless drone of strange sounds, isolation and worries. *What must her parents be thinking?* Merry fretted. *Would anyone ever find her?*

Lying on the window seat, a stack of Morgan's pillows beneath her head and her bare feet pressed against the glass, Merry listened for the ships bells, that strange code that marked the passing of time. Outside the cabin was a world active and alive. From the decks floated the sound of constant movement, footsteps, talking, shouting, and singing. Occasionally, there was music, the sound of a fife or violin. Other times riotous crashing of quick brawls and petty quarrels. The ship was always noisy, a man's world, never peaceful.

Inside the cabin there was silence. Lying alone in her small, rocking prison, she might have been a spider in a web, for all the significance she had on Morgan's ship.

Inactivity had always been her nemesis. Her life had always included a healthy dose of the out of doors. Long hours riding the melancholy grandeur of the Cornish hills, the sun and air sharp against her cheeks. There was always Philip and Kate to make mischief with. Uncle Andrew's sharp wit to challenge her. And her parents, so loving and alive in their private happiness they seemed to exist in.

If Morgan had searched for a punishment, he could not have picked a more perfect one. The walls of the cabin closed in as the minutes dragged by.

If not for Indy, she was certain her first day as Morgan's captive would have sent her into madness. It was Indy who saw to her needs. Indy that brought her meals. Indy who emptied the chamber pot, when at last, need had reduced her to using it.

The first time he had reached for it, she had thought she would die of mortification. It seemed nothing was private aboard a pirate ship. In a tone that had burned her ears, he had barked she would be more humiliated if he let it stew in the stuffy confines of the cabin. He went about his task with his never failing indifference. Modesty, it seemed, had no place on a ship.

As darkness spread across the sky, she watch the clouds grow slowly gray. Gentle streaks of orange and rose laced through them, and then vanished.

Indy found her lying as she had all day, her face a mask of youthful boredom. Her long hair was fanned around her like the feathers of a peacock tail.

"If you don't let me from this cabin, I shall die. I think I am ill. Last month I had a fever. I have not fully recovered, and now this."

She rolled over to watch the boy. He set yet another tray to be eaten alone at Morgan's table.

"You look perfectly healthy to me, Merry."

"How can you be sure? These things can come on suddenly and then...death."

She collapsed back onto the pillows and Indy rolled his eyes. What an idiotic creature she was.

"Please," came her small, wheedling voice, "a little fresh air. That is all I need. One turn around the deck. That's all."

"Do you plan to eat or sulk? You haven't touched a thing all day. Enjoy our fresh supplies from Falmouth, while you can. Later on, it'll be hardtack and salt beef. If you starve yourself, you will become ill. Morgan isn't going to be moved by such childish melodrama. He's more apt to warm your backside, if he finds you enacting a tragedy in his cabin. Blast it, Merry, no one has ever died of boredom before."

"How do you know? It isn't exactly something one would write on a tombstone? Here lies Mr. Jones, dead of boredom, when boredom could have very well been the cause."

"Because if boredom killed, Little One, half the men at sea would be dead."

That low voice.

Merry pushed up from the pillows to find Morgan looming in the cabin. It was then Merry noticed that Indy had set two plates.

"How dare you keep me locked alone in here all day," Merry hissed, her blue eyes slits of rage, as she anxiously followed Morgan's movements.

"If I had known you were suffering a decline from my absence, Little One, I would have come from the deck sooner."

How odious of him to purposely misunderstand her.

"I am more likely to suffer a decline from your presence."

Morgan's smile was insultingly unruffled by that. "See, Indy, your Little One is fine. Whatever you imagined she was suffering, being alone in the cabin all day, I can't see any change in her."

He settled in a chair, his head resting back with his eyes closed, as though he hadn't a single scar on his conscience.

"I demand you let me from this cabin," Merry shouted.

"The door will stay locked, Little One, until I decide otherwise."

"Damn you. If I were a man, you would not be so smug in your treatment of me."

"If you were a man..." the slight turn of his head brought her full view of black eyes sparkling wickedly. "...you would not be in my cabin at all. You would be with the rats."

The sickening suspicion, that Indy had shared their conversation with Morgan, pushed Merry's nerves into a frenzy of mortification mixed with fury.

Staring at Morgan, sun bronzed and wind fresh, all the frustration of the day raged to the surface. She picked up the first object within her reach and flung it at him, with all her might. It was a good thing her aim didn't match her strength. Her mouth made a wide "O". She stared in anxious dismay as

Morgan's shiny reflecting circle nicked the polished wood of the cabin wall.

"That was not at all ladylike," he informed her unflustered.

"I don't care. I wish it had pierced your black, demon heart. I wish…"

It was Indy who grabbed her by the arms to give her a hard shake. "Blast it, Merry, of all the muddled-headed stunts. If that had hit Morgan…"

"I don't care. I hate him. I hate this ship. I hate you."

"Someone should have spanked you a long time ago. I am sure you would have benefited immeasurably from it," Indy grumbled, dragging her from the stern gallery and dropping her heavily into a chair at Morgan's table. "Behave yourself."

Merry did not. She itched to throw something else. If she had not been hungry, if the food had not smelled so good, she would have thrown it at him. Instead, she settled on making a face at the boy.

When the table lay set, Morgan rose from his chair, settled beside her, and watched until the boy left the cabin.

"If you please, Little One, I can hardly dine while you glower at me. Sit and be a good girl for a change. There is no need to fret and brandish that knife, as though you fear I will attack you. It's only a butter knife, after all. So, unless you mean to spread me, I suggest you stop pointing it at my face and put it to use with the jam."

Blushing, she let the knife fall from her hand to drop with a clank against her plate. "I find your treatment of me intolerable. You can't expect me to live alone in your cabin, forever."

"I am heartened to hear you don't wish to be alone. If I had known your changed stance on the subject of my company I would never have left you to your own devices for so long. You need to practice at being more direct, Little One."

She puffed up like a suddenly inflated balloon. "That is not what I meant."

Morgan reached out, fingering one dark curl on her shoulder, and his smile could only be called wicked.

"Would that it were. Here I have been entertaining a delightful image of you pining in my bed all day. Really, Little One, you do know how to crush a man's fantasies."

Crushed was the last thing Morgan looked. His amusement was a thing that filled the room.

Slamming her fork down upon her plate in rage, Merry screamed, "Doesn't it matter to you I have no wish to be here? That I have done, absolutely, nothing to deserve this punishment? That I have a family worried sick over my disappearance?"

"I find that my conscience can be quite a flexible thing, where you are concerned, Little One. Especially since you are the one determined to stay with me."

She sprang furiously from the table and stared down at him like a tiny game hen ready to do battle.

"You have no conscience or human heart for that matter. What am I to you? Another bauble, to add to your plunder. I am no threat to you. You know that. You keep me as a toy, to pick at in your boredom. You have no interest in me as a woman, if you *even* have any interest in women at all, for that matter. But I am not a toy. I don't wish to stay here. I demand that you return me to Falmouth."

Morgan leaned back in his chair and his eyes began to sparkle.

"Oh, Little One, you do like to play with fire, don't you? Are you imagining, because I have not raped you, you are safe from me because my tendencies go elsewhere than women?" He began to laugh softly. "Is that why you think I left you on the bench all night?"

Merry's eyes rounded to their fullest. Instinctively, she took a step back as he stood.

"If you touch me, I will kill you," she hissed with another hurried step.

Laughing, he said, "Oh, Little One. Somehow, I think if I touch you, you'll learn a thing or two about yourself, and most definitely a thing or two about me."

Merry had flattened herself against the wall. He was there, impossible to escape. His handsome face filled the world above her. Unable to fix on anything else, she did not see those long, capable fingers come to her cheek with suave gentleness. The touch of them made her tremble, at once.

"Please. I did not mean to say that."

Tracing the line around her mouth, he said, "Oh, but you did say it, Little One. It would be wrong not to make you aware of how much danger you are in. So, you never let down your guard, unless you wish to. Never forget that I am a man. Aren't you tired of wondering about this? How it will feel for me to kiss you. I am. Give me your mouth."

Merry would have spoken again. In an artful move, Morgan swiftly lifted her face. His lips calmly lowered to hers. With the sweetly measured skill of a well-versed lover, he noted the stiffening shock at first contact. He gentled his lips against her, at once. They were a light, teasing glide, moving in an almost absurd chasteness, that he was surprised he was still capable of managing.

It had been a long time since he'd had to manage this level of restraint with a woman. But it was necessary to make this tiny creature, as rigid as a statue of Lot's wife, into one of lushly made body parts slowly relaxing and pressing forward.

When she brought her body flush against him, on her own, he eased his lips back, *just enough*, letting his fingers coax around her mouth in expert strokes. Beneath the subtle pressure she was too inexperienced to understand, her lips parted and he reclaimed them.

He deepened the kiss in careful degrees as his hands moved in comforting patterns through her curls. When she made a small whimper at the intrusion of his tongue, he deepened and gentled the skilled rhythm, until there was no resistance at all.

The girl made a small, involuntary tremor, but she didn't pull back. Slowly with his fingers he pushed aside the thin gown, sweeping her with their masseur's caress. Then, he turned her head from side to side, dragging his lips across hers.

The ease of her surrender was nearly laughable. Why that should make him feel pity for the girl, Morgan wasn't sure. He eased back, touching her passion-flushed face with only the tip of a finger.

"You are right to be afraid," he said in a slow voice. "Never forget, Little One, that I am a man."

He followed the warning with another expert kiss.

It was not the first time Merry had been kissed, but it was the first time a man had ever kissed her to teach her a lesson. However, the harsh sting of that did nothing to help rally a defense against him.

This was no chaste kiss of a gentleman. This was not kissing marble. This was a *man's* kiss. She was horrified by her body's response and her inability to fight him. The blood seemed to rise in her skin to meet his touch, and everywhere his fingers worked there was fire. Her muscles had ceased to obey her will. To her alarm, she did nothing to stop the beguiling exploration of his hands over her body.

Somewhere far back in her mind, the memory of who this man was tugged at her. The horror of that, finally, gave her the strength to fight the pleasure of it.

Terrified the kiss would not end at a kiss, she acted upon

the first inspiration that came to mind. Galvanized by fear and mortification with herself, not thinking about the consequences, she brought up her knee swiftly. She tried to strike him in that area of the anatomy Grandmamma had suggested, in such circumstances. What she earned for her effort was a numbing explosion of pain as she connected with the hard length of Morgan's thigh.

Morgan's face lifted above her at once, and he was grinning. "That, as I am sure you've already guessed, was not even close to the right spot, Little One. Would you care for me to show you the right spot? You would have done better to simply ask me to stop."

Merry turned red as a turnip. More than a little frightened he would kiss her again, she shouted, "I might have missed, but you had better think again, if you think I will let you..." she broke off, unable to say the word.

Running her flushed cheek with a fingertip, he said, "There is no need for violence, Little One. I am perfectly able to contain my urges at present."

Trembling in fury, Merry screamed, "If you kiss me again, I will kill you."

His reaction was not what she expected. He smiled in a softly tender, amused way. Humiliated and unstrung, Merry aimed another kick at him, which only succeeded to make him laugh more. She was trying to work her hands free to slap his face, when his fingers moved to take hold of her shoulders.

In a flash, she found herself trapped and being carried in his powerful arms across the room. He set her into the lambskin chair, releasing her with the infuriating indulgence of a man patiently dealing with a vexing child.

'If there is any doubt left in you that I desire women, then I suggest you be in my bed when I return," he told her, laughing softly, even as he finished his wine. Those black eyes were oddly gentle as he paused at the door and looked at her. "You can go to sleep without fear, Little One. We're done with kissing for a while. You are a rather unpredictable creature at times. Unpredictable and very safe."

Merry watched his towering figure, hating every inhuman inch of him. She picked up his logbook and threw it at Morgan, narrowly missing his head. He didn't stop and in a moment the cabin door clicked closed behind him.

~~~

Merry was asleep on the window bench when he returned. Morgan had not expected otherwise. He stood above her, staring down into her young face, feeling a pleasant type of smile surface. He noted her features held the most comical expression in sleep.

Kissing the girl had been a mistake. It had stripped away the fiction he'd carried that he did not want her in his bed.

While he was sure it would take little more than a small seduction to have her willingly—*very small*, he amended—it was quite clear her female emotions were still fresh and untried. If he pushed her along too fast, in this, he would harm her.

One had to have a gentle, patient hand when dealing with virgins. Especially, with fragile creatures like this girl, if one wanted to have them without emotional scarring and destruction.

Morgan shook his head, amused and unclear by what motivated him in this. *Age? Vanity? Boredom?* He had absolutely no reason to keep her.

Whatever she'd been doing at *Grave's End* had nothing to do with him. Five minutes in her company and the striking proof of her innocence had told him that. Why had he decided to keep her, when the logical thing would be to return her to Falmouth?

He could buy her silence with the same forces that

controlled all people, coin or fear. Was it Rensdale, his hatred for the man, the knowledge of that vile character sleeping behind such fashionable elegance and what Rensdale's pursuit of her would mean to her, in the end? Or was it the girl, her youth, her beauty, her wild spirit and innocence? Those elements she possessed, in such exaggerated abundance, so far removed from his world?

He understood Merry more than she would ever be able to fathom. His eyes fixed on her, remembering her in his arms. The charming, honest awakening of her young senses, the sweet freshness of guileless passion. The shock of her surprise, and then the panic, the quivering, followed by wild fight.

He was certain the girl had never been kissed before. Her reaction was, among many things, one of dismay. She did not want to be bothered with men, but more so, because she'd liked being in his arms and had never expected to.

Gently raised, surrounded by foppish young boys who could not begin to understand tenderness, it was little wonder her opinion of men was so low. He was sure her beauty and spirit worked only against her. It made a man anxious, determined to master her. This girl did not wish to be mastered.

Push and, of course, the girl would fight. Had even one grasped that fire was often a mask for fragility? That thorns were there to protect the rose? Had he even fully understood that at twenty? Could any man at twenty understand the fragility of a woman's heart?

Morgan settled in a chair, staring at the girl, while another image slipped over his mind. How long had it been since he had thought of her? Why did he think of her now? There had been a time when he had never expected to be free of her image.

The other girl had been less beautiful than this Little One sleeping before him, less wild, less afraid.

Closing his eyes, he let the time trapped picture fully form.

Dear Heart, was I as patient and tender with you, as I should have been? Was I all the things you deserved? If you had come to me now, to the man I am today, no longer twenty and wild and too foolish as young men are prone to be, would I have made you happier? Would you be alive with me now?

Regrets, useless, wasteful things. Like memories, pain, and cruelty, all the things that hurt the living.

I have not loved another woman since you, dear one. But of course, you know. Spirits, gentle spirits, you hover and know all. Are you the one who sent me this girl? Dear Heart, is this your plotting?

The boy was more than enough to manage and now there was this girl in his care. This girl, so young, who did not realize he was a man at all. Who stared at him as though he were only a phantom of legend, not human, not flesh. Innocence, untarnished innocence of mind and body. And the boy, the result of innocence lost through brutality and force.

The sound of her breathing—slow, measured, and calm— pulled him from his memories.

How peacefully Merry slept, her cheeks turned toward the warmth of the stove and tiny fingers tucked beneath her chin.

Nudge me, Dear Heart, if I should step too harshly on her. Climbing into his bed, Morgan indulged another look at Merry and laughed softly. *No, Dear Heart, better to kick me soundly in the ass.*

~~~

Ominous charcoal-gray clouds scudded across the midmorning sky. As soon as the cabin door clicked, Merry sprang from her icy-cold resting place to huddle her shivering limbs beneath the lightly scented warmth of Morgan's bedding.

It was a ridiculously large bed, mounted on gimbals to lessen the feel of the seas rolling, plushy deep with pillows and quilts. When she found herself in its center she suffered the sensation of being swallowed by it.

135

The night had progressed with frosty fingers that gripped at her through the glass. Only the sounds of Morgan's slow breathing had held her on the bench, while her eyes fixed on the lambskin chair, knowing it would be an improvement. The days had grown steadily colder, which tallied five by her count. If the weather continued to conspire against her, the bench, wretched now, would prove unbearable.

No power on earth could force her to suffer the indignity of sharing Morgan's bed. Not while Morgan was in it. Not even the pleasant warmth, which lingered several hours after his rising.

Last night, shaking and miserable, she had watched him reclined on pillows, comfortable still above the quilts, reading endlessly. Those black eyes fixed on the book in hand, slowly swirling his wine glass, a gesture she had come to know as a habit. She cursed him for whatever power he had not to be affected by the elements.

Struggling to maintain her battered dignity, Merry had kept herself from asking for another quilt. Morgan's indifference to the chill was second only in her loathing, to his indifference of her. Foolish pride, perhaps, but her pride was suffering sorely.

She had unpleasantly discovered in her character a basic flaw, unknown before. A total intolerance to indifference. While arousing any man's interest was always the farthest desire in Merry, inexplicitly, she found it unbearably annoying to inspire no interest.

He had kissed her once, in a way that had made her shamefully burn. Now he treated her as though she were furniture. What little conversation he made was short and civil. If he had a purpose for keeping her, at all, Merry could not begin to make reason of it.

Whatever else could be said about sharing a room with a man, Merry was certain it couldn't be said it was the path to understanding that man. Morgan was a creature beyond all comprehension.

For reasons she couldn't begin to fathom, the less he seemed to notice her, she strangely found herself more unwillingly compelled to notice him. Studying Morgan had become an obsession to her. She tried to tell herself it was the natural result of her boredom. There were precious few amusements to be found alone in Morgan's cabin. Perhaps it was the simple fascination of having followed this man's life in the *Times*. She knew if she allowed herself to be honest, the cause went much deeper.

She had come to know well each line in that handsome face, the subtle changes of light in those lustrous black eyes, the moods that they preceded, and the graceful, effortless movement of that goliath body in total mastery of the world around him. Nothing Morgan did ever held the look of insignificance.

On the days Merry woke early, she would find him still in the cabin pouring over his desk. She could no longer deny the striking figure he made. His ruffled shirt was always opened, just the right amount, over his iron chest, *three buttons*. His darkly glossy head was without a single hair ever out of place. The candle assisting the pale early sunlight cast shimmers in those intense dark eyes.

Grudgingly she conceded, he was the most handsome man she had ever seen. She was more fascinated by him than any man she had ever known. Merry found herself watching him more and more, even though she didn't wish to. Perhaps it was because he had a way of giving all things dash.

His garments, while expensive, were of simple lines, their affect anything but simple. He was always fresh faced, fresh groomed in the mornings, though she never seemed to see the process by which he got that way. When he returned from deck

SUSAN WARD

with a light dishevelment from the elements he only seemed to look that much the better. Even in sleep, somehow, he managed to maintain the air of supremacy about him.

His cabin was a place of totally respected isolation and solitude. No one ever dared knock, except Indy, when relaying messages from the deck or seeing to the captain's continued needs. Other than the boy, only Tom Craven, Morgan's quartermaster, ever passed through the red oak door. He never came uninvited, always by summons. Though at times, they shared a conversation or a bottle of wine, she would not call what they had a friendship. She had never run across anyone who seemed to have less of a need for people. In truth, Morgan seemed to have no needs at all.

After five days Merry had studied Morgan, so thoroughly, she knew the meticulous routine of each thing he did. What she didn't know was a thing about *the man*.

~ ~ ~

Merry came awake with a start not knowing what had stirred her, until she lifted her cheek from the soft, pleasant smelling texture of Morgan's blankets. She fixed her eyes on grim reality standing across the cabin.

Morgan.

He was staring out the windows, his back to her. She realized the soft plopping rhythm from the decks was rain.

Humiliated to her marrow he had discovered her snug within his sheets, Merry started to scramble from his bed when that low voice stopped her.

"You don't have to flee in a fit of youthful panic, Little One. I prefer you where you are at the moment."

Blushing, she wondered how he knew she was awake. His eyes never moved to her. She froze like a naughty child having been caught stealing the baker's pies.

"If you think my being in your bed gives you any

inducement..."

His black eyes turned to her and began to sparkle.

"Inducement?" The way Morgan said it made her sound absurd. "Oh, your imagination does have a tendency to scamper off with you, doesn't it, Little One? I wasn't entertaining thoughts of joining you. There's a ground swell coming. Stay put until I tell you."

Merry dismissed his words with the contempt they deserved, certain it was a perverse game of some sort. She had almost climbed from the pillows when the ship suddenly lurched in a creaking pause. It was suspended and then drove furiously downward on a wave into its trough. The force of motion brought her in a dizzying rush down into a heap upon the bedding.

Lifting her burning face from the sheets she noted Morgan hadn't move an inch.

His soft laughter filled the cabin. He turned from the stern windows to give her a small, enigmatic smile. "It would serve you better to trust me a little and not let your thoughts scamper off into the lurid."

"It's only natural for one's thoughts to be lurid when you're around."

As far as blunders went, it was the worst of her life. Known for a quick and clever wit, she couldn't imagine what had become of her tongue. Since Morgan's advent into her life, it seemed to fail her dismally.

Knowing she couldn't seem any more foolish to him than she already did, Merry abandoned what little dignity she had left. She pulled a pillow down over her head to escape that unwavering, amused gaze.

"Go away," she said in an agonized voice, made muffled by feathers and emotion. "Just go away. Aren't you needed somewhere? I thought captains never abandon the deck during times of storm and battle."

"A storm? It's little more than a shower," he said, silky and amused. "I hate to disappoint you, Little One, but I am more a creature of comfort than noble sentiment. I much prefer to stay dry and warm here with you. I have always failed to see what was noble or sentimental about staying topside with my men, just so I can be shivering and wet, like sturgeon, with them."

He picked up the pillow and gave her a blistering smile.

"I am afraid you're stuck with me until nature decides otherwise."

Merry pushed back the tangles of curls and found him sitting a safe distance away in his chair. "You're despicable."

"No, sensible. And while it's probably unkind of me to dash another of your idealistic hopes so soon, if you're lying there praying for the weather to worsen enough to sink us, if the ship were to go down, you wouldn't be free of me at all. I would be the first off. There's no future at all in going to the bottom of the sea with a bunch of wood and rubble, no matter how many pretty prose the poets write about captains staying until the end. Somehow they fail to grasp that it's the staying that causes the end."

"And your crew chose you to be their captain?" Merry scoffed, outrage.

She had read pirate ships were a democracy, and captains were elected by the crew. She had thought the process rather appealing in its fairness. Obviously, Morgan considered himself above all dictates of social order, even those expressly stated in every work on pirates ever written.

As though he could read her thoughts, with no effort at all, he said, "Fortunately, they are more concerned with their profits than my lack of tolerance for discomfort."

"I didn't realize what an adoring following you have among the scourge of the sea," she said, pleased for having managed just the right edge of sarcasm.

"Oh, Little One, I don't bother with adoring, at least not with the scourge. I prefer adoring women and greedy men."

Morgan stretched out and crossed his stocking feet at the ankles. It was then, Merry noticed he'd removed his boots and seemed to be planning to settle in for a while.

When had he done that? While she was sleeping, no doubt. She suffered another blush surfacing.

Morgan opened his eyes just enough to meet her stare.

When finally he spoke, his voice was pleasant and spruce. "I don't think we're quite ready for anything so intimate as isolated hours of conversation. What do you say to a little sport to pass the afternoon?" Her expression of wariness made him grin in spite of his effort not to. "There you go again. Scampering off into the lurid. I was thinking of piquet, Little One. If you're not ready to do conversation comfortably, what makes you think you're ready to do *that* comfortably?"

When she didn't answer, he gave her a dark smile and added, "There isn't a hand aboard ship that can play a decent game, except Indy, and he despises games. I am assuming you know how to play."

Merry glared at him, insulted. "Of course I do."

"I didn't mean it as a criticism." Morgan turned toward her, one dark brow easing upward. "Why, of course?"

Realizing it unwise to divulge any more information about herself than what he seemed so effortlessly to discover through observation, Merry said instead, "I don't wish to play cards with you."

His expression told her that he knew better. In a mild tone, he said, "Yes you do, Little One. Your face lit up at the suggestion of it. You're bored. I am bored. What danger could there be in a harmless game of cards?"

She stared at him hard, as though trying to discover a trick in this. He went to his desk and removed a deck.

"Would you care for me to join you *there* or would you like to join me *here?*"

Merry had taken two steps before she froze. She stood several feet from Morgan her eyes wide with dismay. *Here* was not the table, *here* was on the floor atop his dark Persian rug.

Smiling, he pulled from the window bench several pillows, scattering them into inviting piles.

"You look like a girl who prefers comfort to the hard back of a chair."

He settled before her in a graceful descent of long limbs. He reclined himself on a small stack of pillows in an unselfconscious manner, which somehow managed to be strangely elegant.

"There's no need to worry about decorum here, Little One. We only do what we want, how we want, and only so long as it is pleasurable."

Swallowing hard, Merry held back, reality an impossible to grasp concept.

Is that really the infamous Captain Morgan, sprawled on a carpet in front of me, staring at me with those great black eyes and wanting to play piquet?

For a man of such reported ruthlessness and bloodthirsty villainy, he behaved not at all like she expected. She had expected him to kill her. He had not. She had expected him to—*or at least try to*—ravish her. He had not. He had kissed her once, let her go, and left her to sleep on the window seat.

Blushing at the memory of his lips, she pushed her thoughts away. Piquet? Who would have thought the man enjoyed piquet?

Sinking down a safe distance from him, Merry pulled the pillows in front of her into a barrier. She caught Morgan watching the effort.

It was clear he had no designs on her, so the gesture was foolishly extreme. If he had a reason for keeping her, at all, it was for amusement. He did seem to laugh a great deal at her.

Frowning, she realized she didn't like him laughing at her, any better than she liked knowing he found her undesirable. Shaking her head in frustration, she couldn't imagine why either of those conditions should have caused her a moment's bother.

Picking up the cards, she found Morgan's black eyes assessing her with something akin to a smile in them.

Furious, she grudgingly jerked her cards into order. She balanced herself in a ridiculous pose, on knees and elbows. She looked like a tiny cat ready to spring from danger, in an instant. It was clear she didn't know that her position had pushed her breasts forward from the gown. It gave Morgan a delightfully clear view of their fullness. Unknown to Merry, her lovely little bottom was rising upward in a manner that was inescapably provocative.

His mouth softened slightly by a smile, Morgan asked, "What do you think to wagering? It makes the game more fun."

"I should have known better than to think you wanted to play cards," she hissed. "And what do you propose we wager? I have nothing but myself, and this night dress, thanks to you."

"I wasn't thinking that at all, but if you insist..." He let the words hang, causing her cheeks to color brightly with fury and embarrassment. "...no? We could wager questions. The winner of each game gets to ask a question and the loser must answer. And because I can see your suspicious nature taking hold again, why don't we make those questions connected with your plight of being here off limits?"

Then his black eyes sparkling, ever so slightly, he whispered, "And in the spirit of good will, Little One, you may ask me anything."

Merry didn't for a moment think she could trust him. Yet

she found the temptation to wager an overwhelming impulse. She could fill a book with her curiosities about this man. She was very good at piquet. Even Uncle Andrew said she was masterful at the game. It *seemed* harmless enough.

As though carefully debating with herself, she asked, "You want to bet questions? And I may ask you anything? How do I know you will answer me honestly?"

"Are you expecting to win, Little One?" Morgan replied, amused. "I wouldn't have proposed it if I had no intention of being truthful. Whatever you think of my despicable character, what would be the pleasure in wagering, if it were insincere?"

Merry stared at him for quite awhile and then played a card. The first game went slowly as she seemed to agonize over each card she played. They played without conversation, until he had one card in his hand and she had two. She studied her cards a long time. She slipped down on her stomach to lay on a pillow, her longs legs bent at the knees, bare feet in air, moving ever so slightly back and forth in her indecision.

Frowning, Merry set between them a diamond. Those lovely eyes moved anxiously to his face. Then, flashed with anger as he laid a club, taking the first game from her.

"You are not accustom to losing at things, are you, Little One?" he said.

"I am not accustom to playing with people who cheat without me being able to see it," she returned.

Morgan's laughter was softly amused. "You can't see it because I *don't* cheat. And as I recall we had a wager, the first win is mine."

Merry looked up, smoldering. She spread the cards before her, giving them a sharp inspection. If there was a trick to the cards, she couldn't see it. Breathing in deeply, she lifted her eyes to his.

Smiling darkly, he asked, "How old are you, Little One?"

She searched Morgan's handsome face, wondering why he should want to know her age. Merry tossed her hair back and said reluctantly, "I am nineteen. Why do you want to know?"

His long tanned finger ran the line of her cheek and stopped atop her lips. "The question belongs to me, Little One. I was the winner."

The look in Morgan's eyes was sharp. Merry wondered if he were daring her to slap his fingers away. When she shifted her gaze away from him, he moved his hand slowly back from her, smiling.

"Do you want to play again?"

Merry didn't answer. She grabbed the cards, shuffled and dealt them out. Four games they played. Four games, he won. Four times, she waited anxious and worried for the questions. Four times, he asked her meaningless things she could not fathom his interest in knowing. She answered him each time, not pleasantly, but truthfully.

Another game. Merry's frown had moved to a constant scowl.

"I have never played against anyone who I can't make reason of their moves," she murmured in open irritation.

"Why are you not married? Aren't young girls of your age and birth, usually well settled into the business of marriage by now?"

"I prefer my freedom to the servitude to a man. Especially, since in my experience, I find most men not worth service to."

Merry was staring at the cards, not bothering to give him notice.

"You won't let yourself quit until you win one game, will you?" Morgan asked, amused. "It is better sometimes, Little One, to retreat and save yourself than to push forward into winning, when it will only bring you ruin in the end."

"Just because I haven't won a hand does not mean I am

incapable of beating you."

"You are more than capable," Morgan said, reaching out to touch the tense and angry lines of her face. "You are quick and you are clever, but, Little One, you are not wise."

Merry glared at him. He picked up his cards.

They had been playing for hours, the game out lasting the rain. It was nearly total darkness beyond the stern windows. Sitting in the dim glow of a single candle, she had failed to note the rain had stopped. He had told her she would be free of his presence when the weather cleared. She gave no wonder at his purpose in remaining and playing the game through.

Two more games passed until she won one. Smiling triumphantly, Merry looked into the mysterious face of the pirate captain to find his eyes watching her in unconcealed enjoyment.

Easing upward into a sitting position, his long legs relaxed in front of him, Morgan reached for his wine and said, "Oh, Little One. Such power you have now. One chance to learn the mysteries of a demon. Which way will you go with it?"

He was mocking her and Merry knew he only meant to rattle her into using her question foolishly. Morgan enjoyed mocking all things: himself, her, the world. He might have been content to keep the spirit of the game light asking banal questions, but she had worked hard for this win.

Sifting anxiously through the tidbits in her mind, of all the things she wanted to know, of all the things she couldn't ask because of their danger, she asked, "Why do you hate Rensdale?"

Quick. Clever. Unwise. Morgan arched a brow. "Are we admitting we know the man or still pretending we don't?"

"Neither," Merry replied stubbornly, not realizing that by the question she had told him something else of herself. It sat in her eyes. This girl didn't like Rensdale.

She eased upright, dragging her satiny legs beneath her gown. "One question. It is mine. Why do you hate him?"

Morgan drained his glass and then met her sapphire eyes directly. "Ancient history, Little One. You were just a little girl, playing on the cobbles of Falmouth throwing rocks at boys, when the cause of my hatred for Rensdale happened."

Thinking he meant to avoid answering, Merry pressed, "That's not an answer and you gave me your word to be honest."

He eased onto his knees and took Merry's face in his hands, lightly stroking her cheeks with his thumbs, before he slipped his fingers through the gossamer cloud of her curls.

"You are a very beautiful girl, Little One," he whispered. "Do you want to know why I hate Rensdale? It's an excellent question. It's part of why I hate the thought that he might someday have gotten to touch you. Touch you here." The shock of his words, so paralyzed her she was unable to move away from the light contact of his fingers on her cheek. "Or here." His fingers came against the pulsing flesh at the base of her neck in a way that sent shudders down her. His strokes glided downward, to her collarbone, gently brushing and everywhere he touched she was on fire. "Do you want to know why I will never let you go? So he will never have a chance to touch you, as I am sure he burns to?"

Cutting like a knife through his words were the sweet movements of his hands, drifting in a faintly suggestive exploration that spread heat across her flesh. So many bells erupted in her mind. The answer was dangerous, just as asking the question had been. Dangerous how? Merry did not know, but the bells were ringing loudly, like St. Andrew's Church.

She was almost fainting beneath the burning play of his hands, but was unable to pull from him.

Panicking she said, "You refuse to answer me. You are not

playing fairly."

"It was your question, Little One. It deserves a thorough answer. The answer would mean nothing to you unless you understood the emotion it lay with. I do hate Rensdale. I would never want you to underestimate my feeling of that."

She was trying to figure out something to say, a way to break free of him, since her body refused her command. The light touches made her tremble and they were nothing, meager caresses at best. Furious with herself for having started this, she sent desperate pleas to Heaven he would move away, since she couldn't begin to reason a course to deal with this.

Then, all at once, Morgan stopped and sat back from her. Merry watched his hands falling away, feeling an icy shiver race up her as he stretched to his full height above her. His black eyes settled on her face, liquid pools, beguiling and mysterious. Their steady hold from Morgan's austere face made her heart leap upward in her chest.

"Little One, I have cause to hate Rensdale. The man killed my wife."

~~~

Merry was sitting in the center of the floor, surrounded by pillows and cards, when Indy came with her evening tray. Her blue eyes whipped toward him, wild and full of emotion. She looked like she'd been forced through a cider press.

Good Lord, what had Morgan been doing with her all day? The man had a mania for melodrama at times. Clearly, the girl had been on the pointed end of one of those grim, ruthless games he played so well.

He set down the tray, took her face in his hands and gave her a sharp examination.

"What the hell did he do to you? You look like your hair has been set on fire."

She moved forward and shoved her face within inches of

his. "He didn't bed me if that's what you're hoping for. Did you really put me in his bed out of a need for some sort of revenge against Rensdale?"

"Of course not. I don't even know who you are. How was I to know you had a connection to Rensdale? I just played with Morgan's assumptions, because there didn't seem any other way to help you. I put you in his bed, so I would not have to kill you. Beyond that, there is nothing to this. And I am perfectly aware you share only a cabin with him. You would look a hell of a lot better than this if you shared his bed."

Indy sat down beside her.

"So what has you looking so frazzled if you didn't spend the afternoon romping in his sheets?"

She blushed. "Is that how I look? Frazzled?" Then, just a little curious, remembering how Morgan's touch had raced like a firestorm across her flesh, she asked, "Wouldn't I look frazzled if Morgan had bedded me?"

"No. In my experience it makes a woman look better to be bedded well. Believe me, Merry, Morgan beds them all well. You could fill London with the pleasure-moaning remains of his discarded lovers. The Wythford woman cried buckets down my shirtfront when I rowed her back to shore. It was bloody annoying."

Merry stared at him in flashing disbelief. "You are such a poor liar. It's pointless of you to try to make me less worried and less angry with you. Everyone knows he kidnapped Christina Wythford, using her brutally. He only returned her to her husband after he paid a ransom of twenty-five thousand pounds. It was in the *Times*."

"You've been with Morgan nearly a week and you still haven't realized, nothing is as it seems with him." He met her round eyes and said, "She is his lover, Merry, and has been for nearly two years. She was never his hostage. She comes to him

149

willingly. It breaks her heart each time he sends her away. He kept her so long the last time, he could not return her to her husband without the ruse of ransoming her. He sends them all away. It's best you keep your emotions tight, Merry. Whatever he says to you, strain it through a sifter. No woman ever comes to mean anything to Morgan."

"Your warning is unnecessary. I absolutely despise Morgan. And while I don't know what Morgan plans to do with me, it's not…" blushing hotly, "…*that*. He has absolutely no interest in me as a woman."

The minute she spoke the words, she felt sharp bites in her stomach. The last thing a sane girl should want was Morgan to have an interest in her. Her discomfort was extremely illogical.

Then, the image of his handsome face softened by smiles and laughter in the caress of candlelight as they played cards came to her. She remembered the gentle glide of his touch on her flesh. To her own horror, reluctantly she was forced to admit to herself that she had liked it.

How did he manage that prickling liveliness that shuddered all through her, whenever he touched her? She had never felt it before and didn't want it. It was even more galling, since all the touching had been a meaningless gesture that had accompanied his words *for effect*, and not motivated by any emotion for her, in any way.

He had stopped the caresses in a blink, as quickly as he'd started them, and had been decidedly unaffected by his love-play with her.

"I imagine he can have any woman he wants," she said, feeling instantly pathetic for having said that.

Her small head took on an alert tilt. Her very bright blue eyes were sharp on Indy's face, searching as she waited for her answer.

"Can and does," he said, with tight irritation.

Merry's face stiffened in response to that. "I thought so. I imagine that's why he doesn't bother me that way. Why then, do you suppose Morgan keeps me?"

Indy abandoned the effort to keep his voice polite. "Why don't you ask him?"

"I would better trust an answer from you. The man confuses and unsettles me too much. I want to go home. How can I get him to release me?"

"Try to pay attention this time. Take him to bed, damn it."

"I would rather die. I fail to see how you would think that would accomplish getting me my freedom. Regardless, I won't do it."

"If he beds you, he won't harm you, Merry, not ever. He is strangely gentlemanly, that way. It's the fastest way off this ship for you, since he never wants the flowers around to disturb him once he's pollinated their buds."

Her eyes were flashing daggers at him.

"If you don't like my advice, don't ask for it."

Pollinate, indeed. Indy's words made her blush in fury. A week with the boy had proven no topic was beyond his blunt exploration, even *these* matters. While she may have surrendered to the expanding scope of the conversations she was forced to suffer out of necessity, it did nothing to free her from modesty while having to endure such discussions. Every cell in her body was stinging in mortification.

She pressed her face up to his like an angry weasel. "Clearly, it must be obvious to you your plan is flawed. Why won't you help me? Couldn't you ask Morgan to release me? Especially, since *he* is not inclined at all..." she pleased herself with the ability of her bravado by saying into that worldly face, "... to pollinate me."

The air between them crackled with tension.

Cursing under his breath, Indy snapped, "Damn it, Merry,

don't look at me like that. I can't help you. I don't know how. That is the only plan that has occurred to me. Pollination. If I could free you, I would."

A hush fell as Merry digested his words. The boy's eyes were widened, in a way she'd never seen them before, catching and shimmering with a light within them. They were usually shed of emotion, but his gaze answered her with something almost like regret. The boy wasn't happy he had brought her here, and he didn't know how to help her. Merry took some comfort from that.

She sank down until her face rested on his thigh, and surprised herself when she said, "I'm sorry. I shouldn't snap at you. You are the only friend I have here. You were right earlier. I have no one to blame but myself for being here. I should never have gone to *Grave's End*. This is my just punishment for being so willful and foolish. But now that I am here, I haven't a clue how to fix it. I have never met a man like Morgan before. I don't know what he wants from me. I don't know how to deal with him."

"What did you expect? You're not in London, Merry. He's no dandy, remember that. However you deal with him, be careful," he said.

The warning was sincerely given. There was no point in being cross with the boy over this. She felt Indy's hard knit muscles slowly relax. Picking up his braid, she wound it around her arm, brushing the tip against her lips.

"I suspect you are right. You are younger than I am, yet you are the one always right. Though it should surprise me, not at all. You are very knowledgeable in these matters and I am not. I suppose being on a pirate ship gives a broader education in many areas. How old are you, anyway?"

"Seventeen."

Indy's muscle tightened irrationally, as Merry began to

brush the tip of his braid against her cheeks. He forced down the unexpected rise of desire, with all the reminders of why it was inappropriate.

Against his better judgment, he asked, "So what were you doing in here all day?"

She let Indy's braid slip from her arm and ran her cheek on his thigh. "We played cards. He told me why he hates Rensdale."

"Oh," he said, wishing Merry would move away. He found himself lightly stroking her hair. "What did he tell you?"

"That Rensdale killed his wife."

The truth. Indy had never expected that. Morgan must have accomplished something by the use of it, if he'd been willing to part with it.

Frowning, Merry began to rub her cheek against the material covering Indy's thigh.

"It is hard to imagine," she began softly, faltering a bit. "That a man such as Morgan had a wife, as though he were just some ordinary man, like a butcher, or a farmer. Did you know her, Indy? Did he love her very much?"

"Yes, I knew her, Merry. I knew her well," he said in a voice carefully stripped of emotion.

Indy's fingers slipped through Merry's hair and he watched the curls float downward.

"I miss my family so much," she whispered. "My mother must be worried ill, by now. I want to go home. If I told Morgan the truth, do you think he'd let me go? He said if I answered his questions, I could go home."

"I don't know, since you've never bothered to tell me the truth. It depends if the truth can harm you. If you have no connection to Morgan, nothing about you with meaning to him, he would free you, if you answered him all he wants to know. But, if there is anything in the truth you are afraid of, you must never tell him, Merry."

He put his fingers on her chin and lifted her face toward him.

"You must promise me, Merry. Not to tell him if you have something that needs to stay hiding."

The look of trust Merry gave made him look away.

He said, "Are you tired? Is that why you decided today to use my leg as a pillow? Do you want to eat or would you like me to put you on the window bench?"

Yawning, she lifted her cheek from his thigh. "The window bench. I want to sleep. Don't leave me. I am so tired of being alone in this cabin. Will you stay with me until I nod off?"

Saying nothing, Indy placed her on the bench and retrieved an extra quilt for her. He noticed those round blue eyes on him, as he tucked the covers up around her chin. Swearing under his breath, he sank down beside her.

"What a strange girl you are, Merry," he said, lightly stroking her hair with a scarred hand.

She was the first woman he had ever known that did not fear the touch of his hands and did not ease back, whenever they moved forward.

"I am the one who brought you here. How could you think of me as your friend? Why do trust me so much?"

Merry shook her head. She didn't know. It was a feeling. How does one explain that which by its existence should be unexplainable. She closed her eyes.

"I have always hated Rensdale," she mumbled, on a tired, little voice. "I hate him more now than I imagined possible."

Indy's eyes fixed out the window. "Go to sleep, Merry. Go to sleep."

CHAPTER SEVEN

The single candle had burned low, casting only a hint of glow in the cabin. Indy sat on the rug, one well-muscled leg bent, elbow on knee, scarred face with closed eyes resting in palm, half hidden by the long black waves that touched the floor. His other hand moved through the girl's ebony curls with an infinite gentleness that could almost be tasted.

Morgan hung back in the doorway absorbing the scene. Yet undisturbed, he had not been particularly quiet and made no effort not to have his presence noted.

Weariness, and it seemed to him, some sort of deep thoughtful conflict had brought a touch of animation to the usually lifeless angles of Indy's face. Morgan wasn't sure which it was, exhaustion or thought, that had failed the boy in being aware of him now. That Indy didn't stir was as shocking as the unexpected picture he made.

He sensed it wasn't worth making comment on either to the boy, not yet. Not until he had a better sense of what was going on between Indy and the girl. Clearly, there was something. To dive into the conflicting image the boy was making now, to those long burned in Morgan's memory of the lad with other girls, would only bring another argument to the surface, partly the result of the boy now almost being a man.

Deciding to leave both issues unexplored, he crossed the cabin in an easy stride and poured a goblet of wine.

"There's no need to continue. She's asleep," Morgan observed in a quiet voice.

He smiled thoughtfully as the boy lifted his head, meeting

directly the dark gaze on him, the younger as always unwavering and unrevealing.

"You don't have to rush off. I am going to drink, for awhile, and most probably smoke, before I can rest myself. Join me. We haven't had so much as a civil word between us since Falmouth."

Indy rose with the effortless grace of a small mountain lion, his hand the last thing to move, leaving Merry's gossamer black curls, to rest at his side in a pleasant, careless gesture. Without comment, the boy went toward the door.

"Running again?" said Morgan suddenly.

The boy halted halfway across the room.

"I have not touched her, if you've changed your mind about leaving her here. Is that why you've worked yourself into a frenzy avoiding me on this ship? Regrets over the girl? You might as well say what's on your mind, lad. Especially, since I have a feeling it would do both our souls so much good."

For that he earned a sharp disapproving look from Indy. Betraying emotion, a uniquely new occurrence in their arguments. He artfully altered his own gaze to fix on his glass.

In a steady voice, Indy said, "She's better off where she is or I would move her to my cabin. And if we're pretending to be truthful, you wouldn't let me take back Merry, even if I wanted to. I see the way you watch her. I know you've convinced yourself what you're doing is a kindness, making the inescapable result of your desire for her a less repulsive conclusion for her, if you buffet her emotions enough that she comes to you willingly. Has it occurred to you that the clever raping of one's heart is crueler than the forced raping of the body? A kind man would satisfy his body of her and let her go. If you were in the mood to feed your bloody vanity, why feed it with her in the only way that will cause her lasting harm?"

The silence between them was lengthy. The wind was a

pleasant rhythm against the glass.

Morgan studied the disgruntled youth, finally saying, "My, we did have a lot on our mind, didn't we? If you're in the mood to tally our hypocrisies, you might want to start with your own. You put her in my bed, knowing damn well, I would desire her, when you could have released her at the beach and saved her... what was it you called it?..." Those black eyes were glittering, "... 'the clever raping of her heart?' It's odd, when you gave her to me, wanting me to seduce her for some illogical pubescent revenge against Rensdale, you had no moral conflict with this. Odder still, when I have decided not to seduce her, to provide her only proximity and familiarity to decide her fate, you are wrapped in self-mutilating disapproval. You are not as far from me as you think, boy. We both hurt others to escape those unpleasant realities of ourselves. I have left her untouched and will let her make her way on her own, until I decide what should be done with her. "

Indy snapped out, "Every road ends the same. With your insane vanity and your absolutely fanatical need to recreate others, as you wish them to be, and the decisions yours. When Merry has no will of her own left, when you've proved some point to your ego by owning her heart and soul, you'll send her back like the others. Just as you've held me here, by your cruel manipulations of my feelings for you. You play with people's emotions for your grim need and vanity. You think that makes you not brutal. Consider that hypocrisy tonight, while you sit there wanting her, denying her freedom, and denying yourself the relief of her body."

Morgan's eyes were glittering like fire embers. "Are we talking about Merry or you now?" said Morgan evenly.

"Does it matter? You give us all the same in the end. Captivity and misery and freedom only when you decide we can have it. Because you refuse to admit, that at the bottom of it all, you are someone other than who you pretend to be."

Anger flashed in Morgan's eyes and was quickly concealed.

The boy gave a short laugh and lifted a brow. "Has it ever occurred to you that you may well trap yourself in all this? That this girl might come to have more meaning to you than even you expect? That you might be brought, face to face, with so many truths about yourself that you can't manipulate them away any longer?"

"The girl won't get you what you want, boy."

Morgan drained his glass. He reached for his pipe, stuffing the loose green leaves into it before setting it aflame. Inhaling deeply, he held the pungent smoke, and then let it roll slowly from his lips in a gently swirling cloud.

The cold air topside had not cleared his body of the taste of the girl. He had come to the cabin, knowing the only thing that might possibly leave her chaste on the window bench this night, was the numbing effect of this seemingly innocuous small leaf plant. He had run across it in South America, in his early days of searching for the boy. He knew the dulling of the smoke, too well, not for him to accept the soothing of it now.

Another drag. Morgan felt a slight heaviness of his lids.

"You can't manipulate truth of yourself, at all. You can only learn to live within it. You won't have peace until you're willing to do that, regardless of what you think ridding yourself of me will accomplish," said Morgan grimly.

The boy's laugh came harshly this time.

"As you have peace? You surround yourself with reminders of everything you've lost. Feeding the suffering, only enough, so you can tolerate being here with me and the obligation you feel you can't let go of. You've made even the girl a part of your need to escape the realities of your existence. Would you be denying yourself and playing this game with her, if she were not young, not innocent, and not of noble birth?

You are as much a prisoner of this ship as you've made me a prisoner, of my failure."

Morgan looked at Merry, taking a long drag of smoke, letting it sooth the needs of his body as he had never expected to need help in soothing. Thirty-nine and drugging his body into submission over a nineteen year old girl, like a pubescent boy unable to control his urges and erections. If it wasn't all so grim, he would laugh.

Morgan opened one eye and gave a thorough assessment of Indy, without ever letting the boy see him do it. It was clear this exercise was a product of their own never-ending struggle.

It occurred to Morgan the girl was closer to Indy's age than his own. He could end this now by putting her in the boy's cabin, letting him make the choice of her fate, remembering how Indy had looked lightly stroking her hair. In those few moments, it was as if none of what had happened had left any gruesome residue on him.

His veiled gaze settled back on Merry's figure, sleeping soundly on the bench. Morgan wanted her with an edge he found surprising, since she was the very kind of woman he avoided as a rule.

Was that the point of this? She was an inescapable reminder of his past, linked to the unavoidable demands of the male body no man under eighty could escape with her.

Indy had come to know him well these past five years, but the boy was in for another failure, if Indy thought Morgan's fascination with the girl would get him what he wanted.

Wherever Indy's plotting took him, it would not dissolve his ties to the boy. They were ties that could never been dissolved, nature's unrelenting rule, not a product of his vanity, regardless of what the boy thought.

"You were right earlier," Morgan said, letting the pause develop artfully, before opening his eyes to cut off the boy's flash of surprise. "She is looking pale. She needs a touch of sun in her cheeks. Take her topside tomorrow."

Silence. Morgan eyes were black and innocent. He tossed the intricate gold box of leaves to the boy. Indy caught it with a remarkable quickness of a hand.

"Since you want my rebirth by fire, why should we make it easier on me? I have a feeling you are going to need that, more than I do, before this is through. That's all that's left, since we've been so long from the Caribbean. You are not as unaffected by all this as you imagine yourself to be. Perhaps you are the one who isn't going to like where it takes you, lad."

Indy's eyes were shockingly empty. "Keep it." He tossed the box back. "I have more experience, than you, in suffering the agonies of being forced through events I don't wish to go through."

~~~

Merry was sitting on her knees at the window bench, her nose pressed against the chilled glass of the stern gallery when Indy, breakfast tray in hand, entered the cabin. She looked like a tiny suffering cat, trapped in a cage, desperate to escape.

"I thought you had forgotten me," she said irritably.

"We attracted the notice of a British frigate at dawn, and I was needed on deck."

Merry's eyes rounded. *A British frigate? Was her luck finally to change?*

"Is there going to be a battle?" she asked, unable not to sound hopeful.

The boy took a biscuit in a scarred hand and tossed it to her.

"No. We played with each until about an hour ago. I am sorry to disappoint you."

"Why did we run?" Merry asked, unwilling to abandon all hope.

The boys shrugged. "We're not political, Merry."

He took the bundle from his arms and dropped it on bench beside her.

"Those are my clothes. Put them on. Don't ruin them. Morgan gave me permission to take you topside, for a little air, if you want to. He thinks you need a touch of color in your cheeks."

She sprang from the bench. "Would a moment of privacy to dress be tempting my good fate?" she said.

"Only if you delay. Morgan said a quick turn on deck. Nothing more today, since there's always a possibility we might go into battle. You had better behave yourself, Merry. Do what I tell you. If you cause any trouble, he won't let you out again."

"But, why is he finally allowing me out of here?"

Indy crossed the cabin, turned his back, and gave a curt order to dress.

"Why does Morgan do anything? If you want to know, you would do better to ask him."

Not bloody likely. She wanted as little contact with Morgan as possible. The man confused her, too much, as it was.

"You can turn around now," Merry announced once Indy's britches and shirt were secured.

Indy swept her once with a hard stare and then cursed low.

Merry glared. "What have I done to irritate you now? Is my shirt button crooked? Why does everything I do irritate you?"

"I had thought my britches and shirt would serve better than the Wythford woman's dresses," Indy grumbled, noting how her breasts struggled against the fabric of his shirt. "I was wrong." He shrugged out of his vest. "I should leave you here, loss of color or not. I should have known better than to think you wouldn't be a nuisance. Keep that bloody thing on until you're back in the cabin."

y shrugged into the garment. "You can be
times. It is not my fault your shirt is too
ʳ you to accuse me of being a nuisance

but to be a nuisance, it's an unpleasant
ʸour character and sex. You are going to be
enough of a damn curiosity on deck, without your bosom
popping out to heat up every man within a hundred feet of you.
These are rough men, Merry. You're not in England, damn it.
Exercise some common sense for once."

As they clambered up the ladder through the hatch, Merry
fought the sudden burn of light against her eyes, her senses raw
after having been in doors for so long. She struggled to focus
her gaze and her senses to the dizzying rush of sound and
activity around her.

Everywhere there was noise and motion, men busy rushing
on deck, the brilliant vast sky now gloriously diffuse in color,
and the sharp slap of icy cold wind against her cheeks. Merry's
senses jumped with a tingling excitement.

Leaning back her head, she paused at the top step, staring
at hundreds of yards of sheet white canvas dancing against the
masts. The men in the ratlines, their agile sailors' bodies moving
with a sureness that was oddly graceful, were no longer a muted
sound. Their shouting and singing flooded her ears.

Tilting her face toward the sky, Merry allowed a smile of
pure pleasure to surface.

Indy watched, felt instant dread, and his gaze narrowed.
Every man within eye-shot was fixed on the bloody picture she
made on that top step, face lifting to the Heavens. He'd be
damn lucky to make it through the morning without drawing
steel to protect her foolish hide.

Even Tom Craven had paused beside Morgan to give her a
hard stare. Morgan was the only man not staring at Merry.

Though aware of what the sudden stir around him meant, he made neither comment to put a halt to it, nor gave notice of it.

Indy grabbed her arm jerking her out of her pose.

"Ouch. Why did you hurt me?" Merry hissed, slapping at his hand.

"I told you not to attract the notice of the crew. Don't you have sense at all?"

Her face instantly moved to his as she glared. "I wasn't doing anything."

He cursed again. The boy caught her hard against him with a scarred hand and pulled her with him across the deck.

Merry struggled against the grip and then stopped, glaring at him, as she slipped awkwardly behind him on the damp deck. She tried to jerk free, but fighting Indy was pointless.

She had done nothing to deserve his irritation. The men who did notice her quickly dropped their eyes as they passed. She couldn't image why he was angry with her. The boy was scowling, his face even more fierce than usual.

In no time, Indy had worked her through the maze of rushing men, to a grinning blond youth who looked vaguely familiar to Merry. He sat, back against a mast, pulling a needle in one beefy hand through canvas, with surprising skill.

"Hello, lass, so yer alive and well with us, after all," he boomed in a jovial voice, grinning up at Merry. "I was almost given up me prayers to ever see yer bonnie face again."

Merry stared at him, then remembered. Shay, Indy's partner from the beach. She would have moved onward across the deck if Indy, with not so gentle hands, hadn't pushed her down onto the space beside Shay.

"Why the hell haven't you finished that yet?" Indy growled.

"Plague rot ye, lad, I have got me a good hand with me needle, but not a quick one. So unless ye want the bloody thing to pull apart, leave off."

Then to Merry, with heavy meaning, Shay explained, "It's not that I am lazy, lass, no matter what himself thinks."

He looked at Merry again and his smile was bright, lopsided, and absurdly shameless.

"So, yer still angry with me, lass? And meself, I have been worried day overnight fer ye, since none of us have seen even a hair of yer bonnie head, though every shellback on ship knows that yer here. I wanted to let ye go, remember? Makes me sick, in the pit of my belly, to have such bonnie eyes glaring at me. Can ye find an ounce of pity in yer blessed heart to forgive a dumb foolish Irishman?"

It was hard to remain angry with the young pirate. Merry felt the corners of her lips twitch with a smile. He had wanted to let her go and he did have an uncommonly attractive face, with lively shameless eyes that could be only be termed now as wheedling.

Her smile came, slight, but his reaction was not.

"There, ye are forgiving me, don't try to pretend yer not," Shay said with syrupy satisfaction.

Indy wondered at the wisdom of this and almost reached to pull Merry back up beside him. But he had duties to complete below deck and he had to leave her somewhere. Shay was the only other man under twenty on ship. For that reason, combined with the fact this spot was within range of Morgan's vision if things got ugly. Indy reluctantly decided to leave Merry where she was.

"Ye can run along, lad. I will see the lass don't come to no harm. Morgan is in a rare temper. What the hell is the matter with the mon these days?" Noting Indy's hesitation, he slanted another look and added. "Go along with ye, lad. I will see the lassie doesn't make no mischief."

He gave Merry a playful wink, which brought soft giggles

in spite of how she tried to check them. Indy favored them both with a severe glare.

He said to Shay, "See she doesn't get into trouble or I will skin your hide myself."

Merry watched as Indy crossed the deck to Morgan.

"That frigate is a bloody well-armed one, lass," Shay said, noting the direction of her gaze while he continued his work with canvas. "If she hadn't broken pursuit, it would have been a damn hellish mess. Not that Morgan can't take her. The mon knows battle tactics that most captains of the fleet have never seen, much less heard of. The mon is bloody charmed and ruthless. There's no need to worry, lass. Morgan's order was not to battle and we didn't."

It was clear Shay all but idolized the man.

"Morgan," Merry said, settling her chin in palms with elbows on knees. "I am so weary of that insufferable man. The last thing I want to do is talk about him. Next you'll be telling me he can fly."

"He might at that. If yer weary of the mon, lass, why do ye stare at him? Here I thought ye were glad to see me, and I would be getting a share of yer bonnie eyes on me."

Feeling an unwanted blush, she rapidly shifted her gaze. She *had* been staring at Morgan.

"I despise the man," she stated stiffly.

Shay gave her a wink. "That's good, lass. I like ye. He ain't the mon fer you. More bother than any mon's worth. He's bloody ruthless with the lasses. When he walks the streets, the women flock about him, like he were the last sweet meat on the dinner tray. Want him fer dessert, they do. Common or noble, ain't no difference what they are, every blasted one of 'em. Now tell me, isn't my fion figure just as striking?"

He waited for a reply with a silly expression on his face and didn't get one.

Shay studied her face, and then said, "Ah, so that be the way of it. I heard some of the crew all a'whispers in their hammocks that ye slept on the bench, but the scuttlebutt at times is a crazy thing. I couldn't believe me ears. Do you know, yer the first lass I ever run across that didn't have an itch for the mon?"

Blushing furiously, Merry stated in a voice of absolute resolve, "I assure you the only thing I want from that man is my return to Falmouth."

Her gaze shifted back to Morgan then. All at once he turned, fresh faced and romantically tousled by the wind. Reaction surged upward so quickly, Merry couldn't stop it.

She had shared a cabin with the man for a week. She had watched him in ever mood and turn. She had thought she was over that shock that came when looking at him.

But Morgan by sunlight was another prospect all together. Sun-detailed, the chiseled lines of his face were more flawlessly perfect, more handsome. Less soulless and dangerous. Those black eyes captured light, seeming to hold it, turning it into a shimmering mosaic of rich tones, which had only been hinted at by candle glow. Seeing him now, next to other men, made him all the more inhumanly perfect.

She hated her reaction. Yet, she couldn't stop it. It caught Merry like a cannon ball against her stomach.

Shay sat for awhile, stitching and studying Merry. She claimed she didn't want Morgan, but he'd known that look in a woman's eyes, more clever than her at hiding it. Then there was Morgan who, if rumor had the right of it—and he sensed it did— let the girl sleep on the bench, when her beauty alone would have brought her ruin with any man who could make their member work.

He couldn't begin to fathom it, but any way he looked at it, the situation was better for the lass, if it were left to sit as it was.

Shay invested a full hour of quickly invented, outrageous sea tales to drag her gaze from the captain. Pulling her attention back, canvas done, he decided to distract her by teaching her knots. He was pleased when the effort turned her face to smiles as she clumsily worked the rope. Once Morgan had disappeared below decks, Merry gave the rope her full attention, though it didn't seem to help.

"Blast it, lass, that's the damn silliest rolling hitch I have ever seen. Now pay attention."

Effortlessly he twisted and turned his rope into the knot.

Merry tried again. *Hopeless.* He tried teaching her several more types. They were just as bad. But, the lass was all smiles. Both of them forgetting Indy's warning, the knots turned into a trek to the canons and showing her how to load one.

Merry was covered in gunpowder and laughing uproariously by the time they were chased off by Morgan's gruff gunner barking furiously at them, after the boy had asked if she could fire one. Shay had stopped to pelt him with a wash of powder before they fled the flustered man.

A lesson with a knife followed that had him rolling with mirth on the deck, as she inexpertly attempted to bury it in the wood of a mast. The knife whizzed past the target, just missing the sailing master's leg. Shay only boomed about how well she sank it into the railing.

For Merry the afternoon was splendid. Being with Shay was like floating in the bubbles of a champagne bottle, impossible to resist and providing an escape from her currently ghastly state of affairs. However outrageous her conduct was, it only pleased and urged the boy onward.

He'd raved in pleasure when she'd asked to climb the rigging, clutching her hand in his burly grasp. Before she knew it, she was climbing aloft, hurrying to keep pace on the ratlines with the much surer moving boy. She had done this before, with Uncle Andrew on their journey to America, and as remembered the experience was thrilling.

High above the ship, with an endless horizon of water and sky, the wind rushed her senses. She held the ropes, leaning back, feet braced, hair caught by the current of air and streaming in a dancing dark cloud behind her. As miserable as her current situation was, this was a treasure.

Shay looked down at Merry, smiling in satisfaction. "Damn me, if yer not one of the best I have seen on these ropes. Do ye want to go higher, lass? Let's see if we can't touch Heaven."

Merry's laughter filled the air as she scrambled to continue upward with him.

Indy, coming through the hatchway, found the majority of the crew gathered beneath a mast, the ship in near chaos, not a lick of work being done with a British warship within reach of them. Following the direction of their gazes, he looked upward and saw Merry. Recalling the battle he had had with Morgan to let her from cabin, he wondered how the devil he would ever explain this.

By the time Morgan returned to deck, Indy was in the ratlines, as well. His laughing, jeering crew was almost folded over on the deck in their unrestrained humor. It was clear the boy was fighting to get them down. Shay took direction only moderately well, in the best of circumstances. With Merry's glowing humor egging him on, Shay was unmanageable.

The Irishman was making comical wipes with his leg to keep Indy away from his companion. Indy's face was a thing of thunder, as he rapidly spoke with an animated swing of arm. Merry was doing ridiculous evasive maneuvers on the ropes, rather skillfully, and was laughing like a madwoman. The scene held all the absurdity of a low farce in a London theater.

Morgan's black eyes took in the scene in a single glance. Only Tom Craven wasn't laughing, though there was a telling softness to the edges of his thin lips.

As amusing as it all was, Morgan was irritated with the interruption. Since they were still playing cat-watching mouse with a British warship, it was time to return Merry to the cabin where he should have kept her in the first place.

"Varian, don't you think you should keep the girl locked below in your cabin?" Tom Craven said the instant Morgan was upon him.

"You can't expect her to exist on only doses of alone and doses of me. I think she shows astonishing agility for a girl of nineteen. Who would have thought she could out run Indy on the ropes."

Morgan arched a brow at Tom Craven. Tom's was a reasonable suggestion given the current disruption on ship. His response, therefore, sounded unreasonable even to him.

"Agility be damned. The girl is a madwoman. I have not made comment any time you've kept one of your conveniences aboard ship and let them have the run of the deck. This one, of course, is beautiful, but the others had the good sense not to climb the rigging. Why the devil do you keep the girl? She's not in your style at all, Varian, and she's a bloody nuisance."

"The others had not so much more sense, Tom. Most probably less agility."

"Where will you be with your amusement if she kills herself? I don't relish the idea of having her hide splattered on the deck, regardless of what you decide to do with her."

"As I recall, you wanted me to dispose of her. Wasn't that the content of our discussion last night? Wouldn't her being splattered on my deck tend to settle our disagreement for us? A betraying softening, Tom? What should I make of that?"

That sent a slight flush across Tom's face. Morgan

assessed it and then turned his eyes back to Merry.

He was about to send men up after them, when it became unnecessary. Indy, who had the never failing sureness of a cat, fell from the ratlines into the water. He had made an uncharacteristically foolish move with an arm as he reached for Merry's squirming leg.

Humor gone, Morgan's face was thunderous. He found himself giving the order *to come about* so that the boy could be retrieved from the water.

He was still on the quarterdeck when Indy was dropped, a shivering, splattering wet mess on the deck. Two of Morgan's stouter crewmen held him back from tearing Shay apart. Merry, laughing in unbridled glee, dropped to her knees beside the boy's struggling, snarling figure.

"Blast it, Merry, if you continue to laugh, I will beat you after I finish with Shay. I told you to behave. I should have known better than to trust you with that Irish idiot."

"I am sorry." Merry tried to look contrite, failed miserably, and bit her lip to stop laughing. "You are delightfully amusing when you're angry with me."

Indy struggled against the hold of the men. Fighting to sit up, he sneered, "It's clear you don't have an ounce of common sense in that head of yours. I should spare myself the bother and let you kill yourself, and put me out of the misery of having brought you here."

"I am not the one who fell." Laughing again, she put her face close up to his, and asked, "Are you planning to be angry with me for very long about this?"

The boy looked enraged, disgruntled and frustrated. Why that made Merry want to laugh, she couldn't begin to fathom, but it did.

With a light stride Morgan crossed the deck, his arrival instantly silencing the laughter of the crew. His eyes did a harsh trek across his men and then settled on the three figures on deck beneath him.

"Let the boy go," came that low voice above Merry.

She had all but forgotten Morgan during the blissful whimsy of the afternoon, but having his towering figure looming above brought her back to reality with a harsh thump.

His flexible, placid timbre carried across the deck without effort. "Any man who leaves his duties the next time the girl is on deck will be hanged."

The warning disbanded the crew with a rapid flurry and sent, in a flash, the protection of the boys from Merry in a scrambling of long limbs. Though how she could think of the boys as protection against this mountain of man was anyone's guess.

Morgan stood above her, the crimson circle of the sun a hallo around him, reflecting off of the cool stare of his eyes. For once the reflecting light in those great black eyes was not unreadable. He was studying her like a physician trying to figure out how to remove a wart.

She would have liked to reclaim some dignity by meeting him with a cool stare of her own, springing to her feet, and walking off from him in a manner *dismissing*, but it was impossible. She was never herself with Morgan.

Without a word, he reached out and lifted her from the deck. The contact brought Merry's disobedient limbs into action. She began to fight him, her arms anxiously flailing against him as she was carried to the cabin.

"Take your hands off me," Merry hissed.

"Stop this nonsense before I beat you and spare the boy the effort," was his answer to that.

A furious surge of words rushed Merry's lips and then died there.

Morgan was always so annoyingly perfect, somehow

managing to remain impeccably neat even during his duties on deck. But her squirming had sent a swirling wash of dark gun powder residue from her hands across his shirt—*white today, an unfortunate choice*—and there was a streak like Indian war paint across one high chiseled cheek.

It made him look so human. While her mirth was, perhaps not wise, certainly ill timed, definitely never expected, it proved uncontainable. It had been just that kind of afternoon for Merry.

All at once, she found herself uncontrollably laughing into the elegant features of that frightening face that had just threatened to beat her.

As he dropped her unceremoniously in the center of his bed, Morgan said, "You are a madwoman, do you know that?"

Merry couldn't check the impulse, so peeking through her curls, she flung back at him, "And you, sir, are a mess."

Morgan looked at his shirt. "You have the oddest humor of any creature I have ever known." Then, giving her a hard stare, he added, "And you are the dirtiest girl I have ever held in my arms."

Merry tried to look contrite, failed, and only laughed harder.

"I suppose I must seem odd to you, laughing like this over dirt on a shirt, but you are never anything but inhumanly perfect, sir. A little less perfection and a little more laughter, I think would suit you the better."

"I am not inhumanly perfect, Little One," he pointed out coolly, before reaching for the pitcher and filling the basin. "What I am trying not to do is lose my temper. Your conduct was foolish and reckless. You would do well not to disrupt my ship, again."

"Ah, but you are inhuman," Merry scoffed, wondering where she got the courage to taunt him. "You are inhuman, like all creatures of myth and legend. You are never anything less than perfect. You don't allow yourself to be. That, sir, is a tragedy. Imperfection is what you must risk if you are going to enjoy living."

Merry jerked her curls from beneath her bottom and left gunpowder where her fingers had fluttered. Morgan felt the unwanted pull of a smile, but did a facile frown instead.

"You are an absurd, girl. Now sit still, you little monkey. You are getting gunpowder across my bedding."

Merry's blue eyes instantly dipped to the smudges across his pillow and she began to giggle again in earnest. She was the most beautiful woman he'd ever had on his bed and she was distinguishing herself by being the only one ever to find enjoyment in his sheets by making them a ruin.

Shaking his head, Morgan stated, "You are a lunatic."

Still in the hopeless possession of her giggles, Merry studied her toes, grayed by gunpowder. She took no notice of what he was doing, and said without a shred of the proper caution one should have with such a man, "Then you have a lunatic as a hostage. You should release me. Lunatics are dangerous."

Lifting one delicately boned bare foot in the air, she announced in a melodramatic way Morgan found silly and a trifle charming at once, "I can't imagine why you keep me."

"Have you by chance ever looked in the mirror when your face is clean?"

"My face is rarely clean, sir. I am imperfect. I enjoy living too much to bother with perfect."

Morgan settled on the bunk, dipped the cloth in washbowl, and with patient hands began to work on the grime on Merry's face.

He surprised himself by quietly saying, "Tell me who you are and I will release you."

Merry's eyes shot to his face. Carefully, she responded, "I am a lunatic. Lunatics have no names. I think we are identified by branding. Perhaps you should look for my mark if you are still curious as to my identity."

No less than a score of wicked responses came to his mind from that. Morgan was pleased with himself that he didn't say any of them.

As his dark gaze did a subtle inspection of her, he noted that she was exceptionally well made, long of line and lush of curve, just where a man would want them lush. The last thing this girl should want is a man looking for her mark. It would shock her where he wanted to begin.

"I think you're going to have to soak in a tub for days to get this off," he commented wryly. "What the devil were you doing with Shay to get yourself covered head to toe with gunpowder?"

With creamy satisfaction, Merry announced with a delightful smile, "Learning to load your canons, Captain. I wanted to fire one, but your gunner wouldn't let me because of the warship, and was not at all polite about my request. He's a horrible man. I can't imagine why you keep him *either*."

He inspected her hands and fingers. "Where did you learn to climb rigging so expertly? It is not usually the developed talent of young, wellborn British girls."

"I sailed to America with my uncle once. Or rather I stowed away with him to America. He was even less pleased than you to have me."

Morgan only laughed softly and replied, "You are very good at it, but please don't do it again. You are enough of a distraction to my men if you do nothing more than sit still as you are." He dumped the towel in the bowl. "I think I am going to have to send for a bath."

Morgan was about to rise when Merry eased forward, held

him with the lightest contact of her hand and reached for the towel. She was unsure of where the boldness came from. Perhaps it was just the unanticipated pleasure she'd felt by making him laugh, when clearly he had wanted to be stern.

"Imperfection. Touch of Merry." She removed the streak of gunpowder from his cheek. Smiling into those occult black eyes, she whispered, "There you are perfect and inhuman, once again. You will be your terrifying self when you return to deck."

Then, on stranger impulse, she placed a soft kiss on the now clean flesh. The shock of what she did mortified her. She jerked back from him at once. Why she felt the want to kiss Morgan then was just as strange to her as doing it. Morgan was not a man to toy with.

Locking eyes with the abyss of Morgan's terrifying stare, Merry was half-off the bed when Morgan's hand locked on her arm. He pulled her against him. Before she could stop him, he was kissing her. Her cheeks began to instantly burn with the contact. He let his mouth drag across hers in way that made her body stiffen, then quiver from head to toe.

Unable to work free of his body, Merry soon found herself turned in his arms in a movement that was subtle and graceful, and then lowered into the soft mattress before she had time to realize what he was doing. The weight of his body was balanced above her. She struggled to watch his hands and break free, and it took her several moments to realize Morgan had stopped kissing her.

His laughter was soft. "The next time, Little One, you want to thank a man for washing your face, you will know how to do it properly."

Morgan gently put Merry back against the pillows and let her go.

"And the next time you kiss me, I will kill you," Merry screamed.

Merry watched, anxiously trying to still the rioting currents inside of her, as Morgan rose to his feet with an unhurried elegance of movement that hit her like a slap. She could barely breathe.

"I am going to send for a bath," was all Morgan said, not bothering to even to look at her as he left.

~~~

Descending below decks, the clatter of the afternoon left Morgan with a pulsing headache. He paused at the end of the stairs, the hallway dim, quiet, cool, and pleasantly scented with warm wood musk.

They were a welcome balm after the bright sun, the petty flashing brawls of the men, and the never ending intrusion of sound was unavoidable in the command of a ship. Life on ship had never suited him well.

In his cabin, he managed to maintain the ambiance of a home, out of the necessity of maintaining the illusion that he had one. As that thought filtered through his mind, he spotted a tiny shoe lying outside his cabin door.

It was Merry's. She must have lost it while struggling in his arms as he carried her below. He picked it up and into his senses wafted the scent of her sweet fragrance, mixed with a hint of rose soap. Even the shoe leather carried her flavor.

The last thing he'd expected, at this point in his life, was to have the fate of an untried girl resting in his hands. This morning, he had sat for an hour in the blue light of dawn doing nothing but watching her sleep. There was a winsome playfulness to Merry, even in sleep. Her tiny body was always turning on the bench, her hand swatting at her unruly cloud of hair, or her even white teeth chewing on the corners of the blankets.

A familiar pondering claimed him. Who was this girl? Why wouldn't she answer his questions so he could send her home?

Questioning her only brought stubbornness and no response. He had never met anyone he couldn't make full reason of within a quarter hour, but Merry was a whimsical blend of mismatching pieces. Those pieces were driving him to distraction.

She was a puzzle in every way. She could climb the rigging like the best tar of his crew, having learned it sailing to America with her uncle. That meant she was a girl of means, if not of noble birth. The more he knew of her, if she were nobility at all, it was a modest level of little significance.

Her laughter was a thing of showering lunacy, without a hint of the proper reserve a girl of good birth who moved in society would have cultivated.

Her beauty was unlike any he had seen, but she had altered it, not at all, to turn it fashionable. Her hair was too long, not even short curls cut to frame her oval face. She preferred to tie it in a knot that bounced on her shoulder, charming but not stylish.

Her manners were soft, her voice cultured, her temper a fury, her whim unconventional, her mind educated, her politics treasonous, and her instincts dangerously unaware of the harsher elements of the world. Almost as if she'd never seen them. She was of marriageable age, but romantically untouched, as though she'd never been courted.

What possible connection could this creature have with Rensdale? Where the devil did she come from?

Now, opening his cabin door, his charming puzzle sent the blood rocketing through his veins. He had assumed it was safe to return to his cabin, since Merry had completed bathing. Without any reason to do so, he had expected to find her curled in a chair reading.

Instead, he found her lying on his bed, dark curls fanned

around her, with her tiny feet pressed to the wood of the headboard. She was wearing only his shirt and he could see that she wore nothing underneath it, since it was all too apparent she had pulled it on without drying herself well. It was molded to the shape of the round fullness of her breasts, the flat belly, and the gentle turn of her hip.

She was, by far, not the first woman he'd ever found on his bed. He doubted she was among the first fifty, but oh my, she was the most tempting.

Letting his eyes roam her, he closed the door softly. Merry snapped up at once, saw him, and did a startled flip on his bed that did her no good, at all, at this moment. It made her hair tumble in floating waves over her flushed features and heaving bosom. She had landed in an unfortunate posture, balanced on hands and knees.

"If you are open to suggestions, Little One, I would recommend that if it's your intent to cool a man's ardor *that* is not the pose to strike. At least not while wearing his shirt," Morgan chided blandly, while his blood continued to shoot through his veins and other places.

Merry blushed and sprang from his bed. "It was not my intent to do anything. You startled me."

Her naive, blunt confession was a timely thing. Morgan's smile surfaced on its own.

"I know. You startled me, too. We're even." He focused on the bedding as he tried to marshal his organs into order. "You've also added dampness to the smudges of gunpowder. I don't mind you lulling on my bed in the afternoons. Though it does my ego no good at all, that you are only inclined to do so when I am not in it, but I would prefer if you didn't make a ruin of my bed."

"The gunpowder was your fault. You put me on your bed that time," she pointed out hotly, and regretted the words the instant she'd said them. They had made his black eyes start to sparkle. "If I am too much a vexing nuisance you could return me to Falmouth."

"If you want me to be inclined to return you to Falmouth, I suggest you stop climbing into my sheets. It is more likely to give me hope, so I will be inclined to keep you."

His words made her eyes round in dismay, having the pleasing effect of the cooling of the rest of his anatomy.

"What are you doing here? You never come below deck in the afternoons."

"It's my cabin, Little One," Morgan said softly as he turned to face her. "I am willing to share. Don't expect me to give it up. If I need to come below deck before eight bells to see you in my bed, I might very well make a habit of it."

He bent her a look that turned her cheeks to crimson circles. It wasn't kind to deliberately make her blush. She did it so often on her own. But, he found the cherry-spots charming when they surfaced on her sloping cheeks.

"Oh, why don't just go away," Merry moaned, dropping her eyes disconsolately.

She watched him as he tossed his pillows back into their usual arrangement on his bed and stretched out atop the blankets.

Nervously she asked, "What are you doing?"

"You're quite safe, Little One. *I* have the necessary headache to prevent... whatever it is you are imaging I might be contemplating doing with you." He lifted one of the pillows to his face and breathed in deeply before placing it beneath his head. He laughed softly, and then said, "Touch of Merry. Headache gone. Behave yourself, Little One, if you are determined to pass your afternoon only watching me snore."

Closing his eyes, it was only a moment before Morgan heard his cabin door slammed shut.

179

Dressed only in the captain's shirt, Merry didn't dare go any farther than the stairs of the hatchway.

Miserable and huddled there, she stared at her knit fingers, knowing she was cowering here with less dignity than even Kate had in her skittish hen moments, and thought, *Merry Merrick you have fallen low.*

Leaning her head against the wood wall, she ran her cheek along the cool polished surface and tried to reason a course to free herself of this unpleasant tangle her life had become.

She was trapped on a pirate ship, captive of a man who rattled her in every way and compounded this disastrous state of affairs by behaving, not all, like herself in any predictable manner. Wishing heartily she hadn't been so stupid as to have gone to *Grave's End,* she tried to gather every scrap of her poorly functioning brain to figure out how to undo both vexing states and get back to Falmouth.

She was deep in thought when Mr. Craven came down the stairs. He whipped her with a harsh stare and snatched her painfully from the ground to hold her before his face.

"Let me go," she cried out in desperate fear.

"Stop your foolishness, girl. I haven't ruttery on my mind, but there is any of a hundred men here, who ruttery would be their first train of thought, if they found you sitting here in his shirt. Who the devil let you wander loose? Why aren't you with that stupid Irishman or the boy? Why aren't you in Morgan's cabin?"

"He's sleeping." Mr. Craven's eyes sharpened in unkindly revealed interpretation of *that* and Merry blushed. "Take your hands from me."

He didn't. In the biting hold of fingers, he carried her down the hall, opened a door, and all but tossed her to the floor when he released her.

"This is my cabin. Don't touch a thing or I will blister your backside," was all he said. To Merry's horror he locked her in.

It was Indy who came near midnight to lift her sleeping form from the wood floor just inside Tom's cabin doorway.

His face came into hazy focus before her, as he said, "You're lucky it was Craven who found you dressed like this. I should beat you for being so foolish as to scamper about clad only in his shirt."

Merry cut him off. "Craven is a horrible man. Beat me if you want, I am too tired to defend myself with you. He's already bruised my arms with his fingers. So perhaps you will leave off and consider the beating unnecessary."

Her eyes drifted closed and exhaustion dragged her back into sleep before he could answer her.

He put Merry to bed on the window bench and tucked the blankets high beneath her chin. Rolling up her sleeves he noted the tiny purple marks marring the flawless creaminess of her flesh. Lowering himself to the cabin floor, he lightly stroked her hair. It was sticky from sweat.

She'd pounded on the door for hours because he'd left her there, long after Craven had given him the key, as a lesson, hopefully, that would lead to an inclination for self-protection.

Morgan remained silent through the heated quarrel that had ensued in the captain's cabin between Indy and Craven. He'd heard them both out without a word.

Fixing his black eyes bright with his amusement on the window bench, Morgan said pleasantly, "I think I will keep the girl forever, since she's doing us all so much good."

CHAPTER EIGHT

Someone had left a silver bowl of allspice berries on the window bench where Merry slept. It was most probably Indy, who always let her know, without saying so, he was sorry when he was too harsh with her. He had indeed been harsh with her the prior night, and had avoided her all day because of it.

The berries were a treasure. The ship had taken on fresh supplies when it had taken her on in Falmouth, which accounted for the berries. Because of the vast number of men, these little delicacies of fresh produce were exclusively Morgan's. For Indy to sneak a bowl into the cabin for her was to break a standing order against stealing food and risk punishment.

Merry was curled beneath a quilt, chomping away and staring at the star points beyond the stern windows. The ship rocked pleasantly beneath her as it rose and dipped over the waves. It was a poor ally for her mind that tried to make plans of escape.

Ireland, perhaps I will escape Morgan in Ireland.

The cradle-like motion of the ship made her drowsy mind unable to go farther. They wouldn't drop anchor for another five days. She had time to plan plots, so she decided not to be overly critical with herself for not doing it now.

With the sounds of footsteps from the hallway drifted pipe smoke. Brandon Seton's. She identified the pungent scent and its owner without effort, just as she identified the low voice conversing with him.

Expecting Morgan to drift past the door, rapping it once

with his knuckles, *a habit*, she did nothing to hide the berries. Morgan never brought the crew, except Tom Craven, to the cabin. She should have remembered the warning about 'never'.

In a few moments the door came wide, admitting the two men. Merry flushed like a guilty child, and tried with a not so subtle move of her hand to hide the bowl. The amusement shimmering in Morgan's black eyes let her know she had failed dismally.

Before Morgan said a word, Merry snapped, "I stole it. I was hungry."

She had offered her statements as a protection to Indy, and completely given up protection to herself. Morgan was not alone. The rules about stealing food and their punishments were no stranger to Merry. They would be rigidly enforced, even with her, and especially in front of the crew. Flogging.

The lamp he had brought in, he sat on the table, and Morgan crossed the room to cup her chin.

In an affectionately chiding way, he said, "No you didn't, you little lunatic. I left it for you. Never confess to a crime on a ship. You are the only one on this ship who ever disobeys my orders. You spent your supper glowering at me instead of eating. I knew your appetite would return once you were rid of me."

Caught off guard, Merry blushed, because there were any number of ways to interpret that last statement.

He released her chin and was able to dismiss her from his mind with a *dispatch* she was envious of. Morgan was not so easy to dismiss.

She sat up, curling her legs in front of her. With the blanket, she made a desperate attempt to hide that she was wearing Morgan's shirt. She didn't want Mr. Seton to see her garbed thus and putting *implications* to it.

Her attempts at this must not have been subtle. Brandon

Seton began to wickedly grin as he watched the useless endeavors of her hands.

"I never expected to be jealous of one of your shirts, Varian, but I find that I am," he announced, in a careless way that made him sound amiable, in spite of the rudeness of his remark.

That Mr. Seton was one of the few who called Captain Morgan 'Varian' when they were alone, told Merry this man was among the few men on ship Morgan liked. You could count on the digits of a single hand how many people were allowed to speak his given name. Merry was not among them. It told her which group *she* sat with.

Reading her thoughts with alarming precision, Morgan said, "Yes, Little One, I have Christian name. Even devils come to earth spawned through human flesh, and are burdened by their traditions. You may indulge the tradition whenever you develop the whim to."

The rounding of Merry's eyes made Brandon laugh.

He was rudely enjoying himself, as he asked, "Now, I am intrigued. What does the little flower call you when she whispers at you in the darkness, Varian?"

Morgan's eyes held her in a wandering hold. "I don't give her a chance to call me anything. The words from Merry's lips are, by far, not the sweetest things to come from her lips. I haven't enough ego to risk its thrashing to ask her what she calls me in her mind."

Insufferable man is what I call you, Merry thought before she could stop herself.

Morgan laughed at once, in a pleasant way, and announced dramatically, "Ah, it must be bad. We had better leave off on her before it gets worse, Bran. I will have to work double effort to improve the dismal state I am presently in. Both in where Merry prefers to sleep, and in what Merry prefers to call me."

Morgan went to open a bottle of wine and, not as expected, took out three glasses and filled them. Merry was disappointed with herself that her eyes moved with him.

He was such a fascinating man. Even so insignificant a thing as opening wine she watched in fascination, because he floated before her eyes, mysterious and beguiling.

He handed her a glass and went to his table, making a graceful gesture of arm for Brandon to join him. Looking at the delicate, finely made crystal, *French no doubt*, an elegant detail of his surrounding that were tastefully filled with elegant details to compliment him. She took a sip and watched them alertly.

Morgan's conduct tonight was new to Merry and put her nerves on edge. He was not usually suggestive in his talk about her. He never entertained the crew, except Mr. Craven, and when they were alone he rarely noticed her.

Was it possible her predicament here had grown all the more dangerous? Her eyes rounded without her knowing it, and she held him in a searching gaze, anxious and wary.

Morgan tossed down a card. Merry slowly released her tension since he seemed tame and focused on the game. She slid down like a feather floating to earth, back to a laying position on the bench. She was still watching, still nervous, lying curled on her side, head on pillow, and making nonsensical efforts to drink her wine without spilling it.

He threw down another card, stupider choice, and lost the hand.

They were halfway through the second bottle of wine when Merry realized Morgan hadn't won a hand all night. It was unflattering to her that he was losing because he had beaten her, *without* effort. He kept tossing down cards and had lost a considerable sum of money, for all that it seemed not to bother him.

He threw down a diamond, and she winced without

knowing she had done so facially. It was a hideous play. Morgan wasn't following this, at all, tonight. It took all of twenty minutes for her to figure out Mr. Seton's pattern of plays. His strategy was predictable.

Merry's thoughts were interrupted by laughter, amused and enticing, followed by a whispering command. "Come here."

Her eyes rounded in distress as she saw that the quiet directive of a finger was addressed to her. That she didn't immediately move brought the slow upward ascent of a brow, the kind Morgan made just before chiding that she needed learn how to obey an order. His finger moved again, only slightly. She wanted to tell him to go to the devil, but he had only one standing order with her. Not to flash her proclivity toward disobedience in front of the men.

He had said, *the burden of maintaining command would make it necessary to react unfavorably.*

He'd said that with one of those banal smiles that warned of unlimited possibilities of what unfavorably meant and she didn't want to find out what unfavorably meant. If she let her temper flash now it could have ugly consequences with Mr. Seton in the room. Reluctantly, she pushed up from the blankets.

Morgan settled his chin in the heel of a hand and favored her with a smile that could have raised blisters on the wood of the deck. It was pushing her luck to drag this out further, so reluctantly she sank in a chair beside him, and curled her legs up in front of her.

"I need your help," Morgan said. "I haven't won a hand all night."

Heat rose in Merry's cheeks, since her foolish heart seemed inclined to respond to every moment he set his attention upon her, wanting him to even while she dreaded it. Mr. Seton was watching in fascination in a way not lending to comfort.

It may be unwise, but she said it anyway, "You deserve to lose. You are playing horribly."

He let his gaze wander from her, and herded the cards into a pile that he collected in a single palm.

"What do you suggest I do about my playing horribly?"

"Change to piquet. You are better at playing piquet. You certainly can't be worse."

"It is ungentlemanly to switch games when you're losing. I have a *better idea.*"

Morgan's *better ideas* accompanying a smile were a disquieting thing. Merry tensed.

"Do you think you can be generous with your charms tonight?"

She had no idea what to make of that, or how to respond. She eased a hair back from him.

"I need a touch of Merry."

Openmouthed with dismay, in a frenzy of enflamed and rapid speculations, it was by iron will that Merry didn't hit him as he circled her wrist in a gently holding band of blood warmed fingers.

She felt an utter fool at once. All he did was hold her trembling fingers above the deck and ask her to cut them. She took the deck, divided it, and with an exasperated slap set it before him on the table.

She was exasperated with herself, with her skittishness with him, and what she suspected was his amusement over her skittishness. She was behaving like a spineless ninny. His next words didn't surprise her.

"Kiss them," he said.

She glared at Morgan, smacked the deck with her tense lips, in a way decidedly angry, a touch loud and seemed to only add to his merriment in this.

Furious, she exclaimed, "You got me out of bed to kiss a deck of cards because you are losing. You are a vexing man, Captain."

The eyes he fixed on her were sparkling, like blackberries. "I got you out of bed to kiss me, Little One, but you seemed not inclined, and I am a *flexible* man. Now, Bran is jealous of the shirt, we are both jealous of the cards, and it should be a more interesting game. Which card carries the kiss of Merry?"

He bent her a charming smile before he began to divide out the cards. Merry, desperate to hide the humiliating blush on her face, curled into a tighter ball, cheek resting on knees, staying because somehow she knew Morgan expected her to.

His orders at times were unperceivable dictates, received through keener senses than those of eyes and ears, and always obeyed.

Drowsy in the chair, without thought, she took his wineglass, finished it, and started to run the edge of the glass against her lip in an effort to keep herself awake. Slowly, she felt herself pulled into sleep.

"Are you selling? If you are, I am buying."

Morgan shifted his gaze from Merry to find Brandon's amber eyes running on her *not* angelically.

The practice of transferring women by sale was one he'd never interfered with on his ship. It was a commonplace occurrence in this world at sea, one he tolerated, despised, and did not participate in. He was far from an angel himself. However, he was not a defiler, and that was the ultimate defilement of a woman, to reduce her to a product of commerce.

"I don't think you can afford her," Morgan said, as he took the wineglass before it slipped from Merry's tiny fingers. She had fallen asleep.

More eager, Brandon countered, "Try me. Set a price."

Morgan leaned back in his chair and arched a brow. Brandon was determined. He was eager in his body. He was young. Morgan's black eyes narrowed on the younger man's face.

"I have set a price. It will cost you a single..." he let the pause develop slowly, menacingly, then added dramatically bored, "... a single bullet between your eyes. Depending on how unsure my hand is after two bottles of wine, you may still live to enjoy your purchase. Are you still interested in buying? I find that I am in the mood to sell."

Brandon sprang up from his chair, as though he's been doused in burning oil, but was too cautious to leave without permission. The color was gone from his pretty boy face, his bronze tan looking dull without blood to give it hue.

"I didn't mean to offend you with the offer, Varian."

Morgan smiled darkly. He reached for the glass he'd taken from Merry, filled it, and then took a sip

"I am not offended. It is natural that one of you has inquired, given her visible merits. I have set a price. I am uncomplicated in commerce. Let the men know. A single price. A bullet between the eyes. The price of ownership. The price of a second offer being made to me. The price of touching her. I thought I made that clear on deck today. I must not have. I should practice at being more direct."

Morgan looked up as he gathered the cards.

"Please, sit. I am not done playing with you."

~~~

Merry stretched, coming awake pleasantly bathed in the aftermath of a very restful sleep, opened her eyes and shocked herself by where she'd had it.

A frantic dart of her gaze showed her a pillow undisturbed, puffed up beside her, which she gratefully accepted as evidence she had been in Morgan's bed alone. However, another dart of her gaze told her he was still in the cabin, not a gratefully accepted evidence of the state of affairs of her morning.

Morgan was sitting at his table, picking at his breakfast plate, black eyes reading from a copy of Voltaire's *Micromegas.*

An edition in French, no less, Merry thought peevishly. *He is an educated man. Whatever other things he may be that I am far from fathoming. Why am I in his bed?*

An amused voice cut through her thoughts.

"So, the beautiful detainee wakes. It was worth waiting to see Sleeping Beauty stir in my sheets. You look rather charming there. Stop troubling yourself over why you are in my bed. It is harmless. I drank and played cards until dawn. You fell asleep in the chair. It was a shorter walk with you in my arms to the bed. Don't work yourself into virgin panic. It is unnecessary. I am pure of heart in this, laziness."

She frowned, puzzled by his presence, wondering how Morgan saw her when his eyes never lifted from book.

The sun beyond the stern windows told her it was midmorning. It was an uncommonly late hour for Morgan to be breakfasting.

She gave herself hearty pats on her back for the calm manner in which she climbed from his bed, and her ability to maintain a little dignified composure even garbed in his shirt. She padded across the cabin to curl in a chair beside him.

Picking absently at her plate, she carefully studied Morgan while he ate. Her eyes went on their own to wander the handsome lines of his face, the rich tones in his dark hair, the bronze tan of his skin, and the graceful arrangement of his hands.

She paused for a moment in her study of his hands. They were extremely large hands. They should terrify her. She was surprised they didn't, and then in start, knew why.

They never moved with anything but fluid gentleness, no

190

matter how terrifying he could be at times.

Her gazes floated upward from the tip of a long tanned finger, to the well-muscled bicep, across his broad shoulder, and then along the smooth skin of his neck that ran over a molded chin.

He is a very handsome man, Merry reluctantly admitted to herself. She shifted her eyes to his and found those black orbs watching her.

Blushing and scowling, not watching her knife, she exclaimed, "I demand that you take me back to Falmouth."

"Ah. We are getting this out of the way early today, a change in strategy. Catch me in the morning while I am pleasant. Though not a good strategy today to catch me after I have seen you in my sheets because I will be inclined..." A linger pause, then, "No."

"Ah. Laziness, a single word. I demand that you let me go. You have no right."

Not watching her task, the knife slipped, cutting her thumb.

"Damn you."

Droplets of blood from her finger began plopping to table from the torn flesh that was pulsing painfully. Trying to stem the flow of red, she began to cry fiercely, hating the tears, but there were times when one just didn't have enough strength to be brave.

"You need be more careful," Morgan said softly. He lifted Merry's thumb to brush it once lightly with his lips before he wrapped his handkerchief around it. "I can't let you go, Little One. The rules are set in this. Answer my questions and I will release you."

Merry was beyond caring if she sounded pathetic. She was sobbing, and when she spoke her voice was weak.

"I miss my family. I want to go home."

She didn't look up as Morgan rose from the table. It was humiliating to sit here, crying before him. She felt him run the slope of her cheek with a thumb.

On a whispering soft voice, he said, "I am sorry. I know how you feel, Little One. I miss home, too."

The cabin door clicked closed. Merry could tell by the emptiness of the air around her that Morgan was gone.

He stayed away from the cabin all day. She began to wonder if she were wearing down his refusals. It was late in the night when Morgan's returning presence and a pungent smoke, unlike any pipe tobacco scent she'd smelled before, stirred her from sleep. Her drowsy eyes searched and found him in his chair.

On a tired whisper, hopelessly curious about each detail of this man, she studied his pipe and asked, "That is an odd smell. What kind of tobacco are you smoking?"

Merry had startled him. She could tell by the flashes in Morgan's black eyes. However, the smile that surfaced was wicked and lazy.

On a melting whisper, he said, "Go back to sleep, Little One. I am smoking your innocence."

Merry's eyes rounded in fear and confusion. Morgan laughed softly.

"Go to sleep, Merry. You need to help me sometimes. My conscience is a weak creature. We shouldn't trust it."

CHAPTER NINE

Merry sat on the top step of the hatchway, in a pale pink gown formerly owned by Christina Wythford. Indy had taken all his clothes back, in an effort to discourage her troublesome conduct.

She was watching Shay polish a sword beneath the hazy sunlight of an overcast sky. He was in good spirits. They were preparing to drop anchor in Ireland, just south of Galway Bay in a cove along its rocky shore.

Everything seemed to have sipped a wild spirit. The sea roiled in riotous swirls of crashing, white tipped waves against the rocks. The air capered through the canvas laden of heady flavors as it made the sails flap.

She had stood at the rail for hours, staring in fascination at her first glimpse of Ireland. It seemed an untamed land, a vast sweeping expanse, haunted and magical.

Earlier, Morgan had ordered her below, but seeing her face fall, he'd relented and surprised her by allowing her to stay on the steps of the hatchway.

Across the deck from her, Morgan stood with Tom Craven doing an alert assessment of the wind, followed by the graceful gestures of his arms as he made some comment about the sails.

His dancer smooth strides carried him to the mizzen where he immediately went into discussion with Mr. Seton. Shay had informed her he was the sailing master and the twenty-five year old youngest son of a cotton planter from a place called, Georgia, in America.

Apparently Mr. Seton possessed a genius mind that hid behind the carelessly foppish mannerism of a dandy. He was an uncommonly handsome man, long golden waves framing a face of boyish good looks and bright amber eyes. Whenever he saw Merry, he sent her his dazzling smile. He had gone to sea with Morgan four years past.

Morgan's crew, though in possession of its share of the rough lot, was not always the scourge of the sea, as Merry had expected them to be.

They were, if one were inclined to study them, an interesting and fascinating assembly of men. Morgan not excluded.

Merry's eyes strayed to him again, following the flutter of his dark hair being caressed by the wind. She had stared at him too long.

Beside him, Mr. Seton, facing toward her, had begun to grin in earnest. Thankfully, Morgan's back was to her, or she would have felt completely pathetic. Studying the man was a dangerous compulsion, better to stop.

Shay gave the lass a guarded look, realizing she had stopped talking some minutes past, and then saw the cause standing by the mizzen.

"Sit farther back out of the sun, lass. Ye've got enough burn from yesterday. Did you put that salve on I gave ye?"

Merry nodded, eased back against the polished wood wall and managed a slight smile. "How did you come to be with Morgan? You are such a kind-hearted boy. I would have never expected you and piracy to have made a pact."

Shay looked up in his work then, surprised and pleased by her question. He loved to tell a tale and Merry could tell that clearly this one was going to be a big one.

"It weren't exactly a chosen profession for me, Merry lass, I happened upon it with no choice," he began, his voice fluid and full of humor. "I was thirteen. A foolish, mischievous boy. Me da had left Ireland for America, one step in front of the hangman. I was left behind with his rebel band." He bent her a meaningful look. "They weren't exactly pleased to have me, if ye can believe that. Wasn't good fer much but making people laugh and playing ridiculous games with the other lads. I could invent some wild games, Merry. I was sit'n on hills, like I always did when the men rode out, watching and playing with the children some ridiculous game with rocks and pebbles. There I am, huddled over the dirt, when all around turns quiet. Round eyed, I look up. There was Himself."

Merry was shocked. "Morgan?"

Shay nodded in satisfaction. "Aye. Weren't no ordinary mon, even I could tell that. Spoke like landlord, so of course I feared we were done fer. Just standing there, he was, all in black like the devil, with those black eyes of his a' fixed on me. I was supposed to protect the children, mind ye, and here we had let Himself catch us."

Shay paused to make a few swipes with the rag on his sword as Merry stared at him in frustration. The boy loved to drag out a story at times, and she was intrigued in spite of herself.

Why on earth would Morgan go to the Irish countryside and snatch a boy? An idiotic boy playing with rocks, at that.

"Are you going to go on and tell me the rest, or am I going to have to hit you?"

A wave of pleasant mirth came with the upward tilt of his face. "Ye're not patient at all. I am Irish, so let me be telling me tale me way." Frowning, he grumbled, "Now ye made me forget where I was in the telling."

Frustrated, Merry reminded, "You were only on the hills playing with rocks."

"Ah." He sat back with a lopsided smile. "He gave us all a

once over, fixed his gaze on me, and out thin air, says he, 'Are ye Ian Shay?' I almost died, right there, I did. Here was the devil out of nowhere calling me by me name, no less."

Shay's eyes closed then, and he gave a gentle shake of his blond head.

"I thought fer sure it was the hangman coming fer me, instead of me da. But, there's something in those eyes that would need a stronger heart than mine to lie and before I knew it said aye, 'I, be him.' Without a word he picked me up by the edge of me ragged collar and drug me aboard this ship. When I saw the ship I knew who Himself was. Terrified was I, Merry lass. To have Morgan in Ireland knowing me by name was worse than the hangman."

"But what did he want with you?" The tale made no sense at all.

"I be getting to that if ye be let 'n me. Brought me to his cabin, he did, and worried was I. Ye hear frightful stories about Englishmen and pirates, as a child in Ireland. Morgan was both. I was sit'n there, quivering and crying. It's then me fixed on a boy sitting on the bench scowling at me. Weren't yer normal boy, Merry lass, I can tell ye that. Himself was frightening enough, but the boy and them scars, ye just don't know what fear is until ye've suffered the emptiness of the eyes cutting into ye."

Knowing, excited, being pulled along in the tale, Merry said, "Was it Indy?"

"Indy, himself. Whatever they wanted, I wanted no part of it. Would have left the cabin, if Himself hadn't been blocking door. Then, polite as can be, with those smooth manners, after dragging me here by me neck, says he to me, 'Ye may sail on my ship and when ye reach yer maturity, ye will share in every prize we take. Ye will die a wealthy mon.' Almost fainted, I did. But I wasn't so fixed on run'n then. Then Himself, he adds, 'Ye will have duties, and so long as ye obey my command, ye will have a place in my crew, as long as ye desire one. Until ye are older, ye will have one duty. Ye will share a cabin with the boy, be his companion, and teach him to play.' And he walks from the cabin as though it were decided, leave'n me alone with that fearsome creature."

"Play?" She began to laugh and slapped him in the leg. "I should have known this was going to be blarney from you. How funny it must be for you to daggle me along with that."

"No, no, Merry lass, it's the truth of it," Shay said forcefully. "Aye, I thought it bizarre then meself. Later I understood the madness of it. He wanted the boy to be a boy, and the boy was not. He was a fierce, snarling gruesome thing, that used to spend half his day beating me up and the other half locking me from me cabin. Ye wouldn't know how he was then, by how he is now, lass. Five years has brought a more powerful change than ye'd know. Ye think him terrifying now, but we're almost friends, we are. I thought it chance Morgan came for me. Himself be born with a silver cutlass in one hand, and crystal ball in the other, so I never bothered much about Himself showing up in Ireland knowing me by name. But it weren't chance. Himself come looking for me. Years passed before Himself told me that he owed me da a debt. I stayed on when Himself told me I could go, and got me bunk and quite a bit of money now. It's happy I am that he came for me."

It was mysterious. "Who is Indy to Morgan that he should do such a thing?"

"Nothing at all, that's the strangest part. The old timers say he just some wild ruin Morgan found, by chance, chained on a ship one day. That mon has uncommon decency. Look what Himself has done fer me. Longer yer here, ye will come to know the decency part."

"I don't understand any of this," Merry whispered, looking

197

at her knit fingers.

Shay shrugged lazily. "Neither do I, Merry lass, but that's the mon. Nothing ever makes sense. It's not supposed to. He wants it that way. Look at how he treats ye, lass."

That brought the memory of being kissed by Morgan, and a wash of color on her cheeks.

Indignantly, she said, "He doesn't treat me, any way, at all."

With unexpectedly sharp eyes, he said, "That's the point of it, lass. Ye would have been ruined on any other ship the first night. Raped by the captain then tossed to the crew, what was left of ye left fer dead. But, there Himself has ye. Treats ye like a gentleman, he does. Leaves ye alone because ye not be want'n it, when he doesn't have to do anything that he doesn't want to do. Does that make sense to ye, lass?"

She said nothing and gave a simple shrug. She needed no more things to add to her foolhardy fascination of Morgan.

She settled her chin in hands, focused on the sword, and fought a familiar battle to push him from her mind.

A sudden, flapping chorus from the sails broke her train of thought and caused her to look up. Merry's excited face was tilted skyward, her eyes darting with the trek of a huge cluster of birds soaring low through the sails.

"It's a North American Plover," Morgan said.

She found the captain standing above her, having noiselessly crossed the deck. He was smiling as he waited for her attention.

Skittishness settled in, its ever-present whim from head to toe at the sight of Morgan. She strove for something to say to him that wouldn't come out either clumsy or childish. It was the first time Morgan had ever sought her out on deck. She wondered why he was doing so now.

That made Merry tense.

"I have never seen a plover. At least if I have, I never noticed it," she said, after an embarrassingly long pause.

"That tells me you've not been in Ireland before." Morgan sank down until they were at eye level. "They come across the Atlantic from America."

There was a carelessly charming smile on Morgan's handsome face, but above it, his black eyes had focused on her and were alertly probing.

"Perhaps I have been to Ireland and have just not noticed the birds," Merry retorted, proud with herself that she'd managed it, since the liveliness of her flesh usually catapulted her brain into malfunctioning stupidity.

Her words made him grin. "Somehow I doubt that, Little One. You are a girl who would notice the birds."

Morgan's unexpectedly approving tone Merry found flattering, strangely enough, though she suspected he was not the kind of man who found women who noticed birds appealing.

Against all force of her will, the blush came as quickly as the power of speech deserted her.

"The decks are going to be crowded with men and activity once we drop anchor. I have ordered Indy to put a bath in my cabin. Run along, Little One. Don't make a ruin of my sheets," he said softly. Then, he left them.

Not one ounce of that exchange did Merry's internal arrangements any good, nor did it please her that she obeyed him without pause.

She allowed herself a leisurely bath in the cabin, since Morgan's words let her know he'd be well occupied on deck for hours. She dressed in the change of clothes Indy had left for her.

They were odd clothes, common. A gray skirt, a billowy white peasant style blouse, and crudely made leather sandals.

They were not a lady's garments. She wondered where they had come from, and why the boy had left them for her.

Merry settled on the window bench, combing the knots from her curls, and watched as the ship dropped anchor. An hour later, as the sun was dipping, she caught sight of Morgan's, impossible to miss, towering figure in a boat loaded with men going to shore. He was laughing in evident amusement over something Mr. Craven was saying. He was a heartlessly appealing man when laughter softened his imposing face. She followed him with her eyes until he disappeared from view.

Their location seemed a strange place to drop anchor, since she knew Morgan was meeting the Earl of Camden here. She had expected a seaport of some kind, but they had gone ashore on a dramatic, uninhabited stretch of the Irish coast. Not a village or a port within sight.

As the hours passed, she understood why they'd dropped anchor here. The lush greenery had gone through a startling metamorphosis with the passing day. Bon fires, made high with wood, blazed from the earth, dotting the expanse of land before her, the glaring flames setting aglow a scene of wild gaiety that she could taste even from here.

With the arrival of darkness came hundreds of men to the hills, the majority of the crew mixed with what looked to be Irish locals. Among the revelers, to her annoyance, there were women.

Her eyes scanned the riotous gathering, watching as bottles were raised, seeing instruments being played, though she could not hear them. The wild zeal and vigor of their dancing, their talking, and their shouting was not diminished by distance or the soundless confines of the cabin. Watching it brought a slow hungry burn to her soul.

Indy had locked the cabin door after clearing away her bath, something he hadn't done in over a week. It was clear

Morgan would not return tonight. He didn't trust her not to try to escape.

She pushed back her curls, cursed herself a fool, and tried to pick out his figure amid the crowd. Staring out the window, the hour deep in the night, she fell asleep, as she was, cheek against glass, insides anxiously churning.

She came awake, sometime later, with the feel of something warm in the palm of her hand, and a whispering voice cutting through the cabin silence, "If I have ever seen a face in need of fun, it is yours, Little One."

Merry instantly jerked back her hand. Her eyes flew open to find Morgan crouched beside her at the window bench. She hadn't expected Morgan to come back tonight. Not with the party on the hills. Not when there were women there.

Feeling her pulse escalate, all at once, Merry became aware of a difference in him. Morgan cut a powerfully striking figure tonight.

Studying him, she saw that there was that same aura of energetic boldness, an aura of flamboyance to the manly presentation she had not seen since *Grave's End*.

He was purposely, dramatically, turned out in a cardinal red shirt, parted three buttons at his iron chest, dark breeches topped by high polished wine colored boots, midnight hair, and midnight eyes. He seemed to hold the star-points from the night in the even white teeth of his smile, and the dancing light in the blackness of his gaze. He carried with him the sweet essence of wine on his breath and the scent of heather grass whispering on his flesh. Perhaps it was the wine, the revelry, or whatever he'd been doing ashore, but there was an added vibrancy to his presence.

As much as she hated him, she couldn't escape what her own eyes could see, or the affect it had on her.

Searching his face, she tried to figure out what he was up

to. Morgan was clearly in a good mood. She stared into those enigmatic eyes, wondering what he had meant by *fun*.

Wariness and anger rose inside of her, a bulwark against whatever Morgan's game with her tonight. She snapped back, "I don't wish to have fun. Go back to shore and leave me alone."

"I am taking you to shore tonight, Little One," he said, his tone like a caress. "You are a very wild girl and you should be, at least once, where all things are wild."

"I don't wish to go anywhere with you," she said trying not to meet the alluring darkness of his eyes. "I wish to sleep."

Morgan's answering smile cut through the armor around her heart like a steel spar.

"Would you come with me, Merry?" he asked slowly. "I can see that you want to. I would like to share what's left of this night with you on the Irish coast."

The urge to go with him surged upward out of nowhere and was nearly overwhelming. It would do her no good to fight him in this, but his invitation was melting her resistance, and the temptation was almost beyond her power to resist.

Merry was proud of herself that she was able to maintain her dignity, not jump to accept, and said instead, "Aren't you afraid I will try to escape?"

His grin told her he wasn't.

He said in a melting whisper, "Come with me, Merry. Let me watch you drink of Ireland."

Let me watch you drink of Ireland. Morgan's whispering voice made her shiver.

The man could be appealing to a fault when he wanted to be. Merry hated the fact that every part of her wanted to go with him. Wanted to feel that wildness on the hills that she could taste through the window glass. What a pitiful girl she'd become.

She went with him topside and into a boat.

Ocean spray lightly misted her clothes and hair as she sat beside Morgan, while the men rowed. When the boat reached the shore, he lifted her into his arms, carried her until she was beyond the water, set her on her feet, then casually held out his hand.

She paused for a moment, and stared at those long, tanned fingers. Cautiously lifting her gaze to meet his eyes, those black orbs simmered with amusement. Irritated with herself, she realized the offer of his hand was an order, not a request. Flushing hotly, she took his hand.

It was a dazzling night, luminous of moonlight, fires, and stars. The passion of the celebration swept Merry's flesh even before she was within the gathering. It brought an unreal wakefulness to her senses. The sky above seemed blacker and more littered with brightly glowing stars than any night sky she had before seen. The smell of the countryside, richer than any she had ever breathed, and the air was crackling with strange spirited strains of music. The long pits she had seen from the cabin were filled with chunks of roasting meat and surrounded by dancing revelers, inebriated faces engaged in vivacious chatter and men engaged in the not so discreet pursuits of pleasures.

The women were strange to Merry, their boldness with the men making her drop her eyes in heated embarrassment. She caught enough of a look at them to realize Morgan had dressed her similarly in their costumes. Her simple attire was everywhere.

She swallowed a tight lump in her throat, sharply insulted and humiliated by these clothes, which were his affront.

"How dare you dress me as though I were common?"

Morgan halted in mid-step. "Since I have no idea who or what you are, there is no cause to accuse me of insult."

"I am not common, and you have dressed me as such."

Morgan's only answer was a chuckle that sent shivers up Merry's spine. How foolish she had been to come with him without a fight.

Before tonight he never appeared to take much notice in her. That he was doing so now screamed danger and, too late, she was hearing the warning. Behind that elegant and handsome male exterior was a mind capable of committing any atrocity.

His black gaze flickered over her as he held out his hand again in a commanding, economical gesture.

"You don't want me to leave you here on the path, Little One. You are much safer at my side. Come."

There was no logical reason for her willingness to obey, but Merry found herself taking his hand. Staring at the ground, more than mildly furious with herself, she realized some unfathomable impulse inside of her betrayed her with this man, even in his most aggravating moments.

Frantically, Merry studied the people around her, wondering if she could find assistance to help her escape her captivity. As though he could read her thoughts, Morgan's hand tightened as he guided Merry beside him on the path.

Disappointment settled heavy in her stomach as she realized it was unlikely she'd find any willing to betray Morgan to assist her. All around them, eyes followed with something akin to awe or worship. The Irish celebrated Morgan being here, when logic warned that they shouldn't. She would not find an ally against him among these people. She could see it on their faces when they turned to take note of his towering form moving among them.

There were many tiny clusters within this one giant gathering. They moved past several groups, until Merry's eyes fixed on one gathering and knew instantly that was where he taking her.

High on the hill was a larger cluster where Brandon Seton,

Shay, and Tom Craven were joined by no less than a dozen of the rebels.

It was made comfortable by an open fire pit. Elegant even amid the barren countryside by all those finer, always tasteful, and often out of setting luxuries, which seemed a necessary part of existence for Morgan.

He had impeccable taste in all things, she realized. She recognized the patterns of the china, silver, and crystal, chosen in a manner that could put to shame the finest London hostess. The excellent selection of wines and brandies, and the delicious foods that would be served with the meats sizzling above flames. The soft fur draping the ground, with closer inspection, she realized was sable, its darkness speckled by bright brocade pillows, tossed freely for comfort.

She took it all in, in a sweeping glance that only confused her more. There was more here tossed on the ground than these Irish locals would make in lifetime. Yet it was clear, they resented Morgan not at all. Not for his wealth, or his extravagant displays of himself, or his obvious heritage. He was such a commanding figure, so baffling in this, his ability to be whatever he wanted to be in all circumstance. Even here, where what he wanted to be should not have worked well.

Merry stood rigid at Morgan's side as he made a gentlemanly round of introducing her to the rebel men.

Their stares were openly bold and appreciative of her, without even a mild hint of reserve. The way they looked at her should have insulted her. Yet, she found that it didn't. Their praise-filled words floated around her on musical voices full of vigor like Shay's, voices that were honest and kind. They were rough men, earthy and without adornments, wildness and gentleness somehow blending at once on the surface of their flesh and in their speech. Their manner was flattering of her and direct in their treatment.

Merry liked the men of Ireland, instantly.

Seated tensely at Morgan's side, a little ill at ease in this utterly unfamiliar setting, Merry watched everything unfolding around her. She tried to make reason of why Morgan had brought her here with him.

Color burned her face as her gaze fixed on a member of the crew, apart from the gathering supported against a tree, a young woman in his arms, straddling his bent leg, clinging in a knotted tie of limbs as they were madly engaged in a frantic flurry of kisses and caresses.

Morgan's arm slipped around her, bringing her to rest against his side, the clasp protective and supportive. He must have been able to feel the tension curling in her. When she sought his eyes, their wine hazed depths sent her a smile, and then his fingers brought his wine glass to her lips.

"I know some of this is shocking to you, Little One," he whispered, he mouth close to her ear. "But, if you want to sip of Ireland, you must sip of all of her."

He fed her slowly, brushing the droplets from her lips as his fingers on her back began to move in slow glides. Quickly turning her face from him, she noticed a flood of curious stares studying them from the circle around the pit.

Uncertain at first, Merry was reluctant to be drawn into the rapid and turbulent conversation. On her left was an attractive blond man, who she learned was Shay's uncle and one of the leaders in the rebel band.

Being told of their relationship by Morgan, she could see that there was a connection of blood in the lines of his face and the liveliness of his eyes. He had the same splendidly vivacious manner. It took Ryan Shay little effort to get a smile from her. Once having gotten that, he got the rest in the short space of time it took Morgan to send for a plate of food for her.

Their conversation was intensely fast and far beyond

frivolous, hotly political and focusing on the turbulent events around the world. She was from England, the center of the world and the center of its wars. These men of Ireland wanted her insights and opinions as no man outside her family ever had, discussing such matters that were never discussed with her on English soil. In the stuffy drawing rooms of London, in the constant blur of social amusements, in nineteen years, not a soul had ever asked her what was in her head.

Being a Merrick, she had come by a wealth of knowledge never shared, but nurtured in the quick intelligence of her mind. Fighting to remain silent through the fast moving exchange proved a useless endeavor. Before she could stop herself, she was standing toe to toe arguing politics with the infamous Captain Morgan and a rebel band.

They moved in a flurry from Wellington and the battles in France, to the difficulties Prevost was confronting in Canada, to the problems in Flanders, to Vice Admiral Cochrane and his war in America.

"How can you be certain that if the battles in France end, England won't concentrate her armies on her former colonies, lass?" asked Ryan persistently. "The *Times* keeps stirred the flames of fury toward the United States. When I was last in London, the mood was not to be merciful."

"We don't have men for an invasion force," said Merry in frustration. "We can't even send reinforcements for our positions in Canada. We are wasting men and money, which would be better put to service in Europe. Rather than to support a series of intolerable forces of will, which we have imposed by our Orders in Council. We have provoked a war we are not prepared to fight, for the worst reason of all."

"All reasons for war don't meet the cost of war. What is the worst reason for war, Little One?" Morgan asked, his black eyes alertly searching her and sharp.

"You should know the answer to that better than I, sir," she said, feeling her mood shift and dim, now that Morgan's full attention was upon her.

"Me?" Morgan was smiling. "Why should I know better than you?"

Staring at Morgan, not trusting his tone and fearing his attention, Merry whispered reluctantly, "I am a woman."

"The ability to understand politics is not beyond the female intellect. If anyone here thought that tonight, you have destroyed that incorrect belief, remarkably well."

His compliment made her insides shudder. The touch of his eyes made her burn. When Morgan wanted to beguile, he certainly could. He was not beyond the rare and skillful acts of charm. The clever thoughts he concealed, too often, behind his unfailingly disarming allure he could wield as a hacksaw or a scalpel.

Merry gathered every scrap of coldness that was shooting through her in warning and wove it against her foolish body's unwanted response to the undeniable appeal of the man.

In a voice she hoped sounded cold and disinterested, Merry said, "Because we are fighting a war with America that was born of British male arrogance. You are British. And you are..."

"...arrogant?" His black eyes were sparkling like fire embers.

Wishing heartily that she hadn't been so stupid as to let down her guard with Morgan, she said in a voice embarrassingly thin, "I was going to say male."

He threw back his head and laughed. He brushed a wayward curl from her brow. Morgan's gaze shifted from her to the men and began to sparkle.

"Is she not everything I said she was, Ryan?" Morgan asked, resting his long body more closely against her.

208

Merry's face reddened beneath the touch of Ryan's eyes just as he said, "She's a highflier, indeed, Varian."

The world affairs took a natural turn to the conflict in Ireland. It had been a prelude, the necessity to know where England's energies were drawn as they discussed their current political problems, and course of action.

As she listened to Morgan's practical suggestion on how they should proceed with the Chief Secretary of Ireland, she fell silent. Staring down into her wineglass, Merry realized, as the hours drifted away, she understood Morgan even less.

All afternoon, she'd watched from his cabin the long boats going ship to shore packed full of supplies and leaving empty. He was giving the rebels supplies to aid their struggles against England. If what Ryan Shay had said was true, Morgan was not even allowing them to pay

Having long followed the exploits of Morgan in the *Times*, she could run through his crimes like a butcher's bill. Yet somehow, the world had missed this. Morgan supported the Irish rebels and had done so for half a decade. It only added to the mystery of this man.

Shay had said that Morgan had slipped into the world with a silver cutlass in hand, but after a fortnight with him, Merry knew with certainty it was a silver spoon instead. No matter what words sinister, seductive, or obscurely menacing danced from his lips, the low voice that carried them was unmistakably cultured. She had watched him enough to know that his habits were meticulous. Like a gentleman with a subtle grace he did each thing. His wide and varied reading material, betrayed not only an intelligent, but also an educated mind. Whatever Morgan was, at some point, Merry was certain he had entered this world *British* and *highly privileged*.

Giving supplies to the rebels seemed an intensely personal act against England, when Morgan should have no interest in politics, at all. He was a man of no country. He was a pirate.

She recalled Shay's words earlier that morning: *Nothing about the mon ever makes sense.* Would she ever understand Morgan? And why did she have the fearful suspicion that her fate depended upon understanding him?

Searching Morgan's face alertly, she asked, "Why do you hate England?"

His heavy lids widened, just a trifle, above his black gaze. Delicate surprise augmented his eyes.

She'd listened quietly throughout the discussion of Ireland. More than an hour passed, in deep thought, without her saying a word. Now, when she did speak, it was in direct question of him, when he was not a man who allowed inquiries about himself. It was a bold thing to do, given who he was.

A tremor passed through her body as Merry realized this was not wise. Morgan must have felt it. She unexpectedly found his hand moving to her face, the slow decent of a fingertip across her cheek, and the warmth rising in her skin to meet it. His palm rested in a cup on her face, his thumb gliding the line of her chin as he studied her for awhile.

Finally, quietly, he said, "I don't hate England, Little One, I hate her cruelty. Her cruelty and what she means to do to you."

Flickers of light from the fire bounced against Morgan's great black eyes, and were held there, shimmering. It was unclear to Merry whether the reflection in them was inward or outward. His voice and expression had betrayed neither.

"Me? England has done nothing to me. Only you have."

The amused curl of his lips looked almost to hold a blend of anger and sadness. "I suspect you've spent all your years fighting the wind of British male arrogance, condescension, and the limiting, stifling social rule to protect who you are. You fight so much because you've learned to fight hard to protect yourself, because you are more than what they expect you to be. You have a mind that could argue politics in the House of Commons, but I doubt the London dandies would be pleased to know that, if they were ever wise enough to discover it. England demands that you be little more than a pretty creature who spends her days in marriage, amusing yourself with social gatherings, children and water-colors. You, however, have other wants. England fights to take your freedom and you fight not to let her. The stuff of tragedies. A war where no one wins."

Furious, she countered, "You are wrong. You're the only one to take my freedom."

"Did I take it? Or am I giving it to you, Little One?" he said pointedly. "Would you be in England this night, arguing politics as you have here? Or, would you be dancing, hating it, and fighting to keep free of men who force you to listen to insipid drivel because it is fashionable, and you are not supposed to want more? If you had opened your mouth and proved that you had a brain, would the man at your side be charmed, outraged or censorious? I don't expect you to be other than who you are, Merry. I enjoy being in the company of a woman who, in all ways, reveals herself to be remarkable. Whether socially proper or not, in ways I find to my liking. You tell me, Little One, which circumstance are you free in? The one where you are yourself, or the one where you are trapped into being what others demand? Which circumstance is cruelty?"

Was there anything beyond the discovery of Morgan's heartlessly capable mind? Without knowing anything of who she was, Morgan was perfect in his insights of this.

It made Merry's temper flare because no matter how much about him she learned, she couldn't weave it together in a pattern that made sense. There was no rhyme or reason to be found in him. He eluded understanding as effortlessly as he read the world around him.

As though he could read her thoughts and were amused by them, his large hands fanned her face, holding her beneath his black eyes that were so intense, at this moment, they were too hard to meet. Merry pulled free of him, quickly turning her face.

Rapidly she shifted her gaze away from him. She realized they were being watched, by every man around the pit.

Merry's expression was all too familiar to one man. Shay sprang from his place on other side of the pit. He looked at Morgan and asked if he could dance with her. He nearly fell flat, when the captain lifted his glass to lips and gave a slight move of his head in ascent.

"Come on, Merry lass, dance with me," Shay boomed. "Let's celebrate this night, and celebrate being Irish."

At first Merry declined, no longer in a disposition that desired dancing, furious that Morgan had given Shay permission to ask her. Furious that he'd just treated her as though she were nothing, a possession he owned and could hand off to another, as he was doing so now. But Shay was a force that could not be denied. He cajoled, he wheedled, he implored, and in the end Merry took his hand.

Peevish, Merry went the few strides to the area of the hills crowed with dancing. She felt strange in the music, even stranger, watching the wild movements around her. It was so odd, so full of passion and without control. How would she manage this when even a waltz with her could be disastrous?

Reluctantly she took Shay's hands. For a big clumsy man, he was sure-footed and smooth in this, graceful and certain in his movements. She watched, tried to follow his dancing legs, and then, her own mirth came, making her body less strained, her steps more fluid. The joyful energy bathed her in its warmth. She felt herself surrendered to the wild spirit around her that was so like her own.

Before she knew it, Merry Merrick, the daughter of the esteemed Duke of Dorset, was on the Irish coast, dancing with a rebel band.

Laughing, her leg flurries sent her off balance and his hand brought her body into him. Instead of shocking her, she was surprised she found the contact agreeable. An arm snaked around her waist as Merry was turned away from the boy and pulled into dancing with one of the rebels. It was scandalous, the way the man's arms encircled her waist. She had always hated dancing. She had never allowed men to touch her, but here she found pleasure in matching the jaunty steps, her forehead falling against his chest, her hair a wild cloud around her.

Smiling, Merry lifted her face upward and when she did her caught sight of Morgan still seated on the hill. That black gaze, burning and intense, was unwaveringly fixed upon her.

There was instant reaction all through her body, a pulsing and running of blood, as she wondered how long he'd been staring at her. Color ran her cheeks as his eyes did a slow roam over her and then lifted to hold hers again.

Someone shoved a tankard into her hand, the sudden intrusion welcomed to Merry. She shifted the goblet to hide her face, to hide the flush she knew would be too telling, and took a hearty drink of the wine.

The glass was gone from her fingers as though by magic, and the rebel had both her hands again, dragging her along with him into the press of heated bodies.

She tilted her head so she could see if Morgan were still watching, not knowing what possessed her to do so since she had left the pit angry with him.

Fire shot through her as his gaze met hers again. She tilted her head back, her long curls dancing behind her. Even that added to the odd vividness in her flesh. The pattern of the dance went on, from partner to partner, and back to Shay.

Carefully, she slanted another look at Morgan. He was still watching her, and his long finger began to run the rim of his glass. Almost as if he were willing it, her flesh began to tingle. She could feel Morgan, as though he were touching her, when he was only touching her with his eyes.

Someone grabbed her around the waist, spinning her away from Shay. She tossed her head and made a silly little move with her hip, then look back at Morgan as sharp currents shot all through her.

Quivering, excited, and not knowing why, she moved her body boldly into the rebel, oddly wanting to know if it would irritate Morgan. Then, she looked, the trembling heightened as she searched his face to see if there were a change in him. Nothing could be picked up by her eyes, but it was there in her keener senses. The heat in her body and the trembling of her flesh grew fiercer. She was dancing with Shay, but it was Morgan who held captive all her senses.

Breathless, her cells popping inside her like the crackling embers from wood in flames, her head spinning because she realized she was a little light headed. From the wine, the laughter, the music, the wildness, and the way Morgan had watched her. Merry leaned into Shay and told him she needed to stop for a moment to rest.

Shay was laughing, praising her dancing in his booming voice, as he led her back to the pit.

Merry's laughter died because Morgan was no longer on the sable by the fire. She was about to sink down, when Shay tugged her hand and guided her up the hill.

It was then she took note of the figure in the darkness, long legs curled around a boulder, the posture letting her know who it was, though the man was only a shadow.

"Thank ye for the dance, Merry lass," Shay said. All at

once, she was left with Morgan in the shadows on the hills.

Merry became aware of each detail in slow degrees. They were alone, and the sound she heard was his breathing. The warmth, with the chill of the air against her damp flesh, came from his body. She was standing between his powerful legs, only a hair separating her body from his trim hips and his chest. The fine-boned elegant features of his face were lost in the darkness, but she could feel the burn of his eyes, and a strange sort of tension from him.

She became aware of her own body, just as slowly. She was so hot, pulsing, and charged in every fiber. It was so unlike any feeling she had ever known. She hadn't been touched by him. How was it possible to be claimed by a brilliant awareness of him without even his touch? Bracing herself, her lashes danced opened and she met his tempting gaze. The blood rose like steam over her body. An ache formed in her stomach.

"Are you enjoying Ireland?" he inquired softly. His voice was little more than a husky displacement of air.

She tossed her curls back over her shoulders and lifted his wine glass from his fingers to her flushed face. The heat of his gaze roamed her body like a fire poker, stirring the flames everywhere it touched.

Breathless, she slanted Morgan a look under her lashes. Then, a little silly, a little giddy, and very proud, she said, "I danced in Ireland with a rebel band. Did you see me?"

Cupping her face and tilting it up toward him, Morgan said, "I did not see anything else, Little One. Or, did you not notice that I could see nothing but you?"

What was in his voice made Merry tremble, and the smile to slip from her face. Somehow, her body had come into full contact with his, his face only inches from her, his warm arms around her, his breath a caress against her cheeks.

With shock and desperate eagerness, Merry realized, *he is*

going to kiss me, in front of all these men and I want him to. God help me, I want him to.

As his lips slowly lowered toward hers, she felt herself ease upward to meet him. It was like drinking fire. Every cell in her body began to burn. The contact of his lips was light, subtly erotic, the play of his tongue unhurried and sure, but his hands where another thing, moving with ruthless skill in free exploration.

Everywhere he touched made the blood in her body work harder through her veins. Gentle and pressureless, his fingers played. On her face, her neck, lower, and under the press of his hard chest easing down against her breasts. As he deepened the possession of his mouth, the world around her became a hazy void of blurry shapes and shadows. The only thing focused and real was Morgan.

His palms pressed her urgently closer, his fingers spread like star points, fanning her backside, easing her upward into him, until she was pressed into that most intimate part of him. The shock of it made her sway, though she didn't pull away. His mouth wandered over the inner curve of her throat, and then his face lifted.

Keeping her body collected against him, he murmured. "Kiss me, Merry."

His husky words made her heart pound in the depths of her body with such force. All she knew was a desperate need to have the taste of his kisses running down her throat, his hands roaming her, to twist into that hardness where they touched and she ached.

"Kiss me," Morgan said, running a thumb gently along her blistering lips. The sweet yield of her flesh sent a rocketing shiver along his nerve tips. Whatever small interference his conscience had managed, before today, was now lost in his burgeoning desire for her.

She floated in graceful sureness into him, her lips rolling softly back and forth across his, her finger curled on his shoulders, drawing him to her. The breath quickened in his throat as he drank in the taste of her surrender. They began to deepen and expand the exchange, until the kiss became a flurry of hungrily seeking lips and wandering caresses.

She tried to protect herself with her thoughts, that she had consumed too much wine, the wildness of the dancing she had done combined with the strange eroticism of the play around her had weakened her and left her pliant and willing in his arms for this. But the thoughts could find no strength within her.

The pressure of Morgan's mouth never eased from her. It was slow, erotic, and careful, ebbing and intensifying in disarming waves as she melted to meet each move.

His hands fanning her breasts began to circle in more thorough strokes. Losing herself in the sudden piercing sensation, her eyes drifted closed. As she curved into him, tilting her head into his kisses, and pushing forward her hips, the most intimate part of her moved there. Shuddering with each tease, she felt warm fingers on the bare flesh of her thighs, and the strangely supple mold of her flesh being tucked into the intimate hard angles of his limbs.

"Please stop. I have had too much to drink," she said. Merry didn't even recognize that thin breathless voice as her own. It was almost a whimper.

She protested again as he made to move her, but he lifted her in spite of it, the coldness of the rock a shocking presence, pinning her to him. She had a sudden vivid image of where Morgan was taking her with this, if she didn't stop him.

In a movement made strong by panic and shame, she broke contact, pushing him back, and her away from the dangerous closeness of Morgan's body. It took a moment to speak, the blood was gushing through her veins, and the air coming into her lungs sharp, choking spurts.

"You and your smug games," she screamed, breathing rapidly. "I can't even imagine that I am modestly in your style, as men say. Or that you would be interested in me, at all, if you weren't obviously in need of a woman. You want to take from me, out of manly need, the only thing I have on this earth to give. Myself."

Merry curled her fingers over the sharp edge of a granite ridge and stared at him with moisture-blurred eyes, trying not to show fear. Surely, his reaction would come and it would be brutal. The sudden quiet in Morgan was a frightening thing.

He stopped himself. The girl understood little about men, but she understood this with knifepoint accuracy. Whatever he decided to do with this doe-eyed creature, she deserved better than losing her innocence propped against a rock like a Covent Garden whore.

Morgan made a step back and said, "I should take you back to the others."

He took her fingers in the lightest of clasps and walked silently beside her, back to the fire pit. He assisted her to sit on the sable before he crouched ahead of her, instead of sitting next to her. His breathing came to her, soft and even, while she could barely pull air in and out of her lungs.

Wide-eyed, Merry watched as he reached for his wine. He took a sip and put the glass to her trembling lips, forcing her to drink. The wine dribbled onto her lips, and with a gentle finger he brushed it from her, the touch of his fingers burning against her flesh. She made quick contact with his eyes and then looked away.

Morgan's laughter was quiet and enticing. "I think you've had enough of Ireland for one night, Little One."

She watched him ease up and toss a key to Tom Craven.

"Take her back to the ship and lock her in my cabin. I will

kill you if she's not there in the morning, and emasculate any man who dares to touch, so much as, a single hair on her head."

Pulsing and confused, Merry could only watch as Morgan's even strides carried him away from her. She followed him with her eyes, until she became aware of a woman on horseback. Her gaze strained through the soft glow of firelight to focus on her face.

Now, with the unsettling mix in her warmly liquid cells, was something harsh and cold. She recognized Christina Wythford slipping from the saddle into Morgan's arms, a welcoming smile on her lips as she lowered her face to kiss him.

She was never his hostage, Merry. She is his lover.

She felt the heat of Indy's gaze watching her. When she met it, the boy broke contact first. She didn't see Indy rise, didn't see his harshly warning glare as he took the key from a stunned Tom Craven. She was not aware of him at all, until his hands gently lifted her from the ground, wrapped in the sable skin, to be carried, shaking in his arms as they passed the men on the hills, to the ship.

All Merry's thoughts were floating, disconnected, random, and mercifully so. But when the door clicked behind Indy, they came together, an unfriendly pattern, too quickly formed to deny. Indy had put her to sleep in Morgan's bed. The boy would not have done this if he expected the captain's return.

Reality came, an unwanted intruder to her already raw senses.

Morgan had kissed her. She had wanted him to. Burying her face into his pillows, Merry let herself cry. There was no point in fighting the tears. She would pass this night alone with no one to see, but the strange agony of her body was something she had never expected, a misery never suffered before.

It was cruelly in her stomach, like a heavy rock that turned, over and over, impossible to stop, better left undefined, ignored but bringing tears.

~~~

Christina Wythford eased forward in the bed, her arms slipping around Morgan, her full breasts a pleasant caress against his back. Kissing his shoulder, she lay her cheek where her lips had touched, the gesture quiet, thoughtful as she had been all morning.

"After that miserable Channel crossing and rugged ride to this nowhere in Ireland, why are you leaving me so quickly?" she whispered softly. "I deserve more than one night for all my bother, Varian. Especially, since it passed without you ever being here with me."

Morgan turned in her arms until he faced her. Christina was a vision in the morning. At thirty-six she had moved into her looks from pretty into beautiful.

They had known each other since birth, had been lovers for two years, and carried each other's secrets with the trust of lifelong friendship. She was his lover and his friend, a combination few men ever found in a woman. It had never been quite been enough for either of them.

He ran a knuckle down her cheek. "Camden should have warned you I would not stay this time."

She sat back, pulling up the blankets to cover herself. "He did warn me. I chose not to believe him. Usually I am correct, in all this. However, you're leaving has nothing to do with an urgent need to get back to sea, and everything to do with whatever hovered between us last night."

Morgan's lips softened just a touch. "I am sorry, my dear, especially after you braved the wilds of Ireland. I know how you hate the Irish."

She wouldn't let him divert her. "I don't hate the Irish. I simply fail to understand your affection for them. Really, Varian, giving the rebels supplies to fight England? What has become of you these years? And you don't even allow them to pay you for them. Pirates are not supposed to be philanthropists, a misguided, disloyal, anti-monarchal philanthropist at that."

"I am not anti-monarchal. There has been no organized rebellion in Ireland since the death of Emmet in '03. It is a political movement non-violent. Nothing more."

She ran her fingers through her stylish, short blond curls. "I won't let you waylay me with a discussion on Irish politics. Who was it in your mind last night, while you made such desperate use of my body?"

Christina was direct. She was honest. Two qualities he had always admired in women. He reached to pull on his boots and decided to be direct and honest as well.

"I have a little bird who sleeps on my window bench, who would rather die than share my bed."

Christine's laughter was a soft, pleasant purr. "So, you bed me, not to bed the bird," she stated simply. She kicked him playfully with a leg. "I would be furious if you hadn't been magnificent last night. I hope you don't catch your bird, and keep coming to my bed. Being denied brings out the best in you, Varian. Some woman should have done it sooner. "

Christina never failed to maintain her posture in all circumstance. Even now.

His eyes softening with his affection for her, he took her chin and said, "The little bird is part temptress and part lunatic. You might as well have your full enjoyment over this, my dear, since I can see the pleasure you're getting at the expense of what's left of my ego."

Christina smiled. "You could feed the continent of Europe with what's left of your ego, Varian. Why are men such idiots? If you want her, she yours. You know that. You could seduce the Virgin Mother, if you had the whim and access to her. What is she? Young? Common? Pretty?" Her eyes began to sparkle. "Irish? What's wrong with her that you want her, but won't let yourself have her?"

"Young. Gently born. Beautiful. British," he said succinctly.

A long pause followed only by, "Aha."

Those black eyes began to glitter. "I know what you are thinking, and I have no patience left for that discussion today. This one has worn me out."

Her brow knit, puzzling. "Who is this girl?"

Amused, "Indy put her in my bed. She's the most beautiful girl I have ever seen, I have no idea who she is, or what I will do with her. There, that is everything. Are your curiosities satisfied, my dear?"

Varian was annoyed. Not with her. Only himself. Christina hid her smile.

She went back to him then, and gave him a long, thorough kiss. "You will never be at peace with what you've become, because it is only surface, and we both know that. You try to convince yourself otherwise, to make it tolerable to you. Yet you're unsure it hasn't taken too much of a possession of you. That is why you keep the bird, why you let yourself be tortured by all she reminds you of, and why you want her. You are a wonderful man, complicated as you are, and I will miss you."

She sprang from the bed and began to gather her clothes.

"Go chase your little bird, Varian. I hope you catch her. I have a feeling, when this is through, it will be her who's taught you a thing or two about yourself."

~~~

Merry was curled in his chair, a quilt high and tight around her shoulders. She had all the appeal of a small, aggravated house cat when Morgan returned to his cabin. She was not crying, but clearly she had been. Her face had lost a great deal of its natural

222

beauty beneath the residue.

Morgan settled at his desk. Watching the neat strokes of his pen, he tried to concentrate beneath the heavy stare he could feel on his back.

At his meeting with Camden, he had received the departure schedule and routes of the *Hampstead*. The heightened fighting on the seas with America had caused a delay. He was getting closer to finally closing the trap on Rensdale, and he had no tolerance for another delay.

But, the delay would leave enough time to return to the Caribbean. To hunt for a good prize for the men, and visit his home, before he would have to return to intercept the *Hampstead*. Before Rensdale's raiders destroyed it.

When he was finished, Morgan pushed up and left without a word.

Indy came, saw Merry in the chair she hadn't moved from since the prior night, and set her noon meal on the table.

"You should get dressed, Merry. We are lifting anchor and Shay is looking for you, knowing if he spends the afternoon amusing you, he gets out of doing his work."

Indy didn't put a smile with his words, the boy never smiled, but there was a slight altering of his tone. It was the closest thing to a jest she had ever heard from him. It should have pleased her, knowing what a rare gift an attempt at humor was from him. It made her more miserable.

Merry stayed in the chair, not bothering to reach for the food.

"I can't get dressed. I need some of your clothes."

The tears were back, plopping on her hands. She hated them. She had never been a woman who had been prone to crying. She cried too easily, of late.

"All the gowns are gone. I ripped them up and then I threw them out the window." She looked at Indy then. "They were hers. I won't wear them."

~~~

The expected knock at the cabin door was a welcome relief, halfway through the evening meal that Morgan ate alone at his table. The girl could carry an air of sadness that could smother a village.

Not rising from the table, he gave permission to enter as he continued with his meal.

Tom passed through the door carrying a small wrapped package, a basket and a letter. The age-carved lines of his face were disgruntled, apprehensive, but mildly, albeit reluctantly, amused. Tom stopped, hovering above him at the table.

"What the hell are you sulking about for, Tom? What do you have there? I am tired and am in no mood for anything lengthy," Morgan said, pausing in his meal. "What the devil are you carrying? Have I forgotten my birthday, and you wish to rub it in that I am in possession of another year?"

"You'd need more than one more year to catch me, Varian," Tom said dryly. "Shay brought this aboard ship. It's a gift from Ryan Shay."

"Ah. I expect nothing from them and he knows that. Why would he insult me with this gesture?"

"It's not for you. It's for the girl," Tom said in irritation.

Merry hadn't looked at Tom once since he'd entered, but she was looking now. Her tear brightened blue eyes studied Tom warily, but there was just a hint of curiosity, as well.

He offered her the letter first. Surprise softened her lovely face as she scanned the letter.

Morgan stared at Merry until she finally read the note out loud.

"To my new friend Merry. We are in many ways fighting the same war. I hope you remember kindly your, too-quickly passing moments with us. I know I will, always. With affection and regards, Ryan Shay." There was a post script in French and Merry read that as well in flawless French. "'Through luck of birth, one is king, the other a shepherd, fate sets them apart and only the spirit can change it all.'"

She stared down at the letter. She opened the small wrapped package. It was a worn, though expensively bound, volume of Beaumarchais' poetry and essays. Merry opened the book, touching the dog-eared pages with tiny fingers, and smiled, even while she did an anxious swipe at fresh tears.

Morgan heard her say quietly to Tom, "Thank you for bringing me this, sir."

Mr. Craven continued to hover.

Merry looked up after several moments, puzzled. It was then she took note of the basket. A basket that made little whimpers and scratching sounds.

Reluctantly Tom handed the basket to Merry and said to Morgan, "If you want me to dispose of it, Varian, I will. I know how you despise small animals."

Morgan only arched a brow at that. So the basket was the cause of Tom's excessive reluctance and yes, he did despise it.

Laughing in delight, Merry held a tiny pug up in front of her that was an absurd yapping creation, masquerading as a dog, a red ribbon gaily wrapped about its neck with a tag that said 'Beau'.

"Ah, a dog with an illustrious namesake. I have a trustworthy friend at last in this hostile captivity," she exclaimed, lowering it to her face.

Morgan's thoughts exactly on the matter, though her ingenious use of the word 'trustworthy' in her own innocently unknowing way added bite.

"Leave the dog," was all Morgan said before Tom left. Watching Merry with the pug, he warned, "I am not fond of dogs, Little One. Keep it out of my way. If I find it on my bed I will toss it over the rail."

CHAPTER TEN

The last of September had given way to October many days past as the sleek hull of the *Corinthian* plowed southwestward through the roiling seas of the Atlantic Ocean.

The winds were mild and every inch of canvas was unfurled on the masts as the ship made its way across the white caps farther and farther from England.

All around her was only endless horizons of water. Merry Merrick, who had spent her first nineteen years running amuck on a modest farm outside of Falmouth, had spent her last moments in Europe, oddly enough, on a dramatic hillside in Ireland with a pirate captain and a rebel band, running amuck as well.

If there were a warning in that for Merry, she had no wish to figure it out. She was miserable enough these days.

They were three weeks into their journey to the Caribbean, their alarming destination explained to her not by Morgan, but by Shay. Merry had been so furious with Morgan for that.

She had stormed the cabin, tossing all reasonable caution to the wind, with the full force of her temper demanded her return her to Falmouth. He heard her out in silence and then had said, in a low unruffled voice, that she would enjoy the Caribbean as much as she had Ireland, and calmly returned to his book.

It was the reference to Ireland that kept Merry above deck in an unseasonably blistering sun listening to Mr. Seton's stories about America.

The days had grown steadily warmer as they rode south. Mr. Seton had informed her they were uncommonly so and had gallantly chided it was the charming Merry who had charmed the sun into joining them on this adventure. Even taking the southern route, it was not known to be this warm this time of year.

Brushing anxiously at her hot cheeks, Merry again felt the threatening possession of tears and only with the full exercise of her will managed to prevent them.

In her nineteen years, before Morgan, she had barely shed enough to fill a thimble. Five weeks as his hostage and she could hardly stop them. She suspected these endless buckets were her just punishment for having behaved so repulsively in Morgan's arms.

Merry was pulled from the depressing bent of her thoughts by a shadow being cast across her, with the lowering of Morgan's towering frame. He settled her dog, carefully, into the bed of her lap made by sitting cross-legged in Indy's breeches.

"Merry, when you leave the cabin please take the dog with you," he said in a playfully chiding voice as he touched her cheek.

He always did it the same way, light, with the tip of his index finger, careless, and quick.

"I am running out of pillows. The dog doesn't deserve trust until he's a little older. You'll see the proof of that when you go back below."

The curt rejoinder that formed in her mind never made it to voice. Instead, much to her displeasure, she heard herself say, "I am sorry. I won't forget the dog again."

Morgan brushed his thumb once across her cheek. She was forced to endure the touch, since they were topside. The presence of the crew was a sharp reminder that her disobedience would not be tolerated outside of the cabin.

"Ah, miracles never cease. Either you've finally learned to obey an order or you've been on deck too long in the sun, Little

One. It's too early to be hopeful. I think it's the sun. Don't stay topside, too long, Merry. I find tiny creatures full of mischief charming."

Merry tucked her face against the anxiously lapping mutt to hide the flush of embarrassment as Morgan walked off. Since Ireland, she hovered exclusively in the matter-of-fact state of Morgan's supremely kind manner of inane indifference. There was something unnerving about a man who could make you melt from his passion, then turn course, and completely dismiss you.

Staring at Morgan's retreating back, Merry held the pug, flicking tongue and all, away from her and chided, "If you don't behave he's going to toss you over the rail. You've chomped up your last pillow. You are existing on this ship on borrowed time."

The dog began to make that mournful, whimpering sound he always made when he wanted to chase off after Morgan. The stupid creature adored the man. She made a stern frown and then laughed when the dog whimpered louder. She looked at Mr. Seton, who was smiling at her in that droopy way he had at times when he watched her.

She ignored the look, and said, "This dog has no instinct at all. Morgan hates him and he scratches at the door crying whenever he leaves the cabin. One of these days the dog is going to trot up behind him on the quarterdeck and find himself kicked over the rail. I suppose it's because it makes him look lamblike to have man's best friend adoring man's worst fiend."

Mr. Seton's smile changed from droopy to dazzlingly amused. "It will take more than a scrap of fur to make Morgan look lamblike. Regardless, the dog knows who brought him here, and knows he's not in danger. Instinct intact."

Merry's eyes widen at that. "What do you mean, 'who

brought him here'? The dog was a gift from Ryan Shay."

"Where the devil did you get that idea, Merry?"

Eyes widening even more, she said to Mr. Seton, "He came with a book and a letter from Ryan Shay. Mr. Craven's didn't tell me otherwise. Who are you thinking the dog is from?" And then with a laugh, she added, "Surely not, Mr. Craven. Tell me it is not so."

Mr. Seton's handsome golden brows pulled into a frown at once, as though she were being unaccountably slow in all this.

Shaking his head, he said, "Morgan didn't tell you the dog was from him? There are times the man is a Chinese puzzle that could keep even God baffled. What's the point of bringing a dog as a gift without letting the gift recipient know you're doing it? I will never be able to figure out the man. Do you think a dog would be on this ship, with how he hates them, if he didn't bring it? He spent his last morning in Ireland looking for the darn thing. Left the Wythford tart cooling in the sheets early. She was none too pleased. Every man not doing their trick on ship was out getting their last drop of female hospitality, and there's Morgan looking for a dog. Tully and I laughed ourselves to jelly over that. It was hard not to laugh in his face as he carried the little fluff on ship. Quite an incongruous picture, to say the least."

Merry managed to ignore the proper reaction of modesty that should have claimed her with the implications of the terms 'female hospitality' and 'cooling in the sheets'. It was a necessity of survival in a world exclusively of men not to be modest. Modesty and pirates, the ultimate incongruity.

She settled her chin in the cup of her hand and stared at Beau. Disbelieving, she asked, "Why would he give me a dog and not tell me?"

Mr. Seton did a lazy roll with his shoulders. "I don't know, Merry. Take everything he does with a grain of salt and stay clear of him for your own well-being. Morgan is not lamblike."

Brandon reclined on an elbow, watching Merry study the dog as if to find sorely wanted answers there. As impossible as it seemed, in over a month, Morgan hadn't taken her to his bed. Morgan made his way through the flowers of the field with a machete. Brandon couldn't imagine what prompted the captain to leave this flower intact. There were any number of opinions to be found aboard ship in regards to that.

Some claimed that it was a sign that Morgan had a heart. Others whispered that she was his daughter. Then, there were those who thought he meant to keep her intact to fetch the best price when he sold her.

Brandon wasn't as inventive as the crew. He was also inclined to believe it was only a matter of time when the question wouldn't be debated below decks, at all. The Atlantic crossing was a long voyage and Merry was uncommonly beautiful. As unfathomable as Morgan was at times, Morgan was still a man.

He lifted a hand to scratch the dog's head, careful not to brush against those delicate fingers moving there.

"Are you all right, Merry? You seemed troubled of late. Morgan doesn't hurt you, does he?"

"He treats me like I am his sister. He's more likely to ignore me than harm me. Why would you wonder if he hurts me?"

"You got him heated up in Ireland, then you pushed him away. He is not a man accustom to having a woman push him away. You bruised his vanity well, my dear. I was concerned he may have pushed back."

Wanting to be worldly in this discussion, knowing she was failing because she could feel her blush, she said, "He didn't push back. He is completely indifferent to me."

"Indifferent?" Mr. Seton laughed so long and loudly it

drew stares from the crew. When his ha-has, faded into little gasps, he explained, "Oh, flower, the man threatened to put a bullet between my eyes if I so much as touched you with a finger. That is not indifference."

Merry stared at Brandon Seton then, wondering if she had heard him correctly. It made the way Morgan treated her, all the more baffling. Before she could probe Mr. Seton further about this, he was gone. Someone from the crow's nest had cried 'sail ho,' and the lazy afternoon on ship exploded into well-organized action.

Shortly before sunset, the *Corinthian* had taken a French schooner in a battle that had consisted of a single canon blast. Standing at the port rail, Merry watched her first experience of piracy at sea, surprisingly entertained by it instead of feeling the expected outrage.

The revelry of the pirates and their exuberant frolicking in the longs boats as they went about transferring the cargo made them look more like naughty little school boys up to mischief, rather than scourge committing villainy. The schooner's cargo had held a healthy supply of fine French liquor. Earlier in the afternoon, Shay had tossed her a bottle of Bordeaux, for her ladyship's pleasure, with a silly promise to teach her, no less than a dozen drinking games when he was through.

Now, shortly before darkness would blanket the sky, she leaned laughingly over the rail as Shay tipped from a long boat. That brought a full chorus of blustering from the lad as the pirates in his boat tried to fish Shay from the water. He was making preposterous swipes at Indy as the boy tried to retrieve him from the Atlantic. To her greater amusement, when they managed to lock hands, Shay only pulled Indy into the water with him. She suspected the drinking lesson would be short tonight, since the open bottle that had fallen from Shay's fingers as he plunged from the boat was probably not the first he'd imbibed.

"Oh, Indy is going to be grim tonight," she said softly to pug, as Shay bounced on Indy's head to submerge him in the water.

"Indy is usually grim. It's remarkable how often that he is not so with you."

Merry tried not to blush. Morgan was standing close, assessing her idly. It had surprised her he was even aware she'd been here at the rail.

He'd sat on the quarterdeck with Mr. Craven, through it all, as he watched the men in their duties. At some time before the meager battle, he had changed into his severe costume of all black. It was a brilliant contrast to the gleaming red tint of sunlight cast by the fall of the day, dark waves capering in wind, black eyes dancing rakishly. He hadn't looked at her once all afternoon. It was pride that kept Merry from looking at him more than she could stop herself.

He looked at the wine in her hand and his eyes took on a smile. "Where did you get that?" he asked her. "Have you taken to skimming from my spoils before I have a chance to tally them?"

That made her tense, uncertain if this were a crime aboard ship. It seemed hardly possible, with how many of the crew had bottles in hand. She decided not to tell him that Shay had given it her.

Her silence only amused him. Touching her cheek, he said on a laugh, "I was only teasing. Though, I don't recommend the drinking games, since the men are apt to get a little rough in their conduct tonight when they've finished with their work."

So he had been watching her. Her attendant reaction to that was unwelcomed. "I guess gentlemanly conduct would be too much to expect from the scourge of the sea," she quipped playfully, enormously pleased she was able to do so.

He lightly cupped her chin and said, "It is much too much to expect gentlemanly conduct from the scourge, Little One. It would serve you better to expect rogues and to keep your wits about you. Now run along, Merry, and take the dog below with you, or one of the crew is apt to use it for target practice, if he gets under foot."

Attractive smile creases bracketed his black eyes, but his words had been merely dismissive, one of his lazy efforts to get her out of the way. Dropping the bottle in his hand, she picked up the dog. Merry's sole consolation was that she managed not to run from him.

Her internal unrest was hardly improved by an evening spent alone in the cabin, listening to the men and Morgan's laughter above deck.

Much to her dismay, she found herself near the stroke of midnight in Morgan's chair, devouring of all things Mary Wollstonecraft's *Maria, The Wrongs of a Woman*. She'd plucked it from the shelf, amused by its presence in Morgan's decidedly male domain. Much to her displeasure, she found herself fascinated by the scandalous thoughts pressed on pages. They were, at best, a poor ally for a girl, whose first experience of desire was in the arms of a man, who was ever so wrong for her. Her stomach turned as she fought to focus on the book and turned a page.

The door opened and in from the deck floated music, laughter, and misery. The rosy light of the lamp fell in sparkling points across Morgan. He carried with him the moisture dew of a sea mist that held shimmers on his jet hair, the elegant chiseled features of his face, relaxed and wind fresh, and the darkly tanned flesh of his sculptured forearms where his cuffs had been rolled up halfway.

The cabin was filled at once with his presence, the natural scent of him, touched of tobacco and a sigh of wintergreen.

Both the fragrance and sight of him ran through her like a sultry caress. No matter how she fought it, it was not possible to look at this man and not feel reaction all through her. Sometimes at night, she'd wake just to watch him sleep, and there was still that awe, that fascination of him even when he was doing nothing.

Morgan's eyes fixed on her in a surprised way that told Merry he'd been expecting her asleep. As his gaze dispassionately ran her curled figure in the chair, absurdly swallowed within one of his white shirts, a childish picture she was sure she made, at best.

She wondered if this night would pass, as all the others since Ireland, miserably uncomfortable in his stoic silence. The only time his eyes paused was on the cover of her book. Against her will, she felt color burn her cheeks.

"I am surrounded by scandalous company on this ship. Scandalous thoughts, for a scandalous girl," he said lightly mocking.

Morgan's dark gaze floated the room, settling on the drawers before moving back to her, now with a twinkle in their gemmed depths. She'd demolished the drawers earlier, in frustration of being ordered to the cabin.

"Scandalous of mind and scandalous in decorating. Little One, I think I will keep you forever."

The smile Morgan bent her was infuriating. Decidedly not irritated by her childish compulsion to annoy him, but he was at least talking tonight. Being alone with him in the silence of the cabin, night after night, had been a dreadful thing to endure.

Lifting her nose in the air, claimed by that prickling in her cells that always came with the hold of his eyes, Merry was pleased she was able to convey just the right amount of sauce in her retort, as she countered, "What is a female to do aboard a pirate ship? Do scandalous decorating and read scandalous thoughts, since the Captain never lets them enjoy the scandalous merrymaking, and the scandalous drinking games."

"Ah, you are rankled with me for ordering you below deck. There are more than few, topside, drunk as friars. It's not the drinking games I protest you learning, it's what's likely to come after."

She followed him with her eyes as he went to pour a glass of wine for them both. He handed her the glass, then tapped her on the nose, almost as though he were dealing with a small child.

Furious with his insufferable treatment of her, she snapped, "Perhaps I would enjoy what comes after the drinking games. I certainly don't enjoy passing into old age, alone in this cabin, since you seemed not at all inclined to return me to Falmouth."

Morgan's eyes began to shimmer. "I will have to start censuring your reading material, Little One, if a night with Wollstonecraft has you eager to learn what comes after the drinking games."

Her eyes began to flash at once. "You wouldn't have to censure my reading material, if you'd let me from this cabin, more than a handful of hours a day," she said in building waves of exasperation. "I am restless and I am bored. I don't get enough activity. I am tired of spending half my nights reading in your cabin, just so I may sleep. I wouldn't read, at all, if there was something better to do at night on ship. I can't imagine why anyone would want a life at sea."

Morgan's dark gaze shifted to the pretty picture Merry made in his shirt. He took her fingers then, making them rub lightly on his lips, before he whispered wickedly, "Since you're awake and I am awake, and neither of us have a desire to read, perhaps you'd be eager to play with me the games that follow."

Merry had no idea what to say to that, but she realized, too late, that the husky quality of his voice should have warned her to run.

All she could do was stare at him in silence. Morgan's hands lifted her from the chair in a movement that was swift and graceful. Merry found herself in a firm embrace, suddenly spread across Morgan's bed. The warmth of his flesh surrounding her was a shock, but inside her skin was a body reeling. She tried desperately to strain her hips away from him. All she got for the effort was a hand cupping her buttocks, lifting her up against him. Exploded was the happy fiction Merry had indulged that Morgan was tame.

Clinging feebly to the hope her circumstance hadn't just taken a desperate turn for the worse, Merry said, "If you are done toying with me, Captain, I'd prefer you let me go."

His laughter was quiet and enticing. "We're nowhere near done. As I recall, you are the one who demanded something better to do at night than reading." When she struggled harder, his hands stilled her hips as he ordered, "Don't. We haven't even started the games, yet." For some unknown reason, she relaxed beneath his touch.

She was trying to figure out how to stop him and what had caused all this, as he tilted her head back and laid careful kisses on the smooth slope of her neck. The delicate touch of his lips had a disastrous effect. Then he was pressing his mouth against hers with sweet skill, spreading the rounded fullness, probing slowly with faint and disarming coaxing. The press of his body and the sweet seduction of his kisses, exploded another happy fiction for Merry that her wantonness in his arms in Ireland had all been because of the wine.

But no, it was happening again. Everything from the neck up sluggish and spinning, everything from the neck down boiling like a kettle.

When finally Morgan lifted his head, his breathing sounded

soft and normal to her, while she could barely pull the air into her lungs. His lips went to the sensitive flesh beneath her ears.

"See, Little One, this is not so bad, is it? More pleasurable than reading, for the both of us. Would you like me to make you spin faster? I can you know. Give me your mouth."

How did he know she was spinning? Why did she lift her chin? His kiss, this time, was searing, and then he lifted his face, until his black eyes fixed on her features with knowing sureness.

With hot cheeks, through moist and swollen lips, she whimpered, "How do I get you not to force me?"

One accurate finger was softly following the hairline around her face. "Force you? Such an inaccurate word. I'm not even holding you, Little One. Or hadn't you noticed."

Much to Merry's chagrin, she realized, at some point, he'd withdrawn his body from her and was lying casually reclined on a hip, staring down at her. Her body, on its own, had turned into him. When had that happened?

Holding imprudently to the belief that Morgan would never take her against her will, a belief at present that seemed silly, she whispered, "All the same, I'm not willing."

"No?"

The sudden glimmer in his black eyes told her that had been the wrong thing to say. His hands returned in rich movements against her flesh as his mouth wandered back to her neck.

"If this isn't willing, then never has there been a willing maid. Do you really want me to stop? Why don't we go a little further and then you can decide? I promise to stop if you don't like anything I do."

His fingers forced her resisting lips back and his mouth wandered to hers, slowly stirring and soothing her. He continued the movement of his hands. She felt as though every part of her was touched by deep sunshine. To fight him might have been the urging of her mind, but it was not the urging of her body. With an artfully slow disconnect, he lifted his face until his eyes, smoky with pleasure, could study her face.

Whispering, he said, "See, I always play fairly. Have I done anything you don't like?"

Ignoring both the question with the proper disdain it deserved, and the improper answer that popped into her head, Merry turned her face so he couldn't kiss her again. She would have dropped to the floor if they hadn't been lying on his bed.

Her head swimming, she said thickly, "I want you to let me go."

"How about a diplomatic negotiation?" His eyes only darkened another shade. "I'll let you go if you kiss me."

She wasn't able to answer him because his lips moved with hushed lightness over her neck. Somewhere inside of her there was fight, but it never came, not even when his mouth lowered to the swell of her breasts. She lost herself in the delicious tease of his caresses.

His hands still pressing her to him, his lips on hers, he whispered, "Let me help you. Slowly, Merry, like this. Yes. Oh, dainty flower, you do know how to play. One should never rush the games that follow." Then, he was guiding her mouth back to him. His hands held her cheeks with his face above her. She was just touching her lips against his, when she finally realized what he'd meant all along by the games that follow.

Humiliated and furious, she jerked herself backward into the pillows as she pushed upward against him with her knee and snapped, "Why don't you go back topside and play with yourself?"

The words were hardly out of her mouth before Morgan started laughing, so hard he was choking. Merry didn't know what he saw on her face, but fresh gales of laughter followed. He rolled away from her, lying back against his bed, as if unable to stop it. The way he was laughing made her temper flare. Before she could stop herself, she shouted, "How dare you laugh at me!"

That her temper came at this, of all moments, only made Morgan laugh harder. He laughed harder still when her response to the laughter was to try to hit him. He expertly avoided it, taking both her arms in a single hand.

He touched her face and in his voice there was a smile. "God must have been in a wicked humor the day he created you. You are more amusement defending your maidenhead than I suspect you'll be in surrendering it."

There was an insult buried somewhere in there, Merry was certain of that, though the necessity to flee seemed more important than finding it. She tried to scramble from the bed, but the tail of her shirt was pinned beneath him. On top of everything, he was claimed again by laughter.

The man was deranged. After weeks of ignoring her, he'd practically forced his attentions upon her. Searching his face, she asked fearfully, "Are you drunk as a friar?"

Morgan smiled and said softly, "No, Little One. I am not drunk on wine. I am drunk only on you."

Then, unexpectedly, he smoothly pulled the shirttail that trapped her on the bed from beneath him.

"You best scamper off quickly, Little One. Before my laughter loses its bite and I think better of letting you go."

Why he was suddenly tame again was a mystery to Merry. She went to the window bench and pulled the blankets tightly around her in a protective cocoon. Much to her exasperation, she felt it, that feeling of being touched she sometimes felt when his eyes were on her. Peeking cautiously over her shoulder, she found Morgan reclined on his bed, reading the book that had slipped from her fingers during her flight to the mattress, eyes fixed on a page, wine in glass swirling.

She was losing her mind. His eyes weren't even on her. They were on the book. It was impossible to sleep. It was unnerving, the feel of Morgan's eyes upon her, only to find he wasn't even looking at her. Most nights passed with him ignoring her, just as he was now, reading endlessly through the night, with an air of bloody insouciance. Meanwhile, she battled not to crawl from the tingling sensation of her own flesh.

These hours were like being trapped in a snare she couldn't see. Most of their quiet nights together passed half with her wondering if he were truly a demon and half wondering if her captivity had made her mad.

From the bed, Morgan said innocently, "You can go to bed without fear, Little One. You amuse me, and that's probably going to save your life." Morgan's chin lifted just enough so his eyes could meet her over the book. "But, if you continue to fidget this night, as you do most nights, all bets are off. You need to learn to practice stillness. It would benefit you greatly."

Having no reasonable response to that comment, it would have felt nice to strangle him. There was something unnerving about a man who could romp you around like Buxom Bess the chambermaid, laugh in your face, and grin over glib jibes about idiocy saving one's life. If not for his grin, she might have relaxed, eventually. The grin always foretold of danger.

As it was, her nerves were as taut as a bowstring. All Merry could do is stare out the window and pretend she wasn't here. Behind her she heard Morgan, his steady breathing, the turn of a page. She concentrated on making outlines in the frost against the glass, tracing fanciful patterns. Anxiously, she erased the glass with the cuff of her shirt when she realized she'd sketched a noose. She was wringing out the dampness of her sleeve when suddenly she froze.

What the devil was wrong with her? For some bizarre

reason she was quivering. Why was her body a stranger to her, whenever Morgan was near? She heard the wine in glass, felt the quivering sharpen, and slanted him a look. In a flash, she realized, with a shock, why the swirling glass always irritated her. She burned when they were alone and the glass swirled.

He is watching me. Every time the glass swirls, it's not the glass he studies, it something else. How is he doing it? It is a remarkable trick.

Merry glared at him in fury. She had thought herself losing her mind before tonight, and it took every ounce of her will not to explode.

You insufferable man, you are watching me, though I don't know how you do it. But I feel it on my flesh, no matter where your eyes look, like they are now. I know what that habit means.

She curled on the window bench, her back turned toward him, and realized with a start that Morgan was always watching her and had been from the first night. She jerked the blankets over her head, hiding fully under them and not caring if he thought her childish.

The wind gained ground as the night grew cold, and the creaking, groaning timbers of the *Corinthian* were hardly a good collaborator to sleep. Lying in the early morning darkness of the cabin, restless and awake, she was surprised how often she felt the burn of Morgan's eyes touching her. The cabin was in total darkness because of the brewing storm. How did Morgan see her? And why did he spend his nights awake watching her?

Heavy lids gratefully rescued her from her thoughts.

The next day, Merry was rudely awakened from a fitful slumber when Indy yanked off the blanket. Her eyes were blistered by a blood red sun. Indy said, "Who the devil are you pretending to be now, Merry? Pocahontas in her teepee?"

"You can really be a cruel boy sometimes, do you know that?" she whispered.

There was a short silence. Then he sat down on the bench,

their faces nearly at eye level now, the burnish sunlight exaggerating the hard bones of his face. "What's wrong?" An extended pause followed before he asked, "What has you so frazzled this morning."

"What could possibly have me frazzled? Outside of the fact I'm trapped on a pirate ship and Morgan attacked me. Then, he laughed at me, insulted me, and spent the entire night staring at me in a manner that made me want to climb out of my skin. He warned me that my life is at risk, if I couldn't stop fidgeting, which I can't, because he stares at me. I feel it in my flesh. What could possibly have me frazzled?"

A pause came in which Merry did a lot of fidgeting as Indy slowly arched a brow in note of it.

Finally, Indy said, "Indeed, you are in grave danger." Then, less mocking, he added, "Melodrama won't help. Do you think you can tell me what happened in a single sentence? What do you mean Morgan attacked you?"

Reluctantly amending her previous grievance, she said, "He kissed me."

It was obviously not a serious development for Indy. After a short wait, he asked, "Is that all?"

Having gone from one extreme to the other in this, Merry knew she was making a mess of the whole thing. Factually, every word was accurate, but there was more to it that could not be conveyed by three little words. She nodded.

They sat together and he said, "You're here. It's always been only a matter of time before he took you to his bed. Accept it."

That sent anger bites down her spine. "You make it sound as if I don't have a choice at all."

"You don't. A clever girl would take him to bed, play to Morgan's kinder tendencies, and get free of here quickly." Indy had moved from her to the table, and sat there picking at her breakfast plate with a fork.

In a huff she climbed from the window bench and said in an exaggerated way, "Well, pardon me for not being a clever girl." She sank like a heavy rock into her chair, jerked her plate away from the boy, and started to pick at her food with a fork.

He watched her eat. "Would it really be that bad, Merry?"

"Yes."

Frustrated and angry, Indy snapped, "I think the lady doth protest too much."

Crazily, considering the situation, Merry felt the keen bite of the truth in that, clamped her mouth shut, and fixed her eyes on her plate. She could barely remember the last time she had passed a day without some thought of Morgan. She could no longer convince herself her thoughts of him were entirely appropriate. Her anger sank like an iron slug and so did her pride.

Indy moved from the table without further insult. He said, "You're going to be locked below decks all day. Captain's orders." He gave no explanation and left the cabin.

Locked alone in the silence of her rocking prison, Merry had no choice but to invent ways to amuse herself and spent half the day re-arranging Morgan's possessions. Today's act of irritation complete, she sat curled in his chair before the desk, reading his logbook.

The entries were brief, his writing a precise and elegant swirl. Much to her dismay, she found her finger tracing over the ink on page. Confused and appalled by whatever had prompted her to do that, she jerked her hand back, reached for another log, and slapped it onto the desk.

It noted a year, 1810. Flicking open a page, she thought, *behold the mysteries of a demon*, and then fixed to read a page.

A pirate's life was a remarkable journey of travel. She wondered at the places noted in the sparse entries. What they were like, the people that were there, the adventure this man lived. If only Morgan had put better description in his log, there could have been much to be learned here. She suspected one was not inclined to keep a thorough history in one's own hand of the crimes and villainy one committed.

Pressed on the pages was a map of life that had seemed to have taken him to the four corners of the earth. What there wasn't, was a single insight on the man. She slapped shut the logbook and moved from the desk.

The cabin door opened. Merry looked up, saw Morgan, and retreated to the far side of the cabin. He shut the door with one hand, as his thorough floating gaze moved efficiently to take note of her disturbance of his cabin. Nothing. Not a word.

He went to his desk and began to rummage through the disorganized stack of logs books, set into his chair, and went into work of an entry. The minutes passed in agonizing slowness with Morgan saying nothing.

Unable to endure the silence a moment longer, Merry spoke: "I demand that you release me from this cabin, Captain."

The neat moves of quill continued. He finished his entry before he leaned back in his chair and set his black stare upon her. "You know, Little One, you may call me Varian. We do share a cabin, after all. Captain seems a touch formal given the situation, don't you think?"

"Nevertheless…"

He didn't let her finish. He rose to his full height above her and said, "Why is it with women there is always a 'nevertheless'. Never more. Never less—" His eyes began to glow wickedly. "—never, never, never."

For so brief of statement it had a remarkable number of half messages. Miserably, Merry fought each one that rose in her thoughts. After a short hesitation of her trying to figure out something safe to say in return, he said in an offhand way,

"Demand denied, unless you'd like to try again. Perhaps addressing me as Varian. That might do it. But, I don't think so. Not today. I prefer you where you are."

By late afternoon, watching the sky swirl and changing color through the stern windows, Merry understood why she'd been locked below all day in the cabin. She'd forgotten the blood red sky that had greeted at waking and the warning: *Red sky at night sailors' delight, red sky at morning, sailors' warning.*

A storm. Heavy seas shook the ship with tall waves, and both the decks and passageways would have been unmanageable for Merry. While she was slowly gaining a sailor's footing, she was still far from Morgan and Indy's steadfast strides through any disturbance. Curled in the chair, it took effort to maintain her perch as the ship launched back and forth, side to side.

The evening meal came and went without Morgan. Something about Morgan's absence put Merry's nerves on edge. She could set a clock by Morgan's routine. He was not a man who ever deviated in habit or ritual.

Watching Indy clear away the meal, she asked the boy, "Are we going to sink?"

Startled, Indy stopped in the collections of dishes and fixed a harsh stare on her. "Sink? It's hardly even a storm, Merry. The worst of it's done. We should see smoother sailing by midnight. You should see the storms off Cape Horn. Now those are storms." He continued in his task.

"You wouldn't lie to me, would you?"

Impatient with her, he snapped, "Yes, I would lie to you, but no I'm not lying."

"Then why was Morgan from the cabin all day, if the storm is not worrisome?"

The first question was a foolish one. The second one, merely irritating. Indy's expression was sardonic. "Perhaps he's had enough dealing with your vexing presence. Morgan has been playing cards in Craven's cabin all day." Picking up the tray, the boy went for the cabin door.

"And you best be asleep when Morgan returns. He always drinks, far too much, when he plays cards with Craven. He's not going to have the patience to deal with your nonsense."

Morgan drunk. An entirely new danger. That sent Merry quickly to curl on the window bench, hoping to fall asleep before the captain returned.

In the middle of the night, she was pulled from sleep to find Morgan in his bed and a growing discomfort in her abdomen. She'd started her flux. It was late in coming and she was always irregular. It seemed, at last, she was not going to be spared her curse on ship. Staring out the stern windows at the star cluttered sky, fighting against the icy quiver of her leg muscles and the sharp pains in her abdomen, she pulled her blankets more tightly around her, determined to wait it out until she was alone in the cabin.

She'd rather die than have to explain this to Morgan. Thinking of Netta, her gruff old maid, she felt tears sting in her eyes. There were times when a woman just wanted a woman. This was one of those times. An hour passed before she realized the futility in making an attempt to wait until morning. Her flux having come late, came in full force.

Carefully turning on the pillows, she cursed what she was sure was a male God for permitting it to start at night, cursed Morgan for his slumbering presence, and quietly climbed from the window bench with the quilt pulled tightly around her. Fumbling in the darkness at the knob on the door, she did not find the key in the latch where the captain always left it. After several frantic, rattling attempts to open it, she found Morgan sitting up in his bed watching her.

"If you are finished making that racket, go back to sleep."

Merry tensed. There was something to his voice and something to his face, not familiar at all.

Still, necessity was proving of late to be the mother of courage. "I want out of the cabin. Please, open the door."

Morgan ran a hand through his tousled waves, favored her with an annoyed scowl, and said in a voice of straining tolerance, "You're not leaving this cabin at night alone."

Feeling her shirt stick to her legs beneath the careful drape of the quilt, she took a rallying breath and lifted her eyes to his.

"Please. You must open the door. Please."

Clearly, Morgan thought not. He eased back into his pillows, rolled onto his side and tugged up his blankets.

"Whatever it is, it can wait until morning."

She made no move from the door.

Morgan lit a candle, studied her face, and then asked, "What's wrong?"

There were no words that wouldn't humiliate her to explain this.

"I need Indy."

That made Morgan rise from his bed. He took a step toward her, thankfully clad in a nightshirt, and she quickly lowered her face.

"Why?"

"If you don't mind, I'd prefer not to answer your questions and just have you open the door. Please."

Her cheeks began to warm.

"Why do you want the boy?" When Merry didn't answer his black eyes sharpened on her face. "I won't open the door unless you explain yourself."

Achy, trapped, and humiliated, Merry's temper exploded.

"Hang it, Varian, open the damn door!" she screamed.

The touch of Morgan's eyes turned into a burn, and it cost her a fiery blush, but Merry managed to hold his surprised stare with a determined stare of her own.

She never called him by his Christian name, couldn't imagine why she did it now, when this was an awkward moment at best to test it, and she wasn't at all sure his reaction to it.

She heard a soft laugh above her and felt the mocking touch of his fingers on her cheek.

"Well, well, it must be a crisis. You should practice at saying my name without clenching your teeth, though I must admit the breathless quality gives it a certain *je ne sais qui.*"

He followed the insult by putting the light touch of his lips on the tip of her nose.

Tensing, Merry's senses were flooded with the faint aroma of whiskey. She realized his strange manner was because of drink. His face was more relaxed, less intimating, and though Indy had warned her to stay clear of him tonight, if he were drunk, it seemed to make him only more tame and manageable.

"Open the door, Varian," she repeated firmly.

That made him grin. Softly pinching her lower lips, he said, "My, you are a fast learner at times, quick and clever. Thou are in true, a woman."

That insult, sharp and unintentionally too accurate, made the color darken on Merry's cheeks. She resettled her spine in a more noble posture, jutted her chin, and was surprised when Morgan opened the door without further argument.

Quickly she raced down to Indy's cabin. She could feel the captain watching as she frantically knocked. The door opened to present Merry with the drowsy faced boy. It wasn't until Indy's biting eyes clearly focused on her that it occurred to her it was no easier to discuss the nature of her distress with boy, than man.

Without a word she pushed passed him into his cabin, and quickly fled under the blankets on his bed. It took twenty minutes for Indy to get the issue from Merry and another twenty to get her to stop crying. By the time she was comfortably tucked into his bunk, glass of brandy in her fingers, and cabin door locked behind him, Merry noted the boy was very practical and matter-of-fact about everything. Much better than it would have been if she had to rely on Kate. She rolled over in his bed and went quickly to sleep.

Morgan was sitting comfortably established in a chair reading when the boy entered the cabin. Indy set the bundle he carried on the carpet, poured himself rum, and sank to the floor, his silk robe puffing up around him. He unwound his braid slowly, shaking out the dark waves to fall across his lithe body to the floor. "She's locked in my cabin. I'll bring her back in the morning," he said.

Morgan watched as he pulled a brush through his long waves. After several minutes, the boy explained, "At least the tears stopped, though I can hardly call her mood pleasant."

"Ah," was Morgan's response to that. He favored the boy with a dark smile. "If you ever leave this ship, your future will be secure. You will be able to find employment as a lady's maid."

For that, Morgan got a cold black stare. Turning course, the captain added thoughtfully, "It has been a long time since you've spent a night in my cabin."

Short. Uncivil. "Shay snores."

From the bundle sitting beside him, Indy pulled free a sketchbook and pencils. Morgan's black eyes sharpened with disapproval. "I thought we had agreed you wouldn't do that on ship. There are more than a few who would garrote you if they knew of your proclivity to scribble everything you see."

"You agreed. And I've not sketched for a long time. I needed a new subject. I don't think any of the crew would mind what I sketch now."

Morgan watched in silence as the boy moved the charcoal

pencil in graceful strokes across the blank canvas. "Have you asked her to pose for you?" Morgan asked.

"No. I remember her body by memory, rather well." That earned Indy a burning stare. He continued with the lines of charcoal.

Morgan tossed his book on a small table. "Do you plan to do that all night?"

"Just until I'm ready to sleep."

Climbing into his bed, with a disquieting grin, Morgan said, "If you sketch her nude, you won't sleep at all tonight."

Indy had been expecting exactly that response. He tipped back his head, drained his rum, lifted from his portfolio a finished portrait of Merry, and dropped it on the captain's stomach.

"Sleep with it," he bit off, before he went to the window bench.

CHAPTER ELEVEN

Considering the situation of being trapped on a pirate ship of men, there were little kindnesses by Morgan, here and there, that made Merry's world tolerable. Morgan's treatment of her set the terms of her confinement. Not violated or harmed by their captain, the crew would not dare either. She was permitted association with Mr. Seton, who proved pleasant in company. He was gentlemanly of manner and always ready with a fascinating tale or two.

Away from the strict rules of society, there was nothing Merry couldn't ask, nothing Merry couldn't learn, and nothing Merry could not endeavor, if she so wished to. What limits there were, were the limits Morgan placed on her. While being his hostage was an infuriating circumstance, it walked hand in hand with the first real freedom and lack of censure she'd ever known.

There was a certain irony to that if one had the interest to note it.

Somehow, the boy had worked from the captain, permission to allow Merry to stay in his cabin while her flux ran its course. Exactly how he had managed that, Merry didn't want to know, but she refused to allow herself to believe he had done it with the true cause of her distress. It was bad enough she'd been forced to discuss *this issue* with Indy. The notion that her biological predicament might somehow have entered a discourse between the boy and Morgan was a humiliation she would have felt for a century.

Indy's cabin was Spartan and without personality. His bunk, while comfortable and warm of blankets, did not hold the plushness or the pleasant scent of Morgan's bed. Subtle luxury and comfort ran floor to beam in the captain's cabin. In Indy's cabin there was cleanliness, order, and uncluttered precision.

Everything in Indy's cabin was locked up tighter than a bank vault. Still, it did not stop Merry from passing her days alone in his cabin trying to break into the vaults, which she hoped held clues to the mystery of this boy. Spending her days trying to spring latches and locks proved a pointless endeavor, but on the third day, by chance, she spied in surprise a dark leather ledger peeking from beneath the edge of his mattress. Wondering how she could have missed it, Merry snatched it from its hiding place and began to thumb through the pages anxiously.

The writing inside seemed to be a code of some kind. There were dates on the top of the pages that went back many years. She was sitting cross-legged on Indy's bunk, rushing through pages in growing frustration, when she happened upon a page with a simple sketch upon it. The color drained from Merry's face and her heart stopped.

There was not a lot of detail to the drawing, but oh, there didn't have to be. She was effortlessly able to make out the figures in the mocking-like caricature. Frantic and frightened, she recalled the expression on Indy's face when his eyes had clearly fixed upon her on the beach in Cornwall. Surprise and displeasure. She'd sensed then that this strange boy knew more than he revealed, but the sketch drawn in his ledger confirmed it.

She tried to make reason of when he might have drawn this—she was walking in Hyde Park. And this was not just any picture of her. She did not need anyone to tell her the flamboyant, foppish buffoon strolling beside her was Rensdale, Morgan's archenemy.

The boy had known all along she had a connection with Rensdale, had saved her life, and brought her here anyway. She didn't know what to make of that or how to calculate and prepare for the danger of this. Fearfully, she wondered what else he knew.

Trembling with panic and feeling betrayed, for betrayed she felt, since she'd grown to trust the boy and thought kindly of him. She jumped when the cabin door opened and Indy entered carrying her dinner tray. Without thought, she hurled the book at him and sprang to her feet, as the content of her meal scattered across the spotless wooden floor.

She shouted, "You lied to me. You know I have a connection to Rensdale. And you brought me to Morgan knowing all that. How could you do it, Indy? How could you lie to me?"

Calmly, Indy leaned back against his closed cabin door and crossed his arms. "Of course I lied to you. What did you expect? Thomas Becket?"

How could he so callously admit it to her? Struggling for composure, she asked, "Why haven't you told Morgan the truth?"

Merry watched him as he slowly lowered to the floor and began to collect the splattered food and dishes at his feet. After another equally long, painful pause, he said carelessly, "I have my reasons, Merry."

She darted across the room and shoved her face into his, forcing him to look at her. "Has it occurred to you that Morgan might kill me if he learns the truth? I thought you cared for me in some small way."

Angry at the parts that were incorrect and angrier at the parts that were correct, Indy flung brutally, "Take him to bed, dammit. Perhaps, you'll listen to me now. Save your life and take him to bed. If you want to get back to Falmouth living, the only way to do that is through Morgan's sheets."

"Never. It is not possible to save yourself by destroying yourself. You don't understand what that would mean to me, or else you wouldn't think it such a trivial thing."

"Perhaps not, but I do know one survives only if one is willing to survive," Indy said, his voice severe.

Merry was staring at him like an angry roaster. The air between them hissed with her fury. He made a slow movement to rise. "I've kept your secret thus far, Merry. And I've kept you alive. What worry have you that I won't continue to do both?"

A hush fell. Feeling the pangs from the conscience he thought long dormant, Indy cursed under his breath. "A smart girl would spend her time with what's she learned, and reason the wise move with it."

"A smart girl wouldn't be here at all," Merry said, a touch brokenly.

"No, I don't imagine she would. I know it's not a comfort to you, and you certainly have little reason to believe me, but it will all work about for the best, if you let it. Try to remember, things are not always what they seem. It's not as desperate as you think."

He gathered the tray and caught a glimpse as Merry knuckled her eyes, in that way she had when she was going to cry, and didn't want to.

"Christ, Merry, there's no need to enact a tragedy. Coupling is a perfectly normal part of human existence."

That made her cheeks burn and her eyes flash again.

"No woman has ever died from going to a man's bed," he said, in a feeble attempt at reassurance.

Startled out of her tears and back into fury, she snapped, "That's something only a man would say."

"Perhaps." Indy's smile was uncharacteristically sympathetic. "But that doesn't make it any less true."

~~~

Morgan closed the door to his cabin and slowly began to undress. He took off his shirt, dropped it over the back of a chair, and gazed at the empty window bench. He strolled across the room, poured a hearty brandy, and then stretched out atop his bed. For five days the boy had kept Merry locked in his cabin, ostensibly in consideration of the rigors of menstruation. Morgan more suspected it was to provoke a conflict, though what kind of conflict, Morgan didn't know for certain.

Morgan gazed out the stern windows at the starless night, his thoughts were claimed by a vision of Merry at sleep. He thought of her silken flesh caressed by moonlight and her dark curling hair flowing across the pillow as she clutched the pug against her. A smile rose to his face, as he recalled how her small white teeth were always nibbling on his shirt cuffs.

The last thing he'd expected was to like the girl.

He sipped his drink slowly. The girl in a small way resembled Ann. Was that why the boy had brought her here? The boy disclaimed all memories of the past. Was that a lie? Even after five years, and with the advantage of age, he couldn't read the boy completely.

For all that Indy was the smartest youth he'd ever known, the trauma of his years in captivity, far too often colored the boy's perceptions. It made him cynical, untrusting, and wrong in his observations. Indy was never more wrong than in his observations of *him*. What had he expected by bringing the girl aboard ship? Morgan had his own generous share of flaws, but harming women had never been one of them. The boy should have known that without having dumped Merry at his feet.

Morgan refilled his glass, stretched across his bed, and lit his pipe. Inhaling deeply, he let the smoke swirl through his blood before he released it to swirl in the stillness of the cool cabin air. Another puff and it was no longer the present plaguing his thoughts, it was the past.

The door opened.

Morgan looked up to see Indy there. The boy, without a word, crossed the cabin and stretched out atop the window bench.

Morgan found himself saying, "I want her back in the morning."

Ignoring the order, Indy began to read.

Morgan took another long pull from his pipe. He watched the boy through the white curls floating from his lips, feeling the edges of his anger soothed.

"Tom has been hearing whispering among the malcontents in the f'cle. He feels the girl is becoming a problem that we need deal with soon."

Indy set down the book. "A problem for who? You or the girl?"

After a long pause, Morgan's eyes lifted from the pipe to the boy's.

Mildly, the captain said, "A problem with the crew aboard ship is everyone's problem, lad. She is not safe alone in your cabin any longer."

"As your grace pleases," snapped the boy. Then, "What has Tom heard? You must really think there is danger, or else you would not have mentioned it."

A frigid pause rose between them.

When Morgan finally spoke, his voice was without feeling. "Nothing that can't be handled."

Indy rolled on the bench, the sharp movement causing his braid to fall until it swung above the cabin floor.

"Damn you. Why didn't you take her maidenhead in Falmouth and let her go? What amusement can you possibly find, toying with her until one of the crew kills her?"

Morgan reached for his drink. "It's not my hand that brought her here."

"But it is your vanity that keeps her a prisoner. Don't pretend with me it's more."

"Nonsense." Morgan's smile had taken on a hard edge. "What was it you expected me to do with the girl? I can't decide which irritates you more. That I haven't taken her to my bed, or that I want to. It would serve us both the better, if you simply tell me which, since your pubescent disapproval becomes more muddled each day."

"I am angry because you keep her your prisoner, while you cannot decide between your lust and your honor, and you think that is kindness."

"Well, well, well," said Morgan darkly. "We are dragging out the siege canons tonight and trying to level the village with a single blast. Have I missed my epiphany? Of course I desire the girl. A man would have to be dead not to desire her. Of course I've not harmed her. A man would have to be a barbarian to harm her physically. That I am unwilling to do either proves nothing more than I am human. Is that really all the point there is, to what you have done, bringing the girl here?"

Indy's eyes opened wide and he turned then on Morgan and gave him an even look. "Tell me, Captain, if the girl dies because of your quagmire, what part of you will you consider still human?"

There was a short laugh, a lifted brow. "Shrewd. Oh, very shrewd, lad. But, a better question is, if the girl dies, what part of yourself are you depending upon not to be human."

A long pause. Morgan watched the shifting shards of light in the boy's eyes, though the emotion betrayed was far from readable.

Refilling his glass, Morgan crossed the cabin and handed it

to the boy. He said, "While I'm heartened there is more to you bringing her here than I feared there was a moment ago, the girl won't rid you of me, boy. No matter your plotting, you will not leave this ship until I wish it."

Indy's dark gaze burned in challenge. "You do not read me as well as you think."

The boy drained his glass, handed it back to the captain, turned on the bench, and went silent.

"Interesting," Morgan said in a civil way, sinking down into his chair. "If it's salvation from me you want, boy, you've gotten your tribal ritual wrong. When the natives wanted salvation from the gods, they tossed the virgin sacrifice to her death in a fiery pit. The gods didn't deflower them. Perhaps, you should have slit the girl's throat at the beach, if you wanted salvation from me."

"Perhaps," the boy said calmly. "But perhaps there is a new version of the tribal ritual. The one who finds salvation is the one who deflowers the girl."

Morgan's thundering laughter filled the cabin.

"What a naïve thing to say. How refreshingly young. If I didn't know better, I'd think you were a virgin, as well."

~~~

Merry woke to a midmorning of grayish light and rain. Moving stiffly, she realized with a start she was on the window bench. She had fallen asleep in Indy's cabin and at some point during the night she'd been carried back to Morgan's. Wondering at the cause of this unexpected and far too sudden change, she rolled over to find Morgan reclined on his bed reading.

Propped on his pillows, legs crossed at bare ankles, somehow Morgan managed to look regal, even shirtless and shoeless. His bronze chest peeked from within a flowing emerald banyan, loosely draped over his goliath frame above buckskin breeches.

Morgan didn't look up from his book. "Ah, the beautiful detainee wakes. You've slept uncommonly late this morning, my dear. Your breakfast is quite cold by now."

The endearment hung awkwardly in the unsettled air. Merry pulled the quilt high about her neck. "Don't call me 'my dear'. From you, it is an obscenity."

"There is no such thing as an obscenity. It's a lie made up by the church so that young girls don't sin."

When Morgan finally looked at her, his eyes were gleaming in a way that told Merry she had amused him.

"You can blame the rain, not my low character for my presence." Morgan managed to convey, neatly by his tone, that he would prefer to remain in pleasant solitude with his book. He calmly turned a page and continued to read.

Tossing the rust colored brocade pillow from her lap, she padded barefoot across the cabin to sit alone at Morgan's table.

"Oatmeal." Merry's dainty nose crinkled with real loathing as she stared into the bowl. Beside her was Morgan's empty plate, and she could see the remains of eggs there. "I hate oatmeal. Why did I get oatmeal?"

Manifesting no interest, Morgan said, "Indy brings your meals. Discuss the matter with him if they are not to your liking. Eat or don't eat. It seems a rather simple choice."

"I can't eat it. There are worms in it." That elicited no response. She glared at him, thought about throwing the bowl, and instead reached for the pot. To her further dismay, what poured into her cup was cold and coffee. Staring at him, Merry accused, "Is this my latest punishment? First, you rudely transport me, like a sack of meal, from one cabin to the next without my consent. And now starvation."

"My, we are in a mood this morning, aren't we, Little One?" Morgan said with an air of disinterest, turning another page. "Or, is it my company and conversation your mood desires today? What should I make of that?"

"You should make that I don't like worms in my oatmeal."

"I thought we'd resolved the issue of the oatmeal."

After several more pages, Morgan finally set aside the book. Reluctantly he climbed from the bed, looked into her bowl to see that there were indeed worms there. "Would you eat eggs if I fetched them for you?"

Merry squirmed uneasily beneath the watching wait of his stare. Why was Morgan being solicitous? It was not that he was ever unkind. It was just unlike him to be intentionally kind.

When she nodded, his hand moved carelessly to lift a curl from her cheek. "You do realize you are the first person on this ship ever to be served by its captain? If I see you properly fed, can I expect to return to my book in peace?"

Merry opened her mouth to speak, but no words came out. Hunger won over pride. She clamped her mouth shut and jerked her face away.

Morgan's soft laughter filled the cabin as he let the silky strands of her hair slip slowly through his fingers. "I'm going to take your silence to mean we have a bargain."

He left then, leaving the cabin door open. More than a quarter hour passed before Morgan returned. Merry was still sitting in the chair as his well-muscled arms passed over her, and he set the tray before her.

As his hands moved gracefully back from the table, his palms found her shoulders, in an idle way. Merry was drawn into his gentle hold before she had time to realize what he was doing. As little as she knew about intimacy, there was something in the way his blood-warmed hands touched her that made this meager contact shockingly intimate.

"Bargain met," Morgan said. "Now I expect you to eat and be silent."

And to her further vexation, he dropped a light kiss on her

curls. Merry's eyes followed him in his trek to bed. He stretched back upon the pillows to continue reading. She picked at her breakfast without exchanging another word with Morgan, taking every care to pretend he didn't exist. For some odd reason, his presence in the cabin unsettled her today, more than usual. Morgan was really doing nothing that should have put her nerves on edge.

Finished with her meal, Merry's next dilemma was how to occupy herself. These were the worst kind of days for her, alone in the cabin with Morgan. While he could dismiss her from his mind, dismissing him was something she could never quite manage. The cabin hummed with his presence. Even quiet and still, he dominated the world around him.

She remained stoically silent, curled in the chair, one by one dabbing the crumbs from her biscuit off the table, determined not to speak. She didn't want to give him the satisfaction of knowing she was miserably uncomfortable. Frowning, she wondered why he kept her. In spite of his occasional flirtations, she knew he wasn't pleased Indy had brought her here. She sensed he neither liked, nor hated her. The vast majority of her hours passed snared in his enigmatic, unfeeling presence.

How was it possible a man could make time pass so slowly? Each moment that passed was longer than the one before. It had been only a quarter hour and it felt like eternity. How was it possible this unbearable silence was not unbearable to him?

She could hear every creak and groan of the ship, every footstep, every slapping cable. She turned and looked at him as he turned a page. Even the motion of his hand seemed to pass in irritating slowness.

Without another word, Morgan pushed up from the bed and calmly left the cabin.

For the remainder of the day, the rain kept Merry below decks. She only saw Morgan once, in the afternoon, when he returned to the cabin to enter something into his log book. She had only a moment to wonder how he had left the cabin shoeless in a banyan and returned clad in a shirt, wearing knee high boots.

Merry stared after him as he departed through the cabin door. The door was left open. Another new mystery in her life. Why had Morgan left the door open?

The remainder of the day passed for Merry sitting in the center of Morgan's Persian rug teasing her pug with Morgan's slipper. The dog caught and chomped it, from time to time, as she stared out into the passageway.

Occasionally, a member of the crew passed and looked in, betraying a surprise, equal to her own, that the door was open. She smiled at those she recognized, all except Mr. Craven, who had given her a harsh scowled. She wished she had the courage to throw the slipper at him, but to be honest, she was afraid of the man.

At nightfall she fell asleep where she was, slipper in tatters and pug clutched against her breasts. It was how Morgan found her when he entered the cabin with Tom Craven in tow. He stood for a long time above her, looking at her, before he stepped away from Merry.

He made a graceful gesture with an arm for Tom to sit. Morgan poured them each a hearty whiskey. He could feel Tom's dull eyes, piercingly watching. Which way would his quartermaster go with their most frequent argument of late?

It was Tom who spoke first, into the dark quiet of the room.

"We will reach Bermuda within a fortnight. It is past time to end this, Varian. You can put the girl on a ship bound for England before she is harmed."

A logical solution, thought Morgan. Morgan's black eyes shimmered with amusement. "We don't even know who she is. Why she was spying on my meeting with Camden, or her connection to Rensdale. You would have me release her without even knowing the threat of that? What am I to make of that, Tom?"

Tom made note of the frequency Morgan's gaze strayed to the sleeping girl. The captain seemed unaware he was doing it. "Surely, there are better ways to get the answers you want than this game you are playing. It would serve you better to put the fear of God in her, buy her silence, and send her on her way."

"Do you not think I would have done that, if it would have worked?"

Tom met the black stare squarely. "You have not even tried." Then Tom's astringent eyes fixed on the girl. "You are old enough to be her father." Tom delivered that last comment with just the right amount of disdain. Morgan allowed himself to acknowledge Thomas had done that particularly well.

Morgan looked at Tom Craven without letting him see it. He wondered if his remorse over the girl showed, if Tom saw it, if that was why his quartermaster was so obviously worried over the meaningless, never-ending plotting of the crew.

Morgan's brow skipped upward, mocking. "As I recall, you wanted me to kill her. Now you want me to free her to spare her my bed. You have a rather flexible use of your morality, Thomas. Though, I have always found you Huguenots, flexible."

"It is best to end this posthaste," Tom warned fiercely. "You are stirring too much suspicion among the crew. I know you never believe these threats serious, but have you considered once the danger to the girl? What will become of your game if she is killed by the crew? Is your amusement really worth that?"

"Ah. Your concern is needless, Tom." Smiling, he looked

up from his drink, his black eyes mocking embers. "What do you imagine there is about this girl, that she stirs such unlikely reaction from both you and Indy? I think I'll keep the girl for that. An interesting experiment in human weakness."

Ignoring the taunt, Tom walked over to the table and refilled his glass. The girl turned on the rug, but didn't wake. Rather suddenly, Tom said, "Do you really wish to risk the crew having access to her? Regardless of what she is, no woman deserves that. It was a damn foolhardy move to leave the door open all day."

Morgan cut him off with a wave of the hand. "A good theatrical is often better at managing the men than a hanging. Shay was there. She was never out of his sight."

"And you think you can trust Shay with the girl."

Morgan's smile was disquieting. "But, of course. He would kill any man who tried to harm her."

"You could sell her in Trinidad. She'd fetch a good price. If you will not free her, sell her. You cannot afford a weakness with the crew. The longer you keep her, the more danger there is to you."

Morgan arched a brow, richly amused. "To me?"

"Yes," Tom said pointedly. The skin tightened across his thin cheekbones. "Is she your daughter?"

"Oh, Tom, I thought you were beyond the idle speculation of the crew."

"Something made you stop, in Ireland. More than a few of the men saw."

"Ah, so I embrace incest, but only within limits. I know I haven't always been philosophically consistent, but incest even in moderation would be a debauchery I could not rationalize. Don't work so hard, Tom. There's nothing to it. She's not my daughter. She is nothing at all to me."

"Then why haven't you beaten the truth from her?"

"She won't break. Not from a beating, but if you'd like to try."

Tom dropped his gaze.

Morgan took a moment to assess that, cut short his thoughts, and then bent to scoop Merry from the floor. She half woke, but was asleep again before he set her on the window bench and pulled up the quilts.

"My way is the kinder fate, Tom."

That made the older man scowl. Tom was, of course, right in every worry and counsel, but it didn't mean Morgan would let him know it.

Morgan gestured with an arm toward the door. They walked in silence topside. On deck, Morgan said suddenly, "During my days in France, there was a saying at court. 'The fuck is made all the better by a good hunt'. I admit that it loses something in the English translation, but the sentiment holds true. It's been a long time since I've been afforded the pleasures of a leisurely hunt. Let me hunt in peace, Tom."

Without letting Tom see, Morgan made a quick assessment of the quartermaster's face. Lighting his pipe, he waited patiently for Tom to digest that and make his next cautious move. The words had been deliberately coarse, the sentiment purposely crude, and the result predictable. Tom was unsure and didn't know what to make of any of it.

Strangely, that Tom was unsure did not please Morgan. The longer he stayed on ship, the more he worried that the years had taken too much possession of him. Christina, who knew him so well, had been right about that. Could any man go to the brink of the worst he was capable of doing, and then return to his better self? Morgan's gaze moved like a nightwalker across the crew. Does any man ever know who he is, who he has become, until he has faced both the best and the worst of himself?

He took another long drag from his pipe. What part of him would the girl be? The best, or the worst of who he was? Which part was him, in true? It was a disquieting self-confession to admit that he wasn't sure any more, and to wonder when that had happened.

"So, that is all this is to you? A good hunt?" Tom Craven said in tight-lipped displeasure.

The reproach in Thomas's eyes was masterfully done. Craven was, and always would be, a rigid moralist at heart.

Morgan's ringing laughter flooded the decks. "For God's sakes, no. Only a foolish man would risk his life for the hunt. You, Tom, have forgotten the fuck."

CHAPTER TWELVE

A warm October morning greeted Merry as she went topside. All around her the crew was busy at work. Shay sat at the bow, a lone figure. Something about the jeering from the port side told her the Irishman had done something to get into trouble again. In front of her Morgan stood, tall and flat hipped, his fine boned elegant features taut, without expression as he peered through the glass at something on the horizon. Mr. Seton gave her a sparkling smile of invitation, but to get to him she had to pass Mr. Craven.

Not bloody likely.

She resolved to find Indy. She found him sitting on the gun deck casings, a raucous group dicing near his feet.

Much to her dismay, the young pirate had never looked more unapproachable. His black eyes stared coldly through her. Pride kept Merry from standing there like a fool staring after him.

She left quickly for the spot on the bow where she'd spied Shay earlier. Hurrying across deck, she slammed head first into Mr. Craven. His long, calloused fingers closed painfully around her arms, as he set her back away from his chest.

His thin, dull set eyes held no malice, but then again, they didn't have to. Instinct warned her of his dislike of her and the danger of this man.

"Who the hell let you free?"

It was the kind of greeting she'd come to expect from Craven. Expecting it didn't make it one bit easier to respond to with composure.

Morgan's sudden presence saved her from that challenge. Amusement minced lightly through the occult blackness of his eyes, as he said, "I did, Tom, and we can discuss it in private if you have a care to."

It wasn't really an offer for discussion. Mr. Craven muttered a curt reply and walked off.

A neat movement of Morgan's hand set the tumbling curls from Merry's face.

"You don't have to be afraid of Tom. He won't hurt you. Not unless I tell him too."

She had forgotten, over the interval of being locked below decks for seven days, how terrifying Morgan could be topside. There were no subtle differences on the surface of the captain, to be picked up by her eyes—handsome face, sardonic mouth, and elegant posture—but there was much to be felt in her keener senses. A latent dangerousness, like a resting coiled spring, ready to strike at any moment, and an omniscient awareness tucked behind an unsmiling mask of boredom.

She made to move past him, and felt his hands warm on her shoulders, holding her in place. To her surprise, she was pulled inward into the firm angles of his body and her mouth brought quickly to his. The fast explicitness of the kiss caught her off guard.

Inside of her quivering muscles, she was reeling from the hot run of blood caused by her body's betrayal in enjoying this. When her body became limp to his will, he gently put her against the mast and let her go.

His laughter, quiet and enticing, made her shiver.

269

"I'm the only man aboard ship allowed to touch you, without permission."

He said it in that way, like an order. Without thinking, she snapped, "If that's meant to be reassuring——"

"It's not."

Morgan gave her a smile that's effect was its opposite. She stood frozen in place, watching his retreating back, wondering what the devil that was about.

Merry couldn't stop the faint color that began to stain her cheeks, and quickly made her way to Shay at the bow. She had almost joined Mr. Seton, his conversation would be a more lively entertainment, but there was something in the way the men around him stared at her that had kept Merry from going there.

Sinking down on the deck beside the Irishman, Merry muttered, "What the devil is wrong with everyone today?"

"Too long from port, Merry lass." His burly fingers did a harsh trek over the shredded rope in his lap. "Tempers always flash the last week before we reach land. Worse than a full moon, if ye ask me. Half the crew want'n to brawl, half the crew with their sheets in the wind. Best watch yer step, lass."

Sheets in the wind. Merry was alarmed she didn't need that explained to her. It was clear, whether she wanted it or not, her days aboard ship were accompanied by a salty education. Settling her chin in her hand, she asked, "And which is Morgan? Brawl or sheets? His mood has been more confusing than usual of late."

Stretching his legs before him, Shay thought it over carefully.

"Neither. Morgan is the devil. From where I sit, lass, if ye've got to be someone's property, it's best to be his. At least he's not of a mind to share ye."

"I'm not Morgan or any man's property," Merry corrected indignantly.

For the first time ever, Shay gave Merry a sharp, angry look.

"Now listen, lass," he said to her on a terse whisper. "Ye best let them believe ye are his property, unless ye be want'n to find yerself in a dark corner of this ship busier than ye know what to do with. Even the lad ain't allowed to be with ye topside. Don't want the crew get'n anything in their heads watch'n ye cozying up with the boy beneath Morgan's nose. Dammit, lass, the crew wanted to have a vote on ye."

That made Merry sit back and stare. "A vote?"

"More'n a few didn't think it was right ye sit'n in Morgan's cabin and the mon not sharing. Strictly speaking, lass, yer cargo."

The effect of his words on Merry made Shay's manner softened instantly.

"The last week of a sail is a dangerous time fer a woman aboard ship. It's best ye be know'n it. Stay put, lass. Watch ye I will, have no fear of that."

Before Merry could question him further, Shay had pulled her into the task of his punishment.

Sitting in the early afternoon sun, picking oakum proved a good excuse for keeping her face down and avoiding the notice of the crew. Morgan had left the decks an hour ago, and the men's notice had intensified and changed. Shay's brow had moved to a scowl and remained there. There were winks, predatory smiles, and looks she couldn't even put a description to.

Was life always so unpleasant for a woman in a world exclusively of men? She welcomed the rain when it sent her from deck, so that she could leave without looking like she was running.

Alone in the cabin, Merry rummaged through her pillows and blankets for the book she'd been reading earlier. It had been dreadful topside, and her mood was anything but bright.

Hours later, Merry was still sitting in the chair. Pipe smoke drifted under the cabin door from the watch and someone, somewhere, was singing "A Soldier and a Sailor".

With the coming of night the weather had grown worse again. The light drizzle that had spanked the polished decks, had turned into a furious downpour. The ship lurched beneath her, up and down, in a tumult that matched her own internal unrest.

She touched her lips, feeling Morgan's kiss there. The memory of her own response seared through her brain. There was not a single thing about this man that did not warn danger. Yet, fear as a protector failed her too often. There was no logic to why she was so afflicted by him.

Even after many weeks with him, Merry didn't know what manner of man Morgan was, in true. She was no closer to separating truth from myth than she had been her first night aboard ship.

The door opened.

Without a word, Indy crossed to the table. She noted the tray he carried had more than two plates. The boy went through his tasks in silence, spreading the white linen cloth across the polished tabletop; setting fluted wine glasses before each chair; and arranging the settings with a care that would have rivaled mother.

What was Morgan about now? There were eight settings at the table and polished silver candlesticks set ablaze, to boot. Morgan did not entertain.

She didn't know why, but the sight of the table elegantly

set made her nervous. "Is something going on that I don't know about?"

"Wear your hair up. Morgan is selling you at midnight," he jeered, then seeing her eyes cloud over with dismay, he relented. "Damn you're skittish tonight. It was a jest, Merry. What are you imagining in the foolish head of yours?"

"Shay told me the crew wanted a vote. And now Morgan is entertaining. It seemed odd."

Indy shook his head as he continued with his task.

"There is no need for panic, Merry. Tempers run short. Foolishness runs high. Life on ship is predictable. It's a captain's job to nip them both in the bud, before there is trouble. It's apt to be a grim drama tonight, but it's not directed at you. Try to remember that."

With that, the boy was gone.

Twenty minutes passed before Morgan entered the cabin, his manner careless and relaxed. Somewhere he had changed his garments, he was in his severe costume of black. There was both a gun and a knife tucked into his belt when Morgan never carried either. The unexpected presence of weapons caused her unease to heighten.

Morgan's arrival followed quickly with a knock at the door. Six men entered the cabin. Three men Merry knew well. Mr. Seton, Mr. Colerain, and Mr. Boniface. They were the three most senior crewmembers after Mr. Craven. With them, were other three men she would have preferred never to have known. The gunner Reade, the shipmate Tanner, and a vile little weasel known as Sails.

For all of Morgan's gentlemanly introduction of her, it soon became clear she was nothing in this gathering, though her presence at the table among the men was deliberate. How she knew this, she wasn't sure.

It just came to her as the evening progressed, an abrupt finger tilting up her chin, the way Morgan's gaze narrowed when it met hers. The tight hold of his blood-warmed fingers atop her hand.

The purposeful contact with her was completely at odds with the wispy gentleness of his usual touch, but there was something artful and calculated in the way each gesture was made. Strangely, it brought to her mind the memory of his kiss earlier on deck. Artful and calculated. That was what it had been.

The meal was far more extravagant than what Merry had grown accustom to aboard ship. A fine barley soup and curried rice cakes preceded a roasted chicken, procured from the small supply of livestock kept below decks for the captain's consumption.

Before dinner ended, Merry felt a small measure of her tension uncoil from her body. The grim drama that Indy had warned was going to happen hadn't, and she was beginning to believe that it wouldn't. Nothing had changed. Morgan, with an urbane mask covering his attractive features, seemed satisfied to listen to the conversation over brandy.

It was not really a pause in the conversation, it was more like a breath, where Morgan smoothly injected on a low voice, "A vote."

That effortlessly, he silenced the room. The entire chemistry changed. Merry would have sprung from the table if Morgan's hand hadn't fixed brutally around her wrist, holding her there.

"Which one of you thinks I share what's mine?" Morgan asked. "And, which one of you is foolish enough to think there is safety in numbers to defy me?"

Mr. Seton turned on his chair toward Morgan. "Varian—"

The captain cut him off so smoothly, it was hard to tell that was what he did.

"The problem with you, Brandon, is you fuck your genius to death. It was a rhetorical question."

Morgan's dark, unkindly gaze moved like a stalker among his startled companions.

"A bullet between the eyes. I thought it would end this. It did not. So the crew would like a vote on the girl? I have a better idea," said Morgan with a menacing grin.

He rose to his full height and tossed the gun onto the table. He subjected Merry to a critical survey before he pulled the knife from his belt to stand behind her chair.

"Let's see if one of you can put a bullet in me before I slit her throat."

Merry had no chance to react before he had her curls in a cruel grip and the knife against her neck.

"Try not to move, Little One. I can make this rather painless."

Merry stared in horror at the gun. She became aware of the rapid expansion of her chest that came with each panicked breath. Her eyes anxiously searched the men across the table from her. No one reached for the gun, but no one would meet her gaze either.

It was Mr. Boniface who first moved back from the table. "Let her go. You're scaring the girl to death."

Morgan jerked her hair hard and Merry cried out.

"I would rather slit her throat," Morgan said, "than let any man on ship touch what's mine. Which one of you thinks they can get a bullet in me and live? Or better still, which one of you wants the girl after she's dead?"

A long pause stretched the tension in the room until it was unbearable.

"Oh, my." Laughter stirred from deep in Morgan's chest. "Six of you. And not one of you is brave enough to try it. I thought the circle in the f'cle thought it time to challenge my command and authority. Six to one. Excellent odds. Or, is my crew only brave when they think I cannot see or hear them? Perhaps, I should rethink my crew."

The knife fell away as his fingers slowly relaxed in Merry's hair. Morgan tossed the jagged blade onto the center of the table before returning to his chair and brandy.

A minute or so passed in agonizing silence. Then, Morgan fixed his eyes upon her and said, "Go to Craven, Little One. I'm not finished here yet."

The blood was rustling with such force through the vein passages in Merry's ear she hardly heard him. Morgan's abrupt hand gesture directed her toward the door. It was then her startled gaze found Mr. Craven waiting grimly there.

She couldn't move, even though she wanted desperately to flee. She couldn't feel her legs. She couldn't feel anything. Noises, sights, smells, couldn't penetrate the numbing horror of what she'd just experienced.

Mr. Seton grabbed her harshly by the shoulder and propelled her to the door, into Craven's waiting clutches.

With the touch of Craven, her tears let go.

Mr. Craven gave her a harsh shake of annoyance and when that didn't silence her, he snapped, "Indy. Where the blazes are you. Get over here and take her now. I haven't got time for this nonsense."

She was out-of-control distraught by the time the boy reached her. She fought him furiously as he tried to drag her into the cabin. It had been too much, the knife on her throat. The way the men had stared at her. Morgan. Too much. She lashed out wildly, hysterically.

"Damn it, Merry. Tempers are short. One more scream and Craven is likely to return and beat you."

"I don't care," she screamed. "Morgan was going to kill me tonight."

"Well, I do care."

Once in his cabin, Indy grabbed her flailing arms and pinned her on the cabin floor beneath him.

"Damn it, stop fighting, and listen to me. It wasn't your life Morgan put at risk in there, it was his. Craven is furious. You're fortunate Craven didn't slit your throat himself."

She was breathing in rapid heavy gasps. Indy could see she was beyond understanding him. Cursing under his breath, he pulled her body from the floor, shoved his scarf into her mouth, and promptly tied her up.

There was a harsh knock on his door, and the boy sprang to his feet.

"For the love of God, Merry, Morgan risked his life for you. He was unarmed and challenged those men, with only their fear of him to protect him. That grim drama was about protecting your hide. Now be still. Be silent. Things are dangerous enough at present."

Being bound left little option to do anything else. He waited for her to stop struggling, and when she finally did, he said, "I'll be back as soon as I can. Don't fight the ropes. You'll cut your wrists."

She was imprisoned in Indy's cabin for most of the night. The ship was nosier in the darkness than usual. She heard Morgan's firm tread in the hall, but never his voice. There was a trial topside. That tidbit of news came to her on the heavily accented voice of Mr. Boniface recalling the tale of dinner on a hurried whisper in the companionway.

It was nearly dawn when Mr. Craven unlocked the door,

cut her free, and jerked her to her feet.

"If you make any more trouble, I'll take you topside and hang you next to Reade. Perhaps now you'll learn to behave with a modicum of caution."

Merry's eyes began to flash. How odious of Mr. Craven to blame the events on her.

Before she could respond, he gave her a hard jerk and sneered, "One would think you'd learn to hold your tongue, by now. You best hold that temper in check. If you flash it in front Morgan tonight, he's apt to chew you up and spit you over the rail. He's not pleased beyond half that he had to kill one of his own crew over you."

With that, Craven shoved Merry into Morgan's cabin.

She found the captain stretched out on his goliath bed. He was swilling rum from a bottle, resembling more a boar at a trough than the graceful acts of careless elegance, which were his usual mannerisms.

He continued to drink in silence, studied her for a moment, showing no expression, before he said without a trace of feeling, "I can't have my men plotting in numbers every time they get excited over something. Though, I would have preferred the issue resolved without the hanging."

Merry leaned back against the door and stared at him. There was something in his posture, his demeanor, not at all familiar to her. He looked almost hollow, a sort of soul deep weariness about him, and a strange light in his black eyes, she couldn't begin to decipher. How odd he looks and how unlike himself, she thought. She didn't know what she had expected, but it was not this.

If what Craven said was true, Morgan had killed a man tonight. If what Indy said was true, the captain had risked his life for her. Of all her possible reactions to the night's events, the one to claim her, she didn't anticipate.

She wasn't even sure how it came to be, but she soon found herself atop the bed, curled into his side and weeping. Tears began to run down her cheeks the moment she touched him. He wrapped an arm around her, gently holding her to him as his hand smoothed up and down her back in quiet comfort.

"It will all be well, Little One."

The gentle touch made her cling, only more tightly, to him as she wept. It felt so good, so warm in his arms. The anxiety of the past few hours poured out of her. She did not think of what she was doing, or how odd it was that it was Morgan she should want to comfort her. Every emotion inside of her was raw, her nerves volatile, and the press of her exhausted limbs into his hard structure only intensified her need to absorb it.

She was grateful Morgan didn't speak. He looked down at her head, adjusted her closeness, and let her weep. Gradually her tears slowed, then stopped, but she remained in his arms, tired by her crying. Beneath her ear his heart beat steadily. His warmth melted through her clothing like a caress. The scent of him, a whisper of man, tobacco, and wintergreen, had the strange power to be soothing. She nestled closer to him.

His arm tightened for an instant, and then relaxed in a gentle drape against her back. Merry gazed up at him, his face only inches from her. She could see into the depths of his dark eyes. The flesh of his forefinger ran the gentle slopes of her cheek, lightly brushing away the traces of tears.

"I'm sorry you were frightened."

His voice was lower than usual. Then it wasn't the tips of his fingers on her cheeks, but his hands slowly lifting her to meet him as he lowered his face.

Their lips met and Merry felt herself go soft and pliant, moving forward on her own without his urging. His mouth was sweet and tender, a forceless seduction, causing her fingers to curl around his shirt, holding on as her lips opened, and her senses filled with him.

For a moment everything around her seemed to stop. She was grateful for the void that left her only aware of the gentleness in his kiss, the firm warmth of him against her, the strong arms that lifted her effortlessly, and the heat that snaked through her emotion chilled limbs.

Her limp body was turned into Morgan. His kisses moved to her neck and shoulders as he softly murmured, in comforting tones, words she could not catch hold of. Shivers of pleasure danced through her as feather-light, his mouth touched the line of her jaw, her cheek, her hair.

Finally, Morgan raised his head, pressing his lips softly against her forehead, and Merry realized he had set her atop the window bench.

"All will be well, Little One," he said, before he quietly passed through the cabin door.

CHAPTER THIRTEEN

The next night Merry sat curled in a chair watching Morgan work on his charts. Yesterday had shown the captain to her in a startling new light, and there was still a wash on him of something different she had never seen before. A thousand questions rolled through her brain, though cautioned warned not to give voice to any of them.

He completed the calculation he was making, sitting back in his chair in that way he had before proceeding with his next meticulous action.

"Why did you kill Reade?" Merry asked.

Morgan adjusted slightly in the chair to fix upon her eyes. "To save my own neck."

His tone alone should have curled her blood and stopped her. It did not.

"Indy said you did it to protect me. Made an example of Reade, so that none of the crew would dare harm me."

"Indy says a great many things, most of them nonsense. I can't have men in my crew I don't trust."

A perfectly logical response. Still, nothing made sense to her.

Merry had spent the night trying to connect the pieces of this man into some kind of reasonable consistency and found none existed. Shay was right. Nothing about the man made sense.

Her life existed in proximity with his that should have provided more clarity, not less. She knew his every routine. The

281

precise manner each task was done. What emotions his expressions betrayed, the tell-signs of when to avoid him, and the tell-signs of when he was toying with her. She knew, in fact, each intricate expression of his physical being, but not a thing about his inner being.

What was the key to the mystery of this man?

"What was your wife like?"

Delicate surprise augmented Morgan's eyes. It pleased Merry that he hadn't been expecting that question.

He returned the surprise by answering her: "A pretty little thing. Young, like you."

"Was she French?"

Morgan laughed.

"God, no. British. Though I had to travel to America to find her."

He stared at the chart for awhile. He tossed the plotting divider on the table, sighed, and then turned into her alertly watching gaze to meet it directly.

"Were you a pirate when you met her?"

Morgan's eyes darkened.

"No. Ann would never have tolerated such disreputable conduct."

"Then, what then were you?"

"A foolish man," he said reflectively.

"Why did you become a pirate?"

He picked up the divider in a manner that should have conveyed to her his annoyance.

"Ann died. Society held no charms or amusement, there was nothing to hold me on land, and it is very difficult to find long intervals of solitude to read from the back of a horse. Highwayman would not have worked well. Piracy was the more accommodating pursuit."

She knew that answer was ridiculous and far from the truth. The sudden displeasure in his voice warned he'd had enough of her probing. Wisdom dictated leaving off, but it was almost as though she could see a slight crack into him, and the impulse to run through it was very strong.

"You could have been anything you wanted to be. You are clearly a wellborn and educated man. It wasn't society, or amusement. Or solitude to read. Underneath those artfully constructed layers, you are a sad, bitter man. Only bitterness could prompt one to throw away so many gifts."

Without looking at her, he continued in his task.

"You are beautiful, gentle of manner, quick of wit, and look where it has gotten you. By your logic you would be the most bitter person to walk the earth. The questions you ask do not lend to simple answers. Do not insult me by thinking they do. Do not show me your impertinence again by thinking you may ask them."

It was a warning, no matter how measured the voice was that delivered it. The sudden shift of his mood should have frightened Merry.

Instead she found herself saying, "I am vexing, irritating and impertinent. I can't imagine why you keep me. Whatever will you do with me?"

"What, indeed. That is a question I would not want answered, if I were in your shoes."

"Ah, but these are not my shoes. They are Indy's."

She rose from the chair in a manner dismissive, enormously pleased she had managed not to cower in the face of his pitching mood. She retrieved her brush from the top of his sea chest and sank upon the rug. She unwound the braids of her hair, and then she felt the burn of his eyes upon her as she began to slowly work the brush through her curls. She brushed her hair longer than usual that night. Never once did Morgan lift his eyes from her.

Why does he watch me? Merry wondered.

If it were lust, surely she would be in his bed by now. No man on ship would stop him from taking what he wanted. There was no power forcing his restraint or his often kind treatment of her.

Beyond the occasional touch and inappropriate advance, he never took. She knew, in that moment, he would never force himself on her. He watched her, but it was Morgan who stopped Morgan. Not once had it ever been her doing that had kept her from his bed.

Morgan watched as Merry put down the brush, then it was her fingers in her hair. Through his shirt he could see the outline of her slender back. When she raised her arms there was a glimpse of a round breast, and just a hint of cream-flesh leg and ankle showing.

She retrieved the brush and this time the strokes were slow. Her beauty was a powerful weapon. It often surprised him she never tried to use it. He half suspected she wasn't even fully aware of her effect on men. He was certain in her proper British upbringing, no one had ever warned her what being five weeks without a woman could do to the male anatomy.

Morgan rose from his chair.

"You are a very beautiful girl, Little One. I can never quite decide what price to demand when I sell you in Trinidad."

~~~

Morgan was gone in the morning, not from the cabin, but the ship. Exactly how one disappeared in the middle of the Atlantic Ocean was a mystery tossed on the heap of all the mysteries unresolved for Merry since joining the *Corinthian*.

Indy announced he was keeping her locked below for her

safety during Morgan's absence. When Merry vehemently protested this punishment of isolation, he relented by allowing her visits from the crew. Mr. Seton and Mr. Boniface were frequent haunts in Morgan's cabin. They proved pleasant diversions, and were in good spirits since the *Corinthian* was less than ten days' sail from land.

That they would soon reach land did not put Merry in good spirits. At night, when she lay in Morgan's bed, her thoughts drifted to the captain. She wrestled with endless questions as to what reaching land would mean to her. She wondered if Morgan would, in true, sell her. She had many reasons to be wary of the man. Yet somehow, she did not believe he could commit such villainy. That, in itself, was a silly thing, since she was under no illusion as to the manner of man Morgan was.

Her thoughts grew more troubled as his absence grew longer. On the fifth day it rained. That night Indy surprised her with a fresh water bath from the drops he collected in a barrel. It had been many weeks since she'd had a full bath, fresh water in low supply, and it was a soothing luxury. She washed herself and her hair. She dressed in the garments from Ireland, the only dress she possessed, since she'd tossed out the cabin window Christina Wythford's gowns.

That night at the evening meal, Indy surprised her a second time by gifting her with the presence of Morgan's two young officers at the table. The evening progressed enjoyably as Mr. Seton and Mr. Boniface entertained her with amusing tales of America. They seemed eager to make the event gay. She wondered if it were in response to her increasingly pensive mood, or in response to knowing what Morgan had decided for her fate. They engaged in light-hearted buffoonery and mock battle to make her laugh. Occasionally, she felt Indy's scowl

SUSAN WARD

upon her as she giggled in delight over their humor.

Indy's scowl confused Merry. The festive meal was by all accounts his doing, but her enjoyment of his gift was clearly irritating him. There were times the boy displayed a strange possessiveness of her. He never permitted her a moment alone with either Mr. Seton or Mr. Boniface. She often felt his watching gaze upon her. Was it possessiveness or something else?

He had saved her life, but only to put her in the captain's bed. He had not brought her aboard ship to keep her for himself. Yet, he watched over her.

The meal was over, the table cleared, and when Indy announced it was time to leave Merry alone in the cabin, the two men protested. Settling back in their chairs, lighting cigars with profuse apologies to her, they drew the evening out longer.

Merry soon found herself sitting with them on Morgan's carpet, playing a fanciful game where the names of famous people were written on parchment, licked, stuck to the forehead, and then solved by asking questions of the room.

They were halfway through their third bottle of Morgan's fine Madera, the scowl on Indy's face had become a thing fierce. He had not wanted to play the game. Merry suspected he had only permitted it because she had insisted upon playing.

Every time she looked at the boy, she laughed harder. Mr. Seton, devilishly funny at times, had neatly penned Indy's card "Morgan." Indy's questions, through gritted teeth, coupled with the prompt answers, only added to the hilarity of such a preposterous endeavor.

The ship rocked beneath them like a great wooden cradle, the moonlight danced through the windows. Merry realized that she was a little drunk.

When Mr. Seton put a cushion on his thigh, she sank onto

it without a second thought. The evening had been delightful. Smiling at Mr. Seton, she missed the subtle change on Indy's grim face.

They were all laughing when the door went wide and Morgan entered. With the quick response of a tiger, the boy sprang to his feet and held the captain's gaze as Morgan crossed the room in easy strides.

Merry jerked upright from Mr. Seton's thigh, knocking the pillow off his leg to send Morgan's fine crystal glasses to rattle on the floor. The captain's heavy lidded eyes fixed and narrowed on her, but he only did a brief flutter with his fingers through Merry's hair as he continued to his desk.

"Pretty children," Morgan commented wryly. "Which one of you shall win salvation?"

Merry's eyes rounded at the severity of his mood.

Removing papers from a leather case, Morgan said, "You know, Indy, instead of selling her, we should keep her as an amusement for the men since she has learned to manage so well with the crew," said Morgan suddenly.

"As you wish, Captain," was all Indy responded before quietly moving to collect the scattered parchment and glasses from the floor.

"And take that damn parchment from your forehead. I find it not funny at all," Morgan added, more severely.

A curt nod of his head sent the crew scrambling from the cabin. In a trice Merry was left alone in the cabin with Morgan. He turned to stand above her, staring down at her with eyes more harsh than he had ever directed at her before.

"After Reade's hanging, one would think you'd learn to exercise some caution with the crew."

Morgan was not usually curt with her. She remained in the center of the rug, staring at his back as he settled into work at his desk. His casual mention of Reade's hanging hardly came as a comfort to Merry's taut nerves.

Unsure how to manage this disturbing change in him, she curled into a tight ball, arms hugging knees, staying as she was on the floor, watching him. He removed from the case a large bundle of documents which were transported to his sea chest. He gave her no notice until after he snapped closed the lock on the chest.

Subjecting her to a critical survey, he said, "You can go to sleep without fear, Little One. I'm not in the mood to bite."

That last comment was accompanied by one of his dark smiles. Merry stared and watched as he returned to his desk. She had never once undressed with Morgan near, somehow he was always conveniently from the cabin when she needed him to be. In his present mood, this change was not one she would welcome.

Effortlessly reading her concern and amused by her dismay, he said, "I won't look. Your virgin modesty is absurd, since you clearly lost your disdain of men."

His back was toward her, sitting in chair, and fixed on work. She debated with herself and then sprang from the carpet. Whatever this mood was, instinct warned her not to irritate him further.

She quickly removed her garments and pulled his shirt over her head. She crossed the cabin to the bench, laid down, and almost completely disappeared from view beneath the quilt. She turned on her side to stare out the stern windows. The tension in the cabin and the rocking of the ship were not a comfortable thing for her, at present. The ship lurched beneath her in a sharp movement that Merry could now recognize as a ground swell.

They'd been dead in the water for days, but with Morgan's

return came the return to sails. The ship pitched again, making the lamp light flicker in the room. For some reason, the motion and flickering light were affecting her not at all well. Her vision blurred as the room swirled. She turned on the bench, trying to escape the strange discomfort of her body.

Her stomach turned. Her head throbbed. Was it the ship? Or was something wrong with her? The discomfort of her body won out of over Morgan's mood and her pride.

She rolled over to face him, the motion making her head swim more and her stomach more distressed.

"Morgan?" she groaned.

He ignored her. She repeated his name twice without being answered. His quill continued in his task, and would not even acknowledge her by looking.

Struggling to sit up, then thinking better of it, in a panicked voice she exclaimed, "Varian!"

He didn't look up from his work. "Yes, Little One?"

Damn, the man. Why must he toy with her at this of all moments? She tried to hold herself steady and found she couldn't. It was difficult to focus her gaze on him.

"Is it me, or is the cabin spinning for you, too?"

He looked at her then. "What?"

"Is the room spinning? It will not hold still. Oh, please make it stop." She knew she was going to be sick.

Morgan's dark eyes opened wider. He saw and understood. When she leaned over the edge of the bench and started to make little heaving motions, he crossed he room in two steps, grabbing the washbowl to hold it under her mouth.

"That's what you get," he observed, unsympathetically, as he collected her in his arms, "when you drink with pirates."

Merry struggled against his hold and against the motions of her stomach. This was humiliating. As her body convulsed, tears ran from her cheeks.

Gasping and jerking, she moaned, "I don't want to get sick."

"Don't fight it, Little One. The sooner you get sick, the sooner you'll feel better," he said in a sensible way. Merry promptly vomited into the bowl on his lap. "Better?"

The look Merry gave him made him laugh. She protested as Morgan moved with her to the chair.

"Stop fighting me," he admonished. "Until this passes, you'll feel better sitting up."

He settled with her on his lap in the chair.

It took hours for Merry's stomach to purge. The girl fought even this. When at last she lay calm in his arms, Morgan set the washbowl on the floor. They both fell asleep, as his patient fingers gently stroked her hair.

~~~

The next morning Merry came awake in agonized slowness. Her head was pounding. She was in Morgan's bed. She had a faint memory of him holding her last night, as she got sick in his arms.

He had promised she'd feel better, if she vomited. He had been wrong. She did not feel better today. She felt worse. Her eyes smarted from the light in the cabin, her entire body ached, and she could not recall a single thing after she had started to toss her stomach into the bowl. She did not remember falling asleep or being put to rest in Morgan's bed.

Lifting up the blankets, she was shocked to find herself naked under the bedding. She wondered when that had happened and why Morgan had undressed her. Finding her discarded shirt beside the bed, the foul stench flooding her nose gave her the answer. She must have missed the bowl a time or two.

She couldn't imagine what Morgan's temperament would be today. It was no less unsettling to note, she'd gotten drunk for the first time in her life. Covering her face with the burgundy coverlet she allowed herself a good cry. She was still head under blankets when the cabin door opened.

Morgan said, "God love us all, the girl is still alive. Feeling better this morning, my dear? Or should I say afternoon?"

He said it in a way that suggested he knew she didn't. Peeking out from beneath the covers, she sent him glare, then wished she hadn't. Mr. Craven was with him. The old man gave her a harsh stare as he settled at Morgan's table.

Morgan poured a short pull of whiskey into a glass and said over his shoulder to his quartermaster, "We'll make a pirate out of the wench yet, eh Tom? Especially if you continue to be so careless in your command of my ship while I'm gone. You should be damn glad all she's suffering today is a touch of hangover. The lads had her three sheets to the wind. If she'd been devalued, it would be your head."

Merry didn't know what that last comment meant, but Morgan was now standing over her, hand outstretched, glass in hand.

"Drink. It will make you feel better."

The last thing Merry wanted was more alcohol. She debated the wisdom of his advice since it was alcohol that created her current misery, but Morgan's mood did not pass with the night. Obedience seemed her wisest course, at present.

Tom watched as the girl took the glass, swallowed, and then coughed as the fiery liquid slid down her throat. Morgan stood above her patiently waiting for the return of the glass.

From the look of her expression, Tom was certain the girl had no idea how furious the captain was, or the cause of it. The girl was fast becoming a danger to them all.

He shifted his gaze back to the captain.

Tom asked, "Did you learn anything useful from Hancock?"

Morgan shrugged and poured a drink. "The good Commodore is as much a bore as ever. Though, I admit the amenities he travels with are more accommodating than my own, at present."

Merry missed the pointed smile he bent at her with that comment.

Her thoughts were too busy spinning. Commodore Hancock? Merry eyes fixed wide on Morgan. She wondered why Morgan let slip, in her hearing, such a shocking tidbit about himself. Hancock was a revered American naval hero, charged with protecting the fledgling country's novice fleet, and was often disparaged in Britain for his tactics. A ruthless tactician and brutal butcher, he'd sent more English sailors to their graves than any other captain of the American forces.

What was Morgan doing with a high-ranking, much despised, officer of the American fleet?

"The Americans haven't a notion on how to proceed with this war, anymore, than they have a notion on how to proceed with the politics," Morgan said dryly, sinking his long limbs into a chair. "Though what do you expect from a country of tradesmen and farmers? It's a wonder they haven't fallen under British rule, already. Though, the British are stupid as well. They can't capitalize off an opportunity when it's handed to them."

Noting Merry's interest, Morgan's gaze shifted from the window, focused on her, and his eyes began to sparkle.

"War often forges the strangest alliances, Little One. I have been known to sell information to the Americans, from time to time. The British as well. My patriotism can be bought for a price."

Morgan smiled and shifted his gaze back to Tom. The older man frowned and took a long pull from his drink.

"Then there is no possibility of an expedited peace accord?" said Mr. Craven.

"No. If war didn't provide benefits, I would almost feel sorry for the Americans. We should not have to worry about peace any time soon," Morgan said, in slightly harsh way. He sat quietly, staring out the window for a long while.

For the life of her, Merry couldn't make reason of his expression. There was almost a look of sadness on his face, though she was certain she was reading too much into the expression.

Whatever Morgan was, he was not a patriot of any country, but the most ruthless type of opportunist. War meant opportunity to him, though what opportunities she didn't know for sure. Only that he somehow profited from the chaos of the world. It was a repulsive existence, in all ways.

A knock on the cabin door pulled them all from their thoughts. It was Mr. Seton. He didn't look, at all well, standing in the frame of the doorway.

Morgan didn't look at his officer. "I'm assuming you've finished?"

"Every inch of the gun deck."

Morgan smiled darkly. "Do it again."

When the door closed behind Mr. Seton, Tom Craven leaned forward in his chair and asked, "How long are you going to keep this up? He's been at it all night."

"Until he learns to follow an order, or is too exhausted to follow anything else." Morgan refilled his glass. "It's a good thing he is too pretty to flog." His eyes shifted to Merry. "Don't you think Mr. Seton is too pretty to flog, Little One? It is a good thing you are both too young and pretty to flog."

~~~

The rain came at dawn in lively little drops that pulled Merry pleasantly from sleep. As her senses gradually stirred, she stretched in the warm cocoon of her blankets, not bothering to lift her head from the pillow. The ship seemed to manage only a gentle sway beneath her. She became aware at once that it was uncommonly quiet.

She realized they had dropped anchor overnight. She could feel the change in the ship's motion beneath her, a gently purring animal instead of a groaning and lurching beast. Sitting up, the view through the stern windows brought her instantly awake. They were in the center of a busy harbor packed with ships.

A low voice, "In case you were wondering, that is the Great Sound you are staring at."

Merry turned to find Morgan at his desk, pouring over a sheet of figures, a candle assisting the pale light of dawn. She had not seen him for three days. She'd been locked below in the cabin. He had stayed away. When she'd asked Indy where he had slept, he'd given her one of those harshly sardonic looks and left her.

Feeling painfully awkward in his presence, not knowing why, she curled into a tight ball, pulling the blankets protectively around her, hoping he'd leave the cabin quickly.

Morgan didn't look up. "And yes, Little One, that is the Royal Navy on all sides of us. Imagine the advantage you have over me, now that I am surrounded by the Royal Navy. Lay back and contemplate escape plots. It's early yet."

Ignoring the subtle taunt in Morgan's voice, she said in a stunned way, "We are in Bermuda. It is the base for the North American Station, where the Admiralty coordinates the blockade and is preparing the invasion force for America. Why are we in Bermuda?"

That made Morgan sit back and give her a hard stare. "Ah, geography and military lessons not needed. You do have the oddest assortment of knowledge, for a girl your age."

His words, though amused, were dismissive. Merry got to her feet and padded across the cabin until she reached his desk. She took his coffee and curled in a chair. "Why haven't they tried to blow us out of the water? The bounty on the *Corinthian* must be—"

"Enormous." He went to dump blotting grit from the document he'd just finished into an ornate silver sandbox, and saw that she'd spilled coffee there. He arched a brow, fixing his gaze on the cup in her hand. "I wasn't finished with that."

Merry ignored his chide and asked, "So why haven't they attacked?"

"We went through a metamorphosis before we came in range of the islands," was the calm answer. "Why do you think I kept you locked below decks for two days? I can't let you learn all my secrets that easily."

"Even your secrets are a trick, so what would be the good of learning them?"

"How about for the simple enjoyment of it?"

Fighting her fast rising reaction to that, she did a foolish show of trying to arrange her curls with fingers as to present an air of un-shocked composure. She was more than mildly proud she managed to meet him stare for stare, before he turned his unsettling focus from her. He set down the page in his hand, and gathered together the documents on his desk before he crossed to his bed to shove them into a leather case.

Morgan was always a striking figure, but today he looked different to Merry. He was wearing the intricate white cravat and meticulously tailored trousers that were the costume of the men of her class. While he still looked dangerous and beguiling in his dark splendor, Merry realized he was as flawless in his guise as a British nobleman as he was in the more dramatic presentations of a pirate.

Brow puckering in a frown, she noted that not only his ship had gone through a metamorphosis during her hours locked into the cabin, so had the man. It was startling how effortlessly Morgan could be whatever he wanted it to be. She wondered if it was the result such flawless good looks, or something more.

Biting her lower lip, she asked, "Why are you dressed like that?"

"I have business ashore, Little One. I should be gone two, maybe three days." His black eyes lifted and began to shimmer. "Imagine the mischief you can create without me near."

Near was said in a voice almost caressing. Merry knew it was a deliberate attempt to cut off her questions. Wicked and sensual, it was a manipulation that flashed to rattle her, and often times to divert her. She was pleased with herself that she was neither. Persisting, "What manner of business could a notorious pirate possibly have in Bermuda?"

"I am more a man of commerce than anything else, Little One," Morgan told her, still focused on his task and not looking up. "Do you really view the world in such shades of black and white? I have honest enterprises and dishonest pursuits. I would say that makes me a rather commonplace man."

Commonplace? Morgan was not. *Dishonest pursuits.* She didn't want to speculate on the meaning of those words. The natural implication was not one that settled on Merry pleasantly.

"I suppose the fact you are in the middle of a war, with a price on your head, is only a trifling interference in your dishonest pursuits."

"No, my honest enterprises," he corrected. "War is only an annoyance if one does not understand the rules to get around it. Knowing what you need, where you need it and what is available is the necessity to survival for honest and dishonest men alike. Unfortunately, for the good politicians in Washington and London, the world is full of greedy men."

"I will have no illusions left at all, after you," Merry countered.

"We can only hope," he said with deliberate wickedness, watching her clamp her mouth shut, jerking her pink face away.

He watched as she picked up the dog and allowed it to lap at the remains in his cup. He killed a smile, and arched a brow. She ignored him.

Morgan looked at the document before him and tried to focus back on his task. As he reached for his quill, he studied her, imagining her garbed in something more appropriate, something delicate and filmy like this beautiful girl. Yes, clothes, he must get Merry clothes while ashore.

Morgan was nearly finished in his preparations to depart when Indy came through the cabin door with Merry's breakfast in hand. As Morgan fastened close his case on the bed, the boy noiselessly went through the chore of setting out Merry's plate.

The silence between them carried a heavy strain. The tension in the air reminded her of that first night when Indy had brought her aboard ship. She stared at the men, wondering at their strange relationship. The strangeness that, often times, filled the cabin in the heavy silence that flowed between them. Today, it was nearly suffocating.

"I should be no more than three days," Morgan remarked.

Silence.

Finally, Indy said, "Where can I find you if you are needed?"

Morgan's eyes turned into black embers. The boy knew, damn well, where he'd be.

He said, "Tom has already figured out the bribes for the customs officials. Move the cargo to the Tempest, as soon as possible, pitiful prize though that French schooner was. Keep a heavy guard on ship, but every man is to have shore leave." A pause, and then, black eyes mocking, he stated, "Except you."

Indy swung around and faced the captain with hard, glowing eyes. "And what am I to do about the girl? Am I to take care of her in your stead, as well?"

The silence between them grew nasty and long.

When at last he spoke, Morgan stated blandly, "I expect the girl to be here upon my return, well cared for, and intact. It will be your head if she is neither."

The boy was clearly not pleased. More silence.

"If you have anything more to say to me, lad, I suggest you say it while I'm walking," said Morgan evenly.

He picked up his case and left without a word to Merry.

Staring at the door with glittering eyes, the boy finally moved with his panther-like quickness after the captain.

Livid with frustration, Indy snapped out, "I want you to release her. You arrogant, son of the devil, let her go home now, while she still can."

Morgan stopped, the smile surfacing took on a hard edge. "What is wrong with you? I can't release her in Bermuda. Are you so consumed by your illogical adolescent fits over the girl, that you cannot reason out you are asking for what may, very well, cause her the greatest harm. The world is not a safe place for a woman without protection. She is far safer where she is."

"Protection?" Indy hissed in a voice that was biting. "Is that what you call it, in your mind, this game you play with her? Your protection?"

"I don't call it anything. I've seen to her comfort and I've left her untouched. A rather good stroke of fortune, considering your intent when you brought her to me."

"My intent was not to see her trapped in a prolonged state of suffering."

"If you've a mind to rummage around in moral incongruities, perhaps we should start with yours. We might possibly be able to remedy what's troubling you, if you would tell me why you brought her here in the first place."

"You could release her simply because I asked you to," said Indy fiercely.

The black eyes above Indy became carefully remote.

"Failure, always failure. That is the last thing you have left me free to do. I can't let her go now, not for your sake, not as things stand. There is more than your wellbeing involved in this. Surely, you see that."

"How cleverly you've learned to lie to yourself. We should all be so blessed and talented."

Morgan's expression hardened in unpleasant quickness.

"Do with Merry as you will. I'm going ashore, where I want a meal and to have a woman," Morgan snapped through gritted teeth, continuing on his way.

When Indy stepped back into the cabin, he found Merry slumped against the wall beside the open door. He offered her his hand and she slapped it away.

"Did you think I didn't know why he was going ashore?" Her hands moved with an anxious flutter to swipe at her cheeks. There were tears there. "You can be a cruel boy sometimes. Do you know that?"

To that, all Indy said was, "Whatever escape plots you hatch, please, Merry, don't let them involve fire. You are but a breath away from a powder magazine that could blow us all to

Halifax. Fire on a ship is an unimaginable hell."

She looked at the scars on Indy's hands and arms. "I know you think I'm foolish, but I know that there is no way off this ship, unless he lets me go."

"Good. I wouldn't want harm to come to you."

"And will he let me go?"

"No, Merry. Not ever."

Merry digested that in silence. "What are the chances if I go to his bed now, he will return me to Falmouth?"

"Nonexistent."

CHAPTER FOURTEEN

All the crew of the *Corinthian,* not serving their trick, had gone to shore. Through the locked cabin door echoed their bawdy songs. Sober they left. Drunk they returned.

Indy had chosen to pass the long hours of the night inside the captain's cabin with Merry.

They laid on Morgan's bed, feet pressed against polished wood, making shadow puppets against the wall. She'd been quiet and pensive all day. Something about her expression warned that he didn't want to hear the matters that, so deeply, claimed her.

In the dark of the night, when the ship had gone quiet, she asked, "Does he love her?"

The young pirate stared at her.

"Who are you talking about, Merry?"

"His mistress. Is Morgan in love with his French widow ashore?"

Startled, Indy sat up, staring at her fiercely. "Who the hell told you about Louisa?"

Merry looked away. "I heard Mr. Seton and Mr. Craven talking in the passageway."

Indy laid back against the bed. "No, Merry. He does not love her."

Merry frowned. "If he does not care for her, why does he have her in keeping?"

"Christ, Merry. Do you really understand so little about men?"

She blushed, but continued to stare.

Through gritted teeth, he said, "Convenience."

"How do I get Morgan to release me?"

The young pirate stared at her. She asked this often. It was getting harder each time to hold his tongue. Her blue eyes were like church glass, she lay still as an idol, and there was a disarming desperation to her expression that was new. She looked like a small trapped animal, suffering, and confused.

Somehow he managed to say, "I don't know, Merry."

"I won't stay here with him," she said in an angry little voice.

That statement was full of double-edge meanings. On the surface it was foolish. She had no choice in the matter. Her words had nothing to do with her captivity, and everything to do with her anger at the man. The girl was more emotionally entangled than she was willing to admit.

In an oddly uneven voice she asked, "Why does he keep me?"

The boy pretended to give it thought for a moment.

"I don't know. God knows, you haven't the temperament to be a whore of Morgan's."

After an aching moment of silence, she asked, "What makes you think that?"

"You're not in his bed. If he wanted you there, you would be there." His eyes were hard and full of meaning. Pity roughened his voice. "As things stand, your circumstance is better than you could have hoped for."

She rolled onto her side, her face on the pillow with her

nose only an inch from his.

Brokenly, she said, "I have to get off this ship. As much as I try to deny it, I am starting to have feelings for him."

"This really has been brutal for you, hasn't it?"

She was brushing at tears again. "If affection for a man is this painful, I can't imagine the way love feels. How do people survive it?"

Indy felt heartsick for her, brutally caught in a web of his creation. The events he'd set in motion had become little more than a bottomless morass for Merry.

It had started such a simple plan, but he'd never once considered what would happen if it veered off course, or even what it would mean to her if it succeeded. It had been the logical thing to do back on the beach in Cornwall, a means to spare Merry's life, and a possible way to free himself from Morgan.

For the first time in a life of emotion-free logic, Indy was learning regret. He found it a harsh lesson. His motives, so simple in the beginning, he had never explored with honesty. His feelings for Merry, he had never anticipated. Reluctantly, he admitted, his feelings for Morgan had been there all along, in spite of his denial of their existence.

He forced himself to look at her clearly, the delicate lines of her face, the fragile finely boned structure of her, and the beauty of her. There was no possible way for this to end without harming Merry. He had not considered that at the start.

Even in the lingering warmth of the cabin, his fingers had become icy cold. This was his fault. He could think of only one way to protect her from where this was going. Only one way to make Morgan no longer desire her.

He couldn't look into her eyes anymore. He buried his face in her hair, letting it pass over his face in a sigh. He whispered,

"We're in Bermuda. I can put you on a ship bound for England before Morgan returns."

She gave him a round-eyed look that would haunt him in the months ahead. Eagerness and suspicion fought on her face. Into her indecision, he whispered, "But I want to make sure you are free of him, completely. As things stand, he will bring you back, Merry. We don't want that, do we?"

His fingers whispered over her face, slowly caressing the nerve points, knowing how, and yet, still reluctant because her trust of him didn't warn her of his actions. Her skin heated beneath his touch. Her eyes grew enormous, and he could feel her reaction to him. He was shock by the instant reaction in his own flesh. He could end this now, if he took her to his bed. If he made love to her, Morgan's game with her would be over.

One hand came lightly to rest on her neck and the other to cup the gentle slope of her cheek. Her sweet face drowned out the world around him. Desire rose rapidly within him.

"Merry," he breathed into her hair, "you do want away from Morgan, don't you?"

He placed soft kisses where his fingers had been on her jaw. She didn't pull back, but he could sense the confusion within her. He kissed the creamy flesh of her neck, then touched the sweetness of her skin with his tongue. The taste of her ran straight to his loins.

In a movement more abrupt than he wanted, he had her pinned beneath him. He pushed his flesh forward to let his hardness touch her. Merry jerked, and began to struggle beneath him.

Shocked and angry, her tiny hands pummeled his chest. "Stop that." Dodging his lips, she screamed, "How could you think I'd consent to such a dastardly trade? I would rather drown in the Atlantic than be made a whore by any man."

He eased back and tossed her away from him. He found himself saying, in a nasty voice, "I'm trying to help you, damn it. Do you think I want this? If you share my bed, Morgan will no longer want you."

"And if I share your bed, I will never be free to go home. There must be another way to gain my freedom. Can you not see that your kindness is no kindness at all?"

Indy sat back on his heels, above her. Fighting to reign in the urgent demands of his body, his eyes widened as he dissected the emotions on her face, slowly digesting her final words. What he saw on Merry's face warned him that it was, perhaps, kinder to them both that she had misunderstood his feelings for her.

The air between them hissed from the sound of him furiously pulling oxygen into his lungs. Fiercely, he asked, "Do you love him?"

Merry lowered her gaze and didn't answer him.

Ruthlessly he jerked her face back to him.

In biting tones, he hissed, "They all love him, you stupid girl. His vanity demands it, but he will never love you."

~~~

Merry was sitting in the center of Morgan's bed when the knob on the door turned. Assuming it was Indy, she didn't bother to pull up the blankets or toss the pug to the floor. She regretted both when she saw it was Mr. Craven, carrying in her breakfast tray.

His good brow rose sharply above his austere face. "Don't stare at me all cutty-eyes, girl. If I had a mind to rape you, you'd be raped by now."

His words were hardly a comfort as he set the tray on the table.

"You best get that dog off Morgan's bed. If he sees it there

305

he's apt to give you the back of his hand, and toss it over the rail."

She made a face at Craven, though she didn't feel at all bold. "Morgan would never hit me. He only plays at being evil. He's not an evil man, at all."

Craven gave her a hard stare. Merry climbed from the bed, dropped the dog, and went to the table.

Fiercely, he sneered, "If it suited him, he'd slit you throat to ear. Don't forget that, girl."

He said the warning with such force, Merry should have accepted it as truth, without pause. It no longer surprised Merry that she didn't.

Instead, she asked, "Why are you here? Where is Indy?"

"I sent the boy ashore."

Her eyes rounded as she digested that. "But, Morgan expressly ordered that he stay on ship to take care of me."

Craven grabbed her arm in a harsh hold. "I do as I please, girl, you best remember that. And don't try my patience today. I'm not pleased, beyond half, to be forced to be wet-nurse to the likes of you."

Merry tried her best not to wince facially, while his fingers dug into her brutally.

Lifting her chin, she fixed her wide blue eyes on Craven, and asked, "Then why did you send the boy ashore, if I'm such a nuisance?"

To her surprise Craven released her. He turned away from the table to collect the pug.

"I sent the boy ashore for your protection," Mr. Craven said ominously, fighting to catch hold of the darting dog.

Merry called for the dog, picked him up, and then held him out for Craven. The gruff old man snatched him from her hands in a manner that made the dog whimper.

"My protection? What protection could I possibly need from Indy? The boy would never harm me."

Alertly, she searched Mr. Craven's face. Craven cursed under his breath.

Not answering her, Craven crossed to the door. "I'll be back with the dog. See that you are dressed."

She didn't know what to make of that last order, but Merry chomped down her breakfast in record time. She was sitting in a lambskin chair, clad in the garments from Ireland, when Craven returned with the dog. He dropped the pug, turned a chair at the table, and settled on it with his arms spread across the top of the back. He gave her a thorough once over, with his dull, deep set eyes.

After a long while, he finally said, "Tell me who you are. I will settle a sum on you and send you on your way."

Of all the things she had expected upon Mr. Craven's return, it had not been this. Merry wanted desperately to jump on the offer, but the truth of her identity meant it was hardly likely Craven would see the bargain through. That is, if she could even trust him.

Carefully, she asked, "Why would you do that?"

"If I know who you are I know where to find you if you open those pretty lips of yours," Craven continued in a cruel voice, "and I will find you, do not doubt me, Merry."

Merry swallowed, uncertain if Craven spoke the truth or if this were a trick. It seemed impossible that Mr. Craven would defy Morgan and free her. She sank her teeth into her lower lip.

"I'm not going to sit around and play games with you, girl. This is likely to be the only offer for your freedom you'll ever get. I need only to hear the truth from you. If you don't want to answer me, then your fate becomes your doing."

He started to rise from his chair.

Anxiously, she crossed the cabin toward him. "Why would you help me?"

The expression on his face had never been crueler. "I'm not trying to help you. I don't give a damn about you."

Merry wasn't sure what to make of that and cautioned herself to remain silent.

He was at the door before he said over his shoulder: "Fine, hold your silence, see where it gets you. If you tell Morgan of this, I will lie, he will believe me, and then I will kill you."

Mr. Craven said not a single word later that day when he brought her noon meal. He set it on the table and left without ceremony. When he came to retrieve her plate, strangely enough, he was carrying a small sewing box and a sampler.

He set it on Morgan's bed with a harsh warning, "You're going to be alone the rest of the night. I don't want any trouble out of you."

He took her plate, then the dog and left her.

The hours did not pass particularly pleasant for Merry. She hated sewing, had never mastered the skill, but as the embroidery was her only distraction, other than the books, she started to work on it anyway.

Late that night she heard Mr. Craven's acidic voice in the passageway outside her door.

"Damn it, boy, go to your bunk and sleep this off. If you make any more trouble, I'll chain you in the brig until Morgan returns."

"I'll see that he doesn't," the voice belonged to Shay.

"You best make sure of that. Keep him locked in his cabin until he sobers. My temper can't support another one of his fits of weeping."

The closing of Indy's cabin door ended the trail of Mr. Craven's words before she could understand the argument.

Only minutes passed before she heard Mr. Craven's firm tread moving toward his cabin.

She was sitting in Morgan's chair, clumsily jerking needle through cloth and making a mess of the sampler, when she smelled Mr. Seton's pipe smoke from the hallway. She tossed the tambour on the window bench and anxiously crossed to the door.

"Mr. Seton," she hissed through the red oak.

She heard a husky laugh then the sound of a body, none too steady, sliding down the wood to sit on the floor.

"Flower, what are you doing awake? Wish I could find a way to pass through the sentinel to visit for awhile."

"Sentinel?"

Brandon Seton laughed drunkenly. "Mr. Craven. You, Flower, are persona non grata today. You best watch your head when Craven's around. At least until Morgan is back."

"But why? What did I do? I heard Indy and Craven arguing in the hallway. What were they arguing about?"

After much probing, reluctantly, Mr. Seton admitted that yes, it had been about her, and that she best keep her oar out of it. She continued to press, then heard Mr. Seton's labored rise to his feet.

"Damn it, Flower, the lad has been ordered to stay clear of you. And that's all I can tell you because that's all I know. I'm drunk as a sailor, Merry, or I wouldn't have talked to you at all."

Chidingly, Merry pointed out, "You are a sailor." Then, "Why shouldn't you talk to me?"

She heard what she thought was his forehead landing heavily against the door. A loud sigh.

"Craven is in hell's own mood. I don't know what you did, but you're lucky to be alive. Morgan may be the devil, but Craven is his wrath. Be careful."

Merry laid back against the red oak door listening to Mr. Seton leave. Morgan wasn't the devil, at all. Why was she the only one on ship who could see it?

There was only one evil man on the *Corinthian*. Craven was the devil, and Merry didn't doubt all things evil in-between.

~~~

It was the dead of night when Morgan returned to ship to find Merry curled in his bed. Even if he'd been inclined to join her, she hadn't left him any space.

She was on her side, lying crossway on his bed, his shirt twisted tautly around the line of her hip, her legs bare, and blankets in a heap at the foot. There was just enough moonlight to illuminate the creamy flesh of her face. The vision she made would have been perfect, if her rose petal lips hadn't been slightly apart and her airy breaths ones of light snoring. The gasps were not dainty, at all.

He watched her for a moment. Lightly, he touched her palm to feel that her skin was slightly cool and gently pulled up the blankets.

Quietly, he placed the bundles he'd carried in on his table, and found, laying open, a book on ship design. Amused, he lifted it and settled in his chair. Merry was almost through it. He opened it to a page with the corner folded back, tilting it toward the moonlight, and noting it was a section dedicated to the design of his own type of ship.

Nothing, it seemed, passed the girl's notice. Two months at sea and she was already deep into analyzing the differences in the vessels she'd seen. Whimsical she may seem on the surface, but her youth hid a mind that would have been termed gifted, if she had been born male. Through her virgin panic it didn't always show clearly, he knew that when she was more seasoned, more composed than youthful, her nimble intelligence would prove as compelling as her beauty to any man wise enough to appreciate it.

She was still little more than an uncut diamond, even at nineteen, but fully cut, she would sparkle magnificently.

A sound from the pug drew his attention to the window bench. Crossing the cabin, he grabbed the mutt, and pulled free from its teeth the edge of a sampler. He couldn't imagine which one of the crew gave Merry this. This was not something Indy would have thought of for her, and definitely not the sewing box with its polished marquetry cap.

Tambour in one hand, he tossed the dog from the cabin. He examined Merry's efforts and saw that embroidery was not one of her talents. It surprised him, since needlework was usually the first accomplished tasks of any well-bred English girl. The stitches were uneven, impatient in their appearance, and even he could tell they weren't done correctly.

Careful not to wake her, Varian undressed. Noting it was nearly morning, he pulled on attire appropriate for ship. He settled into his chair and found himself watching Merry again.

She was a beautiful woman, young and spirited. He reluctantly admitted his fascination with her went deeper than the fact she was young, beautiful, and new. He felt the return of desire, as sharp and insistent as it had been before he'd left the ship. What would she do if he joined her in bed? Would she melt in his arms, or would she fight him?

He had no idea. He only knew that whatever it was that kept him from taking her was dwindling fast.

Wondering what he should do with her, strangely, it was an image of Ann that floated upward through his musings. The sudden picture of Ann, a frequent haunting of late, made the women he'd been with on shore seem vile and jaded.

It surprised him how often he thought of Ann these days.

Stranger still, how his thoughts of her were tangled with his thoughts of Merry. Every day it was more Merry, than Ann, that surfaced from this tangled web of his memories and the present.

He spent the remainder of the night in his chair staring at the girl. Shortly before dawn, he left her.

CHAPTER FIFTEEN

The *Corinthian* was back at sea. Curled in Morgan's chair, Merry glared at the dresses laid neatly on the captain's bed, pulling the needle in and out with angry jerks through the thin sampler. The gowns had coincided with the unexpected loss of Indy's garments.

Whatever the purpose of Morgan's gift, she did not want it. She wanted only her freedom and return to Falmouth.

The cabin door opened and she started. It was Morgan.

The pug sprang from the window bench and trotted to him, whining for attention he would never receive.

Taking no notice of her glare, Morgan said, "We are out of range of the islands. Get dressed. You may go topside if you wish to."

Merry made another jerky move with the needle. "I can't dress. I need clothes from Indy."

"No."

"Then I prefer to stay here. I will not wear those garments."

Morgan settled at his desk and instantly turned his focus to work.

"Then I will take back my shirts. I have the advantage in this, Little One. Eventually, I win. I always do."

313

A knock on the door proceeded Mr. Craven's entry to the cabin. There was a sullen look on his face and a breakfast tray in hand.

Morgan said, "I don't wish to be disturbed the rest of the morning."

Mr. Craven promptly left the cabin.

Merry sat as she was and fixed her anxious gaze on her sampler. Morgan's tension was a palpable thing. Mr. Craven had brought the morning meal instead of Indy. Something definitely was amiss.

Morgan sat at the table and looked at her.

"Would you join me, Merry?"

It was an order, in spite of the slumberous softness of his voice. She dropped the pug, padded barefoot across the cabin, and sank into the chair across from him.

Morgan gave her a hard stare, then picked up his fork. "Now you can tell me what happened aboard my ship while I was ashore."

The question was unexpected. "How would I know? I was locked in the cabin."

His eyes seemed to sharpen. "Were you?"

She flushed. "Yes. In Mr. Craven's care."

The sudden flash in Morgan's eyes made her instantly tense.

"Why was Tom Craven taking care of you?"

"I don't know. I assure you the idea wasn't mine."

Everything aboard ship had changed after Indy's offer to free her. She hadn't seen the boy in days. She had fretted more than once over what Mr. Craven knew. Now, Morgan suspected…what? What did he know?

She felt the blush start to creep slowly downward from her cheeks. She focused on his plate.

"Look at me," he said.

Merry lifted her chin, willing herself to make full contact with his eyes.

"I don't grapple around in blind space," he warned in cutting tones.

She stared at him and in her mind flashed the memory of Indy kissing. Something must have flashed in her eyes as well, because Morgan's face hardened like stone.

"Whatever is done is done, Merry. The boy has lands. Enormous wealth. No matter his peculiarities, I assure you, there are few families who would not consider him a fine match."

Frowning, Merry searched his face for some clue as to the direction this was going. Why was he telling her this?

When she didn't speak, his eyes grew only more searching.

"If the boy harmed you, I can fix it, if you'll let me. I can't help you unless you're honest with me."

The harshness of his tone turned everything inside Merry instantly cold. It took her a moment to attach full meaning to his words. Had Morgan just offered to force the boy to marry her?

Staring at him, all her emotions began to boil like melting waxwork.

She sprang from her chair and whirled back to face him in fury.

"Are you offering me the boy as a husband? I am not your property to dispose of at whim. And what do you expect in payment for this generosity? Me, in your bed?"

Burning embers rose in Morgan's black eyes.

"In case you need reminding, I don't need to bargain, Little One. If I wanted you in my bed, you'd be there."

His words hit her like a slap.

A pause.

Then she hissed, "Why don't you toss me over the rail and be done with it? Any fate would be preferable to this miserable circumstance with you."

It hardly seemed possible, but the burn in his eyes grew fierce, and the lines of his face hardened more. Rising from his chair, he crossed the cabin in two strides.

Morgan's lips were closing in on hers. That effortlessly, she was in his arms. His mouth devoured her in a way that turned her to putty. It was a fiery kiss, scorching with anger, and hunger. His hands moved across her trembling flesh in a manner bold and without restraint.

Morgan had never kissed or touched her like this before. She could rally no defense again him. His hands molded her intimately against him, in manner that clothes did nothing to shield. The fire of his mouth was sending fire through Merry.

She felt herself being lifted into him, closer, closer. She was shocked by her own frantic willingness to let him mold her flesh to the hardness she felt in his breeches. That dull ache exploded as a raging inferno all through her. Her body desperately craved every drop of this man she could consume.

Her disobedient flesh wanted nothing more than to move against him. But, her temper sent her skittering out of his arms, and across the cabin, until a lambskin chair was between them.

Breathing raggedly, she screamed, "You and your smug games. If I were willing to trade any part of me, I wouldn't be here. I would be on a ship bound for England now."

Despair had risen on her hot face.

"You don't know how it feels to be trapped and toyed with for weeks on end. You play with my heart and you play with my flesh. You are masterful at it, knowing exactly what you do to me with each move you make. I don't even know who, or what you are. You are going to hurt me, if I don't learn quickly. I want to go home where I belong, while I still have a right to belong there. I won't belong there if I share your bed."

"Merry..."

She cut him off desperately: "At least the boy made the offer of his bed in exchange for my freedom. At least his trade was honest. You want me for no other reason than your vanity, before you give me to another man."

A hush fell. His eyes widened, as she had never seen them before. Curling her fingers over the top of the chair, she stared at him with anger-blurred eyes, trying not to show fear, for surely his reaction would come and it would be brutal.

At last into the crackling silence of the room, Morgan said, "My, a lot did happen here while I was ashore, now didn't it? Craven did not know for certain if you'd been harmed. I am relieved to know that the boy didn't harm you, Merry."

Then, to Merry's utter shock, he returned to his meal. This time when he spoke, his voice was an easy flow, so unlike him. "Come sit so we may talk about this sensibly."

"I don't want to talk to you," she said from behind the chair.

His glowing gaze swung quickly to her. He set down his coffee cup. His fingers formed a long curve beside it. "I imagine not. But, you will sit and we will talk."

Merry wandered around the chair, trying to overcome the rioting emotions inside her, as she tried to figure out what Morgan was about now. Picking up the pug, she held the dog tightly to her as she studied the captain. She sat down, a careful distance from him, in the lambskin chair.

His voice, coming to her from across the cabin, was webbed with amusement. "You have a few things to learn about men, Little One. If you think that speech would have stopped me, or any man, if I were really interested in taking you to my bed."

She stared at him. For some reason, that remark had the unpardonable power to hurt her. In plain words, he confirmed every anguished thought that had plagued her these past days. He did not want her.

It was why she was not in his bed.

It was why he did not harm her.

She was nothing to him, an object of indifference and insignificance. She could see the truth of that, too clearly, on his face.

Her heartbeat was tolling in rapid distress.

He began, "In this part of the world, it is extremely dangerous for a woman unprotected. So, I am more than mildly pleased that you are here, and not alone on a ship bound for Falmouth."

Morgan stared at her. His stare seemed to bore into her as though to make sure she understood this. She nodded.

"So, the boy offered you your freedom if you would go to his bed?"

Now, at all moments, she felt embarrassed. Merry nodded.

"What is there between you and the boy that he should risk his safety to help you?"

She shook her head.

He studied her for a long time. Then, he asked, "You do understand the boy risked his life saving you in Cornwall?"

"I knew nothing of the boy before that night," she replied truthfully.

Morgan rose from his chair.

"Whatever you are trying to hide, Merry, it is pointless," he said with heavy meaning.

Merry's eyes rounded, but she remained silence.

Morgan sighed. "The truth will come out in time, Little One. It always does."

With those words Morgan seemed to promptly dismiss her from his thoughts. He went to his desk and immediately turned his full attention on his work. An hour passed without a word from him.

Merry watched him, submerged in misery and confusion. He had no feelings for her, at all. His temper, his laughter, and even his passion were meaningless expressions of the man. He used them to manipulate her, and he did not even want her.

She stared at her fingers knotted in her lap. She was nothing to him and never would be. Indy was right. He would never care for her.

It was what she wanted, she told herself. However, Merry could barely hold back her tears until Morgan disappeared through the cabin door.

~~~

The last days of November gave way to December, as the *Corinthian* continued on its journey southward through the warm Gulf Stream.

The water was full of sea creatures, varieties too numerous for Merry to count. Sometimes, Shay would drag her topside to watch a streaming pool of green jellyfish or other tropical treasures he thought might amuse her. At night she could hear the song of the dolphins and whales, their voices strange and melancholy, as she lay in the darkness on the window bench. The Caribbean air was warm and heavy, and the world of the ship a familiar tune that vibrated in the humid air around her.

She'd been with Morgan three months. Their destination was unknown to her. Falmouth seemed so long ago. Bramble Hill was a dream. This was reality, and slowly this was all there was.

~~~

The afternoon Caribbean sun filled the cabin with an orange patina, as Merry jerked awake to the sound of a warning volley shot from the *Corinthian*'s canons. After pulling on a muslin gown of white with narrow stripes of coquelicot, she raced across the cabin and climbed through the companionway to find the ship in well-organized activity

Morgan was in command on the quarterdeck. The ship was running hard to the wind, in pursuit of a sleek privateer flying the colors of Great Britain.

She spied, against the port rail, Shay and Indy.

Reading her thoughts with alarming precision, Indy snapped in irritation, "Don't launch into a patriotic defense of Britannia, Merry. I'm in no mood for it today. That's an American schooner. She's not British."

Her eyes widened at his sharp tone. The boy had been out of temper with her since Morgan's return. As it was, she ignored his curtness and looked to Shay.

More than a little skeptical, she asked, "How do you know that ship isn't British?"

"Morgan wouldn't chase if she were," said Shay, settling back against the gunwale.

Studying the schooner, still not convinced that it wasn't British, she asked, "But the flag…"

"It's a trick, Merry," Indy snapped continuing with his duties. "We've been playing cat and mouse for hours, now. If Morgan's information is correct, that is not the British ship *Arab*. An impossibility, since the *Arab* was captured in the Chesapeake. She is the American schooner the *Heritage*. The warning volley was Morgan's signal that it was time to talk."

Merry frowned. "If that's an American schooner, why should they wish to talk to Morgan?"

Shay pointed to the mast. It was then she noticed that above her proudly flapped the bright flare of color from the American flag.

"As of this morning, we are the *Sea Breeze*," Shay announced.

Nothing remained around Merry that would warn that this was a pirate ship.

"And what happened to the *Sea Breeze*?"

"Captured near Bermuda. It's not common knowledge, yet." Watching her face, Indy added, "You can buy anything for a price, even information on a Baltimore letter-of-marque trader presently in the custody of the Royal Navy."

In her early days on ship, Indy had warned Merry it wasn't safe to ask too many questions of the crew. She was never to inquire as to why Morgan never took an English ship. She was never to inquire about anything she saw. As Indy put it, her continued safety and chance for freedom depended on never knowing too much about the activities of the *Corinthian*.

So why the sudden change?

Sharply assessing his face, she couldn't imagine his recklessness in telling her things she wouldn't dare ask. "Won't Morgan be angry you told me all this?"

"No," was the abrupt, non-informative answer.

She settled her chin in her hands and watched the boys continue in their duties.

An hour later the *Arab* was laying close off the leeward and had signaled it would talk. Morgan left the deck with Brandon Seton. Soon, Mr. Seton returned handsomely dressed as an American privateer captain. He climbed into a ship's boat with a small crew that included Mr. Boniface. Tom Craven was in command, and Morgan had suddenly disappeared below decks.

By dusk wind, sea, and rain made it impossible to remain above deck. Merry was more than a little anxious to stay topside, since Mr. Seton had not returned, though many hours had passed. He'd disappeared on the *Arab*, not to be seen again.

By the time she left Indy and Shay, Merry was genuinely worried for Mr. Seton.

Entering the captain's cabin, she found Morgan casually reclined on his bed, reading. For a broken part of a second she wondered if anyone would believe that the infamous pirate Morgan was not only literate, but also an irritatingly voracious reader, though, she found the voracious part particularly annoying in light of the dangers above.

He didn't look up as the cabin door swung closed behind her, a little more loudly than she had intended. Resisting the impulse to snatch the book from him, she picked up the pug, dropped a kiss on its nose, and then settled, with bottom on heels, atop Morgan's bed.

Of course, Morgan continued to read. Face to face with him, launching into a discussion about Mr. Seton went from seeming a little difficult in her mind, to something that was impossible. She was trying to organize her thoughts into a careful disclosure of her worries when Morgan's low voice cut short the effort.

"While it pleases me the frequency you climb atop my bed, Little One, I should point out, it does me no good that you never climb within it." Morgan gave her a smile, closed the book, and then fixed his eyes upon her. "There, you have my full attention. Get on with it, Little One. Since I know I will have no peace with my book until you are heard."

Arming her nerves, she said, "I wish to speak to you about Mr. Seton."

It was a clumsy opening, but it was the best she could

manage.

Morgan's interest in her vanished at once, and he retrieved his book. "Is that what's got you so riled, My Dear? I thought it was something important. Can it be that you think Mr. Seton is in danger, and you've come to plead for his rescue? If you are open to suggestions, I know exactly how I would like you to plead."

Cherry-spot blushes burned her cheekbones. Merry was just angry enough to snatch the book from his hand and throw it on the floor.

She furiously stammered, "Oh, for once will you stop, Varian. You can't imagine how infuriating your Morgan dramas are, at times. You don't have to resort to wickedness every time you wish not to answer my questions. It doesn't shock me any longer, so you might as well stop it. I'm worried about Mr. Seton. He went below deck on the *Arab* and has not been seen since. How can you sit there calmly reading with an enemy ship off the lee, and a member of your crew being held hostage?"

Surprise flashed in Morgan's eyes, then was quickly concealed. "Interesting," he said in a civil way, as his gaze combed her face. Then, lazily looking about for the book she'd tossed he added, "There is no need for your concern, Merry."

Frustrated, Merry retrieved the book and handed it back to him. "How can you be so certain he's not in danger?"

With a disquieting grin, Morgan said, "Do you know how Brandon came to be with me? He was a rising star in the American War Department, with an unfortunate inclination to sell to the English the departure schedules and routes of American ships. I admit to having purchased information from him, a time or two, myself. He joined my crew one step ahead of the hangman. Whatever his predicament, Brandon is more than capable to manage it on his own. Traitors are remarkably resourceful. He has proven most valuable at getting me what I want, without having to engage in battle."

She shook her head in abstract disbelief. "I don't believe you. Mr. Seton would not be a traitor."

Those clever black eyes brightened at once as his smile took on an edge. "No?"

"No."

There was a short laugh, an arched brow.

Merry ignored the taunt and began, "As I was saying—"

She never got a chance to finish. With a deceptive grace of movement, Morgan leaned into her to claim her lips. She tried desperately to remain unaffected by his touch. All she got for the effort was carefully placed kisses on her eyelids, which had drifted closed without her knowing it, before his lips moved lower, pressing his mouth to hers, spreading the stiff line until her lips slowly softened to the urging sweetness of his probing kiss.

When he stopped, Merry's eyes flew open to find Morgan smiling at her. "Now, go away. You are irritating me."

Within a half second, Morgan was reading again.

She crossed her arms. Clinging, hopelessly, to some remnant of dignity, Merry said, "I wish you'd stop playing this game with me. We both know that your flirtations are nonsense."

His vivid black eyes sparkled. "Nonsense? You consider a kiss from me nonsense?"

"Yes. I don't even know why you play this game with me."

Morgan pinched her chin and said, "Economy of effort, I suppose. I can silence you with a single act that gives me pleasure."

The only response Merry could manage to that was to make a face at him, before she picked up the pug that was now whimpering for Morgan's attention. She studied the captain for awhile, then she climbed from the bed, and began to fidget around the cabin.

She was restless, restless of body and restless of mind. She couldn't completely convince herself that worry for Mr. Seton was its cause. She had felt this unrest for weeks now.

She fiddled with the instruments on his desk. She looked at Morgan. She searched the vast horizon of blue out the stern windows. She looked at Morgan. How did men survive the world of sea? She dropped heavily into his chair. He gave her no notice and continued to read.

More than an hour passed. Eight bells came and went, without Indy brining their dinner. At last, she was unable to bear the silence and the tension, convinced things had gone badly topside, she pushed out of the chair and began to move about the cabin again in loud, agitated movements.

It was then, from behind the book, she heard, "No."

She froze at the door. "Ah, he speaks. What do you mean no?"

Morgan snapped shut the book. "Stay put, Little One. The decks topside belong to the men right now."

She didn't know what to make of that. She sank back into her chair. He rose from his bed, poured two glasses of wine, handed her one and then moved to stand in front of the stern windows.

By way of conversation, Morgan said, "What do you say to joining me on land, Little One? You do seem a trifle restless of late. Cabin fever, perhaps."

Something in how he looked at her made her blush.

When she didn't answer, he added, "I would enjoy some time on land."

His words, friendly, were also intended to end the

conversation. He reclined back on his bed, slowly sipping his wine.

The sky beyond the stern windows was pitch black before Merry heard Mr. Craven, Mr. Seton, and Mr. Boniface talking outside the cabin. A sharp knock on the red oak door made Morgan look up, though he didn't rise from his bed as he bade the men to enter.

Morgan's eyes, dark and intense, fixed on Mr. Seton in a hard stare. "Well?"

Brandon Seton looked nervously at Merry. From certain tentatively, tactful glances she'd received from all three men, it seemed Mr. Seton was waiting for Indy to collect her.

She was never permitted to remain in the cabin when Morgan's three senior officers met with him.

It was obvious Morgan knew the cause of Mr. Seton's reluctance, therefore, no one was more surprised than Merry when he snapped, "Get on with it. Speak. What the devil took so long?"

"Honest men or so we thought," came Mr. Seton's cautious response.

Morgan calmly arched a brow. "Well?"

There was a brief pause as Mr. Craven gave Merry one of his malevolent stares. Morgan's gaze moved among the three men, fixed on Tom Craven, and then began to sparkle.

Meeting him stare for stare, the captain said, "I'm really getting tired of waiting. Are you going to tell me or not?"

Mr. Craven favored Morgan with a blighting gaze. Finally he said, "You were right, Varian. She was the *Heritage*. And among her cargo was a shipment of Rensdale's gold bound for *Ile de la Tortue*. They surrendered the gold without fight, and it is now in the hold."

"Ah," said Morgan, moving to his table to pour himself

more wine. Knowing what Tom's reaction to this would be, Morgan's smile turned lazy and potent as he ordered, "Change course for *Isla del Viento*."

CHAPTER SIXTEEN

A week later the *Corinthian* reached the *Isla del Viento*. Merry stood at the port rail beside Mr. Seton, as they pulled into a harbor populated with ships. It was Morgan's island and they were Morgan's ships, over a half dozen of them.

She stared in awe at the verdant saucer of land, with its white coral sand beaches, backing up into luxuriant greenery speckled of crimson-tasseled blooms of cashew trees. There were unspoiled forests spotted of coffee and cocoa growing for export. The occasional field planted of indigo, a parcel here or there, for the support of the small number of families who lived on the island and tended them for him.

Morgan's home, if this were indeed his home, was one of the most beautiful places Merry had ever seen. On a hill above the bay was Morgan's villa. The villa sprawled in fretwork splendor and wooden porches, bathed in sunlight, surrounded by fountains, and well-raked walks of crushed limestone. Elegant and spruce, it was as magnificent as was the man who owned it.

For the first time Merry realized Morgan was not just a pirate. Whatever else he was, he was an extremely wealthy man. It only added to the mystery of him.

Watching the busy activity on the docks, Merry said, "I don't understand any of this. How does one come to own an island, and why does one stay at sea, when one has all this?"

Mr. Seton looked at her, amused. "Morgan likes to say that

a thief, who is only a thief, dies a poor man."

"A thief, no matter his wealth, dies a thief," she snapped, exasperated. Then, her eyes of horizon blue became very wide. "But, how did Morgan come to own the island? It would take enormous wealth to purchase all this."

There was a slight hesitation, and then casually Mr. Seton said, "I wouldn't say purchase. I would say acquired. Morgan acquired the island. How does Morgan acquire anything he wants? As I heard it told, the island belonged to the Deverell family for generations. Morgan killed Lord Deverell over a woman, took his home, and uses his name, when it suits his purposes. That's all I know, Merry. So, don't ask more. Morgan is apt to cut out my liver for having told you this much."

Her gaze shifted to the colors of Great Britain flapping from a flag overhead then to the prow, where *Windsong* now sparkled in crisp, newly painted white letters.

"So here," she began cautiously, "he is Lord Deverell?" Then, more sharply on an anxious whisper, "Who is Morgan really?"

Brandon shrugged. "He is a hundred different men, with a hundred different names. No man more real than the next. The second you think you've solved the puzzle, you are wrong, and the puzzle changes. Be careful with him, Merry. None of his manipulations are real. Trust none of them. He is a puzzle with no end."

The grim edge to Mr. Seton's warning made Merry tilt her face upward to search his eyes. Her days, it seemed, were destined to be full of nuisance warnings she could make no reason of. She'd had a different warning only a morning ago from Shay.

On the next day's tide, the *Corinthian* was going back to sea under Mr. Craven's command, the hold rich with coffee, cocoa, and indigo bound for warehouses in Bermuda. She was to be alone with Morgan for weeks on the island. After giving her that information, Shay had advised her sternly, *"Watch yer step, Merry lass. Alone with the mon on land is a curse, not a blessing."*

The barking of the pug pulled Merry from her thoughts. She turned to see Morgan emerge from the companionway with her bag in hand. Her pug followed close, bouncing at his heels, as he paused to give final instructions to Tom Craven.

A second stop was made where Indy sat making aggravated swipes with a knife against wood. Merry strained, wishing she could hear it. The boy looked positively hostile. He wouldn't even look at her, and had turned away, ignoring her stare.

Then Morgan crossed the deck, extended his hand to her, and they were off. Even wrapped in warnings from the crew, and freshly bathed in Indy's harsh stare, she was more than a little excited. It had been three months since land, three months on ship, and now she was here on an island in the Caribbean.

She made barely three steps off the plank before she stumbled to her knees. Hovering there, trembling and her brain sloshing, finding her feet was an uneasy task that strangely eluded her.

Before she could stop him, Morgan had her in his arms and was carrying her.

Squirming in alarm, Merry screamed, "Put me down."

Morgan laughed and continued to walk. "I'm not going to stand on the docks while we wait for your head to clear. After any long period of time on a ship, your body makes an adjustment to the sea's motion."

"You could have warned me," she countered peevishly.

"Yes, I could have. But then, why do you think I never worried you'd run and escape me. You wouldn't get farther than two steps from the ship. I could track you down with nary an effort."

Merry's brows lowered in a scowl.

Over Morgan's shoulder, the *Corinthian* got smaller and smaller. Overhead, a lone hawk soared above, watching them, before it disappeared into the jungle. By the time they were at the beach, she was ready to try her feet again and demanded Morgan release her.

"Are you steady?" Morgan asked when she didn't move.

"I am perfectly well to manage," she said with an obstinate lift of her chin.

"Then why are you still?" Morgan asked gruffly.

"The sand. I've never seen anything like it."

Merry sank to the ground, but this time to take off her shoes. The sand was a heated bed of gossamer brightness, deep enough that when she stood, she sank to her ankles in it. Gathering her skirts in her hands, giggling, she walked, then ran across it.

Her face of happy wonder lifted to him. Morgan's chide for her to hurry along never made it to voice. He'd walked this very beach this morning, never sparing a thought about it. Now with Merry, ivory toned, sun warmed sand was a pleasant experience that took *forever*. She lifted it in tiny hands, allowed it to drip through her fingers, and then wanted the feel of it against her bare legs.

It took an hour to get from the beach to the villa. Everything they saw came new to her. Nothing escaped her notice or curiosity. She couldn't pass a palm tree without touching the texture of the trunk, and lowering to giggle, as she carefully examine the pointy tips of a fallen frond.

She asked a hundred questions, missing not one new treasure around her, whether it was a silk-cotton tree or a tropical flower. Every detail found home in her mind and touch. Fingering the soft petals of an orchid was enough to make her smile in joy. A brown pelican skimming low across the bay was enough to make her halt and stare in happy wonder for minutes.

She'd laughed in delight as a conch shell of swirling pink was tucked into her curls at ear, waited eagerly at his urging to hear the song of the sea. Beaming, she asked with sweet shyness that he carry it, because she wanted to keep it for her cousin Kate.

Taking the shell, hoping to move her along in this, getting Merry to move at anything other than Merry's pace, proved impossibility. He managed to get her only a few feet down the path before he watched her scamper off, fascinated by the array of flowers lining the base of a cashew tree. His smile, unknowingly, held equal elements of affection and exasperation as he waited for her.

Half hidden in a bed of scarlet lilies, Morgan heard her say, "I can't imagine why you ever leave here. You are a wealthy man. Why do you stay at sea? Why piracy?"

He was amused by her question, and not bothering to hide it from her. "As opposed to what? Being a gentleman plantation owner here? How do you think I acquired all this, and the source of my wealth?"

She rose and followed him. "You have enough wealth to be free to become anything you wish to."

She wasn't sure, but his smile seemed a touch sad at the edges. "None of us are free, Little One. Freedom is the illusion of the young. One does not acquire freedom from wealth. The majority of the people on this earth are trapped by the same three things, poverty, necessity or society."

"Which one are you trapped by?"

He surprised himself by being honest. "Necessity."

He casually held out his hand. She took it, letting him guide her along the path. He was strangely quiet until the villa came in sight. At the edge of the path that bordered the front lawn, he stopped and turned her toward him.

He said, "Remember. There is no Morgan here. These are respectable people and their safety depends upon you, Merry. One wrong word, and I will have to act unfavorably. We don't want that to happen, now do we, Little One? You will find them delightful company. For *their* safety you must address me as Lord Deverell or Varian. Understood?"

"And what happened to the real Lord Deverell?"

Calmly, coldly, he said, "I rid the earth of him and good riddance it was."

"How can you talk so calmly of killing a man? Why did you kill him?"

With a disquieting smile, he said, "Necessity."

She started to walk again, fighting against the lump that had suddenly risen in her throat. The pleasant wash of the morning had caused her to forget the dangers of this man. She continued to follow with less enthusiasm and more wariness.

Exiting the jungle, they were soon on velvet lawns plush and green, brightened by flowerbeds. Gaily scattered Chinese Chippendale benches and chairs speckled the grass, and to Merry's surprise, a wide variety of children's toys.

Sunlight spilled across the brightly shingled roof. They had but barely reached the graveled carriageway when the front door burst wide. In the opening stood a woman, pretty, blond, crying and laughing.

As she anxiously dried wets hands on her apron, she exclaimed, "Varian Deverell. You could have given me notice."

A steady stream of children and dogs bolted passed her

skirts and down the short flight of steps.

Strong and healthy, bronze from the sun, the children surrounded Morgan in a bouncing horde of youthful enthusiasm.

A pretty copper haired girl of eight, with dancing brown eyes, caught Morgan's notice first.

"Mama said we'd have a surprise for Christmas. She didn't say it would be you."

Morgan had her in his arms and lowered her face until his nose touched hers, the gesture silly and affectionate, so unlike him. "Poor, Lily. Are you sorry your surprise is only me?"

Confident and charming, she leaned back and said, "I am if you didn't bring me a present."

Laughing, he said, "Well, that depends on the lot of you. Have you been good for your mother?"

Glowing smiles and nods rewarded Morgan's words. To Merry's surprise, he was both willing and able to keep up with their racing chatter.

Children. Who would have thought Morgan liked children, she thought in wonder.

His affection for these children showed clearly on his face and they wouldn't have flocked to him if it had been false.

Merry was pulled from her thoughts to take note of an irresistible lad, with a dirty face, tugging on Morgan's coattail. Merry watched as he set down Lily to lift the child into his arms, telling him with a smile he was the grubbiest child he'd ever seen.

The toddler's sharp-eared mother was quick to move to retrieve the boy, but Morgan only laughed and kept hold on him. "No, Emily. Really, it's fine. I'd be grubby too, if someone were cooking me candied peppermint in the kitchen. What is that, Walter?"

A boy of five leaned into Morgan's lowered and offered ear. In a whisper, he asked, "Who is the lady?"

They all looked at Merry, at once.

Morgan said charmingly, "Where are my manners, Walter? This is a very special passenger of mine. Mistress Merry. She's come to spend Christmas with us."

Morgan turned to Merry and said charmingly, "Little One, this is the Randall family. Mrs. Randall, her precocious daughter, Lily, then there is Thomas, George, Walter and the grubby one, Charles." His dark eyes did a thorough once over of the boys. "Yes, that's everyone."

The two women regarded each other for a moment with mutual interest. It was the children who saved Merry from what was indeed an awkward moment. Their mother was clearly not pleased Morgan had brought her here, but the children, island isolated and unaccustomed to visitors, enthusiastically pulled Merry into the house.

The villa was beautifully made in the Spanish style and furnished with a discreet elegance that instantly reminded Merry of Morgan's cabin aboard ship. The interior floors of breadnut timber sparkled and smelled of orange polish. The cream-washed walls surrounded vast arched windows, artfully dimmed by jalousie blinds. The sweetly fragrant air moved lightly through the rooms to cool them. The simple perfection of every detail so artfully camouflaged that its owner was a pirate, that in fact, one could tell absolutely nothing, at all, about the man who lived here. Unless one wanted to make note that everything was perfect and correct.

There was nothing of Morgan's personality here, except his strange ability to be exactly what he wanted to be, in any circumstance.

Standing in the center of the main foyer with the children,

Merry looked askance to see Morgan entering the villa with Emily at his side. She noted the possessive hand that claimed his arm. Sharp spears gnawed at her stomach as she wondered if this woman was yet another of Morgan's mistresses. He seemed to have one on every continent in every port.

Their heads were bent low, and Emily was speaking in a rapid flurry of whispers. Merry caught only two sentences.

Emily's voice broke with her displeasure as she snapped, "You brought one of your women to my house, Varian."

Then Morgan's stern reply, "You forget yourself, Emily. It is my house."

With a stiff smile twisted, Emily stepped from Morgan to the children, clapping her hands to shoo them away.

"All right, my little heathens, enough, back to your studies. Let the poor girl catch her breath. No, Thomas, you cannot go fishing with Lord Deverell. Studies. Now."

The children were gone in a flash of long limbs that soon left the foyer in an awkward silence.

Mrs. Randall turned to Merry. "I'm sure you'd like to freshen up, Merry. Do you mind if I just call you Merry? We don't stand on formality on the island. Would you like me to send a girl for a bath? I know it is the first thing I always want when I reach land. Let's get you settled in a room, shall we?"

She had Merry's bag, and her waist by an arm, subtly forcing her toward the stairs.

Morgan said, "The Emerald Room, if you please, Emily."

Emily turned, stiffened, and froze. "No. It is not...I mean, it is the only chamber in the house not presentable, and has not been renovated as the rest of the rooms. It is completely unsuitable."

Morgan arched a brow. "Is it clean?"

"Of course."

"Put her in the Emerald Room, Emily. It gets a pleasant breeze in the evenings. Then, come to me in the study. We can finish our discussion there."

Morgan didn't wait for Emily's response. He disappeared down a long corridor toward the back of the house.

In the custody of Emily, Merry was led up a creaking wood staircase to a bedroom on the backside of the house. The blond was anxiously gnawing her lower lip by the time she opened the bedchamber door.

It was, if nothing else, an interesting room. The tent bed was the most peculiar thing Merry had ever seen. The gilt sphinx settees were horrid. And all the tables had dreadful crocodile feet with large statues of scantily clad women playing harps scattered across them.

Pausing at a table, Merry's noticed a book, fixed her eyes on the cover, blushed, and looked away. It was then she saw the mirror hanging above the bed, an occurrence she couldn't begin to make reason of.

Then, Merry's bewildered study fixed on a large portrait of a woman strangely arranged with a swan.

Emily's face was cleverly expressionless. "You can see why I didn't want to put you here. The decor is supposed to be in the Egyptian fashion. If you ask me it looks like…" at Merry's stare of confusion, she broke off and smiled. "…well, never you mind what it looks like, my dear."

Emily went to the bed then, and busily went about unpacking Merry's small bag.

"The woman in the portrait. Is that Lord Deverell's wife?" Merry asked.

Emily flushed. "God, no. Ann was a lovely girl. That creature was mistress to the old Lord. He was an artist. She was his model."

Merry blushed. She was not sure what to make of Morgan putting her in this dreadful bedchamber.

Then, as if a thought surprised her, Emily's face snapped up. "Lord Deverell told you of Lady Ann?"

Merry shrugged and sank down on the bed. "Some."

"Such a tragedy. But, never you mind."

Emily was at the windows adjusting the jalousie blinds when Merry finally got the courage to ask.

"Mrs. Randall? Why would there be a mirror above the bed?"

Emily met Merry's unwavering glance, blushed, and then seemed to unbend in rapid waves.

Laughing, she said, "Vanity, I suppose. No one has been in this room so long, I forgot that wretched thing was there."

She smiled to herself as she went to the door. She paused to turn back to Merry, and was decidedly more friendly.

"Helga will bring you your bath, and if you require anything else, don't hesitate, my dear."

Downstairs, Emily went straight for Lord Deverell's study and shut the door. He was sprawled on a couch reading and didn't look up at her.

Frustrated, she snapped, "You can be a horrid man at times, Varian Deverell. You didn't have to play one of your foolish games and put her in that ghastly room to prove your point. You could simply have explained who the girl is, and why she is here."

Varian closed his book. "I should not have to explain myself, at all, to you."

Emily sank down beside him. "Fine. I should have known better than to think you'd bring one of your women to spend Christmas with my children."

Morgan arched a threatening brow at her. Emily ignored

it.

Then laughing, pink cheeked and smiling, she added, "I'd forgotten about the mirror above the bed. Poor little thing, she asked me why it was there."

Morgan only laughed at that. "I hope you didn't explain, Emily."

"Of course not." She pushed her strangling blond hairs from her face and fixed her eyes sharply on Varian. "I'm not going to let you divert me, Varian. Who is the girl?"

~ ~ ~

Merry was helped to bathe by two of Morgan's young maids. To find herself in the custody of gentle women, after so long exclusively in the care of men, was a strange and soothing comfort. They scrubbed her limbs, washed her hair, patted her dry, and then carefully draped her in a blue satin dressing gown.

An angry whinny from outside caught her attention and she went out onto the terrace. Morgan was astride a black horse, which jigged, snorted and fought his efforts to control him.

The angry beast reared once, but Morgan dug his spurs into him, as he struck the animal between the ears with his crop. He pulled him into a tight rein, spurred him, and fought until the animal settled into the force of his command. Then, he was off in a cloud of dirt, into the jungle, and out of view.

It was Lily, spying on her from the far side of the balcony, who pulled Merry's attention away from Morgan.

"Lord Deverell won't be back for many hours. Do you want me to come visit for awhile?"

Merry smiled. "I'd like that very much."

The little girl darted into the room to jump atop that ghastly bed. She fixed her chin in palms and gave Merry a curious study. "Are you going to marry Lord Deverell? Is that why you are here?"

Merry glanced up in surprise. "No, I'm not marrying Lord Deverell. Why would you ask me that, Lily?"

Lily gave a careless shrug. "I hear mama and papa talking at night. They are always whispering about how Lord Deverell should marry again. Now you're here, so of course I wondered, is she here to marry Lord Deverell?"

Trying to change the subject, Merry asked, "Where did Lord Deverell go? It looks like there is nothing but jungle out there."

Lily's eyes sharpened, at once. "Oh, that is a mystery. There is a village on the other side of the island, though we are never permitted to go there. Lord Deverell always takes off in the morning, for hours on end. We are not to ask, and we are not to follow. Mama would not be pleased."

There was nothing cute about that disclosure. Merry had been with Morgan, long enough, that she didn't have to think hard to come up with a multitude of unpleasant possibilities to solve Lily's mystery.

Merry gave a pert nod, though she felt far from light-hearted.

Watching Merry change into a gown, Lily said in a dramatic way, "I'm going to get married, someday. Lord Deverell has promised to take me to America and I shall find my husband there. Is that why you are going to America? Did Lord Deverell promise to find you a husband?"

Startled, Merry responded, "I'm not going to America, Lily."

"Indeed you are. Lord Deverell said so. So of course, it seemed logical that he was taking you there to find a husband, since you will not be wedding Lord Deverell."

"I have no plans to marry, ever."

That confession clearly perplexed the little girl. "Why ever not? I want to marry. Don't you want a husband? Children?"

That question Merry chose to ignore, though the question brought to her an unpleasant pondering. Would it have been better to stay and marry than never to see her family again? That she asked herself at all, was foolish. She could not undo the events of the past.

When Merry finished dressing, Lily eagerly grabbed her hand, tugging her along out of the bedchamber. "Mama told me to fetch you, at once, when you were ready."

The air outback was genial, as Merry was guided into Morgan's terraced garden. There was an unmistakable British look to it, with the neat lawn edged by limestone walkways, the fountains, the benches, and the iron frames dripping with lavender blossoms.

The older boys were studying at their mother's feet. Young Charles was asleep on a blanket beside her. Emily was busy, a large basket of garments beside her, needle moving efficiently in delicate fingers as she mended a man's shirt.

The smile Emily gave her over her shoulder was warm and friendly.

"Ah, I get a rest at last," she said in a satisfied way setting aside her work. "I waited to have tea with you, my dear. Perhaps, you'll sit with me while the children finish their studies."

Merry sank into the chair beside Emily, as Lily went back to her books and grass. Watching Emily's neat moves with the teapot, a thousand uncertainties roiled through Merry. What was Morgan's relationship to the Randall family? Why had Morgan brought her here, since this was clearly one of his careful guises he should not have wanted her to have knowledge of?

Sipping her tea, Merry didn't realize Emily was calmly studying her as well.

Merry smiled. "Lord Deverell seems most generous with your family."

"He is that. Tell me, what do you think of Lord Deverell?"

It was more than a casual question. "I don't think of him, at all."

Emily laughed. "Aside from the fact that he is not a man that a woman could ignore, your answer is very much a smart one. The less a woman thinks of a man, the better it is for the woman."

Having no idea what to think of that discreet warning, Merry finally said, "Your children are lovely. You have a magnificent family, Mrs. Randall."

Emily's gaze floated her children, as she smiled in satisfaction. "Thank you, my dear. I am a lucky woman. I should hate if anything were to change that."

Something in how Emily said that, made Merry's cheeks redden.

Emily carefully tucked her mending back into the basket and rose. "If you'll excuse me, my dear. I must attend to supper."

~~~

Merry did not see Morgan again until dinner. He was hunkered down in his study working. Emily made a constant effort to the keep the children and Merry from disturbing him.

Twice Merry passed the open study door, surprised to see him hovered over papers on his desk. There was something oddly normal about the pattern of Morgan's day. Morning ride. Tea. Long hours in the afternoon, industrious and working in his study. An ordinary man, not a myth at all, but real.

Dinner was a boisterous affair. The children, all except

Charles, were permitted at the table. They laughed and talked in an easy flow that held the flavors of a family.

After dinner, Morgan joined them in the evening parlor, brought out a chessboard and set it on the table beside Emily. Something in their manner told Merry this was a familiar routine.

She watched them play until the evening grew late. The irritation of being ignored grew unbearable. She promptly excused herself from the room.

Merry was sitting on her bed, braiding her hair when she heard familiar footsteps beyond her door. Expecting him to pass by, she was startled when Morgan entered without knocking. For all his politesse in front of Emily, his gentlemanly manner obviously did not extend to her. Deeply gasping, she exclaimed, "You could have knocked."

He gave her a look that made her feel foolish without even an effort. "I apologize. I forgot where we were."

She tossed the unfinished braid over her shoulder. "So much for the gentle care of pirates."

He fixed her in a humorous regard that made her blush. "I am wicked past redemption, Little One. Would you like me to leave? Would you like me to start this over and knock? Or, would you like to join me in an evening of the stars?"

An evening of the stars? Her foolish heart responded to that in a doubly foolish way. From the back of a chair, he retrieved a robe. She was disappointed in herself when she put it on.

He extended his hand and peevishly she accepted it. He guided her out onto the darken balcony, down a narrow staircase, and then, she felt foolish a second time, since Thomas obediently sat on the back lawn waiting for them.

"Do you know the names of the stars?" Thomas asked.

Merry sank down beside him, shaking her head. "No, not a one. Why don't you tell me the ones you know?"

To Merry's surprise, she found she was fascinated as Thomas went on to point out the constellations, and showed her how to draw a line from Mizar, the second star in the tail of the Great Bear, to find Cassiopeia. He showed her the Little Dipper, and then enthusiastically said, "That's the North Star at the end of its handle. It's the most special star in the sky. Do you know why it's important?"

Charmed by the boy, Merry asked, "I don't know, at all. Why don't you tell me?"

With satisfaction, he said, "It is the only star in the sky that is constant. There is more, but I can't remember."

After a moment, she chanced a look at Morgan, and found him watching her intently. "It is the star that guides all captains on their journeys. But more importantly, it is the star that guides them home."

There was something in his low voice that made her shiver. Looking up into his chiseled face, something in how he was staring at her made her heart drum faster, her cheeks grow hotter, and a strange tingling sensation to course through her veins.

Making a silly face at Thomas, she said, "Then, I will let it guide me on my journey to bed."

She sprang to her feet and hurried up the stairs.

Alone in her room, she tossed and turned all night. She laid awaken listening for Morgan's firm thread. Hours passed before she heard him enter his chamber.

Sleep eluded her as she listened to him moving about, then to hear if he remained alone in his chamber or if Emily joined him. Much to her displeasure, that was how Merry's first night on the island passed. Alone in bed listening to Morgan.

~~~

True to Lily's disclosure, Morgan rose early every morning and was off on his horse into the jungle. Merry breakfasted alone in her bedchamber. But by midmorning, Morgan returned, and sometimes he fetched Merry for a walk, if the children hadn't already claimed her.

Her days began to wax into a comfortable pattern with him, of morning walks and afternoon talks in the garden. On rarer occasions, a quiet game of chess followed after dinner when Emily excused herself early.

For all Merry's internal unrest, *Isla del Viento* was a lovely place, and her days almost idyllic. With the Randalls, Morgan was never Morgan, not even a glimmer of the pirate captain rose to betray his persona as Lord Deverell. He was only those subparts she now considered Varian.

This new persona was as dangerously alluring as Morgan had been on ship. There was an irresistible charm to his ability to savor the simple pleasures, to be found in abundance, on the island.

While logic warned Merry this adventure should not have been pleasant, there was nothing to her days she considered disagreeable.

On this morning two weeks later, she found herself in a small boat with the older children as Morgan rowed them toward an underwater landscape of limestone caverns. He'd set a fish pot the day before with Lily. The girl had roused Merry early that morning, eager to discover what treasures she had trapped.

Listening to Lily's racing chatter, Merry focused on the starfish speckled walls and the brilliantly colored fish that swirled in the deep green water.

More often than not, when Morgan invited Merry to leave

the villa, the children were with them. It seemed to Merry as though Emily deliberately maneuvered this. She wondered at the woman's relationship with Morgan, since clearly she never wanted Merry alone with him.

It was obvious they shared a deep affection between them, their manner causal and friendly. Yet, Merry knew for certain that Morgan never passed a night in a room with Emily.

She looked at the children, all dark eyed, a mixture of light and dark hued hair. She felt her stomach turn with the suspicions that had haunted her for hours on end.

Two days ago, she had mustered the courage to ask Emily, directly, her relationship to Lord Deverell. Emily's answer was far from a thorough disclosure, and only added to the suspicions Merry couldn't bank.

She'd been sitting on a stool in the kitchen watching Emily busily at work, and surprised herself by saying, "Lord Deverell seems to be a very fond of your family. Who are you to him?"

Emily's face snapped up from the bread she'd been kneading. She smiled. "I am his kindness, Merry."

At Merry's frown, Emily slapped the bread dough once against the counter, formed it into a ball, covered it, and then sank down on the stool across from Merry.

"I was born on the wrong side of the blanket," Emily explained. "That dreadful creature in the portrait in your bedchamber was my mother, the old Lord her benefactor. When Lord Deverell inherited the estate, he found me here not provided for. His kindness possessed him to take on the obligation of me. He saw to my education, and then saw me well settled in marriage to the Captain. He has permitted me to raise my family here and to treat his home as if it were my own."

Merry sat back, staring at her. Few men would take on the

obligation of a woman unrelated to them. Pensioning off the bastard daughter of a man he'd murdered made no sense.

"But why? Why would he do such a thing?"

Emily smiled blandly. "Who knows what possesses a man to do anything? You would have to ask Lord Deverell, my dear. I really couldn't tell you."

"It is almost Christmas. When do you expect Captain Randall to return? The children seem most eager to see him."

Emily rose, wiped her hands on her apron, and she said, "He will be here when he is here. A captain's wife must always be patient, and know that the sea has its own timetable, unconcerned for the wants of a woman."

Merry was brought back to the present by the raised voices of the children, and the sound of splashing water. Across from her, Morgan and Lily were leaning over the side of the boat.

Soon, the pot was pulled free by his capable hands, a woven cane-work box designed to trap sea creatures. He set in the center of the boat, and the children were atop of it instantly. There were six fish, though an occasional sea shrimp could be found now spotting the floor of the boat.

Across from him, Merry watched as he patiently identified them for the children, trying to answer the rapid fire of questions.

When the children's inquisitiveness had been satisfied, with glowing eyes, he asked, "So what say you? Do we roast them over a fire or return them to the sea?"

The children heatedly demanded their release. Merry watched in amusement as the pot was quickly returned to the water, and the creatures promptly released.

From the caverns, Morgan rowed them to a small cove, well from view of the villa. He carried Merry from the boat to shore and the children scattered like leaves on the wind.

"Now off with you," Morgan announced to the children. "I wish to eat my meal in peace."

The children obeyed without pause. Merry spotted, in surprise, that a picnic had been laid out on a greenbelt several yards away.

The meadow they entered was tranquil, but Merry slowed, wondering why Morgan had done this. She had not been alone with him for many weeks.

Her eyes darted to see where the children had gone. Lily was busy with her gathered flowers, making a colorful chain wreath, far from view in the greenery that edges the beach. Thomas had found something to amuse himself with in the tide pool, on the other side of the cove.

They were in view, but not close. She took a small measure of comfort from that, even as a part of her thrilled at this unexpected moment alone with Morgan. The days of his careful distance from her had miserably confirmed his lack of affection for her. The painful twisting of her stomach had confirmed, for Merry, things she would not permit herself to admit, yet.

Morgan's hand on her arm caused her to draw a single breath that was out of rhythm with the others. When she shifted her attention back to him, his eyes were hooded fire embers, a potent smile lingering on the surface of his mouth.

"Alone, at last," he said, not taking his gaze from her face.

At the gentle urging of his hand, Merry sank to her knees beside him. Merry watched as his well-formed fingers rummaged through the basket for the wine and the neatly wrapped fare.

She realized this lunch had been packed for *them*, most probably by Morgan's German housekeeper. Merry didn't doubt Emily would never have accommodated a request from him for this.

Accepting the wine glass he held out for her, she said, "You're very fond of the children."

He laughed softly, as he continued to prepare a plate for her. "Why does it sound as if that surprises you? I happen to like children, Little One."

Her wide doe eyes sharpened on his face. "But, you seem particularly fond of these children."

Morgan stopped in what he was doing and gave her a hard stare. "For a man my age, I can hardly say that I haven't had my share of dalliances. But, I have no bastard children, Merry. Not a one. And Emily is many things to me, but she has never been my mistress."

For some strange reason that delighted her very much. To cover the confusing wash of her feelings for him, Merry focused on Lily in the distance.

Morgan hid a smile, and continued with his task. In a gesture he'd come to know well, she set down the glass, hugged her knees until she was curled into a tiny ball, and rested her chin there.

Wanting to divert himself from the thoughts he was having, he asked, "Why did you stow away to America, Little One? It has been teasing my curiosity for months. How old were you? Was this recent? You do enjoy such unlikely entertainments for a girl your age."

Merry made a face at Morgan as though he had insulted her.

"I was nine, you insufferable man. My brother had given me a picture book for my birthday. It had wonderful stories about the wild land and the savages. I wanted to see Indians and my father wouldn't let me. So when my uncle had to go on business, I simply went with him, hiding in the luggage box in his coach. It was more difficult getting on that ship than yours.

I had to wait until night. I was cold and very frightened, and more than a little hungry. I snuck aboard and hid in the galley until they pulled from port."

Morgan laughed. She savored the rare pleasure of the fuller sound of it that could only be found in true amusement. "Did you get to see your Indians, Little One?"

Knitting her delicate brows in disappointment, she shook her head. "No. That is the worst part of it. We went to the American capital, and I only got to see a brief flash of the city, before my uncle locked me into a room. I was in a hotel for two months, with a dour faced old woman as guard who would not let me have any fun at all. It was miserable being locked away from the world."

"I think your uncle was wise to lock you away, Little One. You are an excessively curious and willful girl. It gets you into trouble. What happened when you got home? I imagine your parents were displeased with you."

She nodded and her eyes rounded. "My mother cried and lavished kisses all over my face. I was standing there shaking in her arms thinking, 'I was so afraid to come home, so afraid that they would be furious that I could not enjoy the ship on my return voyage, and this is all they've done.' Then, she handed me to my father, who gave me the worst spanking of my life. So you can tell Indy I have been spanked, though perhaps not often enough, and it did no good."

Merry was laughing with her memories. The smile she gave him was breathtaking. Morgan's gaze studied her young face then traveled the length of her. Taking in her slim, shapely body, and the fast rising heat within him, reminded him it had been a very long time since he'd been with a woman.

Leaning in, he lifted her chin and claimed her lips. Without a single recognizable command from either of them, she was in his arms. This kiss was far from a simple kiss. They kissed, hungrily and long, with a caressing intensity that left her limp everywhere, and suddenly beneath him on the blanket.

"I didn't bring you here for this," he said almost to himself.

Then his hands moved in slow patterns on the sides of her gown. The breath quickened in her throat and in his. The erotic glide of his hands made her skin quiver as he continued to devour her lips.

With his palm, he pushed aside the line of fabric that covered her shoulder, moving his kisses there to her creamy softness. Dragging her into his arms, he turned until her body covered his. His mouth returned to hers, feeling the sweetness of her blooming sensuality, the unaffected way her body answered each move of his.

When his hand moved beneath her gown, up her bare leg, he heard a startled little gasp, but she did not pull away. She only melted more against him.

He turned her beneath him, back against the blanket. Merry intimately molded into him with all the completeness that was possible, since they were both fully dressed. Even with the layers of fabric between them, the contact held enough thoroughness to make her ache in places she had never known she could ache. Hot waves swirled all through her body as they kissed and kissed, their mouths desperate and hungry, her tongue playing in frantic answer of his, as she let his hands dance freely across her trembling flesh.

Merry knew where this was going, but the spray of kisses on her passion damp flesh above her lace bound breasts only increased the desperate urges to let it go where she wanted it to. She knew she needed to stop this, uncertain how she had let herself go so far and afraid of going further. Her body was ruthlessly demanding the conclusion, even while the rapidly forming warnings commanded her to stop. This growing hunger in her flesh did nothing to make, less harsh, the fact she could never permit this to happen. Those were her thoughts, even as her hands and mouth never faltered in meeting his quest, and only seemed to urge him onward.

"Please," she whispered. When that brought no response, she did it again, louder into the trap of his lips.

Morgan was not even aware he had her half undressed, until Merry's tremulous voice permeated the ragged chorus of his own breath. He felt her tiny body beneath him jerk, tense, and then almost tragically surrender to his touch.

Opening his eyes, Merry was a beautiful blur beneath him. Her passion kissed features were a blend of anxiousness and arousal, though on every delicately molded line was want to stop this. In his soul rose the damning warning that this act completed today would not be completed well. Aroused in body she was, sure she was not.

As hungry for her as he was at present, he couldn't do it. If he made love to her now, she would regret the giving of herself, regret him, and hate him for it. While he wasn't at all certain what he wanted from her, he knew for certain he didn't want that.

As slowly as his body had surrounded her, Merry became aware that Morgan was withdrawing it from her, with a gentle disconnect that added to her inner upheaval. Her flesh screamed for the return of contact, even while she was grateful that he'd worked his body from her, knowing she could never have managed any of this if it had been left to her.

Merry was lying face flushed beneath him, shivering like a fool, thankful he'd stopped and in agony that he did. That he didn't even try to urge her onward, although it was the last thing she should want, left her miserable and humiliated. Immersed in the agony of yearning, she had left it to him to end this strange torment inside of her, and for whatever reason, he had stopped.

Merry closed her eyes, not wanting to meet his gaze. His low voice, whispering through her tumult, had a raspy tender quality to it. "You are in a surprisingly reckless mood today, Little One."

Merry felt him gently ease away, and then, the sun burned where his body had been. Her eyes flew open and it was then she saw him lying back against the blanket beside her, one well-muscled arm covering his face. His tanned flesh showed a light flush, and his dark hair had tumbled forward in wanton disarray.

When he sat up, she could see in his eyes shards of burning blackness. She dropped her gaze. He said, "Finish your meal, Little One. I should get the children and take you back to the house. Any more sun and you'll be red as a lobster."

She looked at Morgan, then. For the briefest of seconds, she saw the expression on his face before he could conceal it from her. He did not want what had happened between them.

She turned away from him, letting her hair tumble forward to hide her face. No man had ever hurt her more than this. To her greater dismay, she wondered how she had permitted herself to care for a man who would never care for her in return.

He rose to his feet. "I'll collect the children while you finish your meal, Little One."

She didn't look up, obediently nodding.

She was quiet in the boat as Morgan rowed her back to the villa. Morgan looked at her not once, and seemed content to fix on Thomas's sprawling tale of what he'd found in the tide pool.

The house was bursting with the sounds of excitement as they returned. The instant they crossed the front entry, Lily left at a running pace, disappearing into the main parlor.

Hanging back in the doorway, Merry watched Morgan crossing the room. So Emily's captain was real, Merry thought, before she was pulled into the celebration to be introduced to the short, fat, smiling figure of Captain George Randall.

CHAPTER SEVENTEEN

Christmas day rose with a brilliant sun, a vivid blue sky, and not a hint of winter in the air. Christmas in the Caribbean was a magical thing.

The servants and the island families had received their presents the night before. They'd gathered on Morgan's rolling back lawn for a celebration the entire household shared. He was a surprisingly gracious, attentive host and, to Merry's surprise, the island families all but, adored him.

The children would have their gifts in the morning.

Sounds came early and loud in the house the next morning, since the children had been forced to wait. Merry had only managed to don a dressing gown before Lily flung wide her door.

"Hurry, Mistress Merry. Lord Deverell says we must wait for you," Lily exclaimed, grabbing Merry by the hand and dragging her downstairs at a half-running pace.

An hour later, Merry was sitting in the middle of a busy, boisterous family, which much resembled the Merrick clan. Tucked into the warmth of celebrating children, it was easy for Merry to forget she was only Morgan's hostage. They climbed on her lap, pulled at her to show her this or that treasure unwrapped. There was pleasure in simply watching them and their enthusiastic want to include her in this.

The exchange of gifts swirled back and forth. Morgan had been most generous with the Randall children. It was not until

355

she heard Lily, sitting on the arm of Morgan's chair, that Merry did not feel a part of what was happening.

"But, where is Merry's gift?" said Lily, when there was not a single package left untouched.

Morgan's dark eyes floated the room, returning to the little girl. "Ah. It does seem we are one short."

That made Lily glare at him. Then, Morgan's eyes shifted to Merry as he whispered into Lily's ear, "There is a small, black box in that drawer over there. Fetch it for me."

The little girl climbed from his lap, went to the drawer, and brought it back to him in satisfaction.

She said, "It is wise you did not forget. I would have been angry."

In mock-seriousness, Morgan shook his head. "Then, it is a good thing I would never forget Merry. I did not plan to do this now. Go away. You are irritating me."

He crossed the room to Merry. Her eyes were round in her face, huge upon him, as he slowly lowered to the floor in front of her. She cautioned herself not to make more of this gesture than she should. It was no doubt only part of this fiction he maintained with the Randalls.

Still, her heart would not respond obediently as she felt his eyes upon her. She opened the gift. A large blue sapphire sparkled brilliantly in its setting. Merry stared at the pendant in disbelief.

"This is for me?" she asked.

He laughed softly. "Of course. It is the exact hue of your eyes. Who else could I make such a gift to?"

"Ah. It's beautiful," Emily said, and then added pointedly to Morgan, "A sapphire. How extraordinary."

"The North Star," Morgan corrected, keeping his eyes carefully diverted from Emily. "When I saw it in Bermuda, I could not think of it belonging to anyone but you, Little One."

Merry lowered her gaze from him, her heart a confusing blend of hurt and longing. The North Star, the star that sees every sailor home from their journey. An odd trembling possessed her. She did not know what to make of his words, the gift, or that he had thought of this many weeks ago.

He removed the dainty chain from the box and unclasped it. "Would you like me to put it on you?"

Merry said nothing and lifted her hair. His arms slid over her shoulders, her heart pounding as the warmth of his fingers brushed the flesh of her a neck.

When he eased back from her, he lifted her chin. "It looks most beautiful on you, Merry."

She could not meet his gaze.

"It's lovely. Thank you," she murmured.

She sprang to her feet and hurried from the room. She didn't know why, but she was in tears before she made it through the terrace doors. What were these strange feelings inside of her? How did one make them stop?

She was standing at the edge of the porch, brushing her tears, when Morgan's even footsteps sounded behind her.

Morgan said, "I am sorry. I don't know what I've done to upset you. It was not my intent, Little One."

Even without looking at him, his voice told her he was telling the truth in this. It made her reaction all the more perplexing and foolish. How was it that a gift from man had the power to make her cry? What could she say to him that would not sound foolish?

"I miss the rain," Merry sobbed. "And stormy days with everything cozy inside. And my family. I never thought I'd spend a day without them. I miss my home more than I ever thought I would. So many remark that Cornwall is stark and eerie. It is not. It is peaceful."

Morgan didn't ask. He lifted Merry in his arms and settled in a chair with her curled upon his lap.

"Cornwall is peaceful, Little One. You are right. And you are right to want to go home."

And with that Merry curled into Morgan and let go more tears.

~~~

The end of January saw the return of the *Corinthian*, but only Tom Craven and Indy came to the villa. The rest of the crew had scattered across the island.

The day before they were to set sail, Merry hurried into the dining parlor to find only Emily and Captain Randall there. She'd awoke early, hoping to catch Morgan still breakfasting. She had hardly seen him since the ship's return.

She stared at his empty chair. "Where is Lord Deverell this morning?"

Emily's smile was strained. "We most probably won't see him today, my dear."

Captain Randall continued to eat and gave a nod. "It is a dark day, indeed."

Merry shifted her gaze to Emily. They were both in somber moods.

"There is nothing to be troubled about, my dear. It will pass. It always does. Now eat," Emily said, and then absently added, "When we saw you, we had so hoped these dark spells would be behind Lord Deverell."

Merry sat back in her chair and studied the Randalls. "Dark day? Why is everyone so grave?"

Emily dabbed at her eyes and forced a smile. "Never mind, my dear. I want this to be a happy day. It is your last day on the island. I think we should have a party in the garden. Wouldn't you like that, George? Yes, that is what we need. When you finish your meal, Captain, you will see that my pianoforte is taken to the garden."

~~~

It was the sound of Merry's laughter that pulled Morgan from his darkened room. It was like a siren's call, inescapable, even in the grimness of his mood. The day marked the tenth year of Ann's death. It was the day he faithfully devoted to her and all he remembered.

Morgan sat on a Chinese Chippendale bench in the brilliant sunlight of afternoon, staring into the terraced garden at Merry. Emily had had his pianoforte carried to the lawn; the glossy surface now filthy with the treasures discarded from Merry's hands. There was now a scattering of seashells, leaves and the petals of scarlet lilies.

Even from a distance, Morgan could clearly hear the words Merry was singing in a clear voice, not quite as lovely as her face. Her anti-monarchal selection stirred a remnant sense of discomfort, since it seemed time could not completely obliterate the politesse of his youth.

She was charming in this, as lovely as she was in all the things that she did. So much so, even the staunch loyalist, George Randall, sat charmed as Merry entertained his children with mocking references to the large girth and villainy of England's ruling prince.

Her song was British home grown. It was most probably the product of the young, radical republican set that haunted the English countryside. It was definitely British, not American. It accounted for its cleverness, since the Americans had no flair at all in their wordplay or satire.

Her treasonous little ditty over, Merry began to laugh uproariously. Morgan wondered, yet again, who this girl was.

What did it mean, her affinity for the anti-monarchal and her clearly expressed sympathies for the Americans? Was she English merchant class, perhaps?

The blockades, that restricted trade, harmed on both sides of the Atlantic. It was the merchant class that was particularly vocal in stirring the flames of civil unrest. Perhaps Merry was not nobility, at all, and merely moneyed.

"The girl has become a problem, Varian. It is past time to resolve the issue of her," announced Tom Craven.

Morgan's opaque gaze transferred slowly to meet Tom Craven's blighting stare. Tom was carelessly relaxed against the balustrade of the villa's porch, one leg bent, swinging, watching Merry, as well. His strict eyes were not quite generous in their assessment of her.

"Is it the boy? Is that why you keep her?" Tom added, less provoking.

The boy. This was a new theory. Morgan found it as unpleasant as the rest. It was a logical theory. Before Merry, Indy would have given the girl no notice at all, scarred and frigid as he was. The only contact the boy allowed with anyone was casual. Infrequent and rapid encounters with mature women of a certain order. Yet with Merry, there was a gentleness of manner Morgan had never before seen in the lad.

Sighing, Tom remarked, "I don't know you anymore. What could there possibly be about this girl to interest you, Varian."

It had been a long time since they had attempted to speak to each other in total honesty. The ghost of what their friendship had once been, of who they had once been, hovered between them.

"You are too harsh in your perceptions of women at times. Harsh, but amusing. During my days in London she is exactly what I pursued."

Tom's pale gray eyes sharpened. "You are not in London, Varian. Don't try to put a noble wash on this. You are maneuvering her to maintenance in a house on Green Street. Be truthful with yourself for once. Do you imagine yourself entertained by her any longer than you have been entertained by the others? What becomes of her then? By the time you tire of her, she will leave here knowing too much of who you are. She may, very well, destroy us all with those parts of yourself you give her in reckless lust and whim."

Morgan cut him short. "I've already made my decision. We will discuss it no further."

Tom swore softly under his breath. "Goddamn her. I knew she was a curse the first moment I set eyes on her, with what she is, and the way you looked at her as she hovered on your bed."

"If she is a curse, Tom, then she is my curse. Surely, I deserve one," Morgan said evenly as he rose. "Come. I must go to the village before we join the others at the beach."

Tom's gaze narrowed. "Perhaps, you should take the boy to the village, as well."

Morgan's smile took on an edge. "He finds his own amusements. Don't examine too closely, your opinions of her, Tom. She is all our curse, my friend. All our curse, since the time when God first made Eve for Adam."

Morgan made a fast stop at the piano. Merry had been glancing skyward toward the wild twitter of a bird, which darted across the trees. She didn't note his presence, and startled when his hand found her shoulder and his lips touched her hair.

"Thank you for the song, Little One," he said, smiling at her.

Merry was disappointed to find that Morgan's light kiss

could send her again into internal disarray. His touch had been only casual. His comments amused.

There must be a better way to manage with a man. These waves of uncontrollable feelings were like shackles at times.

Into her silence, he said, "Enjoy the afternoon and your birds, My Dear. We return to sea tomorrow."

His black eyes shifted to Indy.

"Come, lad. Tom thinks a walk to the village will serve you well."

Indy's eyes glittered. Captain Randall coughed nervously. Emily colored, rather prettily, on her cheeks. It was Merry's clear stare that made Morgan look away and quickly leave them.

A heavy silence ensued while Indy stared off at the captain. When her questioning gaze fixed on Indy, the boy sprang up on his feet, running slowly until he caught Morgan on the edge of the lawn.

Shifting her gaze, Merry found Emily watching her. The older woman quickly dropped her eyes.

Merry's spirits were hardly elevated by an evening alone in her bedroom. Morgan had not returned from the village. There was to be a party at the beach. A British man-of-war had dropped anchor off the island. Lord Deverell was required to make welcome to the officers there.

Shortly after supper with his family, Captain Randall left to join the festivities. Emily was clearly not pleased by this. Prior to his departure, Captain Randall had forbidden both women to leave the house.

"Why has Captain Randall ordered us not to go to the beach?" Merry finally asked, after a strained hour sitting with Emily in her parlor.

"It is better for a woman to know as little as possible about what men do in their private amusements."

Emily continued to keep her gaze locked on her sewing. Merry stared at her, trying to make reason of Emily's uncharacteristic mood and response.

Then, exasperated and angry, Emily said simply, "Lord Deverell brings women from the village for the pleasure of the British officers."

In an angry huff, Emily tossed the shirt into the mending basket, and promptly retired.

Alone in the quiet house, Merry went to bed.

Sleep eluded her. She had been with the pirates long enough that none of this shocked her now. It wasn't maidenly outrage that kept her awake through the hours of the night. It was more the anxious churning of a woman's heart, which could not be stilled with the reminder it was foolish to be so despondent over anything Morgan did.

What a strange power men possessed to so easily claim the thoughts and emotions of a woman, without want or effort.

At midnight, she climbed from her bed and padded barefoot out onto the balcony. Her fingers curled the balustrade.

There was only darkness, indigo fields, and jungle in front of her. There was a dot of light in the distance, the slave colony that Morgan had warned her about. From the beach she could hear the music and revelry.

It made her feel warm and agitated in her flesh. It instantly brought memories of Ireland to her. The memory of how it had felt to dance in the firelight, to have Morgan's eyes upon her, and then her wantonness in his arms as her body strained into his as he devoured her with his kisses. If he kissed her that way tonight, would she stop him?

She felt that ever present restlessness takeover her body. She did nothing but think of Morgan these days. The more she thought of him, the more this urgent need grew into a free-flowing possession of her that never seemed to completely quiet.

She did not want to think of his flesh and touch, she could not stop herself.

She did not want to want him, she wanted him all the more.

She wanted to maintain the security of her anger at him, and found herself forgiving each and every cut as they came. Whatever this affliction was, she wanted to be done with it.

After years of avoiding men, she had found herself trapped by one.

~~~

Morgan returned to his room alone. There were any of a dozen women at the beach he could have selected for this night, seasoned, eager, and knowing in relieving the hungry demands of his flesh. He had chosen instead to smoke, a vile indulgence he despised, and to return alone, his flesh raging, to an empty bed

He still had the bottle of Cici in his hand as he settled in a chair in the darkened corner of his room.

Cici was a harsh drink that made its way to the island from Chili. A rough gin made of corn, the maize chewed by toothless women and left to ferment in water. It was hard on the stomach, hard on the palate, and rapidly intoxicating. It suited his need, and his mood.

He didn't know for certain the source of his turmoil. Was it this day? Was it his conversation with Tom? Or, was it the man he used to be, always watching and slightly repulsed by what he'd become. That thought had hardly finished before he saw Merry float through his open French doors.

Merry did not see him in the chair. She would not have

gone into the room if she had.

She glided toward his desk, stopped, and then began to move her barefoot back and forth across the rug, as her soft fingertips gently floated across the items on his desk. She was wearing a sheer, sapphire lace nightgown. She didn't know it, but she looked very tempting and very beautiful. Her wild disarray of curls fell loosely about her shoulders, her fingers moved in artless flutters across his possessions, the delicate lines of her body, clearly silhouetted by the soft candlelight.

Morgan knew he should send her from his room quickly. His soul raged. He had a fiery hunger for the girl. A dangerous combination.

Merry glided before his gaze to his bed. She lightly touched the coverlet, before lifting his pillow and pressing it to her face. He watched her in silence, understanding better than she what had brought her here.

The desire between them was very strong. It seemed to only grow with each passing day.

It was the pug, suddenly yapping and running across the room that drew Merry's attention to him. She flushed guiltily and into her silence he said, "Pretty, pretty Merry. Where did you come from? Why are you here?"

Her eyes rounded in dismay. She stared at him. He could see the desire, not fully concealed, in her sapphire eyes and the indecision on her face.

Merry crossed the room, sank down in front of Morgan, and took away the bottle. "I am here because you will not let me go."

"Ah, then we are even, yet again. You will not let me go, either," he said.

She touched his face, gently, tentatively. "Go to sleep, Captain. You would do well to get some sleep."

She set the bottle on the table, and made to move toward the door.

"Don't go. I don't wish to be alone yet," he ordered.

Before she could make it to the door, he crossed the room in three steps. In no time at all, he had her in the chair, on his lap, and her body pressing sinuously into him. He lifted her hair and touched his lips against her neck.

Into her ear he breathed, "Do you know you make my life a torment?"

Carefully, she said, "You have only to return me to Falmouth, if I am torment."

His laughter was soft and of something other than humor. "So like a woman."

Running his thumbs over the rise of her lips, he finished the touch with a probing kiss. Her unrestrained breasts made lush contact with his chest, the slightest movement made her rub against him. A shudder passed through her body. He felt it, and lowered to gently kiss across her lace covered breasts.

He kissed her once on the lips and drew back, waiting for her to look at him. When she didn't immediately, his fingers spread over her flushing skin.

Her bluebell eyes went wide. "If you're done playing your games with me, sir, I'd like to go to my room."

He grinned. "I'm nowhere near done, My Dear. Is there a young man in Falmouth that you care for, Little One?"

She shook her head. "No."

Morgan was silent for a moment. "Surely, you had many suitors. Surely, there was someone."

His eyes burned into her now, even as he held her gently, stroking her shining hair. She ran her tongue along her passion plump lips, searching his face as if unsure how to answer him.

Finally, looking away, she whispered, "One suitor. I did

not care for him."

"Remarkable. Do you have any idea what a beautiful woman you are?"

His fingers, firmly on her chin, forced her resisting gaze back to him. After a moment of kissing her, he whispered. "Do you like that, Merry?"

"I do not think that's the issue here."

Easing her back against him, his mouth on the silky flesh beneath her ear, he said, "What is the issue here?"

"That I should return to my room."

She tried to climb from his lap.

"We return to sea tomorrow," he said. "I need to resolve what I should do with you."

He felt her try to pull back from his flesh.

"You could return me to Falmouth."

"Can I?"

He lifted her hair, letting it fall across his face, while his moving hands on her back brought her mouth to his again. All her fragility and sweetness were flowing into him. Whatever his more honorable inclinations were demanding, his male inclinations had other thoughts.

In the warm space that separated their bodies, somehow his hands had undone the fastenings on the front of her gown. The ribbons fell a loose tease against her flesh. The blue strands moved with the rapid intakes of her breath within the lush crevice of her rose tipped breasts.

"I can never take you back to Falmouth. Do you think me a fool? You know too much of who I am. And I know too little, so much less than I want, of you."

He made another neat, fast move of their bodies to the bed. She tried to pull away, but with strong, gentle hands he held her against him, feeding the flesh he so wanted to consume with the fervent kisses of his mouth. When her resistance gave way and left her pliant beneath his touch, his hands moved upward on her bare skin, paused, and then covered her breasts.

"Please. I will not do this. You must let me go," she begged, moving her hands in a forceless way against him.

Her face came hazily into focus before him, the soft shining eyes, and the desperate anxiousness of her features. Desire rose in his body with a fierceness that had not visited him in many years.

Softly laughing into their kisses, he rolled until he covered himself with her flesh, savoring the joy of being surrounded by her. It had been too long since he'd felt the fire like this. He missed the sweet thrill of gentle hands touching him lovingly, of honest passion in lush flesh, and the pleasure of sharing both his heart and body at once.

"Varian."

His name on her panting whisper sent a rocketing shiver along his stomach and hips. His hands molded her back against him.

She whispered his name a second time, and that only brought her lowered to the bed. His knee held one of her legs in a warm cradle. To her dismay, he was above her, his long, tanned fingers working the fastenings of his own clothing.

"You must let me up."

She struggled as with one hand he steadied her body. The other began to stir back her tangled hair that clung to her lips and eyelashes and cheeks.

"Please. What must I do to make you stop this?"

He buried his lips in her hair. His voice was but a ragged whisper, "Let us make love all night so that this suffering inside of me will end."

Moving his hands down to hold her hips, he pressed his

throbbing flesh against her as he brought his mouth to hers, once again. He felt her move against him, even as her hands tried to work between them against his chest.

"Please let me go, Varian."

As though from far away, her stricken tone pierced his senses. Still he continued, his fingers searching within her soft hair, his motions growing deeper, longer, until she was damp and helpless, struggling against the demands of his lower body, and hers.

Feeling her yield, he felt his senses explode. Her lips were meeting his with a passionate want to equal his own. Her hands roamed anxiously the supple muscles of his back and shoulders. He felt his pulse quicken under the innocent motions of her fingers.

He whispered his desire for her, working free the fastenings of his breeches, breathing her name to urge her onward.

All at once, her tiny body stiffened. She jerked back from him and she hissed, "Let me go. I will not let you bed me in a drunken stupor and want of another woman."

The anguish in her voice was enough to clear his head. Morgan stared at her. Tears of humiliation were burning down Merry's cheeks, and her face was a tensing of hurt. In an instant, he realized what he had done.

Abruptly he released her, and with purpose he left the bed. It came to him in an inescapable shock wave, what he'd nearly done and why he had nearly done it.

Morgan faced toward the wall, his posture frozen. There was much inside of him running loose he was trying to bring under control.

Merry screamed, "I may be nothing to you, but I deserve more than being raped by a drunken fool, while being called another woman's name. I would rather you toss me into the sea than ever have you touch me again."

Morgan looked at her then, his eyes as severely bright as fire embers. "I will never let you go. Never."

Brushing frantically at her tears, she screamed, "And I will hate you until I die."

His gaze fixed on her as emotion rose sharply through him.

"Go, Merry," he ordered harshly. "Go now. Lock your door. It is not safe for you tonight."

Morgan watched Merry run from the room. *What a fool I am*, he thought. *What an incredible fool.*

He had not seen it before this moment, but it had been there all along. Oh, on the surface it was only a whisper tucked cleverly inside of her brilliant extremes, a quiet suggestion to nag at his brain. Tonight it was in the room with brutal clarity.

It was why he kept her.

It was why he wanted her.

It was why he couldn't have her.

It was all there, plain to see. Her sweet innocence. Her naïve gallantry. Her sharp intelligence that hid behind her youthful face. Her grace. Her beauty. The gentleness of her manner that existed in a laughing effervescence that made her beauty a thing beguiling.

Merry was a living, breathing creation of all he had once loved, in an exaggerated form that even he could not dismiss by will.

The boy had read him well in this. There was sudden sureness as to why Indy had brought her to him. Oh, it had been wrong to underestimate the lad.

He sank down on his bed, cradling his head in his hands, wondering how he could not have seen it. Indy's plotting was so glaringly obvious that a blind man could see it.

The boy had been brilliant in this.

~~~

By midmorning, Morgan had concluded all remaining business on the island and was eager to return to the *Corinthian*.

Merry had missed breakfast. She had refused to come when Emily had gone to fetch her. Splitting hangover and all, Morgan knew he was going to have to deal with her. His even strides carried him up the stairs with no noticeable hurry or reluctance, though he was claimed by both, and more than mildly, not wanting of this confrontation.

He found her as Emily warned he would.

Merry was curled on a windowsill, staring out at the yard. Tiny arms hugging legs, her cheek resting on knees, and for all her stillness she had the look of a tiny cat, ready to strike at a moment's warning. He noted her breakfast tray untouched. Without a word to her, he shoved her belongings into the small case retrieved from the armoire.

Bag in hand, standing so close to her that it was impossible for her to not know he was there, he said, "Come."

She refused to look at him. She didn't move. Succinctly, this time, he said, "You have dragged this out as long as you can."

He could hear the exhaustion in her breathing. If the remainder of her night had been half as miserable as his own had been, he couldn't imagine where she got the energy to continue with this.

"It will do no good to fight me, Merry," he said.

She resettled her body in a more noble posture, lifting her chin. "If you don't mind, I would like to know where you are taking me."

"I fail to see how that matters at this juncture."

371

"Of course, you would fail to see," she answered, with a sarcasm that was withering. "You fail to see many things. I will not board your ship, unless you give me your word it is taking me to Falmouth. I will not stay with you."

In spite of how wretched he felt, he almost laughed. She'd learned, in a handful of hours, how to fight like a woman, to fight with her tongue. Her observations added to the sting and his reluctance to take her by force to the ship, on the heels of what he had nearly done to her.

"Battle done," was his laconic answer, as he took her arm, propelling her toward the door.

She tried to pull out of his grip, unsuccessfully. When they joined Emily on the front porch the band of his fingers softened. The opportunity was not lost to Merry. She jerked out of his hold.

"I will not go with you," she hissed. "I have had enough. I will stay here with the Randalls, since you will not return me to Falmouth."

Morgan's eyes darkened ominously. "You will come, or I will carry you back aboard ship, Merry."

She met him stare for stare. "Try you might, but today, I do not think so."

Morgan studied the stubborn set of her features. He did not doubt it a slight effort to take her against her will, but he did not want her fighting him, and perhaps, being harmed in the process.

"Do you really want me to humiliate you by carrying you aboard ship? Or will you behave yourself for once? Will you be reasonable if I apologize? I was drunk and unclear. I was drunk. I am sorry."

His words far from soothed her heart and only stirred greater her temper. She shouted, "I do not need your apology. I am your hostage. You seem to be unclear about a great many things."

His handsome face stiffened and Merry was unsure, but she thought that she'd just stung him with that. Such a thing had never happened before. But his reaction was gone before she could make reason of it. He took a step back from her.

"As you will. Stay." He looked away from Merry, in a manner dismissive. He said to Mrs. Randall, "She is never to leave this island, Emily. Not ever. It will be your head if you defy me. She best be here when I return next winter."

With that, he walked off, leaving Merry on the porch staring after him. As soon as he was from sight, she let her tears pour. It was what she wanted. Why did it feel so miserable to have gotten her way? She felt an arm slip comfortingly around her waist and turned into Emily's waiting embrace.

Emily said, "He is a hard man, Merry, but a good one. Go after him. He is a proud man. He will not come back."

Shaking her head, frustrated and hurt, Merry cried, "I am his hostage. Did you not hear what I said? What power does he possess that no one can see what he is, or will help me?"

Emily began to dab at the tears on Merry's face. "We are all hostages of the men we love, Merry. Why should you be different?"

Fire rose in her cheeks. Miserable and exhausted, she snapped, "I do not love him."

"Ah, who is being foolish now, my dear?"

~~~

Merry had cried herself to sleep in Morgan's villa, and awakened in Indy's cabin the next day. Beside her laid a note. *Yes, I kidnapped you a second time. The first experience compelled me to drug you. Don't throw anything at me when I bring you your breakfast. I'm in no mood for it today. Morgan is a thundercloud. Step carefully.*

373

She'd been kidnapped twice in under six months' time. What were the odds of that? she wondered. So, Morgan was a thundercloud. She was to step carefully. She had no intention of stepping, at all. She'd remained in the boy's cabin three days, until finally, clearly fed up with her, he scooped her from his bunk, took her down the passageway and dumped her on the floor in Morgan's cabin. He finished the insult by locking her in.

Thinking of that day a fortnight ago, Merry felt the possession of fresh tears. Hearing a familiar sound moving briskly toward the door, she shoved her handkerchief into her nightgown, and turned to stare out the window.

February found the *Corinthian* at anchor in a forbidding cove on the coast of Spanish Florida. There were other pirate ships there, and much to Merry's consternation, American warships, as well.

It was not as lovely of a place as Morgan's island had been, but a slovenly settlement of shabby tents, naked children, pirates, and only partially dressed native women. Not even the nightly bonfires that accompanied the pirates' revelry were able to lend it an air of pleasantness.

What few memories she had of America, they were not like this. She wondered if the rest of the country had fallen to such great disrepair.

That's when Indy explained this was Spanish territory, but he had assured her, the expanse of land beyond the stern windows was America.

Pug jumped from her lap and scurried across the cabin to Morgan. The stupid beast all but worshipped the man. In her present mood, if she could have left the cabin, she would have tossed the dog over the rail herself.

Another tear.

It plopped from her eyes and rolled down her cheek, and

for the life of her she couldn't seem to stop them.

That night in the villa, alone in her room, she had admitted to herself she loved him. It was pointless to lie. She had hoped if she stopped her inner pretense, perhaps it would bring quiet to her senses. It had been an imprudent hope.

Waking up on ship, only to be confronted with the truth that it was Indy who had brought her here, had turned her tears into a raging current she could not check.

More tears. Damn. It was humiliating to cry in front of him.

It did not surprise Merry that Morgan did not speak. She heard a chair scraping against the cabin floor, and the strain of well-knit muscles against fabric as he settled at his desk.

The broken feelings of loving him had spiraled them downward into days of all but silence. Their discourse consisted of two sentences at best, usually in the morning if she bothered to rise with him.

"Will you eat?"

Answer, a slow shake of her head.

"Will you dress?"

Answer, second slow shake of her head.

After that he left her alone each day.

The rustle of papers meant he was at work, and gave her a chance to slant a careful glance his way. Frowning, she took note he was dressed as Mr. Seton had been, when he'd boarded the American privateer. Buckskin breeches, knee high boots and simple white shirt of a rough sort of cotton. She noted the garments flattered him.

Did Morgan intend to board one of the American warships? How did he always manage his fictions so expertly? She fought to banish her worry over his recklessness. Worry for him was a foolish endeavor. He commanded all things as effortlessly, as he commanded her.

She made another guarded glance his way, hating that every part of her wanted to end this now, to curl in his lap and cry as she had done Christmas Day. It was all his fault, it was he who'd hurt her. It was not fair he was the one who passed his days in normalcy.

Only pride kept her silent on the window bench.

The cabin door opening made Merry jerk, and quickly turn her face before Morgan could take note of her watching him. It was Indy.

"So, you still intend to go on the *Adventurer*?" asked the boy.

"I should be no more than five days," Morgan said. He rose from the desk and gathered his papers, shoving them into a leather case. "She is to remain locked in the cabin."

With that, he left her. Once his footsteps faded away, she picked up her book and rocketed it as hard as she could at his empty chair.

"Charming," was all Indy said. He set the book on the table beside her untouched meal.

"I will not stay locked in this cabin another week."

"Oh, praise Heaven you can speak. I feared you'd been struck mute by the drugging, and I'd be reduced to suffering your communication signals forever."

He turned the chair around and sank down on it, draping his arms across the top. He began, "Morgan said you had to stay locked in the cabin, but he did not say alone. If you will eat, I will bring Shay to you. Or, would you prefer Mr. Seton, or Mr. Boniface."

She shook her head and looked away.

He said, "You can refuse to eat, but all you will do is make yourself ill. You are here. Accept it." Then, cursing himself a fool, he added, "Now listen, Merry, do you think I could have gone back for you if he hadn't given me the order?"

"It is supposed to improve my mood to know he ordered my kidnapping a second time?" she said angrily.

Indy went for the door.

"When you finish that bowl, I will bring you what company you want. But I expect there to be no more melodrama out of you."

At the door he paused, staring at her and shaking his head. His temper won out over his concern for her, and he snapped, "Damn it, Merry. Do you really understand so little about men? The man brought you back. Even you should be able to figure out what that means."

It took another day, but Merry was more manageable after that.

The morning Morgan returned to ship, Shay was in the cabin, sitting in the center of the floor trying to amuse Merry by building a card house.

Morgan paused in the doorway, drinking in the sight of her. She was fighting to be bright of mood for the Irishman, and failing at it miserably.

"Get out," Morgan barked.

He stood above Merry until the cabin door closed. He sank cross-legged with his shins touching her knees. On a whispering command he said, "I am going to take you in my arms, put you on my lap, and you will not fight me."

Her body was weightlessness, and pliant in his hands as he lifted her off the carpet. Her body melted into him as his arms circled her. The tears started to flow again the instant he touched her.

"What must I do to stop your crying, Little One?"

"Take me home."

"I can't take you home, Little One." He buried his lips into her hair to trap his words. "It is not your time to leave me."

Continue the story with the rest of the Deverell Series:
<u>Face to Face:</u> **Book 2 of the Deverell Self ries Release date 11/3/2014**
<u>Love's Patient Fury</u>: **Book 3 of the Deverell Series Release date 12/1/2014**

For all my current and future releases visit my website: http://susanwardbooks.com
Or like me on Facebook:
https://www.facebook.com/susanwardbooks?ref=hl
Or Follow me on Twitter: @susaninlaguna

Please enjoy this excerpt from Book 2 of the Deverell Series, <u>Face to Face</u>:

The tears burned as they rolled down her cheeks. There was a long pause in which nothing changed, not his hands or his kiss. Then, Merry felt his body tighten. He stopped the furious outpouring of passion and set her away from him.

Varian stepped back from her and his black eyes were glittering in a soullessly unreadable face. "I didn't mean to frighten you, Merry. However, there is a limit to what I will tolerate of you. You may refuse me as long as you wish, Little One, but do not dance beneath my nose and play games with me."

"I will do whatever I please, you odious insufferable man! You're a fine one to talk about playing games. You have done nothing but play games with my heart and flesh since my first night aboard this ship. If you touch me again, I will kill you. I was wrong about you. It is Varian who is the fiction. It is Morgan who is real. And Morgan I despise."

It didn't seem possible to Merry, but both his face and his eyes hardened even more chillingly. Varian said, "If that were true, Little One, you would have been in my bed the first night. Do you know how desperately I want you? Enough to wish Morgan were real and because he is not to be trapped in the torment of living with you."

"If I am a torment return me to Falmouth" Her voice had degenerated into a feeble whisper, heavy with her misery and desperation. A tear choked sob interrupted her words and it took her a moment to continue. "Take me home. Please. You are like a spider, spinning a web around me and I am caught in the web. I know you are going to devour me. I know it because I want you to, but I can never let you. I don't belong with you. I don't belong here. Take me home to Falmouth while I am still able to leave you."

In excruciating frustration, Varian ground out, "You are more bother. More pain. More irritation. And more pleasure than any woman I have ever known. You are every element of the universe, brilliant and extreme. When you are angry you are hurricane at sea. When you laugh it is with the wild resonance of a raging windstorm. When you are sweet you are like marzipan. When you are calm, you are an English autumn before a fire. You have the beauty of a perfect molded china doll. The lushly sloping curves of a Venus statue. The delicacy of crystal. The will and stubbornness of iron. I can't imagine what the passion will be when we finally share it. Even the torment I savor when it's given by you because it is you and you make me want it."

Frightened of him, but more frightened of herself, Merry whispered, "I will run from you the moment there is some place for me to run, Varian. I only returned to ship with you in hopes that you would take me home to Falmouth. I can't remain with you. You must know that."

The touch of his hand on her cheek, after his fury, startled her. It was quiet and tender and wistful. "You won't run, Merry. We are one. One, but both of us incomplete, because you are young and stubborn and think there is a choice in this. You think you can get all you want, as you want it, instead of how it is. You fight the wind head on, instead of letting it carry you were want to go. I gave up fighting you on *Isla del Viento*. You, it seems, require longer. Don't make it too much longer. You are squandering the happiness of our lives."

Stunned, Merry watched as Varian's unhurried stride took him from the cabin, leaving her there, trembling, furious, and frightened. Her body hungrily yearned for his kisses and his touch, and her heart ached for his return. She should have been relieved that he left but, now that he was gone, all she wanted was him back.

Angry and frustrated, with an anxious sweep of her arm Merry sent the crystal on the table to crash against the floor.

Please enjoy this excerpt from Book 3 of the Deverell Series, <u>Love's Patient fury</u>:

She dealt. Merry was in that pose again, on elbows and knees, like a cat ready to spring. This time Varian allowed himself to enjoy it. They played without conversation; she threw her cards down in fury and won the first game. They played two more in silence and she won both of them.

Picking up the cards, her blue eyes fixed on his face with rapidly forming suspicion. "Why do I always win now?" Merry asked with measured slowness.

Varian's eyes were black and innocent. Thoughtfully, he replied, "You won before as I recall."

Frowning. "Only the last game. You won nine games to my one." Merry was working herself into a glorious temper. Varian knew she would figure out about the cards if he played with her and be furious. Mimicking his voice to perfection, she hissed, "'You are quick, you are clever, but, Little One, you are not wise.'" Fairly shouting, Merry accused fiercely, "Damn you, how did you cheat, and don't bother to tell me that you didn't."

Varian reached out then and brushed a knuckled down the cheek of her angry face. He wanted to touch her. So he did. It would only aggravate her further.

Calmly, Merry hated it when he was calm, he said "You're behaving childishly."

Merry slapped his hand away. Again his voice: "'Oh, Little One, in the spirit of good will, you may ask me anything.' I could ask you anything because you would only let me win once. How did you do it? Why did you cheat me at cards?"

Varian said nothing, but as Merry rapidly studied his face his voice came to her in memory: *Little one, have you really shared my life for nearly a year and not realized that everything I do has purpose.*

"The questions. They weren't meaningless at all." Varian's expression was lightly interested, as though she were trying to work a riddle. Merry stared at him, searching through her memories of that rainy afternoon. *There were nine questions. He had won nine games. He had cheated to win. What were they?* She rallied them off, slowly, one by one, and together they formed perfect logic.

Merry sat up then, trembling with fury and screaming in a voice surely heard all through the house, "You calculating son of the devil. You asked me questions that would tell you how to make *me* desire *you*. You got me into your bed with what you learned cheating me at cards. You keep me in your bed with what you learned cheating me at cards."

Varian was relaxed. He was amused. He was deliberately not contrite. He spread the cards in front of him, backs up and lifted his eyes to meet her. "This, Little One, is not my deck. You are quick, you are clever, you are..." he let the pause artfully develop and cut it off just right, "more wise. You watched my hands. You should have watched my eyes, Merry. Yes, the questions were to learn how to get you to desire me. You were a woman a man could not seduce without all-out battle. It was better for us both if I left the seducing to you, the same way now I leave it to you and your whim to come to my bed when you wish to."

Or enjoy one of my current contemporary romance releases:

The Girl on the Half Shell

The Signature

Rewind

One Last Kiss

EXCERPTS

Please enjoy the following excerpt from The Girl on the Half Shell:

The room is so quiet it is deafening.

I find Alan on his bed, casually reclined against a stack of pillows, dressed only in flannel pajama bottoms, and reading—of all things—the *Wall Street Journal*. There is a fire lit, the silver candlesticks flicker with flame, the bedcovers invitingly turned down as if in preparation for some sort of romantic scene. But he is focused on the *Journal*.

He doesn't look at me and I feel stupid hovering by his door, so I start to wander around the bedroom, trying to still my frantic pulse. It's a good thing that it's an interesting room, otherwise my deliberate study would seem silly.

Even Alan's bedroom is something I find weird and demands a certain amount of mental analysis. It looks like something from a nineteenth century English manor, elegant to the point of being almost a touch prissy. There's an antique mahogany king-sized bed facing the fireplace; floral wingback chairs with pillows positioned before the hearth; and high-tech conveniences camouflaged in antique furniture. There's a Monet on the wall; tall, polished sterling silver candlesticks; crystal; and fine, leather-bound, first edition books of classic literature. I sink down before a small, mahogany table where I find a stack of newspaper: *Barons*; the *New York Times*; the *Washington Post*; and the *Daily Telegraph*.

The warmth of the fire surrounds me like a caress, but I am quaking like a leaf. I wasn't sure what Alan expected after he walked out of the kitchen. It would have been logical to assume that I would leave. But he knew I'd follow him. I don't know why he's ignoring me now. I look at the lit candlesticks—he wanted me to follow him.

I bite my lower lip and stare at my knotted fingers. I stayed alone in the kitchen for what seemed like ages, and now that I've done exactly what he expected me to do, *nothing.*

I struggle for something to say to break the silence. "You do have seven bedrooms. I counted them twice. But there are seven only if I include yours."

He folds the *Journal*, tosses it on the table and fixes those penetrating, mesmerizing eyes on me. "Is this the room you want?" he asks, his voice gentle. "I meant it when I said you could have any room. It doesn't have to be my room for you to stay."

Does he not want me in his room? A ragged breath forces its way from deep in my lungs. "Do you want me to go?" I murmur.

"Of course not. I want you here." His voice is husky and his eyes are wandering in a leisurely hold that is tender and oddly comforting.

Thank you for reading. You might enjoy a sneak peek into Chrissie and Alan's future, with <u>Rewind</u> A Perfect Forever Novella. Available now on Amazon:

He doesn't laugh. Instead, his gaze sharpens on my face. "I am being nice, Kaley. I came to you. I got tired of waiting."

What? Did I just hear what I think I heard?

Before I can respond, he says, "How's your afternoon looking? Do you have time to take off and come see something with me?"

My afternoon? There is something. I'm sure of that,

but I suddenly can't remember a single thing.

"What do you have in mind?"

"I want to show you where I've been living. What's I've been doing? I think you'll find it interesting."

Interesting? Why would I find it interesting?

"So, do you think you can cut out for a few hours?" he asks, watching me expectantly.

I focus my gaze on the table, wondering if I should go, wondering why I debate this, and what the heck I have on calendar that I can't remember. God this is weird, familiar and distant at once, and I haven't a clue what I should do here.

I stare at his hand, so close to mine, on the table. Whoever thought it would be so uncomfortable *not* to touch a guy? It doesn't feel natural this space we hold between us, spiced with the kind of talk people have who know each other intimately. What would he do if I touched him...?

His fingers cover mine and he gives me a friendly squeeze. The feel of him runs through my body with remember sweetness.

Suddenly, nothing in my life is as important as spending the afternoon with Bobby and for the first time, in a very long time, I don't feel like a disjointed collection of uncomfortably fitting parts. I feel at ease inside me being with Bobby.

I stop trying to access my mental calendar. I smile up at Bobby. "I've got as much time as you need."

Bobby chuckles and his hand slips back from me. He

rises and tosses some bills on the table. "Just a few hours, Kaley. I'll have you back before the end of the day."

I rise from my chair and think *not if I figure out fast how not to blow this.*

Or enjoy the first novel in the Perfect Forever Novels: The Signature. Available Now. Please enjoy the following excerpt from The Signature:

She became aware all at once how utterly delightful it felt to be here with him, alone on the quay, with the erotic nearness of his body.

She closed her eyes. "Listen to the quiet. There are times when I lie here and it feels like there is no one else in the world."

"No one else in the world? Would that be a good thing?" he asked thoughtfully.

"No. But the illusion is grand, don't you think?" she whispered.

Krystal turned her head to the side, lifting her lids to find Devon's gaze sparkling as he studied her. He shook his head lazily. "No. The illusion wouldn't be grand at all. It would mean I wasn't here with you."

It all changed at once, yet again, and so quickly that Krystal couldn't stop it. The ticklish feeling stirred in her limbs. Devon's words, as well as the closeness of their bodies, should have sent her into active retreat, and instead she felt herself wanting to curl into him. *What would it feel like if kissed me? Would I still feel this delicious inside? Or would that old panic and fear return?*

Laughing softly, Devon said, "I'm not used to relaxing. Can you tell?"

"I wasn't used to it before Coos Bay, either. There is a different pace of life here. At first I thought there was no sound. That's how quiet it seemed to me. Then I realized that there is music, beautiful music in this quiet."

After a long pause, he murmured, "You'll have to bring me here every Saturday until I learn to hear music in the quiet."

Krystal smiled. "Once you hear the music it's perfect."

"It's perfect now to me." His voice was a husky, sensual whisper.

He was on his side facing her. *When had that happened?* An inadvertent thrill ran through her flesh, and she could see it in his eyes—the supplication, the want, and an unexplainable reluctance to indulge either.

Devon was no longer smiling, his eyes had become brighter and more diffuse. His fingertips started to trace her face with such exquisite lightness that her insides shook. For the first time, in a very long time, she felt completely a woman and wanting.

Was it possible? Had she finally healed internally as her flesh had done so long ago? Was she finally past the

SUSAN WARD

legacy of Nick? Was what she was now feeling real?
Should she seek the answer with Devon? Or was it better
to leave it unexplored?

"You are a very beautiful woman," he whispered.

She watched with sleepy movements as his mouth
lowered to her. It came first as a touch on her cheek,
feather soft between the play of his fingers. Her breath
caught, followed by a pleasant quickening of her pulse.
She was unprepared for the sweetness of his lips and the
rushing sensations that ran her body. His thumb traced the
lines of her mouth, as his kiss moved sweetly, gently there.

His breath became rapid in a way that matched her
own, and his mouth grew fuller and more searching. The
fingertips curving her chin were like a gentle embrace, but
their mouths were eager and demanding. Flashes of desire
rocketed through her powerfully. Urgency sang through
her flesh, a forgotten melody, now in vibrant notes. She
found herself wanting to twist into him. Reality begged her
to twist back.

ABOUT THE AUTHOR

Susan Ward is a native of Santa Barbara, California, where she currently lives in a house on the side of a mountain, overlooking the Pacific Ocean. She doesn't believe she makes sense anywhere except near the sea. She attended the University of California Santa Barbara and earned a degree in Business Administration from California State University Sacramento. She works as a Government Relations Consultant, focusing on issues of air quality and global warming. The mother of grown daughters, she lives a quiet life with her husband and her dog Emma. She can be found most often walking at Hendry's Beach, where she writes most of her storylines in her head while watching Emma play in the surf.

Spare a tree. Be good to the earth. Donate or share my books with a friend.

45906139R00223

Made in the USA
Lexington, KY
18 October 2015